alt.sherlock.holmes

This book is a collection of three novellas reimagining Sherlock Holmes and John Watson in different settings in modern America, from the Dust Bowl of the early 'thirties to the glitzy- and trashy-world of reality TV. You'll encounter the Great Detective as a carnival owner and fortune teller, as a drugged-up bohemian and as a smart-mouthed New Yorker.

The short stories in which these characters first appeared—"A Scandal in Hobohemia," "All the Single Ladies" and "Half There/All There"—are taken from Abaddon Books' acclaimed anthology *Two Hundred and Twenty-One Baker Streets* (2014), and are included here as bonus content.

An Abaddon Books™ Publication
www.abaddonbooks.com
abaddon@rebellion.co.uk

Omnibus edition first published
in 2016 by Abaddon Books™,
Rebellion Publishing Ltd, Riverside House,
Osney Mead, Oxford, OX2 0ES, UK.

10 9 8 7 6 5 4 3 2 1

Editors: Jonathan Oliver & David Moore
Cover Art: Sam Gretton
Design: Sam Gretton & Oz Osborne
Marketing and PR: Rob Power
Head of Books and Comics Publishing: Ben Smith
Creative Director and CEO: Jason Kingsley
Chief Technical Officer: Chris Kingsley

ISBN (UK): 978-1-78108-423-6
ISBN (US): 978-1-78108-424-3

Printed in Denmark

alt.sherlock.holmes

JAMIE WYMAN • GINI KOCH • GLEN MEHN

ABADDON
BOOKS

WWW.ABADDONBOOKS.COM

a scandal in hobohemia

JAMIE WYMAN

THE CANVAS TENT held in heat like an Alabama kitchen, though it didn't smell nearly so pleasant. The odors of dust and grease paint mingled with the smells of pungent herbs: patchouli, sandalwood perhaps. But there was no mistaking the funk of a blue drag somewhere beneath it all. That scent—the reefer—brought back all sorts of memories. Some good, others best left in the trenches.

She'd sent me in here alone, and though Agent Trenet didn't say it, I knew she meant to test me. No genius needed to figure that out, this being my first case. I turned in a circle in the tent, focusing on all the tiny details: the way the stitches on the psychic's garish red scarves were fraying; the coffee stains on the rickety table peeking through the moth-eaten silk cloth. Fingerprints smudged the glass orb in the center of the table. How anyone could read the future through all that oil and muck was beyond me.

But then, I wasn't Madame Yvonde, Seer of All and Mistress of Fate.

According to the painted banners and smooth talkers at Soggiorno Brothers' Traveling Wonder Show, the Seer was a direct descendant of Cassandra herself. "She can lead you to fame," the barker had said, "guide you to money. Help you seek that which you most desire."

I didn't want fame, and I didn't need money. What I needed, strictly speaking, was a man. Or at least his name. Trenet seemed to think Madame Yvonde would lead us there, and with her being my superior in a multitude of ways, I didn't bother to make a fuss. I stood in that sweatbox of a tent and waited.

Madame Yvonde paid me little mind. Probably on account of all the spirits and such vying for her attention. She shuffled about, a rotund bundle of bright scarves, grimy homespun and arthritic old bones. With her came an eye-searing stench of rotgut. Padding from one corner of the tent to another, the hunched old hag murmured gibberish and lit a number of ivory candles. The bracelets on her wrists and the tiny coins at her wide hips jingled with every ponderous step.

"Now," she said as she slithered behind the crystal ball. "You don't believe, do you, sonny?"

I put on my best, most innocuous smile. "Excuse me, ma'am?"

"Don't ma'am me, boy." Yvonde's voice was deep as a well and just as dark. She withdrew a cob pipe from the folds of her dress and brought it to her lips. She spoke through gritted teeth as she lit it. "You come in here wearing a suit like that, it says you're educated. Educated man don't listen to spirits or stars unless he's desperate. And you are not desperate. Not yet."

"I'm looking for someone," I said neutrally.

She brightened and let out a puff of tobacco smoke. "Oh! Well, then I might be able to help you after all. Come." She wrapped on the table twice. The chair across from her slid away from the table, and a brown work boot withdrew beneath the cloth. "Have a seat and we'll see what we find."

With the stiffness creeping into my left thigh, I didn't so much walk as hobble over to join Yvonde. Trying to keep my discomfort to myself, I bit down on my lip as I slipped uneasily down into the chair. Scooting closer was a whole other bargain that I wasn't prepared to make without a shot of whatever liquor the Seer had beneath those rags of hers.

In the flickering candlelight, Yvonde's face wavered in and out of focus. Layers of pancake smeared over fishbelly-white skin. The makeup flaked at the edges of every deep wrinkle, particularly around her lips where she'd stolen the pink off a peony to color her flabby mouth and bony cheeks. Those pale eyes of hers—all done up with black paint like a kewpie doll—drooped and fluttered. One of her false lashes threatened to fall off at any moment. I could see the fibers of her wig coiling out from beneath the scarf on her head.

Yvonde held out a bony hand and snapped her fingers. "Cross my palm, sonny."

"I paid out front," I said.

"You paid for the circus. Now you pay for the pleasure of my company."

I pretended to wrestle with the notion of parting ways with my hard-earned dollar before reaching into my coat and plucking a bill. I handed it to her, and she crumpled it in those skinny fingers. Yvonde grinned around her pipe as the money disappeared. That smile held a sinister edge, but her teeth were straight and white as a Connecticut Sunday social.

"Now, you were looking for someone, were you?"

An arc of cards appeared on the table. The drawings were intricate, and had probably once been lovely. Now they were just as faded as the rest of this damn circus. Yvonde tapped a card.

"The World," she breathed hoarsely. "You are a traveler. No roots, just boots. Stomp, stomp, stomping on the ground."

I bristled, my blood running cold. She came close to making me think of old times.

"I'm not here about me."

"Aren't you? You're looking for a man, but you haven't stopped to consider that you're searching for yourself. Aimlessly going from South Carolina to Alabama. Over an ocean and back again. Boy, you've just been rooting along the Southern states like a dog hunting for a master that's left him behind."

"A master?" I snarled, balling my fist on my lap. "That supposed to mean something?"

She waved me off with a jingle of her bracelets. "I don't give a flop about negroes, boy. Your money spends just as well as the next man's. But you've chosen the hardest fields to plow, haven't you, soldier?"

Her cold eyes fixed me with a challenge. *Tell me I'm wrong*, she seemed to say. We both knew that I wouldn't. Couldn't. We stared at one another, sharing only that meaningful look.

"What else?" I asked.

With a flourish of scarves and skeletal hands, the arc of cards vanished. Only three remained on the table. The World still stared up at me.

"The Empress," Yvonde sang as she slid the card toward me. "Lovely thing that you can never touch. Wouldn't want to get her pretty blonde hair dirty with those dark hands of yours, would we? Not that she's noticed you. She's too busy with her eyes on some other prize."

The old gypsy slammed her knuckles on the next card, a sound like a gunshot. I didn't jump, but my hand flew to a sidearm that was no longer there.

"The Devil! You seek him out, but beware, little soldier. Hellfire awaits you down this path."

"Hellfire," I whispered, "is behind me."

Her lip hitched up in an ugly sneer, smoke curling up from the pipe. "Sure it is, soldier."

The curtain behind Madame Yvonde twitched with a breeze, and I coughed at the smells stirred around. The pipe, the reefer. Shalimar perfume. Maybe the black powder was my imagination, but that tent filled with the odor of sulfur. Shots fired more than a decade before rang out in my ears. Shells and screams, and a woman singing along with Duke Ellington.

I stared at the Empress and let my fingers trace the inked lines of her face. I wasn't thinking of the blonde slinking into the tent, but I growled just the same. "Damned old gypsy."

"Still want to smile and tell me you don't believe? Or are you going to pass me another of those crisp new bills so I can give you *real* wisdom?"

Agent Trenet had come in silent as night, but when she spoke her voice was loud like the crack of dawn. "Or you could drop the bullshit."

My partner stood behind the Seer. A straight razor gleamed in the candlelight, poised against Yvonde's throat.

The Seer's eyes rolled back in her head and fluttered dreamily as she drew in a long breath through her nose. With an obscene purr, Yvonde clutched at my partner's hand. When she spoke, her voice was a low, throaty rumble. "Oh, Adele, it is wonderful to see you again."

"You haven't seen me, Sanford, your eyes are closed."

Agent Adele Trenet pocketed her razor and stepped away from Yvonde, leaving me more than a little befuddled.

"Sanford?" I asked.

Yvonde opened her eyes. Agent Trenet tugged at the scarf on the gypsy's head, removing both scarf and wig in one gesture. Russet curls sprouted from beneath a shoddy bald cap. And now, without the cover of all the rags about her head, I noticed Yvonde's very prominent Adam's apple.

"Sanford?" I repeated.

"Crash," the gypsy said. Now that I listened, the voice couldn't be anything other than a man's.

"His name," Trenet said sharply, "is Sanford Haus."

Yvonde/Sanford took the agent's hand in both of his. "Now, now, Pinky," he said, dropping his lips to the backs of Trenet's fingers. "You know how I loathe that name."

"And you know I hate it when you call me Pinky."

Trenet tried to pull her hand away, but Sanford held fast

"Let us have a look, shall we?" The gypsy turned Trenet's hand over in his and peered into her palm. Though he only traced the lines there with a single finger, the act was potent with meaning and lust. It made me uncomfortable to watch.

"Oh, what's this I see?" Sanford sang cheerfully. "You're hunting again, Adele. Looking for something to make you whole and fill you up."

My partner rolled her eyes.

"And I see just what you need," Sanford said. He looked up at her like a wicked puppy. "A man, strapping and brilliant. One you'd travel to the ends of the earth to find. And it seems you have found him."

As the fortune teller brought his lips to her hand again, Trenet wrenched loose. "Never, Sanford."

"Crash," he whined, bounding up from his chair. He tossed a cloak of scarves and rags to the floor, and stood at his proper height. His capped head brushed the ceiling of the tent. I boggled at how only moments ago, he'd folded most of that lanky frame into the image of a hunchbacked hag.

"Agent Trenet, who is this?" I asked.

Before she could answer, the gypsy spun to face me and thrust his hand across the table. "Vagabond. Performer. Owner and proprietor of Soggiorno Brothers Traveling Wonder Show. I am Crash."

"He's a thief and a liar," Trenet spat. She tossed a lock of blonde hair out of her eyes and put some distance between her and Sanford Haus.

Rather than bristle at the accusations, Haus smiled. He lifted one shoulder in a dismissive shrug and regarded me with interest. "And you, soldier boy? Have you a name?"

I winced as I got to my feet. Shook his hand as I replied, "Jim Walker."

"Jim? Well, isn't that just dandy?"

"How did you know?" I asked.

"Know?"

"That I am a—was"—I corrected myself quickly—"a soldier?

All that stuff about South Carolina? Alabama? Did she tell you?"

Trenet plopped into the chair I'd just vacated and crossed her arms over her chest. "Here we go."

"You walk with a stiff leg," said Haus as he began to divest himself of Madame Yvonde's ample hips. "The footprint of your right is significantly deeper than that of your left. You've had an injury of some sort that has led to amputation. While that might be more common for a farmer, you dress too well for someone working the fields. You're of an age to have served in the Great War, so I can presume soldier."

Haus shimmied out of the costume while he explained. Beneath all those rags and scarves was a stained undershirt, brown trousers and suspenders. Sanford's arms were ropy sinew and milk-white marble. He threw off the bald cap and tousled his red curls.

"Now, there are very few regiments that are accepting of negroes. It's clear by your accent that you are a northerner. There was one regiment from the North that saw enough fire that might account for your leg, and that was the 369th out of New York. They mustered in South Carolina. I made a very educated guess that you had been part of Harlem's Hellfighters. You confirmed this suspicion when I needled you about Hellfire."

My jaw hung open. "You... that's..."

But he went on, enjoying the sound of his own voice. "After you returned from the war, you spent some time at Tuskegee in Alabama. I can tell that by the ring on your right hand, with the school's seal."

"Incredible," I gasped.

"Now we get to the fun part. When you fished out your money, you made the mistake of flashing your badge. I am more than familiar with Pinkerton Agents," he said with a nod to Trenet. "Considering our previous associations, I could only assume that Adele was with you. I stacked the cards and played to that knowledge by giving you The Empress."

"And the Devil?"

Sanford Haus bowed. "I am what I am."

Agent Trenet let out a whoop of laughter. "You only wish, Haus."

"My wish has already been granted," he smirked, sliding his thumbs up and down his suspenders. "You're here, Adele. To what do I owe the honor?"

"Well, for starters, your brother sends his regards."

Haus flopped into his chair and rested a boot on the old table. Taking another drag from his pipe, he muttered something dark that should never be said in front of a lady. "How is dear Leland?"

"Leland Haus?" I blurted out. "The head of the Secret Service? If that's your family, Mr. Haus, that would make you a very rich man."

Sanford's smug grin and flippant wave of his hand was all the confirmation I needed.

Agent Trenet nodded. "Sometimes Director Haus prefers to keep an eye on his wayward sibling, make sure he's keeping his nose clean while playing dress-up in the gutter."

"I'm happy here," Sanford snapped. "Leland needn't worry his tender sensibilities about little old me."

"He hopes you'll come home and—"

"Yes, I'm sure he does. Now, Adele, why are you really here? I hardly think Leland's mommy complex would be just cause to send a couple of Pinks all this way. What do you have?"

Trenet smiled despite herself. Reaching into her shoulder bag, she produced a photograph and held it to her forehead. Mimicking a spiritualist, she called out, "I see the Hermit." She slapped the picture onto the table.

Sanford gave the picture the most meager of glances. "A dead hobo. What of it?"

"Ah-ha!" Agent Trenet fished out another photo and laid it beside the first. "He was murdered with this."

When his gaze took in the knife in the picture, Sanford Haus went still and silent. He steepled his hands beneath his chin and pondered, his eyes gone hard. He stared and stared at the photographs, unflinching and barely breathing. For long minutes, the only sounds came from the midway outside, muffled by the tent. When the carousel started up a new waltz, my partner turned her own leer onto the gypsy.

"Problem, Sanford?"

This shook him from his reverie.

"Crash," he chided.

Then he was up, gathering all the pieces of Madame Yvonde from the floor. "This is a conversation for the back yard. Dear Adele. Mr. Dandy"—he thrust the bundle of rags into my chest—"follow me, if you please."

He proceeded to lurch through a tent flap hidden behind a map of the human skull. I followed, watching as he once again unfolded that beanpole frame. I drew in a breath of clean, fresh air. The night was cool and breezy: a welcome change from the musky tent.

Stretching out those long legs of his, Sanford took off at a brisk walk, leading us through a maze of tents, ropes and canvas stalls. Soon, the music and hustle of the carnival fell away to background noise and I found myself in a small shantytown. Trucks, wagons, tractors, even a couple of repurposed box cars. Few people lingered here, but those who did were obviously carnies. Here a woman in a sequined costume shared a cigarette with a dwarf. There, a man broad as an elephant scraped the last of his dinner from a tin plate.

Haus brushed off the occasional call of, "Hey, Crash!" without acknowledgement. As we passed a chuck wagon, Sanford piped up, "Mrs. Hudson!"

A dwarf with wild copper hair and an ample bottom raised her head. "What'll it be, boss?"

"Three coffees as black as my soul, if you please."

"Don't know that I've got anything that dark, Crash, but I'll see what I can rustle up. And will there be anything for your guests?" she joked.

Sanford gave Mrs. Hudson a wry grin. "Where's Arty?"

"Last I saw he was tagging along with a couple of bally broads and a butcher. He should be at the kiddie show by now, though."

"If you'd be so kind as to send Mars on over to the kiddie show, then. I need to have a word with Arty *tout suite*."

"Aye, Crash," Mrs. Hudson said as she waddled away from her cart.

Sanford hadn't broken stride. I struggled to keep up, my prosthetic leg wobbling and chafing.

With a leap, he took three stairs up to the door at the back of a gypsy wagon. The thing had been cobbled together with various pieces of other things. I recognized the eaves of a farmhouse, a wall built of aluminum, a couple of railroad ties. The door had come from some apartment or other. The numbers 221 clung to the peeling paint, as defiant as Sanford 'Crash' Haus himself.

He pulled a key from a chain around his neck and unlocked the door. "Good sir, gentle lady, I welcome you to my home." With a wide, sweeping gesture, he indicated we should enter.

As the door shut behind us, I dropped Madame Yvonde to the floor and hobbled to the nearest chair. The ache in my leg had become a tight vice, a hot brand of pain settling around the joint where my knee had once been. If the bone-deep throbbing was any indication, we might get rain soon.

Sanford rooted around and produced a cigar box. Opening it, he offered it to me. "Would you like some?"

I blinked at the papers and mossy green herb therein. "I'm sorry?"

"For the pain, obviously. If you've need of something stronger I can provide that as well."

I waved him off. "No, thank you. Not while I'm working."

He snapped the box closed. "Talk to me, Adele. What do you know?"

"The vagrant was Enoch Drebber. Before the Crash, he was an accountant in Salt Lake City. He and his family lost quite a lot, though. They became Lizzie tramps, traveling, looking for work. Then the family car busted and they took up with a Hooverville outside of Omaha, just in time for that mammoth dust storm to plow through this month."

Two quick knocks on the door interrupted Agent Trenet's story. Haus opened the door where Mrs. Hudson stood with three tin cups on a wooden platter. She gave a bow and exaggerated flourish. "Your service, dear sir!"

Haus moved lithely through the cramped space of his wagon, fetching the cups and doling them out to Trenet and myself. "Excellent, Mrs. Hudson. Thank you."

"Johnny is on his way to take Arty's place. When I see the kid I'll send him your way."

"Fantastic."

The dwarf's eyes landed on me and sparkled with lascivious delight. "Crash, do call if there's anything your guests need. And I do mean *anything*."

Mrs. Hudson gave an impolite wiggle of her rounder virtues and rolled back into the night.

Trenet smiled into her cup of coffee. "Well, well."

Haus shut the door. "You were saying. Mr. Drebber found himself outside of Omaha, destitute and most dead."

"Yes," Agent Trenet continued. "Well, it so happens that his death coincides with the date your particular mud show slunk out of town."

"Coincidence."

"Perhaps, Sanford—"

"Crash."

"—but it's not the first crime to turn up on your route. Three weeks before that, Mary Watson was kidnapped less than a quarter mile from your tent. Pinkerton agents are still looking for her."

"Never heard of her."

"Two weeks before that, Calvin Bailey was found dead."

"Calvin Bailey? We oil-spotted him in Duluth!"

"Oil-spotted?" I asked.

Haus rolled his eyes. "Oil-spotted. Red-lighted. Means we left him behind and all he saw was the oil spot where the truck had been."

"He worked for you?" Trenet asked.

"Until I found out he was using his job as a balloon vendor to find little girls, yes. As I say, we left him behind."

"Well, he was found dead on the Kansas-Missouri state line."

"Serves him right," Crash said, rolling a cigarette. "Wasn't me or mine, I'll tell you that. We're no Sunday School, but we generally keep clean."

"You're sure?"

"We haven't pulled close to Missouri this trip."

Trenet's pretty face scrunched up with confusion. "But your posters..."

"We had to take a detour due to bad weather, Adele. We missed that stop entirely. Planned on hitting St. Louis on our way back to Peru."

"But you recognize the knife," she said pointedly.

Haus took a long drag of his roller, staring at me. Studying me. Without taking those cool eyes off my form, he exhaled a plume of blue smoke from both nostrils like a lanky dragon. "Is it wooden?"

"Excuse me?" I asked.

"The leg. Is it wooden?"

I nodded. "Hollow. Iron foot, though. Why?"

"Dammit, Crash!" Agent Trenet was on her feet. "Have you been listening to a damn thing I've said?"

Haus gaped at her, but mischief danced in his gaze. "Why, Pinky, you called me Crash."

She let out a frustrated growl and kicked at his shins.

"Yes," Haus said through his laughter. "I recognize the knife. It's identical to the ones Arty uses in his act."

She yanked the cig from his lips and raised it to her own. "Tell me about him."

"Barely old enough to shave. Born into circus tradition to a burlesque dancer and an inside talker. His dad got red-lighted before I bought the show, but his mother—Baker Street Baby—will be onstage in an hour or so." He nodded to me. "You'd like her. Has a penchant for peacock feathers and parasols."

"How do you figure I'd—"

Trenet cut me off. "What about the kid?"

"Arty's a sword-swallower and knife thrower. Goes by Arthur on stage, plays up the Excalibur legend."

"Do you think he could have killed Drebber?"

"Adele, my dear, given proper motivation, anyone could kill."

"I suppose that's true. Just talking with you makes me homicidal most of the time."

"You flatter me. What else? Any other evidence found with Bailey or this Watson dame? You must have more than just my tour schedule and a knife."

"Coffee cans."

Haus's face scrunched in genuine concern. "Come again?"

"Coffee cans," I said. "Found at every crime scene. Each of them contained a letter and a handful of objects."

"Objects such as?"

"The can found with Calvin Bailey's body had a taxidermied dog's paw. Drebber's held the knife. A third can turned up at Mary Watson's home. Inside was a necklace fashioned after a snake."

Haus launched himself out of his chair, and in two long strides he was out the door.

"Crash!" Trenet called after him. To me she muttered, "Come on."

We followed him at his blistering pace—well, I hobbled as quickly as I could all things considered—as Haus led us back toward the siren song of the carousel and hawkers. He swept the folds of a tent apart with his long hands and barked to the assembled crowd.

"Everyone out."

Though there were murmurs and complaints, no one dared argue with the glare Crash passed. Of course, his painted face was rather ghoulish, which might have had something to do with their compliance.

Haus had led us into the sideshow tent. Tables and ramshackle shelves were covered in little curiosities. Jars of amber fluids and specimens—two-headed lizards and the like, as well as fetuses—were caked with dust. One such jar contained only a thumb. A wooden box on a table nearby held a bit of rock. The card in front of it heralded the item as the Mazarin Stone. There were other such relics; a beryl coronet, a tree branch from Tunguska, the stake used to kill a vampire.

"What's this about, Sanford?" Trenet asked.

He led us to an empty bell jar and plucked the card from its display. "The Devil's foot is missing. Tell me, did the paw you found look anything like this?"

I eyed the photograph. "To a tee."

Haus tossed the card and hissed another black curse. Flipping his hand toward an ornate jewelry box, he snarled, "And the Borgias' torque is missing as well."

I padded to the box and read the card. Apparently, the necklace usually kept there was the property of that most notorious family. The card said that Lucretia used it to deliver poison to her rivals. And it was modeled after a scarlet snake.

"Matches the one found at Watson's scene," I muttered. "Right down to the speckles on the snake's head."

"What did they say?" Haus snapped at me.

"The snake?"

"The letters, damn you! The letters found with my stolen property?"

"Just the same two words, every time: *memento mori*."

Haus seethed with palpable rage. The tendons in his fists popped as he clenched. "Arty."

A grizzled old bearded lady joined us. "Boss? There a reason no one been by my stall in five minutes?"

"Where's Arty?" he bellowed.

Agent Trenet took Crash's temper in stride, but the bearded lady jumped back, startled. "Ain't seen 'im tonight. He never showed up for call. He's probably drunk behind the wheel."

Crash growled and spun on his heel. Over his shoulder he called, "Tell the talkers to let the towners back in. Business as usual."

He was a hound on the hunt, leading Trenet and me back into the strange back alleys of the circus. The equipment housed here had seen better days. Trunks of props were open. I saw a few performers grab what they needed, then dash back into tents. Though my thigh ached with the fire of Hell itself, I felt the old rush of excitement that came with having a mission; a goal. Hadn't felt that surge since a time when I had both legs, but that night—stomping through the carnival's backlot—I felt more whole than I had in damn near twenty years. This might have been my first case for Pinkerton, but I was hardly a greenhorn.

That swell of confidence helped to mask the pain and lit a fire that let me keep up with Crash and his spidery legs.

"Where are we going?" Trenet called.

Crash had no time for explanations as we came up on a looming disc. Small metallic triangles glinted from its surface— the points of knives. We were looking at the back of a knife wheel. And one of the exposed blades—this one exceptionally long—was red with blood.

Crash was the first to round the wheel. He spat a few salty words, then kicked up a cloud of dust.

Arty sat in a reeking puddle. The sword—Excalibur, I

presumed—had been thrust through his mouth, pinning his head to the rotting wood of the wheel. His face was fixed with a terrified expression. I raced forward and knelt, the prosthetic protesting as I did. I checked the boy for a pulse, but it was a futile effort.

"Marks on his wrists," I said. "He was bound."

Haus paced with mounting anger. "What else?"

I leaned in close to sniff the boy's waxy face. "Chloroform."

"Someone drugged him, tied him up and did this," Trenet surmised. "When did you last see him, Sanford?"

"Just before the gates opened," he answered. "Sometime after two in the afternoon."

I stood up, took out my handkerchief and spoke from behind it. "The blood has been clotting for a while. Flies are on him, too. A few hours. Six at the most."

"And everyone's been working the show since then. Not a soul to find him."

"Jim," Trenet said, her voice nasal as she pinched her nostrils shut, "you stay here with the body and Haus. I have to call the local police."

"No!" Crash barked. "No police."

"Sanford, I have to."

"You can't."

"It's my job!"

"Locals get sight of coppers on my lot, they'll assume the worst."

"They'd be right!"

"They'll stop coming and my people will lose money. If word carries too far, we could lose the rest of the season."

"You can't seriously think I'll just let a murder—the latest in a string of them, I might add—go unnoticed."

"He's not a towner, Adele. He's not even a gaucho like me. Arty was born in the circus. Let the circus deal with it."

The war between Crash's reason and Adele's conscience

played out on her face, and I understood both sides. All of the consequences weighed against one another and Trenet simmered.

"I let you clean this up, Sanford, there's gonna be some conditions."

"Name them," he said.

"You let me in on any evidence found, so I can keep this on record as part of our case."

"Done."

"Second, I get alone time with every one of your people. If someone is stealing from you and leaving the items at crime scenes, following your route, now killing one of your performers, I want to know if it's someone in your show."

"It's not—"

"That's how it's going to go down, Sanford, or so help me God, I will shut this show down myself and feed you to the local cops with a side of cotton fucking candy."

I jumped at the lady's language, but it didn't stop me from smiling. The other Pinks had told me Adele Trenet was a firecracker, but it was another thing to see her in action. Crash seemed to appreciate her as well. The slightest of dimples formed on one cheek as he stuffed his hands into his deep pockets.

"Fine, Adele," he said. "We'll play it your way. You can start talking to Mrs. Hudson back at the crumb car while Dandy, here, helps me deal with Arty's remains."

"Shouldn't I go with her?" I asked. "Your people don't much care for outsiders."

"Adele's not a stranger to my crew. They might not care for the badge, but no one will give her too hard of a time."

"I can handle them," she agreed.

"You can handle me," he added with a provocative waggle of his eyebrows. My partner glared at him, and he held up his palms in surrender. "Fine. Work first."

She rolled her eyes, but couldn't hide her own smile as she started for Mrs. Hudson's crumb car. As we watched her jog along the back lot, Crash let out a pleased sigh and rumble of approval.

Haus and I quietly extricated Arty from the wheel, and I tried not to think about all the things my partner wasn't telling me. She wasn't crooked or a bully, like some of the other Pinks, but something didn't jive. For starters, her connection to Leland Haus. The Secret Service and our agency didn't play nice together. But she had some connection to the Haus brothers. I assumed her dealings with Leland involved money and investigations on the sly. But with Crash? Well, I didn't much want to think on that.

Not that a woman so snowy would be seen with a man dark as cinders such as myself.

We were filling the boy's grave when Crash spoke up. "So tell me, doctor, how long have you been with Pinkerton?"

"How did you...?" I stopped asking the question when Crash just gave me an incredulous look over the handle of his shovel. "Right. This is my first case."

"Doesn't seem to suit you."

"Maybe not," I answered truthfully. "Can't keep soldiering. Tried to put down roots and be a good doctor, but, well, that didn't work out any better. Thought I could put both those skills to use with the Agency, though. Not sure it's not another bust." I piled more dirt on top of the grave and patted it down with the blade of my shovel. "Now you tell me something: do you reckon this is one of your folks doing all this?"

Crash shook his head. "Whoever the character is, he's not job."

"You're certain."

"One of the deaths occurred in a town we skipped. He couldn't have known we would wildcat around the weather, any more than we did. And being fifty miles to the south is a pretty good alibi for me and mine, don't you think?"

I nodded grimly. We were no closer to finding the Devil than I'd been when I walked into Madame Yvonde's tent.

The dirty work done, Crash and I shambled to his wagon wrung out as old cloths. As he went to open the door, it jerked.

"Locked," he said, tone dark. "I didn't have time to lock it, Dandy. We ran out in a hurry."

I leveled the shovel in front of me and gave Crash a nod. "Let's see who's inside, shall we?"

Gingerly, he slipped the key in the door and turned the lock. We burst in to find his wagon unoccupied. It was precisely as we'd left it earlier—Madame Yvonde's rags still strewn about the floor and our joe gone cold in the tin cups. One thing, however, was different. On Crash's bunk was a yellow, rusty coffee can.

Crash picked it up and cradled it in one arm while opening it. His fingers snatched the paper out and he let the can fall to the floor.

"'How good it is,'" he read, "'to have a real opponent for my game.' That's all it says?"

He flipped over the page and chuffed out a rueful laugh.

"What?" I asked.

"Have a look."

I took the paper. While the front had only the single line of handwritten text, the back was all flourishes and tiny drawings. Like something from an illuminated manuscript, the figures were ornately detailed. They decorated large letters.

Memento Mori

Something about the drawings bothered me. One of them—a mermaid—was too long. Her body stretched the length of the old paper before joining up with her tail. And another, this one a teddy bear, was bifurcated. One half of its body was on either side of the page. My gaze fell across a seam in the paper. A crease. It had been folded many times. I followed the crease as I brought my hands together. The mermaid shrank into a more average body. The teddy bear became whole. A new word appeared.

"Moriarty?" I asked.

"What's that?"

"I was about to ask you." I looked up from the paper and offered it to Crash. He pocketed something—a pearl, from the looks of it—and put the can down. I hadn't even noticed him pick it up. I began to realize that Sanford Haus was full of talents.

Crash took the picture from me, unfolded it and re-folded it again. Several times.

"Moriarty," he whispered. "Moriarty."

I turned at a knock on the door to see Agent Trenet lowering her hand. "Something you've found, boys?"

Crash swept the can to her. "Another note from our killer. Seems he's enjoying himself."

Agent Trenet looked at the paper. "A game? That's what this is to him?" Peering into the can, she frowned. "There's nothing else here. He always leaves something else, like the necklace or the foot. Crash, was there anything else?"

"Just the paper," he said, lips pressed thin and colorless.

Weary, Agent Trenet brushed her hair over her ear. She grabbed her earlobe with surprise. "Damn! I've lost an earring."

"Could be anywhere," Crash said quickly. "It's likely gone out on the lot somewhere."

As Crash swept Agent Trenet out of the wagon, I noticed the pearl in her other ear.

My stomach fell. How had her other earring landed in that can?

In that moment, my years of wandering ended. All of the steps I'd taken—from Harlem, to South Carolina, to the beaches and trenches in France, to Alabama and now to this mud show in the middle of Arkansas—all roads seemed to have led to this moment. To this puzzle with the answer already filled in. A decision was made as I followed them out, although I'd not even asked myself the question.

"Moriarty," I said under my breath.

"What was that?" she asked.

Over her head, Crash gave me a stern glance.

"Nothing, Adele," I answered.

She shrugged and ran toward the crumb car, where a beefy man with a broad moustache waited. "Excuse me, Mr. Mars. A word," she called.

I lingered behind, watching the work of a Pinkerton Agent at the top of her game, now a pawn in someone else's. *Moriarty.* Our killer. He was there, somewhere at the circus, watching us. He'd followed us enough to pluck up the pearl earring when Adele dropped it. Had slipped into Crash's wagon and had been kind enough to lock up on his way out.

The case was here. The answer to it all was here. Not on the road or behind a desk at the Pinkerton home office.

Crash put his hands in his pockets and sidled up beside me leisurely. "Payday is every Friday. First of May like yourself would get three aces a week for your pocket. Until we get something else square, you can kip in my bunk."

"Excuse me?"

"Unless you would rather stay with Mrs. Hudson. She'd enjoy that."

I laughed. "A dwarf and a one-legged negro. That belongs in your freakshow for certain, Crash."

"Everyone works," he continued. "Normally I'd start you as a candy butcher, but that requires a lot of walking the lot. No, you're not a vendor. Though you might make a good talker. Inside talker, I'm thinking. You catch details. You're not as good as me, but then, who is?"

"Humble son of a gun, aren't you?"

"You can start tomorrow, Dandy. I'll introduce you around tonight while Adele is questioning my folks."

"Wait, wait," I said. "I didn't say I'd run off and join your circus."

"Of course you did," he said. "And you're going to. It's settled."

"Shouldn't I think about it?"

"You've already decided."

I had, of course. But... "And just how do you know?"

Sanford Haus smiled wide as a Cheshire cat. "You called me Crash."

the case of the tattooed bride

JAMIE WYMAN

one

"BEST OF ALL mornings to you, my dark-hearted friend," Crash sang as he barreled into the vardo.

A gale cold as the hinges of Hell followed him into the wagon.

I grumbled one of the more colorful turns of phrase I'd picked up from Mrs. Hudson, but most of the words stuck in the cottony numbness of my mouth. Prying my gummy eyes open, a vision of my damnable roommate came into focus.

That particular day he'd bundled himself up in an old wool coat and a blue scarf that had seen better times. A leather satchel slung across his body bumped against the narrow doorframe and the wall as its wearer spun his back to me. As his nickname suggested, Sanford "Crash" Haus would never be mistaken for a feather-footed angel.

My hammock swayed when he slammed the door behind him. I groaned in protest, but kept my curses to myself. Mostly.

"Didn't wake you, did I, Dandy?"

"I'm fairly certain you woke everyone from here to the Devil's door and back again."

"Then I must try harder next time, if I'm to rouse Mephistopheles himself," he snickered, ruffling snow out of his ginger curls.

Crash's movements about the tight space were a dance: fluid, yet punctuated by percussive accents of the destruction that came part-and-parcel with him. The satchel fell to the floor, spilling its contents with a gentle whispering, as Crash reached to the shelf above my hammock. The cigar box slid easily into his hands.

I closed my eyes, adjusting to the pain of being awake far too soon for my own liking, while my friend rustled through papers and skunky herb to make himself a morning repast. The rasp of the match was enough to relax something in me. Smoke filled the small wagon, and I massaged the stump of my left leg.

"The cold makes it worse, doesn't it?" Crash asked quietly.

I nodded. "Winter ain't my friend."

"Perhaps you should've stayed in Alabama."

"Humidity's no good for me neither. Besides, I let the leg tell me where I go and what I do...? Might as well have died in the war. Now," I said, lurching upright in the swaying hammock. "What's got you marching out into the snow before the sun's had time to put on her face?"

Haus grinned at me, his pale, smooth cheeks wrinkling. "Mail."

"Mail?"

"Indeed." He bent over and upended the satchel. Letters poured out, littering the floor of our wagon. "Mail. We'll sort it out here and deliver it to the rest of the camp."

"What's this *we*?" I asked wryly.

Crash folded himself up on the floor, one hand sifting through the envelopes while the other held the joint oozing its blue smoke. "Of course. What else did you have planned for today?"

I rolled a shoulder in concession. With the Soggiorno Brothers' Travelling Wonder Show pulled into its winter berth just east of Peru, Indiana, there weren't crowds to fleece or balloons to fill. Just a bunch of drowsy carnies looking to fill the hours between dawn and dusk until the next tour began.

I took up my prosthetic and stood on two feet. With the mess Crash'd made of everything, hobbling from one end of the wagon to the door proved to be a feat worthy of a barker's busking. *See the one-legged man! Look how he hops and skips!* I threw a swath of fabric—turned out to be one of Crash's gypsy costumes—over my shoulders and headed out into the inhospitable December morning.

The camp wasn't a Monet, but I'd be a bald-faced liar if I didn't say it was a mighty pretty sight. We'd had a week of snow, and circus folk being an industrious sort, tracks had been carved throughout. Roads spanned from this tent to that wagon, to the large fire pit we shared some nights. Most of the footprints frozen into the mud and slush led to Mrs. Hudson's place.

Other than the sinuous trenches, the snow was pristine. A crystalline crust had formed over the top of everything, making it glitter and shine in the wan daylight. The most colorful tents had been stored away, of course, so as to not damage them before the next season. But against the slate-grey sky and black, naked trees, the wagons and trailers of the carnies gleamed jewel-bright.

Even the rickety old vardo belonging to Haus looked like it wore its Sunday best—well, apart from the peeling paint and the brass numbers dangling askew on the borrowed door. Wherever 221b originally stood, the address now belonged to Crash forevermore.

And to me too, I suppose. In the handful of months I'd lived with him, we shared the accommodation about as well has a couple of surly sardines in a can. Every day he promised we'd find something more suitable that I could call my own, but nothing had turned up. Or a problem sprouted on the lot. Or we had to duck out of a city too quickly. When we pulled into Peru, it was just assumed I'd stay with him.

I peered around the quiet lot, eyes landing on Mrs. Hudson's place. Hers was the largest, most ornate homestead. Smoke curled up from the chimney pipe of the "crum car"—what the carnies called their commissary. It looked to me like someone had taken the old caboose off a train and thrown a Mississippi kitchen into it. From the railing at the back, the lovely dwarf would dole out heaping plates of her wares. Off to the side was a small shelter with a few benches for people to gather and eat around a fire. Soon those canvas flaps would open to all who had an appetite.

Squatting behind it all, wide and ample as its sole occupant, Mrs. Hudson's canvas tent was all faded stripes and patchwork. Discarded pennants snapped in the biting wind, shaking off the frost.

Where Crash's wagon was a cold, hard edifice, Mrs. Hudson's tent looked like a warm, soft place to land. Much like the woman herself. But those thoughts weren't for entertaining.

"Not a snowball's chance in the pit of Hell, Jimmy," I berated myself.

After dodging patches of ice, and doing my business in the nearby outhouse, I carefully took the stairs back into the vardo.

Crash had kindled a small fire in the stove, complete with a pot of terrible coffee brewing on top. Even in the short time I'd been out, Haus had managed to turn some of the chaos of the mail pile into discernible order. But I'll be damned if I could understand his system.

Taking up a stool nearby, I surveyed the heaps of post. "So what've we got?"

Smoke trailed from the roller in his hand as he indicated each category. "Everyone's got their own stack, you see. Mr. Mars; Miss Collette; the Canaga sisters. You get the idea. We'll sort it out, divide the stacks and deliver them like a couple of postmen." He paused and shot me a mischief-laden glance. "You can take Mrs. Hudson's. I'm sure she'd enjoy the visit."

I snorted my response.

"And, if I'm not mistaken," he continued, "you'd enjoy it as well."

I leaned over and took up a couple handfuls of unsorted envelopes. "What I'd enjoy and what's proper ain't always the same, Crash."

Without looking at me, he raised his eyebrows incredulously. "Why, Dandy, you cad! And just what improper things do you wish to do to our dear Mrs. Hudson?"

"You know what I mean."

His grin was a mite too lascivious. "Pretend that I don't. And don't," he added loudly, "skimp on the details."

"A gentleman doesn't speak of a lady like that, Crash."

"I'm no gentleman," he murmured. "You'll not offend my sensibilities."

"Yeah, well I might offend my own."

"How so?"

"Do I need to spell it out?"

"Apparently, you do."

He knew damn well, but seemed to take pleasure in making me say it aloud. Never did understand that about him. I sighed, weary. "I'm a negro and she's…"

"A well-endowed dwarf."

I hung my head and brought my hands to my temples, the growing ache there. Impossible carnie bastard. "There are rules, Crash."

"The rules are different here, Jim."

I kept my mouth shut and mulled it over. Mrs. Hudson had made her feelings clear since the moment she set eyes on me. Unabashed flirtations at the chuck wagon, extra helpings of dessert… the dwarf would tell anyone with ears she fancied me. For the longest time I thought it was a joke, some sort of prank on the new guy at the circus. After a while, though, I realized she meant every word and illicit promise. Didn't matter a lick that I found her charming, lovely and altogether fine as the smile on an angel. There were some things that a negro like me couldn't ever enjoy, and a woman with snow white skin was one of them. So, like fantasies of regrowing my lost leg, I put away my ideas regarding Mrs. Hudson and went on living.

I spat an oath I'd never utter near my grandmother, and swiped the joint from Crash's fingers. Taking a drag, I closed my eyes and let the cannabis ease the pain in my leg and the lump in my throat. My thoughts swam on an eddy of blue smoke, and warmth seeped into my limbs. I felt loose and at ease.

"Oh, ho!" Crash sang. "Speaking of fine women..."

I opened my eyes to see Haus raising an envelope to his nostrils. He inhaled deeply, eyes rolling back in ecstasy, then purred, his voice a low rumble in his throat. "Oh, Adele."

"Miss Trenet writes to you?" I asked, a bit of jealousy making my ears hot.

"Hang on," he said, ignoring me. "What's this? Why is it addressed to you?"

I plucked it from his fingers and checked the scrawl on the envelope. Sure as sin, there was my name in Adele Trenet's fine hand. The letter inside, I found, was written on Pinkerton stationary. *Business, then*, I thought. And so it was. Every last word pertaining to the last case she and I had worked on together for the agency.

> *Sebastian, my new partner, fidgets like a ferret and isn't quite as polite as you, Dr. Walker. I do hope that your current surroundings haven't robbed you of that kindness.*

I smiled, despite myself. While I hadn't practiced my trade in quite some time, Agent Trenet was one of the few souls of the world who still called me "doctor."

"It's got to be here!"

I eyed my roommate to see him pawing through the mail feverishly, sputtering, "Where are you, you devil!"

I returned to reading Adele's letter.

I thought you should know that there are no new leads in the strange case of our killer. No new deaths. No more coffee cans. And no earthly idea what this "Moriarty" means. I'm still looking, though. And I trust you to do the same. You might not be a Pinkerton agent anymore, Dr. Walker, but you've a fine, agile mind. If you see or hear anything about Moriarty, do call me post-haste.

"Damnable mail!" Haus blurted out. "Where is it?"

"Where's what?"

"My letter from Adele, obviously. Why would she write to you and not to me?"

"Maybe she didn't have anything to say to you," I said quietly, sliding the letter back in its envelope.

"Nonsense!" Crash snatched the letter from me and his gaze darted across the page. "Nothing. Not a word? Not a single word or thought for me?"

Disgusted and disappointed, he tossed the letter back to me, and went back to his task of arranging mail for the rest of the residents of our strange camp. A pile near the fire caught my eye. The topmost was addressed to Crash—well, to his given name of Sanford Haus, anyway—and bore an intriguing postmark.

"Looks like you've got your own letters to peruse," I remarked.

Crash followed my gaze, then snorted with derision. "Those? They're nothing."

"A stack from the head of the United States Secret Service is hardly nothing, Crash."

"Whatever my brother has to say on any matter is of absolutely no matter. Not to me or mine."

"Could be important."

"Leland and I have very disparate notions of what's important."

I laughed. "For the rough-and-tumble carnie you try to be, you sure do sound like him sometimes."

His head shot up. "What?"

"Your brother, Director Haus. You sound like him sometimes."

"You've met him?"

I nodded. "Once. Didn't take much notice of me. Though I've got one more working leg than the president, apparently a man needs two good stems to work for the Secret Service."

Crash shook his head. "Imbecile. My brother is a complete and utter moron."

He took up the stack of letters—presumably all from Leland—and made to toss them into the fire.

"Wait! Aren't you even going to open them?" I asked.

With a patronizing roll of his eyes, he slipped out of his Crash Haus persona and into that of Madame Yvonde, seer and psychic, as he brought the topmost envelope to his forehead.

"Sanford," he croaked in Yvonde's voice, "you're an embarrassment to the family."

He flicked it into the fire and plucked up another. "Come home. Take your rightful place..."

Flick. Pluck. "End this ridiculous game."

Flick. Pluck. "Sanford, you ungrateful basta—oh, hello, Moira."

This envelope interested him. He let all the others fall—along with his Yvonde schtick—then tore into the paper.

"Who's Moira?"

"My niece," he muttered. As he scanned the letter intently, his mouth formed the words. I'd rarely seen him so keenly invested in anything that didn't have two legs and blonde hair. When he'd finished reading it, his mood had grown even more sour. "There. Have a look. Evidence that Leland and I value different things entirely."

The handwriting wasn't as adept as Adele's, but Moira's cursive was elegant. Practiced and precise rather than relaxed and routine.

Dearest Uncle Sandy,

Washington D.C. is lovely in the summer. And while it's entirely true that the Capitol is an aesthetically pleasing site, I find no joy in it.

Dear Millicent has taken up piano. Her stubby fingers make an appalling racket for such a finely tuned instrument. I've offered to tutor her, but Mother insists that I learn to paint instead. Honestly one can only stare at trees for so long before one would rather take the brush to her own eyes rather than canvas. Baby Willard is walking now, a fact that vexes his nanny no end.

While my younger siblings indulge in playtime and walks in the park, I am mired with the minutiae of society. Scads of names I'm supposed to commit to memory and titles I should care about. Vapid young ladies meant to be my peers, but I find we've nothing in common.

It bores me!

If I dare voice this opinion, Father dismisses me. Or worse, curses you for putting such foul thoughts into my head. He has agreed, however, to take me with him on some of his jaunts with President Roosevelt this season. I should enjoy being able to see new places in our fine country.

Father speaks of you sometimes, and it's never fondly. But I think that's because you did something he doesn't understand. You gave up this silly game of pawns and politicians. The rules and niceties that come with wealth and status. You gave it all up and went to a place where our family name means nothing.

I think I understand that, Uncle Sandy.

I think you would understand me. You always did.

I know that your schedule is rather full—delightfully so! But I do hope that you might find the time to write back. Or better still, visit us. I would so love to hear all about your adventures. Perhaps you could come for Christmas! The capitol is rather lovely when the snow falls.

Your faithful niece,
Moira Grace Haus

"Why didn't you go?" I asked, carefully stuffing the letter back in its envelope.

Crash's attention was on the ends of his hair as he unspooled a curl and pulled it down before his eyes. Absently, he replied, "Go? Go where?"

"Home. To visit your family. Christmas was last week, Crash."

"This is my home."

"This," I said, holding up the letter, "is your kin."

The look Crash gave me, you'd'a thought I held him at gunpoint. He eyed the envelope warily and narrowed his gaze on me. "And what of your family, Jim? If it's so important, why were you here with the rabble for Christmas?"

"Only family I've got are ghosts or them that don't want to be seen."

"Well you can count me in the latter group where the Haus family is concerned." His voice was tight, with an angry hiss. His eyes blazed. "I want nothing to do with my brother or our lineage."

"But Moira?"

Sanford turned his back to me and pounded a fist against the wall. Cans and boxes rattled.

I softened my approach. "This niece of yours sounds lonely, man. She needs somebody."

Silence stretched between us, filled only by the crackling of the fire and Crash's tense, trembling breathing. I waited while he worked his fingers into fists. Squeezing. Releasing. Fidgeting a bit before squeezing again.

Finally, he tossed a few scraps of conversation over a quaking shoulder. "She'll find better than me."

I couldn't help the smirk that came over me. "You're saying there's better than Crash Haus in the world? Mark the date and color me surprised."

This lightened his mood a bit, and his familiar bravado returned as his mouth hitched up in a grin. "Not today, there isn't."

Crash snatched the letter from Moira out of my hand and placed it gently in a cigar box over the stove. This one, unlike the rest of my roommate's stashes, was filthy with dust and soot. I'd never seen him bother with it before. I wondered just what else he kept in there that he didn't want to look at.

two

HE TOSSED THE stack of letters from Leland into the fire and watched the paper curl into cinders, then went back to sorting out the rest of the mail. We'd nearly finished with the small piles when Crash's head jerked up. Those piercing eyes squinted, and his pale skin flushed.

"No!" he called to no one in particular.

In a flash, he was out into the blistering cold on a scent of something he clearly didn't like. He looked a damn fool in nothing but his trousers, suspenders and a sleeveless undershirt, waving his arms and carrying on like a howling loon.

I followed him as fast as my prosthetic leg would allow. When I caught up with him, he was staring down a black horse pulling along a wagon not dissimilar from our own. This one, though, was well-kept; bright blue with white canvas in the windows. The boxy thing wasn't as ornate as some of the vardos around the lot, but the paint was fresh and something about the clean lines drew the eye to it with wonder and curiosity. Lanterns creaked and something in the undercarriage wheezed as the wheels ambled over the snowy path.

"Get gone!" Crash shouted. "You're not welcome here."

The horse didn't seem to care one way or another if it was welcome or not. The driver—a bundle of black coats and scarves—seemed even less impressed by my friend's assertions. But he drew the horse to a halt all the same. Clouds of breath steamed out of the folds of the driver's coverings, from the horse's nostrils as it snorted and tossed its mane.

"Get out!" Crash continued to bellow. He stomped along toward the rear of the wagon, banging his fist against the slats as he went. "Go on, turn this heap around!"

"Did you miss me?" a voice shouted happily from within the wagon. The door flew open and a long-legged skeleton launched out. He wore a purple coat, a top hat, and a smile that dashed away when Crash punched at the wall again. "Do not lay another finger on my home, Haus," he said, his accent fine as Queen Victoria's.

Crash simmered so hot I thought he'd boil right through the snow around us. "Get out," he repeated, voice low and menacing. "Get off my lot."

The stranger leaned his elbows against the railing of his wagon and brought his face down closer to a level with Crash's. "I'll do no such thing. This berth has been my home longer than it's been yours, gaucho."

"Gaucho?" I asked.

His handlebar moustache twitched as he spared me a quick glance. "Oh, fantastic, you've spawned another of your kind."

Crash crossed his arms. "I'm owner of the show. I decide who takes up with us."

"Is that so? Or maybe you're chasing off the *real* talent and all you can muster is a gaucho like you. And a gimp-legged one at that."

I didn't know what a gaucho was, but I didn't like the way this pompous vermin tossed the word about at me. "And just what's that supposed to mean to me, limey?"

"You weren't born into the circus life. Neither of you." With a glare in my direction, he spat, "Pretenders."

"What does it matter?" Crash tossed in. "You were born to

it, and it certainly didn't help you foster any sort of talent. And if we're such a rotten show, why bother with us? No, Professor, you want something."

Professor? I thought.

"As it happens," Professor Skeleton said, smoothing his moustache with spindly fingers, "I am on the run from nefarious persons unknown."

"And you mean to bring trouble to me and mine?"

"On the contrary, I hope to evade these ruffians by putting myself in the least of likely places: with you, Crash, my most stalwart foe."

Seeing that my friend was still dubious, the Professor added, "Besides, try as I might to discern the meaning of certain messages left behind, it seems I'm just not clever enough for the task."

The Professor dipped his chin, a liar's smile sparkling in his eyes as he waited for Crash to rise to the bait dangling before him.

Crash stroked the stubble on his chin. "Messages, you say?"

"Oodles of them," the Professor purred, stare keen. His fists tightened around the railing.

The chill air tightened with anticipation, waiting for Crash to give a yea or nay on the matter. Contrary to my expectations, my roommate stepped forward and said, "Fine. You park your wagon and stay here until I get this little matter of yours solved."

The two men shook hands.

"Thank you, Crash. Perhaps you're not such a ridiculous man as I'd thought."

"Ridiculous or not, I wouldn't get too cozy. I'll likely have your messages deciphered by sundown, at which time you can feel free to swing on down to Hell."

With a wry smile, the Professor brought his hands together and bowed. "We can only hope you're so quick-witted, Master Haus."

As he ambled back to our wagon, I snatched Crash by the suspender. The strap snapped against his skin and he winced. "What's that about, Dandy?"

"What's *that* about?" I said, hooking a thumb to the Professor's vardo.

Behind us, the Professor shouted, "Maeve! Swing the wagon 'round and try not to get us stuck in the snow. Last time it took you three hours to dig us out!"

Crash pawed at the air. "He's nothing."

"He's baiting you with that fish story about ruffians and messages, Crash. And you're taking it. Never pegged you for a mark."

He whirled on me then, features becoming frosty and sharp. "Listen here, Walker."

I flinched at the use of my actual surname.

"I know exactly what that man is. Better than you. Better than at least half the people on this lot, truth be told. I know damn well not to trust him with so much as a cabbage. But I'd have him where I can see him rather than lurking somewhere behind me. Savvy?"

"Enemies closer," I muttered with a nod.

"Something like that. Now you can hand down advice on my family. You can tell me to put the damn violin away at three in the morning. But what you won't do is tell me how to run my business. Never take me for a mark, Jim Walker."

Crash stalked away then, his footsteps crunching through the snow.

three

THE MOOD IN our cart was only slightly warmer than the outdoors, but I think that was more on account of the fire than anything else. We quietly set to our task of sorting out the rest of the mail. When every envelope had been put into a pile, I tied each of them up with a bit of twine and grabbed my coat off the hook by the door.

Crash shrugged into his moth-eaten coat and threw the scarf around his neck again. "I'll take this half, you take the other."

I doffed my longshoreman in his direction. "Aye, Cap."

He shook his head at me, expression still grim, then barreled out into the cold. As I trekked from tent to wagon, I praised the strong backs that had carved out the paths through the snow. The drifts were knee-deep in some places and if I'd had to gimp my way through them... well, the whole Wonder Show would've seen a one-legged man freezing his ass off while he flailed about in the powder. Would've made for one helluva snow angel, but I prefer living to dying of hypothermia.

Anyhow, I got the letters to their folks and trudged along the slush toward Mrs. Hudson's cart. Right about the same time, Crash trundled up with the Professor and his driver.

Said driver was much smaller on the ground than when manning the horse. I guessed him to be about four and a half feet tall. And that was about all I could say on the matter. He was still wrapped head to foot in heavy black clothes, a massively long scarf, and a fedora. He took tiny, brisk steps to keep up with the others.

The Professor still wore his purple tail coat, but had chosen to leave his top hat behind. Snowflakes clung to his handlebar moustache, and a red tinge kissed his nose and bare chin. Getting a better look at him, I judged him to be hungry. Oh, sure he kept his dark hair and moustache immaculate, the nails on his hands clipped to precision. But with cheekbones that could slice a man's throat, and a sallow complexion, the Professor looked about as starved as a hyena in Heaven. I wagered that if I pulled back that coat I'd see the man's ribs.

Crash's expression was surlier than it had been before we set out on our deliveries.

"Breakfast," he grunted, the word billowing out of him on a cloud of mist.

"Oh, vittles do sound good. Don't they, Maeve?" The Professor looked to the black shadow behind him, but didn't bother waiting for a response. "I don't know that we've had a hot meal this week at all, since *someone* can't seem to keep a fire lit."

He spat something through his teeth as he pulled off the driver's hat and snatched off the scarf. While the Professor wound the muffler around his own face, the driver was revealed to be a young waif with dishwater-grey hair and skin like a new pearl. She turned her grey eyes to the ground as she bundled into herself for more warmth.

"Sorry, Mr. McGann," she murmured.

"Sylvestri!" He shouted. "I've told you a thousand times, girl, when we're out of the wagon, it's Professor Sylvestri."

"Sorry, sir."

He didn't hear her second apology. Instead, he'd turned on the charm and fixed me with a gleaming smile. "Ah yes, you are Crash's friend. We weren't properly introduced earlier. I'm Professor William Patricius Johann Petroff Christobol Sylvestri. Man of the world, harbinger of fortune, and proprietor of elixirs and restorative tonics."

He offered his hand, but I didn't take it. Crash thrust a pile of letters into my palm. "Don't think I didn't notice you neglected to take Mrs. Hudson's mail. Now turn around, Dandy, and give the woman what she wants."

Haus gripped me by the shoulders, spun me around and shoved me toward the crum car, where the ample Mrs. Hudson waited for us, her customers.

"Good morning, good lookin'," she hollered at me. Her plump face spread into a smile that could melt the iciest of winters.

"Good day to you, too, Mrs. Hudson."

That smile of hers faded only slightly, but the joy in her expression doubled. "Darlin', how many times am I going to have to tell you to call me Martha?"

Before I could stop the words from comin' out of me, I said, "Maybe I just like callin' you missus."

Lily white skin blushed the color of summer peonies, and the freckles splattered over her nose burned. Hers could never be mistaken for typical beauty. Small of height, but round of virtue, Mrs. Hudson had more curves than a spring has coils. Dark, redder than wine, the curls of her hair whispered against the softness of her chin.

"Mail for you, Ma'am," I said quietly, passing her the stack of envelopes.

She accepted them, but tossed them to a chair behind her. "What can I get for you today, my dear, darling Dandy?"

Taking out my wallet, I held out a couple of dull coins. "Toast, bangers and coffee, if you please."

"Mrs. Hudson!" The Professor chimed in as he barged up to the rear of the Missus's cart. "Have you really stayed with this rabble since Haus took over?"

Martha's comely face darkened with disdain. "McGann."

"Sylvestri, madame."

"Your name's McGann, and I'll have none of your arsing about. What do you want?"

"What is the soup of the day, good lady?"

"Whiskey. And if you flash me an extra ace I won't piss in it first."

"Mrs. Hudson, you spoil me," he said, thumbing through a tattered billfold. He gave the dwarf two crisp bills and ordered up a plate nearly identical to mine. When Mrs. Hudson served up our food, though, I'd received two sausages more, and my toast dripped with butter. My coffee was piping hot, while McGann's idled without a wisp of steam.

Crash and I took ourselves to one of the benches over by the fire pit. McGann soon straddled the bench next to us, leaving his young shadow to stand in the cold looking for something to do besides shiver.

"Just like old times, eh, McGann?" Crash asked, his tone smug.

The Professor straightened his tie. "Clearly, the lady is having a discomfiting morning." I cocked my head and listened as he spoke, his accent wavering. "Why, she's probably suffering from her monthly courses and is so overwhelmed by the joy of seeing me after so long an absence that she has no clue how to respond."

So as to not have to look at the git's gaunt face, I let my gaze drift to his shadow. The girl stood staring at the snow, her expression distant. A fact not lost on Crash.

"Maeve, is it?"

She looked to the Professor as if seeking approval. When he didn't take his attention away from his breakfast, she gave Crash a meek nod.

"Won't you sit down? And where is your breakfast? Surely you're hungry, too."

Maeve remained silent as snowfall, her grey, haunted eyes darting about for a response.

"Mrs. Hudson!" Crash called out. When the dwarf's curls bobbed into sight, Haus held up two fingers. She nodded and disappeared back into her crum car.

"Now!" the Professor said jovially. "Haus, my good man, shall I tell you all about these mysterious events?"

"How old are you, Maeve?" Crash asked.

She burrowed deeper into her overlarge coat and murmured, "T-t-twelve, sir."

"And how did you come to be in the company of Mr. McGann, here?"

"Haus," the Professor interrupted, "I'll have you not encourage poor behavior in my ward, here. She already has the unfortunate habit of using my Christian name in public, and I'm trying to break her of it.

"And if you must know," he added indignantly, "I caught her trying to steal food from my wagon. She'd taken to some of the more hospitable hobo trails, but had not learned that there *is* a code of ethics among their ilk. So I, being the kind soul I am, took in the waif, gave her a hot meal and the promise of an honest wage."

The more he talked, the more I thought of the soldiers I fought beside over in the war. Boys from England crying themselves to sleep in the trenches, telling me tales of their sweethearts back home. Or sisters. Some were only old enough to have loved a mother.

And this Professor's voice rankled. It scraped against the memories I had of those lads and chafed me raw. I don't know that I'd have liked him had we met at the gates of Heaven itself.

When he stuffed a sausage into his mouth, I noted, "Whereabouts are you from? At first I thought you might be out of London, but somehow a little bit of Newcastle slipped in."

His eyes betrayed nothing. McGann smiled and his answer slithered out. "Ah, have you been to my island then?"

He brought his mug to his face, but his nose curled as he noticed something floating in the drink. He tossed the contents out into the smoldering embers of last night's fire.

"I've been around the area a time or two," I said obliquely. "Truth is you don't sound like any Tommy I ever met."

"Pardon?"

"That's a'cause he's not," Mrs. Hudson said brashly as she waddled through the snow. She presented Maeve with a steaming mug that smelled suspiciously like the chocolate the good lady kept in her own private stash. Along with it was a plate full of food. Twice as much as Crash and I ate.

She swatted at McGann to get him to make room on his bench, then urged Maeve to sit. The girl did as she was told and then stared at the food, eyes wide as saucers.

Mrs. Hudson crunched through the snow to stand beside me. "This one's puttin' on airs to make 'imself seem more legitimate."

"So I'll ask again," I said. "Whereabouts are you from, Mr. McGann?"

He rolled his eyes and something seemed to slough away, like he'd shed a skin of sorts. His shoulders dropped, and his long, sharp angles seemed to relax. But he didn't look comfortable. Not in the slightest.

"Good ear on this one, Haus," he admitted, his accent shifting to something from the Scottish highlands. Reaching out and taking Maeve's mug, he added. "Hope you've got him workin' a bally."

Mrs. Hudson fumed. And she couldn't have been more threatening if she'd been fifty feet tall and breathing fire. She stalked over, retrieved Maeve's mug and placed it in the girl's fist. Then she scooped up grey, muddy snow from the ground with McGann's cup and thrust it back at him. Without a word, she returned to my side. I gladly made a little more room for her on the bench.

Crash's smile was one of keen amusement. "Go on, then, McGann. Tell me all about these ruffians and their cryptic messages. Spare no details."

For the next hour or more, the Professor regaled us with florid tales of vandalism and terror. Like a true showman, his spiel was loud, bringing out the bleary-eyed occupants of the Wonder Show's campground. Mrs. Hudson tended to their feeding while McGann took it upon himself to entertain the growing mass of carnies with his most curious story.

Apparently, sometime round about the Fourth of July, persons unknown burgled his wagon. They broke the windows, left gouge marks in the walls and floor, but took nothing. As the Professor told it, he needed no further persuading to vacate town quickly and moved himself along. A few weeks later, however, he returned to the wagon to find Maeve in hysterics and fresh paint marring his beloved wagon.

"And what did it look like?" Crash asked, his fingers steepled beneath his chin as he listened intently.

"Yellow," the Professor said. "And why should it matter?"

"Not the color, dolt, but the shape of it. Did someone merely splatter a can of paint on your vardo or did they leave a message?"

McGann's eyes twinkled and he hunched toward Crash conspiratorially. "There's the rub. It seems I'd offended a pack of hobos. They painted stick figure signs on my beloved home, besmirching it with their simplistic sigils."

"Stick figures?" Crash murmured.

"Indeed. Symbols that appear to indicate a dancing man. Or," he said, stealing another sip from Maeve's hot chocolate, "when viewed upside down, they are quite sad and confused flowers."

"And is that all, McGann?"

"How do you mean?"

"Two separate occasions a handful of months ago; are these your only interactions? For if they are, I still don't understand why you'd come running here."

"Not at all, Crash. Not at all. They've kept a close watch on my travels. The brigands broke in again and destroyed more of my property with the same symbols. That was after the wedding in Birmingham, wasn't it, Maeve?"

She nodded sheepishly. "As you say, Mr. McGann—Sylvestri!" she added quickly.

The Professor waved off her gaffe and went on, luxuriating in the sound of his own voice. "The most recent occasion was the worst, Crash. Just last week I woke to the terrible noise of my horse shrieking in agony. I staggered out to find the poor beast flailing in a pile of its own blood, the strange stick figure man dancing a macabre jig on its flank."

I shuddered at the thought, remembering all too well what it felt like to be cut without the luxury of anesthetic or a good shot of rotgut. Crash, however, stared into the middle distance, pondering the problem before him.

"And the gouges in the floor and walls of your wagon. They are the same symbols?"

"Aye," McGann said. "All of them different, and each one carved like a sinister warning to do harm upon my person."

Crash unfolded from the bench and fixed the professor with a hard expression.

"Show me."

four

The interior of Professor McGann's wagon proved to be only slightly more accommodating than the one I shared with Crash. A bed had been built into the rearmost recess atop a pair of spacious steamer trunks on their sides. A worn green rug had been thrown over the slats of the floor in front of the stove. Shelves held all manner of things from the mundane to the curious: mason jars full of clear liquid, vials of amber fluid, brass spheres and clockwork dancers. Every inch of wall not devoted to storing his wares, however, was plastered with McGann's face or name. His smile oozed from posters and playbills next to signs and advertisements shilling "Sylvestri's Scintillating Serum" or the Professor's abilities as a mesmerist, hypnotist and numismatist.

"Numismatist?" I jeered. "Didn't know coin-collecting was something to tell the world."

McGann's cocksure smile waned, but he was quick to recover. "I collect as many coins as the marks donate to my coffers, good man."

The fake accent was back again, along with the sense of unease skittering under my skin.

Haus only had eyes for the green rug. He squatted down, stare intense enough to burn a hole through the tight weave. He stroked the floor with the tips of his fingers.

"Is this where she sleeps?"

"Hmm? What?"

Crash's sigh was heavy and reticent. "The girl, McGann. Maeve. Is this where she sleeps?"

"Ah, yes." The Professor resumed inspecting his own reflection in a small mirror. "I keep to the bed and she has her place by the fire." His eyes grew wide, scandalized, and he turned his full attention to Crash. "Are you insinuating that I've had improper dalliances with her? Haus, you disgust and insult me with these—"

"Shut your gob, McGann. If I thought any such thing, you'd already be on the road out of here with naught but your horse and a kit to match Godiva's."

This didn't seem to ease the Professor's mind at all.

"Where did you find her, by the way?"

"As I said, she was little more than a street urchin trying to rob me."

"Why take her in?" I asked. "Why not leave her on the trails and move along?"

McGann became uncharacteristically silent. "I don't know, really. It's been some time since I had a travelling companion."

"You were lonely," Crash mused.

"Aren't you?" The Professor shot a glance to me, looked me up and down with enough derision to leave a slime trail. "Well, perhaps not."

Rather than answer, Crash threw back the rug to reveal the scars on the floor.

The floorboards were marred with—just as the Professor had said—stick figure men. There were two figures, hands joined, limbs mirroring one another as if dancing.

"You also mentioned the walls were vandalized?" Crash asked.

McGann peeled away an image of his own leering face to reveal a similar pair of carvings. They'd been gouged through a layer of patterned paper, leaving a tattered, splintered texture.

"Now I see why you've got the posters on the wall," I said.

"They are far more appealing to the eye than what lies beneath," McGann agreed.

"That," I said, "is a matter of opinion."

Still squatting, Crash studied the wagon. "Is it just these?" he asked with a loose gesture between the two carvings.

McGann shook his head sadly. "No. There are more beneath most of the adverts."

Crash sprang up and massaged the walls, fingertips gliding over the posters like he was a blind man trying to read the tiniest of ripples. For a time, the only sounds were the rickety squeak of floorboards beneath his weight, the light hiss of skin across paper, and Haus's hurried breath.

"They're almost identical," he remarked. "Always in pairs. Not quite symmetrical. You've painted over the one outside, I presume."

"You presume correctly, Crash. I needn't travel with such a mark. The gods alone know what sort of message that might send to some. Is it a brand? An order to do bring me ruin?"

"Hobo signs," I said.

Crash smiled. "Do elaborate, Dandy."

"Well, the roadmen have their own code. They don't like outsiders to interfere with their business, but they are more than happy to help with one another. Not all of 'em can read, of course, so they use symbols left in the dirt or painted on signposts to let the rest of their ilk know what's about."

"Warnings?" Crash asked, still inspecting the walls.

"Sometimes. They might warn each other off if there's been a local crime, or if there's a particularly unhappy dog that might take a knock out of 'em for trespassin'. Other times, they like to share the good news and point one another to places where they can get a few hot squares and a day's wage."

"Can you read these?" McGann asked.

I shook my head. "I never lived rough."

"Then how is it you have such knowledge?"

I didn't feel like tellin' this cat I had friends who couldn't make it after coming home from the war, friends who'd served their country and could now only survive by scavenging and hopping inside box cars. Instead, I just told him, "I know folks."

"I'm sure you do."

"Where was Maeve?" Crash interrupted.

McGann rolled his eyes. "What's this now?"

"Maeve. If she sleeps on here," he said, punctuating his words with a downward jab, "directly above these rather violent gashes in your floor, where was she when the carvings were made?"

"How the bloody hell should I know?" McGann whined.

"You said she was your ward. You live here, too. For God's sake, man, where was she?"

"I presume she was here, sleeping, while I spent some time out cavorting. When I returned, the girl was in hysterics. I could barely get two words out of her, but those words were clear enough that she'd been frightened by the vandals responsible."

"She was unharmed?"

"I..." he stopped to think a moment, eyes rolling to the ceiling. "Now that you mention it, I'm not quite certain."

Crash slapped the Professor and blazed out of the wagon, shouting, "Imbecile!"

McGann—stunned and mute—gaped at me as his cheek turned a rare shade of pink. I made myself scarce so as to not show him my glee. Crash had done what I'd been aching for since the Professor first rolled up on the lot. And truth be told, I was a mite bit jealous that it was Crash who got to pop him one.

Crash stalked back into the shelter by Mrs. Hudson's crum car where the dwarf was refreshing Maeve's cup. He'd just drawn a deep breath to start his questioning, when Artemesia Proust and Jonathan Mars waylaid my roommate. Mars put his considerable bulk between Crash and young Maeve, though

I don't suppose it was specifically to keep the two apart. The strongman's face was red, and his eyes moist. But a smile beamed through his thick, black beard.

"Crash, you're just the man I need to see," Mars said, almost out of breath.

"Jon, I'm a tad busy. Can it wait?"

"It won't take but a moment, Crash."

He reached out a hand the size of my cap and curled his thick fingers around Artemesia's wrist. The Wonder Show's tattooed lady slid beneath his arm and settled there like they were two pieces of a puzzle. Her smile even matched his.

"Crash," Mars began. His barrel chest swelled to the size of a steam engine. "I've asked the lovely Miss Proust here to be my wife."

Her tiny hand stroking her lover's arm, Artemesia gazed at him adoringly. "And I've said yes."

Those within earshot gasped. Whispers passed the news and soon a chorus of congratulations surrounded the happy couple. Hell, I found myself grinning like an idiot; no wonder Mars was so pleased.

I could see the ropy veins in Crash's neck. He tightened his jaw and flashed a glance past Mars. I looked, too, and saw Maeve bundling herself tightly in that overlarge coat and shuffling off to her wagon, her steps tiny but hurried. Disappointment was a cloud over Crash's face, then, but when he spoke his tone couldn't have been more sincere.

"Jon, that's wonderful. Most heartfelt congratulations to you both." He placed a chaste kiss on Artemesia's temple before shaking Jonathan's meaty paw. Eyes darting toward Maeve's retreating form, he added, "Is that all you needed?"

With a simple upward tilt of her head, Artemesia asked Mars a silent question. He nodded his response and she engaged my roommate. "Well, it's just that... well, I don't know that there's been a wedding since you came to us."

"I don't think so, no."

"You see, here in the circus we've a tradition when it comes to nuptials."

Crash waited for one of them to continue, but when neither Mars nor Miss Proust offered further explanation, he asked, "You're not leaving, are you?"

"Oh, no!" Artemesia exclaimed. "We wouldn't dream of it."

Mars bellowed, "Crash, there is no place we'd rather be than right here with you and the rest of the Wonder Show. Which is why we want you to send us around the carousel."

Haus narrowed his eyes. "I'm sorry? I don't understand."

"It's our way," Artemesia explained gently. "We don't go in for churches and the like. When a man and a woman want to bond together—for life or just a season—they ride the carousel together for everyone to see."

"Generally speaking, Crash," Mars carried on, "the person who starts up the ride sort of acts as best man and preacher."

His voice trailed off and the small crowd around us grew silent. The levity of the moment shifted, became something somber. A tick or two later than me, Crash caught on and understanding seeped into his cold eyes.

Lines scored Crash's forehead, driving his brows closer together as the brilliant man puzzled over this simple—yet sacred—request. I couldn't be certain, being so new to the show myself, but I guessed that the carnies didn't often ask one not born of their ranks to participate in their rites of passage.

Crash cleared his throat, opened his mouth to speak but closed it again. He swallowed hard. "You... you want me...?" he croaked.

The Professor took that moment to barge in. "You know, I would be more than pleased to wed you both," he said, voice booming. "After all, I am part of the family. I was born to the trade, part of this show, and I also happen to be a man of the cloth."

Crash didn't honor him with his full attention. "Any church that would have you should rethink its adherence to a god with such low standards of excellence and piety."

This drew snickers from the assembled mass. Artemesia and Jonathan couldn't have been more serious, though. Artemesia placed a hand gently on Crash's arm.

"Please, Crash. It would be our genuine pleasure if you'd do this for us."

Haus's fingers clasped hers. "I'd be honored."

A whoop went up around the camp and clusters of folks began hugging and kissing each other. Mrs. Hudson—after congratulating the couple—waddled around the scrum and looped her arm around mine. She pulled me down and planted a heavy kiss on my mouth.

"Looks like we're going to have a wedding!" she said.

Crash grabbed me by the arm and pulled me out of the celebration. I let him, stunned as a deer as I was from that kiss.

"Come on," he urged, turning me toward our wagon. "We should talk."

As we left I heard Mrs. Hudson say, "Professor, you help me hitch my wagon to Dandy there, and your dessert's on the house for the rest of your days."

five

THE NEWS OF the impending wedding spread with such a quickness, and with such warm fondness, it was almost enough to melt the snow on the camp and bring in an early springtime. Behind the closed doors of our vardo, however, Crash had little on his mind but the Professor's problems.

He paced—which in the tight wagon was little more than a slow spin—fingers steepled beneath his chin, muttering to himself.

"Means... that's no help at all. Anyone can find a paint can or knife. Opportunity? With McGann rolling from city to city, any number of people could find the wagon accessible. So let's examine motive."

"Spending an ounce of time with him," I offered, "is motive in and of itself, wouldn't you say?"

"Too many!" he shouted, kicking at a box of costumes. "The man offends any and all he comes into contact with. There's nothing special about the methods used to vandalize his property, and our perpetrator had every chance available to get to the wagon unobserved. There are too many options!"

"Perpetrator? Not buying the 'gang of ruffians' tale the Professor's layin' out?"

"No more than you are." Crash opened our door and let

out a piercing whistle. "Mr. Mars, Mr. Cubitt, and Mr. Slaney. Could you join me in here, please?"

In short order the three crunched across the lot from Mrs. Hudson's stall and stopped at the foot of our rickety staircase.

"Diamond" Joe Cubitt—a roustabout dark as sackcloth but soft as an angel's feathers—patted his bald head then thumbed his suspenders. With a voice straight out of the lowest octaves of Heaven, he asked. "You need something, Boss?"

"Yes, gents," Crash said amiably. "Come in. All of you, please."

Mars and Cubitt eyed one another warily. Individually, they were broad as oxen. Yoke them with Mr. Slaney, the carousel operator, and the three could haul a train car.

"You sure, Boss?"

"Yes, of course, come on." He then turned to me and handed me a poster from the floor and a bit of the spirit gum he used to hold on his wigs. "Here, Dandy. Hang this on the wall there."

One at a time, the lads took the stairs and squished through the narrow doorway. By the time all three of them stood in the wagon, we couldn't shut the door behind them, so tight were the quarters. The wagon sagged and the floorboards groaned with the additional weight. The closeness was awkward as the simplest act of breathing meant that one man's body would expand to fill the crannies between him and his neighbor.

Crash, standing at the center of the room, dug into his pockets and fished out a stick of chalk. Then, making no attempts to mind the comfort of his cohorts, he squatted down. I couldn't see him through the bodies, but I heard the sound of the chalk scratching the floor.

"Now, Mr. Mars," Haus said cheerfully, eyes to the floor, "when did you and Artemesia intend to wed?"

The great lummox looked as though he wanted to scratch his beard, but he couldn't lift a thick arm to do so. "Oh, well, with the New Year coming up, we'd thought maybe it would be a fine way to celebrate."

"Dandy, the poster!" he reminded me.

I jerked, butting up against Slaney. "Right." I turned slowly, jostling Slaney and Mars in the process. Back to them all, I tried to raise my arms, but found it harder than expected.

Crash went on. "That's two days. Think you'll both be ready by then?"

I adjusted, trying to tear off a piece of the tack with my teeth, but ended up elbowing Slaney in the face. The paper fell to the ground and I had no clearance to pick it back up again. The space was just too confining. I squirmed around to face the lads again, murmuring an apology to Slaney.

"Oh, yes." Mars beamed.

His face flushed, and I wasn't sure if it was from excitement or the fact that the heat in the ill-sized wagon had shot up severely. Sweat beaded on Diamond Joe's pate like a string of pearls. I felt moisture pooling at the small of my back.

"Right, then," Crash proclaimed. "Slaney, can you and Diamond Joe see to the proper set up of the carousel in the clearing just behind the camp?"

Slaney nodded.

"It'll take some time to dig out the storage shed doors, but we should be able to start building tomorrow. Assuming that suits," Diamond Joe added with a glance to Mars.

"Aye," Mars muttered.

Crash tried to clap his hands, but ended up thudding against the strongman's thighs. He sprang up from his position and nearly clocked his head against Diamond Joe's chin. "Fantastic. Gents, I'm glad we talked. Go on about your day and we'll discuss the nuptials a tad later. I've some business to tend to."

The three extricated themselves and cool air whipped in through the open door. I let out a breath and dabbed at my moist brow.

"Couldn't've said all that with them outside?" I asked, tossing him the spirit gum.

"Couldn't have proven my point if I'd done that."

"What point is that precisely?"

Crash smiled smug as a cat and pointed to the floor. He'd drawn a small circle and scrawled the barely legible words, "Not A Gang," on the boards.

"You," he said, "couldn't hang a poster. Far less vigorous and demanding a task as ruthlessly carving a series of menacing stick figures into the wall. And this"—he indicated the circle—"was all the space I had to work with without drawing on our friends' feet."

"You picked the three biggest sods on the lot," I countered. "What if the professor's ruffians are smaller? More average?"

"Like us, for example?"

"For example."

Crash scratched the back of his neck and shut the door. "I will concede that there were perhaps two men who violated the sanctity of the Professor's home, but no more. If—as he supposes—Maeve was in residence, that would mean three people were in the wagon at the time of the attack. Three people scrambling about—two in a frenzy, the third in fear for her safety. Any more than that and the ordeal becomes cramped beyond plausibility."

"And the horse?"

Haus lolled his head up so as to consult the ceiling, but squeezed his eyes shut. "Damn, the horse! It would take more than one person to subdue an animal large enough to lead the Professor's wagon."

I nodded, though he couldn't see me. "Precisely."

"But!" he shouted, staring at me with wide, feral eyes. "These attacks were separate. While linked by the sigils used, each one escalates. Paint on the outside led to breaking in to carve out the symbols within the Professor's home, which led to killing his horse. The attacks increase in severity and complexity."

"Which might account for needing more muscle to carry them out," I offered.

"Precisely," he whispered. "But we're still left with any number of variables. Identities. Motives."

"And the meaning behind the symbols themselves."

Crash began dismantling the order of the shelves, clattering about as he searched for something. "About that, Dandy. You said you thought they might be hobo signs?"

He found what he was looking for: a stubby pencil and a fistful of blank paper. Once more he squatted, brought the papers to his knobby knee and began scribbling.

"The roadmen have a language that's similar enough in style," I said. "Stick figures, simple meanings. And they leave 'em on any flat surface with whatever might be at hand. If someone living rough took offense to the Professor—"

"Not entirely outside the realm of reality."

"—then he might've seen fit to leave messages on his person."

"Do you think you can find someone in your personal network that would know this language?"

"Suppose I could. Or there might be someone down at the boarding house in town. I can't imagine too many of the roadmen wanting to be out in the thick of a winter this rough."

"Excellent." He sprang to his feet and stuffed the papers in my pocket. Swatting me on the shoulder, he said, "Get down there and see what you can find."

I took a look at the papers. He'd jotted down, from memory, the sigils carved into the Professor's abode. "Me?"

"Who better for the job?"

"Now?"

"The sooner this is resolved, the sooner that sorry excuse for a human being is off my lot. Yes. Now."

"And just what are you going to do while I'm hoofin' it into town?"

Sparing me very little of his attention, Crash studied himself in the small shaving mirror over the bunk. "Someone needs to talk to Maeve. And I'll be damned if she's going to sleep one more night on that bastard's floor."

I gazed up to the small, rarely-disturbed box above the stove. The one in which he'd stashed the letter from his niece.

"Remind you of Moira?"

"More than somewhat, Dandy."

I nodded. There wasn't much more to say, so I got to the doing that needed done. I grabbed my coat and bundled myself up, hat pulled low and scarf wound tight. Cane in hand, I began the trek into town to see a man about a dead horse.

six

You want to find a hobo, the best place to go looking is near the railway. I followed the tracks into town and saw nary a soul on my walk. Of course, that just meant that everyone else in Miami County was a damn sight saner and smarter than me.

I saw some hint of road folk, but only by their language. Symbols painted on, or carved into the rail signs. Nothing that matched the marks on the Professor's wagon, but obviously meant to be seen and understood. A picture of a train. A series of circles with arrows coming off of them. A circle with a slash through it. And one that bore some strong resemblance to a duck.

When I hit the first signs of Peru, Indiana, I left the track in favor of Wabash Road. Soon enough, Patrick's Boarding House came into view. Fact of the matter was, you couldn't miss the thing if you were a blind man. The seat of hospitality sported bright green wood slats and orange shutters. The eaves were bright blue, and the door an unfortunate shade of red most often reserved for certain dens of impropriety.

A crude drawing of a cat had been drawn in the snow, and carved discreetly into the wood of the porch.

I beat the sludge off my boots with a few blows of my cane. As is the way with frozen limbs, my remaining foot complained as if I'd stabbed the thing with a hundred tiny needles. I hobbled up the stairs, then wiped my feet on the worn mat.

The door flew open before I'd had the chance to knock.

The woman standing there was a wisp of a thing, with withered brown skin that hung from her bones like leather. Her iron-grey hair was pulled back into a tight bun, though bits of it tried mightily to escape. She eyed me with a fierce curiosity.

"Well, son?" she croaked.

I took off my cap. "Ma'am, I do apologize for troubling you, but I was hoping I could buy a cup of coffee and rest a bit before I get back on the road."

She nodded. "You won't be needing a bed?"

"No, ma'am."

"And you've got money, you say?"

"I've got a few aces."

She yanked the door wide and warmth swam out of the house. "Get your damn fool ass in here now, boy. You look half-frozen and I'll have no one dying on my doorstep on account of this terrible cold."

"Much obliged," I said with a smile.

I stepped inside and chafed my hands as she shut the door behind me. The inside of the boarding house was no less unique than the exterior. The proprietress appeared to have a particular fondness for doilies and anything with the slightest hint of a pink rose on it. The ewer on the sideboard, a framed picture on the wall, curtains and table cloths; all of them were decorated with floral sprays of varying severity. The armchair in the adjacent parlor was striped blue silk while the walls were papered with a dusty red damask.

"I'm Elise Patrick," she said, her words clipped. The lady smoothed her apron before whisking past me and leading me through the hall. "But that's Miss Patrick to you. There is no Mr. Patrick. There never was and never will be. I will not accept disrespect in this house. You treat me the way you'd treat your favorite auntie and no worse, and you can stay as long as you need."

We turned a corner into a gleaming white kitchen. A pot was on the boil, presumably for the evening's meal. A man twice the height of Miss Patrick—and at least twice her bulk—stood chopping tubers.

"Julius," Miss Patrick called, "this one needs some joe and a bit of that broth in him before I'll turn him back out into this weather."

The man looked up and I saw he had the face of a soot-stained cherub, little more than an overgrown boy. Julius nodded fervently. "Yes, ma'am."

Miss Patrick crooked her finger at me and led me into the dining room. She pulled out a wooden chair and pointed to its seat. "Sit you down, boy. Get off that leg before it becomes a problem."

You don't argue with a scowl like that woman wore. I put my better end in the chair *tout suite*. She gave me a firm, approving pat on the shoulder and set to putting cream, sugar and a small plate of cookies on the table.

"Now what's your name, son, and what brings you this way?"

"Jim Walker." I put a cookie in my mouth so I could think of what to tell Miss Patrick. Though the Wonder Show tried its best to keep good with the townfolk, and Peru was no stranger to rovers like ourselves, I never knew how one would react to housing a carny, something I'd become in a matter of months.

Julius came along just in time with a cup of coffee and a piping hot bowl of broth—chicken, by the smell of it. He only stayed long enough put down his wares before returning to the kitchen and his potatoes.

"Thank you," I said, wrapping my cold hands around the mug of coffee.

Miss Patrick leaned in closer to me and sniffed the air. I

caught a whiff of my own funk—reefer and the odor of having walked a few miles with one leg. Her plum-colored lips pursed disapprovingly.

"What are you about, Mr. Walker?" she asked.

"Ma'am?"

"You ain't local, but you've got no bags. You're too clean to be a railman, but you smell like the Devil's sweat."

I swallowed a mouthful of coffee and let it stoke my insides to warmth. Perhaps truth would be best. Some of it, anyway. "I take up with the Soggiorno Brothers' show that's made camp about five miles east of this very table."

Her smile was wry, revealing a gap in her yellow teeth. "A circus boy, eh? You gonna juggle for your supper, Mr. Walker?"

I shook my head. "No, ma'am. I don't perform, I just help on the lot."

"What's a job like that pay a man?"

"Three dollars a week and ever-changing scenery." I stretched out my prosthetic leg and massaged the ache in my thigh. As I thawed out, the pain began to seep into my muscles something fierce.

She heard the metallic joints clatter, Miss Patrick, and looked down. Her face showed the slightest panic, so I tugged up on the fabric of my pants to let her see that she needn't fear the metal rod that served as my tibia.

She fixed me with her watery eyes and seemed to stare into my mind. Her withered lips trembled. "The war?"

"Yes, ma'am."

Miss Patrick nodded solemnly. "And you walked all the way here from that circus camp?"

"Yes, ma'am."

She swatted me on the head as she passed by into the kitchen. "Damn fool boy, you need a sandwich now, too."

*   *   *

AFTER SETTING WATCH on me until I'd eaten as much as man can hold, Miss Elise Patrick refused to take my money. I'd held the coins out to her, but she put a hand over mine and pushed it back to my chest.

"You done paid for your meal, soldier."

I nodded my gratitude and pocketed the cash. Miss Patrick sat down beside me. "Now tell me, Mr. Walker, what brings a gentleman like you here on a day like today?"

Reaching into my coat, I produced the papers Crash had scribbled on and laid them on the table. "I need someone who can tell me what these are."

Miss Patrick retrieved a pair of spectacles from her apron pocket and looked down her nose at the drawings. "Look like something Flapjack would write on the wall."

"Flapjack?"

"One of my regulars. When he's road-weary, Flapjack comes back this way and stays—no longer than a fortnight, y' understand. But he draws things like this. Messages to other tramps and bindle stiffs like him."

"Do you know what they say?"

She shook her head. "They're not meant for me to read."

Disappointed, I stuffed the papers back in my coat.

"Don't look so glum, soldier. Flapjack's in residence. I'm sure he could help a fella out."

My smile turned to a wince as I stood up. "Lead on, Miss Patrick."

The lady of the house made her way up a set of old, creaking stairs. Pictures lined the walls, some photographs gone yellow and faded. As if it was a script she couldn't help but repeat, Miss Patrick said, "We have five rooms upstairs—that's five beds for payin' folk. Julius and I quarter in the attic. Each room has its own bed, linens and light. There's a radio in the parlor downstairs, and a bathroom at the end of the hall. A man staying here *will* make use of the bath before bedding down or

I will have Julius take the hose to him. I'll not have my sheets spoilt."

"You run a tight but accommodating ship, ma'am."

She knocked on the third door on the left and called to the room's occupant. "Mr. Hilton? Flapjack, are you decent?"

A rumble answered.

"Mr. Hilton, I've a man out here that could greatly use your knowledge of the roads."

The lock clicked and the door swung open. A shaggy head poked out into the hall. "Alright."

Miss Patrick smiled. "Flapjack, this here is Mr. Walker. Be good to him. Oh, and when you've a mind to it, wash up and come down for some vittles."

Bleary as a bear woken in January, Flapjack Hilton waved a paw at Miss Patrick's retreating form. Shuffling back into his room, he grumbled, "Come on."

I followed him in and found the room precisely as advertised. A bed; a small dresser with fresh linens and a lamp atop it. In comparison to the rest of the house, the room was remarkably plain. Cream walls and soft, blue blankets. Flapjack's luggage—consisting of a large leather bag like the one Crash used for mail carrying—rested on the floor next to a pair of boots. A jacket hung on the hook on the wall.

Flapjack pulled back the heavy curtains and daylight poured in. He was a stooped fellow, his shoulders arched with a neck that jutted out, suspending his head perilously in the open air. He wore a stained undershirt, trousers, and a pair of socks that desperately needed darning.

His hair was long, shaggy. What might have once been blonde was grey and looked as though it'd been cut with the dull edge of a knife rather than proper shearing. His beard wasn't much fairer. Patches of silver grew through the thick mass of hair. When Hilton faced me, I saw the leathery texture of his cheeks, the reddish tinge to his nose. He'd been outdoors more than in, it seemed. A glimpse of his watery blue eyes made the breath catch in my chest. This was a man weary to his bones. Haunted.

"Mr. Hilton," said I, "I won't keep you long."

When all I got from him was a grunt, I reached into my pocket and offered him the pages of scribbling. He took them and laid the barest of glances over them before tossing them to the floor at my feet.

"What of 'em?" he snarled.

I sighed and picked up the papers. "Do you know what they mean?"

"Look like a kid drew 'em with 'is own drool. Why should I know?"

"Remind me of something I saw on the road once. Not too different from the cat I saw drawn outside this very house."

"Ask plain, spook, or stop wasting my time."

I bristled at the slur. "Are these road signs, and if so can you tell me what they mean?"

"What's it to you if they are?"

"They were carved into the flank of a horse and a man's home. Whoever did it put a young girl in danger. I'd like to make sure she stays safe."

"She dark as you?"

"I don't see that it matters one way or the other, Mr. Hilton," I said, keeping my voice calm. "She and her guardian have asked me to look in on the matter as a personal favor. I'd take it as a kindness if you could answer my questions."

Flapjack's eyes narrowed and a sneer oozed over his face. His right hand made a move for his waistband, and a familiar hot, pricking sensation flooded my body, just beneath the skin. The acid taste of adrenaline tingled at the back of my throat.

I raised my cane just quick enough to knock the thrown knife to the floor. Its tip sank into the boards with an ominous *thunk*. The sinewy hobo lunged for me, arms raised and fingers curled as if to take out my throat. He spat out slurs, invoking the ugliest of words for a man of my complexion as if he'd invented the damn things.

I stepped to the side and tripped up Hilton with a well-placed blow of my metal leg. As his shin went out from under him, I shifted my weight just so and whacked him one on the back of the neck with my cane. Like a choreographed dance I'd learned long ago, it came bubbling up in my memory. In a few movements and a dash of seconds, I had Hilton on his back, the cane in my left hand pressed to his throat and his own knife kissing his lowest rib. Though he put up some struggle, Flapjack soon found that it was growing difficult to breathe, let alone speak or call out for help. Or use any more of those epithets of which he was rather fond.

I brought my mouth down to his ear. "This is the quickest way to a man's heart," I hissed. "Up under the ribs. A single poke and I'd have your blood all over Miss Patrick's lovely floor. I'd rather not do that, you understand? Nod and tell me you understand."

Hilton nodded feverishly, his thrashing calming down.

"Good. Now, you're going to help me and this little girl out, friend. You're going to be quite the hero. So tell me. Are those pictures I showed you hobo signs?"

He nodded.

"Was that so hard? No. Now, tell me kindly, what do they mean?"

I eased up the pressure with the cane so that he could take a breath. Through gritted teeth, he growled, "First two are road speak."

"Go on."

"One of 'em's 'orphan.' The other's 'murder.'"

"What about the third?" He shook his head. I pressed the cane to his chin, forcing his head back against the floorboards. "What about the third?" I repeated.

"I don't know!" he spat. "Never seen it before."

"Mr. Hilton?" Miss Patrick called through the door. "Is everything alright?"

I shifted my weight off him and Flapjack didn't need an invitation to roll away from me. I palmed his knife and—with a move I'd learned from Crash—slid it into the waistband of my trousers. As Miss Patrick opened the door, all she saw was her new friend lifting himself off the floor, papers in hand, with the aid of his trusty cane.

"Mr. Walker, are you alright?"

"Just dandy, ma'am," I sang cheerfully. "Mr. Hilton here was quite helpful. I was just on my way out when I took a bit of a tumble. Happens from time to time with this old thing." I tapped my cane on the metal leg.

She ushered me out the door and I saw no more of Flapjack Hilton.

"Julius!" Miss Patrick called. "Julius, boy!"

The large lad met us at the bottom of the stairs, a potato in one hand and a small knife in the other. "Yes, Auntie Elise?"

"Put down that potato and see to Mr. Walker here. He's got no business walking back to his homestead on a leg like that."

Julius nodded and returned to the kitchen, but only briefly. As Miss Patrick guided me to the foyer once more, her arm looped through mine, she chided me about not taking care of myself. "Don't you be making trips like that on your lonesome, boy. What if you'd fallen out in the snow by the tracks? No, I'll just not have that on my conscience. Julius is going to take the Packard and see that you get safe home."

I smiled with relief. "Ma'am, you are too kind."

seven

WHEN I GOT out of Miss Patrick's Packard, it was nearly dark. The camp, however, breathed with the warm glow of our huge communal fire. It seemed that the residents of the Wonder Show had decided to throw a beastly houley to chase away the night. I heard Slaney and Hoss playing their drums. Mars and Cubitt were singing off-key to the sounds of Cassie Clay's squeeze box. And there at the center of it, Crash fiddled a gypsy reel.

The cacophony of voices and laughter and instruments gave voice to the wagging tongues of the flames. The shadows flickered across the tents, wagons and, I soon found, in the wide gaze of young Julius's eyes. He gaped at the campground, mouth hanging open.

"Boy, you'll catch flies that way," I warned.

He closed his gob and dared to blink. When the camp didn't disappear, he looked to me. "You live here?"

I gazed again at my home. 'Twasn't hard to see why the boy was so enthralled. The revelers danced sinuously, limbs jutting out of the scrum to take a new partner and pull them close. The thick blanket of snow caught the firelight and glittered like a dragon's heap of gold. The music, the savory smells of Mrs. Hudson's cooking... in many ways the camp was a more intoxicating sight than the carnival itself, with all its banners, lights and carousel song. It could beckon to the most stalwart of souls.

"For the time being," I said, unable to keep the smile from my face.

I dipped into my pocket and pulled out the money Miss Patrick had refused to take for my meal. "Julius, I thank you kindly for the lift and your auntie's hospitality."

"I can't be acceptin' that, sir."

"Please," I said. "As a favor. I don't like charity, boy, and I hate the idea of getting something for nothing. Slip it into her coffers or buy yourself a sweet roll from the bakery in town. I don't care what's done with it, but I'd be offended if you didn't take it."

He stared at the bills, then back at the camp longingly. After pondering something that weighed heavily on his mind, Julius took the money and stashed it in the glovebox. "Sure thing, Mr. Walker."

"That's a good lad."

I slid out of the car with about as much ease as an elephant. Before I could shut the door, Julius called out, "Mr. Walker!"

"Yes?"

"Could I... come and visit y'all sometime? When I'm not working, town gets a little..." His voice trailed off and his chin fell. He didn't want to insult his aunt and her establishment, but for a young man, sometimes the small town just ain't enough to keep his attention.

I nodded. "Sure thing, Julius. Come on out and if you don't see me, tell 'em you're a friend of Dandy's."

His face screwed up in confusion, and I didn't bother explaining. I shut the door, turned my back on the Packard and hoofed toward the fire in my ungainly fashion.

"Dandy!" voices sang, welcoming me to the party.

The music kept on, but a few dancers stopped their spinning to clap me on the shoulder or wrap their arms around my neck in greeting. The Professor had even come out of his den to join in the festivities. He seemed to be doing delightfully well with one of the koochie girls. A flask flashed from his hip and I could smell the rotgut from five foot away. Next to him, ever his shadow, Maeve sat staring at the blazing bonfire. If not for the reflection of the flames, her eyes would've been dull as stone. Her young face fell in an expression far too sullen for one so young.

Crash, fiddle to his chin, fixed me with a sly grin. He bobbed in time with his tune, sketching a light bow in my direction before turning back around to continue the reel with his fellow musicians. A hand too small for a regular-sized adult took my wrist and jerked me to a bench near the fire. A tankard shoved its way into one hand while a plate landed in my lap. Before I could catch a breath, the shindig had engulfed me and accepted me as one of its own.

Much like Crash and the circus itself had done, a few months ago.

I'd not felt such a sense of community since my days fighting in the cold of France. Nor had I drawn on that soldier's anger, or his unflinching ability to hurt another human with the same skill as he could fix one up. Not in nigh unto twenty years. However, that very day in Flapjack's room, the past rushed back to me and Lance Corporal Walker reported for duty like the spry greenhorn I'd been when I first enlisted.

My hands began to shake something fierce and my drink dribbled down my coat. The firelight—which before had been so welcoming, warm and peaceful—flashed and pulsed like artillery fire. The drums boomed in my ears, the voices screamed... all of the noise pressing in on me, dredging up specters and goblins from the past life of a soldier. A Hellfighter.

I pressed my hands to my eyes, trying to blot out the night, but that only intensified the ghostly visions of battlefields and men bleeding their last drops on foreign soil.

Peru, Indiana, fell away from me—or rather I fell away from it, tumbling into a void. Gone was the cold winter night, replaced with the hot, damp skirmish outside Château-Thierry. Smells of black powder, sweat, coppery blood and the miasma of death shoved me, buffeted me on the gale of memory.

The boys were shouting. Some of them cryin' out for their mamas, others screaming for medics who wouldn't make it in time. Laying in mud stained crimson until someone could box them up in pine and send them back to weeping sweethearts.

"Hellfire's behind me," I murmured to myself. "Hellfire is behind me."

"Jim." A soft voice cut through, reaching into the mire of my memories and gently pulling me closer to home. "Jim, open your eyes."

I jerked back into the present and Mrs. Hudson was waiting for me, her stare a pair of guiding stars. Her tiny hands burned on either side of my face. Though the party kept on—Crash's violin climbing higher up his scale at a blistering pace—Mrs. Hudson and I seemed to rest in a pocket of peace just big enough to hold the two of us.

"Jim?"

Words bubbled up in my throat but choked me. There were too many. And how does a man explain the things he's done for his country that would put him out of the esteem of his Lord and a lady? I sagged there on the bench and felt the old anguish sweeping over me.

My head fell, heavy and weary, and it was Mrs. Hudson's shoulder that caught it.

"Come on," she said soothingly.

I let her guide me to my feet, set my course and lead me to the warmth of my vardo. The party droned in another world outside the door of 221b; inside, a man would've wept himself to a thousand pieces if not for the woman holding his shoulders.

eight

After my... episode, I swam in blackness—the sleep of those that don't have the energy to dream. I don't know when Mrs. Hudson left, only that she did. Hell, I didn't so much as stir when Crash returned.

When I opened my eyes on the morning, they were raw, the lashes crusty and brittle. Wind howled outside, whistled over the stovepipe and rattled some of the less sturdy parts of the wagon. Every so often a powerful gust gave the vardo a shake, the springs creaking beneath me. Even my hammock got to swaying.

I couldn't make out if it was daytime or night, nor if I'd slept for a night or a whole year. Crash had pulled the blackout curtains over every cranny. I wouldn't have been able to see my hand in front of my face if I'd been lily white. I heard Crash snoring, though. Great draughts and snuffles rolled in a slow rhythm beneath me.

I might've dozed that way, just listening to both kinds of wind and drifting along in the gloaming, but it's hard to say. Sooner or later, though, someone pounded on our door to wake Ol' Scratch 'imself.

Crash jumped, a bony appendage striking me in the spine. I went rocking, and when he flailed out with both arms the momentum got the better of me. I fell gracelessly atop my roommate, causing both of us to grumble and growl.

"Jim!" Mrs. Hudson called from outside. "We need you!"

Crash and I untangled ourselves and he crawled to the door while I used my prosthetic to lever myself up. He opened the door just about the time I achieved the status of a biped.

Holding an arm over his eyes against the grey light of morning, Crash let out a horrified moan. "Goddammit, Mrs. Hudson, what in the names of the seven whores of Hell do you mean by making such a fuss at my door?"

She snorted and rolled her eyes. "Dramatic ponce," she muttered. "We need the doctor."

"The Professor is in a different wagon, you daft—"

"Not that idiot, Crash! I'm talking about the doctor!" She punctuated this with a jab of her stubby fingers toward me. A few steps and she was grabbing me by my trouser leg and hauling me toward the door. "We've got a problem, Jim."

"Crash," I said over my shoulder, "my bag."

Though I heard him grouse about it, he didn't refuse. Mrs. Hudson led me through the drizzle at a pace that made her jiggle and shake in an all too pleasing a fashion.

"What's wrong?"

"Mars. Got himself bloodied up."

"How?"

"Burglar."

Shit. "Is Artemesia alright?"

"Shaken. Furious."

Mrs. Hudson didn't take me to the tattooed lady's wagon, though. Instead we veered left of it to the behemoth tent of Mr. Mars. A small crowd had already massed outside, their breath fogging me as I passed. Without bothering to jingle the bell outside, the dwarf tossed back the flap and yanked me in after her.

Mars lay in his over-sized tick with Artemesia sitting at his side. The strongman's ruddy face glistened with sweat, and his eyes were glassy as a doll's. His great chest lay bare for all to see, though the rest of him was covered with a blanket. I saw the wound on his left flank, just below the rib cage. Someone had sliced him one, not terribly deep, but enough to bleed and make the Devil's own mess. Smaller cuts were visible on his upper arm, and a puncture was scabbing over on his palm.

"Why the hell didn't you come get me sooner?"

Mars looked at me sheepishly. "Thought it was nothing. Until it weren't."

Crash stumbled in behind me with my black bag in hand. I took it to Mars's side and opened it, taking the time to look at each wound individually. Crash, suddenly sobered by the sight of his bleeding strongman, hovered behind me.

"What happened?"

Artemesia's red-rimmed eyes found mine, then rose to Crash. "Someone broke into my wagon last night, Boss. Jonny heard the ruckus and came over to check on me. Caught the bastard's knife a few times."

"Did you see him?"

Mars shook his head. "Too dark. Too fast."

"Crash," I barked. "Take out the biggest tankard you can find and bring me some clean snow. Artemesia, I need you to get me some clean rags, towels, scarves, whatever you've got. Both of you, make sure it's all clean!"

Without question, they set to my instructions.

"And someone get some water on the boil!" I shouted. As I dug through my bag for what I would need, I said, "Mr. Mars, next time you have so much as a papercut, I'd like to be privy to that information, do you understand?"

"Aye, Doc." Mars let his head fall back and his eyes close. All the better that I could do my work.

"Excellent. Mrs. Hudson, darling?"

"Yes?"

"You got any white lightning in that car of yours?"

"As much as you need."

I eyed Mars's considerably frame. "We're going to need it. And some whiskey, I think."

"There's a bottle of rye next to your bag, Jim."

She set off to get the booze and I put the bottle in Mars's hand. "Take a pull."

"Already been sipping at it," he said.

That could account for some of the redness on his cheeks and nose, possibly a measure of the sweat pouring down his face.

Artemesia flew into the tent with an armful of fabric.

"Crash!" I roared. "Get your lanky ass in here."

A few moments later he appeared with the snow I'd asked for, along with his cigar box of intoxicants. He looked at me knowingly, and I nodded.

"Alright," said I. "When Mrs. Hudson gets back, Artemesia, I need you to lay out all of those rags, you hear? Then I need you to soak these needles in some of the moonshine."

Artemesia nodded.

I took one of the handkerchiefs she'd fetched and brought it to Crash's side. Quietly I asked, "You bring what I asked for?"

He bobbed his head and passed me the cigar box. I flipped the top and sure enough, next to the reefer we shared was a phial of white powder. Glad to know he understood my meaning when I asked for "snow."

"Crash, I can't handle the stuff if I want my hands to be worth a damn."

"What do you need me to do, Jim?"

His steely eyes were somber and serious. And what's more, he was waiting on me to give him ironclad instructions which he would follow like gospel—something I'd rarely seen in my time with Sanford Haus.

"I need you to rub the cocaine around the wound in his side, alright? But wash your damn hands first."

Without question he did as I bade. I filled the handkerchief with snow from outside and tied it into a pouch. When Crash had finished, I handed Artemesia the icy pack and urged her to put it on her fiancé's side.

Meanwhile, I prepared myself for the minor surgery of stitching up Mr. Mars. I washed my hands, got my needles as clean as a baby's soul and set out the thread.

By the time I returned to Mars's bedside, he was calmer. The cocaine had eased a good portion of his hurts, and the whiskey would take his mind to a more mellow place. Examining that great gash, I found that it looked far angrier than it had a right to. The cut wasn't all that deep, truthfully. Long and bloody, sure, but it didn't puncture the chest wall. No need to worry about his organs being damaged, but his flesh was mighty torn up. The stitches would be all he'd need, though. That and a few days off his feet.

I grimaced, imagining this might ruin some of the wedding night fun for him and his bride.

While I stitched up her man, Artemesia sat to his other side, dabbing his forehead with freshly cooled cloths.

"I was dead to the world, you see," she said quietly. "Didn't even know there'd been a break-in. But Jonny's such a light sleeper. A feather dropping would wake this lout up."

She sniffed and I glanced up to see she'd started crying.

"He's gon' be just fine, Miss Proust," I assured her. "Ox like this one won't be down long."

From the corner, Crash asked, "Did you see them, Artemesia? Get any glimpse of who slashed at him?"

"No. It was too dark."

"Did they take anything?"

Peripherally I saw her shake her head. "Not a thing. Bastard ruined my wedding dress, though. Sonofabitch," she spat.

"Can you show me?" Crash asked.

I pulled away from my work so that Artemesia could vacate

the bed and not jostle my hands. When she and Crash took off, Mrs. Hudson took their place in the tent with me. She didn't say a word. Didn't stare at me or try to peer over my shoulder. Her presence, though, was calming and steady. She radiated a strength that others lacked. Sure, Crash exuded authority and leadership. But Martha Hudson offered something else: stalwart serenity in the face of fear. Like she'd weathered my storm the night before, she stood there now, bringing peace with her.

I'd just finished sewing up Mars's side when Crash burst into the room.

"Dandy, look at this."

He held Miss Proust's wedding gown. The lovely lace frock would've been a sight on the tattooed lady's delightful form, it's true. But the creamy fabric had been marred with black stains.

Drawings of two stick-figures standing beneath a cross.

nine

By the time Mr. Mars was sutured, bandaged and snoring to bring down the walls of Jericho, the morning's drizzle had turned to a moderate snowfall. With a biting wind snapping its jaws into any who dared venture outdoors, most of the carnies had the good sense to stay in their homes.

So, of course, Crash insisted we snoop around Miss Proust's wagon sleuthing for clues. "Before the snow has a chance to cover it," he'd said. I stuffed my hands in my pockets and turned my nose to the ground, searching for any hint of a reason to be upright.

"Artemesia said she didn't hear anything," Crash informed me. "That Jonathan roused her sometime after three-thirty or so."

"Did she say if they came in through the door?"

Haus nodded. "The dress was hanging just inside the door and to the left."

We loomed over the stairs, gazing at the muddy shapes on the steps. "Crash," I said heavily, "any prints we might've been able to find have been spoiled a hundred times over. You and Artemesia popped up and back a time or two. Jonny, too. God knows who else."

"The paths aren't much better," he confirmed darkly. "We've been up and down them all day, we'd never find a clear set that we could tie to our vandal."

He leaped up into Miss Proust's wagon and eyed the doorknob, the floorboards.

"What's the door frame look like, Crash?"

Haus ran a hand down the wood. "Clean. No splintering. Don't think they took the trouble to bust it open with brute force."

"Lock picker?"

"There are some scratches on the plate," he said. "Just as easily made by a set of tools as by a key held by a drunk. But there's no sign that someone hunched before the lock and took the time to fiddle it. Most likely, Dandy, that Miss Proust simply left the door unlocked for her fiancé's convenience."

"I'd ask her, but I think she'd bite the head off of anyone who intruded on her right now."

Crash eyed Mars's tent, clearly debating if he should take the chance of disturbing a woman who'd just had her dress ruined the day before the wedding, and her fiancé knifed in the process.

"Don't do it," I warned.

He blew out a cloudy sigh. Then he shut the door behind him and skipped down the stairs with nimble ease.

"Dammit, Dandy," he cursed. We shuffled toward our wagon. "Do you ever tire of being right?"

"Why do you think I so enjoy your company, Crash?"

He smirked. "We didn't get to chat yesterday about your venture into town. You left the party rather early. And abruptly. With company."

I shook my head. "Not like that, Crash."

"Wouldn't mind if it was, you know."

I didn't want to get into a rehash of my less-than-stellar evening with ghosts. "Did you talk to Maeve and the Professor any more while I was hauling my ass along the tracks?"

"I did. What did you think, I'd just sit on my thumbs?"

"The thought had occurred to me."

"Damn shame you think so little of me."

Crash retrieved the key from around his neck and unlocked our vardo. "Shall we trade information, then?"

"I reckon. And maybe you can tell me what you think about those stick figures dancing on Miss Proust's dress."

"Excellent!" The door slammed behind him. "Let's chat."

I sank into my hammock and let it sway a moment. Crash stoked a small fire in the stove and soon the wagon was warm enough to thaw my thoughts.

"I met with a roadman at the boarding house who was kind enough to tell me that two of them signs have meaning to his folk."

Crash danced in place and plucked at the strings of his fiddle. "Oh, do tell."

"One of 'em, the one carved into the floor of the Professor's wagon? Means 'orphan,' if this one is to be believed."

"Fascinating. And the other?"

"'Murder.'"

"Spectacular!"

Crash whirled about and put the violin in its case.

"How is that spectacular, Crash?"

"Well it's more fun, obviously. More interesting than any of the alternatives, really."

I pinched the bridge of my nose. "You don't honestly find this whole ordeal more fun for the hope of murder and death, do you?"

"What else were we going to do with the time?"

I closed my eyes and sighed, weary. "What did you find out?"

"Ah-ha! That's another bit of fun, you see. It turns out that there is more to the Professor's story than he'd care to tell us."

"No shit?"

"Surely you can contain your sarcasm for a moment or two more, Dandy. It is rather unbecoming. Anyway, McGann did find his ward trying to rob his vardo. That much is true. But he failed to tell us that the girl suffers from acute amnesia."

"How so?"

"When I spoke with her, she confided that she had been living rough for the better part of a year prior to her run-in with the Professor some six months ago. So that's eighteen months of her life that she can remember vividly and with ease. Anything *before* her time on the road? Lost."

"Lost?"

Crash nodded cheerfully. "She has always been Maeve—the street urchin. She can't remember a home, a family. Where did she come from? Was she born full-fledged on the street like some hobo Athena? It's delicious, Dandy!"

"You realize you're taking delight in the fact that a girl can't remember her kin?"

"Yes! It's a puzzle! A glorious puzzle!"

"Is that all you found, Crash?"

"Well, for the time being. I am going to write to Adele and see if she'll do me a favor."

"I'm sure that's all you're going to ask," I grumbled.

He smoothed his eyebrows and looked smug. "A man can always hope."

I rolled on my side, putting my back to him and his lecherous glee. I spent the day drowsing, sleeping off the surges of adrenaline and ignoring my roommate's clatter. By the time nightfall rolled around, the snow was coming down hard, with a wind howling to the moon.

THE PROUST/MARS UNION had to be postponed on account of the ground being whiter than the most pristine virgin's wedding dress. A blizzard came through and coated our little camp with more snow than I'd seen in all my days of living. The paths connecting the tents and wagons filled with fresh powder and treacherous ice. Anyone with a lick of sense hunkered down and kept to the warmth of their home.

After the first day of being snowed in, we'd run through what little food we kept in the wagon, but it was genial enough. Our windows iced over, but we stuck our heads out from time to time for fresh air. Like groundhogs, the carnies poked up from their dens to check on the weather, on one another. Since the wedding had been diverted into 1936, we spent the last hours of 1935 listening to the others in the camp. Music, discordant but lively, came from around the grounds. Cheering, laughing. Sounds of joy. Crash and I held our own celebration with some reefer, sharing secrets men daren't speak among civilized folk whilst simultaneously attempting to solve the problems of the mad, spinning world.

On the second day, Haus seemed intent on playing his fiddle in a terrible harmony with the braying wind. Though the gale shook our vardo to the point I thought the hodgepodge wagon would disintegrate to flinders, we survived with the roof still over our heads.

However, come sundown, Crash and I were like a couple of bears sharing a cave—and neither of us was too particularly keen on being awake in the dead of winter. I was content reading a stack of tattered pulps, but a toasty fire in Crash's brainpan led to trembling hands that even a drag off a spliff wouldn't quiet.

Instead of smoking his mind to peace as was his nature, Haus took up most of the floor dissecting some contraption that looked like a cross between a frying pan and a child's guitar. What little body there was on the thing was swamped by a rectangular metallic plate across the lowest curve, covering the strings. A neck longer than a giraffe's stretched up to a head with six tuning knobs and a plaque declaring the thing a Rickenbacker Electro. The strings should've been taut down that neck, but Crash had surgically spread them apart so they stretched off in all directions.

"Do you mind?" he snapped at me.

I stared at him quizzically. "Do I mind what exactly?"

He didn't bother to look up at me, just kept his eyes on the Electro and sneered. "That incessant scratching. It's like having my ears scoured with a steel bottlebrush."

"It's pencil and paper, Crash," I sighed.

"It's distracting. We've been trapped in this wagon for a month—"

"It's been three days."

"—and my mind is a flowering garden of possibilities. Ideas. Work. Never a stagnant moment. And yet you insist on introducing thorns. They snag my attention, pry me away from my work, tear at my very sanity. Briars you've wrought with the lead of your damnable pencil."

I blinked at him in utter amazement—a sight lost on him on account of him still studying his unusable frying pan. "You might be the most dramatic sonofabitch I've ever laid eyes on. You know this about yourself, right?"

"Bothersome fiend," he spat.

I grinned and went back to my scribbling.

"What the devil are you doing anyway, Dandy?"

"It's called writing, Crash."

"Writing?"

"Yes. A form of communication where one uses drawn letters to spell out words and phrases, and generally have a conversation with a person not directly present at the time of composition. You might want to try it sometime," I added. "I'm sure Moira would be pleased to hear from her wayward uncle."

Silence. Sweet, glorious silence from Haus.

I peeked to see if he'd keeled over dead. No such luck. He stared at the wiry guts of his project. "What are you writing?"

"A letter. Or a journal entry. The two aren't all that dissimilar for me," I admitted.

"Explain."

I tucked my pencil into the small sheaf of papers I'd put together, rolled it up and stashed it into my bag. "Back in my

Army days a lot of the guys wrote home to their sweethearts. Or their mamas. I didn't have either, but it was dreadful to try to keep all of those stories in my head. I needed to tell someone about the trip into Château-Thierry, about the first time I killed a man, or lost one in the medic tent. Or how our unit single-handedly introduced jazz to the British boys."

"So you wrote letters to who?"

"No one in particular. Myself, mayhaps."

"Does it help?"

"Sometimes. It's like they say, confession being good for a soul. Mine won't ever be pristine, but I might be able to scrub off some of the dirtiest spots with a little bit of lead or charcoal from time to time."

Crash nodded humbly. "Scribble on, my friend."

I regarded the roll of papers. I'd been writing about my time with the circus. Specifically my time with Crash as a friend. Thinking about it, I decided I didn't need to dwell there when I had a living specimen of Sanford Haus before me.

"What's that contraption?" I asked.

"An electrified guitar," he said proudly.

"Where'd you pick that up?"

"Found it in storage a few days ago when we went to dig out the carousel. Glad we didn't try putting that thing together. This snow would've been frightful on the gearwork. You have no idea the things that are in that shed, Dandy!"

"What good's an electrified guitar?"

Crash studied the frying pan. "Well, I'm not sure. But the mechanisms are simple and intriguing. I don't care so much for the guitar itself, but what else could I do with the concept? Would my violin take a similar wiring and give off the same distorted sound? Can I create illusions of sound using a few magnets and wires?"

I shook my head. "Your mind does strange things, Crash. Strange, but fascinating things indeed."

ten

AFTER TOO MANY days of snow and grey clouds, the sun decided to make one hell of an entrance. Opening the door on the camp was like staring into God's own heart. The sunlight blazed white and holy off every flat surface, turning the snow into fire, and the ice into glittering diamond.

The biting wind had died down, and while the day was a brisk one, the cold weren't too terrible. It felt good to be out, stretching my legs—even if the drifts were taller than me in some places.

Diamond Joe and a few of his hands had set to the grueling work of re-shoveling the camp walkways, and smoke rose from Mrs. Hudson's cart. For the first time in what seemed too long, the camp was bustling and living again.

Of course, that's just about the time trouble came to call.

I sat near the small cook fire drinking my coffee and talking about nothing special with some of the other folks when a ruckus erupted from Mrs. Hudson's repurposed railcar. Pots and pans clattered about while the woman herself shouted a blue streak that would make Satan blush.

I didn't hesitate, nor did Slaney with his huge shovel. We ran around the back end of the cart and found a scrum of tramps trying to force their way in. Mrs. Hudson whacked at 'em with her best frying pan, both hands wrapped tight around the handle. She struck one of the hobos in the hand and swung back to clock him good in the shoulder, too. His arm hung slack and he went down into the snow with only his pain to keep him warm.

"Hey, rube!" Slaney bellowed. His voice echoed around the camp, and soon more shouts took up the alarm.

"Hey, rube!" came the carnies' cries. A bell began ringing, too. A veritable call to arms.

Slaney dove in, shovel swinging left and right with reckless abandon. I flattened myself to the car and came up on the backside of a chap that had a mind to rob my favorite woman on this earth. He'd climbed into the cart and began putting his hands on anything that weren't bolted down. Mrs. Hudson swung at him with her pan, but just missed his kneecaps. His reach, however, was long enough. He lashed out a hand and shoved her on that fine rump of hers.

My vision went red with ire and I didn't need any more excuse to send this man back into the snow with the nothing more than the bones God gave him. And I wasn't too particular if those bones were intact at the time.

I grabbed the tramp by the back of his collar and yanked, while at the same time my right foot kicked at the back of his knee. A joint popped as he reeled, and I let him fall to the floor. My boot found his ribs. Twice. As he doubled in on himself and rolled to protect his stomach, I took him by the belt of his trousers and balled up my fist in his scraggly, dishwater hair. With a roar, I sent him flying back from whence he came. He took out a couple of his hobo mates.

"Jim," Mrs. Hudson called.

I stalked down the stairs and made for the bastard who'd dared lay hands on her form.

He was trying to push himself up, but he broke through the snow and planted his face in the powder. Good, maybe it would numb up his jaw before I gave it a whack or forty.

I kicked him in his arse and he sputtered.

"That's the one!" someone shouted. "The blackie ol' Jack took a hating to!"

When he would've called me something worse, the sound of a shovel meeting teeth told me that Slaney thought it best our new friend discontinue his talking. This did draw some attention to me, however. Attention I didn't quite need when I was staring down the crimson tunnel of my rage at a writhing piece of trash.

"Joe, get Dandy's back!" Mrs. Hudson called from behind.

I reached into the snow and wrapped my fingers around the scum's throat and yanked him up to his feet. He spat in my face.

"Top o' the mornin', Flapjack," I said, ignoring his salivary problems. I reached into his coat and found a loaf of bread. A couple of raw sausages. A slice of the cheese Mrs. Hudson stocked especially for Hoss.

"They're trying to steal from us," Slaney called.

And just as soon as the fighting started, it stopped. A roustabout took each of the tramps around the neck or arms and put them in a hold that couldn't be broken. Play time for the big boys was over, it seemed. Which just left me standing there eye-to-sorry-eye with Flapjack Hilton.

"Jim," Mrs. Hudson said. "Jim, back away."

"Dandy," Crash said calmly.

I kept my grip around Hilton's throat tight and looked over my shoulder. Crash and Mrs. Hudson stood a few feet away. His face was placid, but hers flushed red. The fear glittering in her eyes stoked my anger and I hauled a fist into Flapjack's face.

"Jim!" she shouted.

Crash placed a hand on my shoulder. "Dandy, let go."

"They tried to steal from us," I growled.

"I know."

"And he raised a hand to Martha."

Crash blinked, swallowed hard, but tightened his fingers on my arm. "Dandy, she's fine. See?"

Her hand on my back was warm and comforting. At her touch the anger drained from me and I practically fell into her arms. She helped me step away from the hobo.

Flapjack grinned at me, teeth bloody. "Dandy, is it? So you're a queer *and* a nigger?"

In a blur, Haus's fist crashed into the hobo's stomach, and a massive uppercut from the showrunner sent Hilton flying back into the snow.

IT DIDN'T TAKE long for Diamond Joe and his roustabouts to tie up the tramps and stack them by the fire. I sat on a bench, Martha at my side. With one hand she held my arm, with the other my fingers.

"What were you doing?" Crash asked me. "We have our own kind of justice here. Our own way of handling things."

"He tried to hurt Martha. Tried to steal from her."

"Oh, Jim," she said. "He wouldn't have been the first slime to do it."

"But he's damn well going to be the last," I stroked her cheek, rose petal pink beneath my black hand.

Crash cleared his throat. "It seems he had some sort of vendetta against you in particular. Is there something you failed to mention?"

I shrugged. "He wasn't too keen to help me out when I visited the boarding house, so I gave him a nudge."

"A nudge?"

"I can be quite persuasive if I have to be, Crash."

He smiled dryly. "Noted. Care to help me interrogate this lot before we send them off to the tracks?"

"If it's all the same to you, Crash," Martha piped up, "I think he's going to sit this one out and stay right where he's at."

She squeezed my arm and I nodded.

"Very well," Crash said with a bow to the lady.

He whirled around and clapped his hands together. "Slaney! Put a couple rods on the fire!"

The tramps' eyes widened in unison.

"Gentlemen," Crash announced, "I'm going to ask you a few questions and you lot are going to sing for me. If I like the tune, you all go home with naught but a few bruises, a few scrapes, but otherwise healthy. If I don't... well, I'm sure someone can think of *something* interesting to do with your teeth."

Diamond Joe's heavy boots crunched up through the snow and he loomed there, a shadowy promise. With about as much effort as it takes to bat an eye, Joe hefted his sledgehammer and rested it over one shoulder.

Crash let Joe's presence fall over the assembled tramps before he spoke again. "Now, boys. We had some trouble not one week ago. Some vandals came in, roughed up one of mine and, to put the candle on the cake, they went and ruined Miss Proust's wedding gown hours before her nuptials. You lot wouldn't know anything about that business, would you?"

As one, the hobo line up shook their heads. All except Flapjack.

"Why don't you ask that darkie about it?" he sneered.

Crash kicked Hilton in the jaw. Calm, cool as lemonade, he then put his boot on the nearest bench and leaned down to inspect it. He licked his thumb and polished the toe.

"I don't like your tone. Especially in regards to my friend over there. Other than the colors God painted him with, you got some beef with him?"

Flapjack spat out a gob of blood and glared up at Haus. "Your *friend*," he said with an oozing emphasis, "came round with some yarn about him trying to help out a Maeve with her problems. Was blaming highwaymen and speaking some balderdash about signs."

I bristled against Martha. "I never told you her name," I growled.

"Don't recall sayin' you did."

"You said Maeve."

Flapjack's eyes narrowed with disgust. "It's what our ilk call young girls, ijit."

Crash held up a hand to stall me from getting my dander up again. "He was telling you the truth. The same vandals that set on us have given a friend of ours and his young companion some trouble."

"Ain't you just fucking saints?"

"I might just be the angel that delivers you to God, that's for damn certain, son."

Flapjack stilled. Thinking about the sinister tone in my friend's voice. "I told him what I know. Some of them are signs."

Crash whistled. "Miss Proust! Could you bring me your dress, if you please?" He squatted in front of Flapjack. "While she's bringing you another sign to read for me, you're going to tell me why you decided to pay us a visit today."

Hilton said nothing. He clamped his mouth shut and looked away from Crash with sullen defiance. From down the row, however, a timid voice popped up. "Flapjack said we'd get some grub if we knocked over this place. Got word of it from the dar—" He stopped and eyed me before continuing, "the kid at the boarding house."

"Oh, do tell," Crash said. "What was it worth?"

Another tramp—this one barely more than a bag of bones and ratty hair—spoke up. "Said this feller here nearly dirked him. Said if we helped him even the score we could take whatever food we needed."

"The snow's been rough. We haven't had much opportunity for work or a decent meal in a long time."

Miss Proust appeared with her sullied gown. Crash held it up before them.

"Gents, does this drawing mean anything to you?"

They nodded. The skeleton answered, "Two people under the cross, holding hands? Means they're married."

Crash was quiet a moment. "Last question, gents. Are any of you going to come poking your noses around my lot again if I let you walk?"

They shook their heads in a frenzy. All, of course, saving Flapjack.

"Come on," Crash chided. "All your lads know this is bad business, friend. You wise up and listen to them. You going to come 'round my lot again?"

Grudgingly, he shook his head once.

"Excellent! Mr. Slaney, do the honors of untying them. Hoss, Joseph, please make sure they keep their manners, then you three can escort them off our property."

"On it, Boss," Joe grumbled.

Crash put his back to the scene and sidled up in front of me. He stood there thumbing his suspenders, looking mighty proud of himself.

"What was that?" I asked, voice low.

"What was what?"

"That performance. You played him like he was your fiddle." He beamed.

"Never heard you bring out that one before."

Haus shrugged. "Sometimes a mark needs Madame Yvonde. Sometimes a hardass pit boss will do the job nicely. It's all a matter of reading him, finding his weak spot and exploiting it. Now you simply must tell me what it was you did with a knife on this fellow."

"Found his weak spot," I replied darkly.

"Very persuasive indeed."

eleven

AFTER ALL THE hubbub with the tramp gang coming in, most folks around the camp had some energy to burn. Thankfully there was still a wedding to be had. Martha took off in the big ol' truck with a few others for the sake of stocking up her kitchen for the feast and to ward off any future famine due to another snowfall. While they was off running for supplies, there was still the fact of the bride and groom needing their carousel. Slaney, Diamond Joe and many of the strongest backs on the lot turned their attentions to the massive storage shed wherein the attractions of the Wonder Show slumbered. A couple of the show's firebugs took it upon themselves to help clear the land by breathing like dragons over the snow. I don't know that the act of breathing on it did any better a job of dispersing it than a simple campfire would've done, but the pyroheads seemed to enjoy themselves muchly. And I've found it best to let them have their fun lest I get scorched one way or another.

It was a lively day for our sleepy little circus. Lively indeed.

I looked in on my patient, to find Mr. Mars grumbling about the pain in his side, though I was pleased to see that his sutures were healing just fine. Just to be on the side of caution, I changed his dressings. Didn't want him to come down with some smelly infection for his wedding.

Come mid-afternoon, the carousel's skeleton—consisting of eight or so wedges meant to be put together like pieces of a pie, and a slew of rails, cables and poles—had been excavated from storage, and the woman of my heart returned to make everyone a hearty dinner.

Out by the fire that night, the dancing was infectious. Don't know if the morning's visit and subsequent brawl brought out the celebration in people, or if it was just a bug that longed for spring and warmer times, but everyone in the camp came out to revel in the joy of music and moonshine. I saw the Professor getting on with a bally broad, sharing a hip flask, and spinning her round and round to one of Crash's gypsy reels. Maeve sat by the fire laughing with one of the younger jugglers, eating taffy from a tin he'd offered her. Hell, I even let Martha pull me up for a reel or two. We danced about as well as a one-legged man can with a comely dwarf, but managed not to fall over one another.

I laughed, whirling her around one more time. As I sat I brought her down on my lap. "You are light on your feet, Mrs. Hudson."

"Oh, don't start with the 'missus' again, Jim. I was getting to enjoy you calling me Martha."

"You've never told me; where is ol' Mr. Hudson?" I asked.

"Gone to Heaven with half his platoon."

I nodded. "Long time," was all I said.

"Long enough."

Martha laid one on me then, full and slow. Her breath blew into me like the kiss o' life, sweet and languid as warm honey. A minute or a year later, she pulled away, a smile twinkling in her eyes.

She slid off my lap and took both of my hands in hers. "Come on," she urged.

We walked to her tent and she drew back the flap. Before I followed her in, I looked over my shoulder. Had anyone seen us? Did I particularly care? There, over the fire, I caught Crash's eye. His grin was sad, but he gave me the barest of nods.

I dipped into the tent and let the flap fall behind me. In the weak light of a single lantern, I found Martha. My arms wrapped around her, hands feeling those soft curves, and we danced a different kind of waltz together, me and the missus.

SHAMBLING OUT OF Martha's tent the next morning, I beamed brighter than sunlight. Martha'd been up and cookin' for a bit already. Long enough that most of those not too hungover had made their way to the fire for breakfast. The lot smelled of eggs, bacon and a roast of coffee that set my mouth to watering.

Some of the roustabouts had come and gone from Martha's cart. From across the camp I heard their hammering, the rhythmic chant-song as they worked on erecting the carousel. It was little more than a wide, fat pole sticking up from the ground yet, but already some of the sledge-gang worked to bring over beams and wires.

Anyone not working was by the cook fire. I looked around the assembled mass of folks and noted one conspicuous absence.

"Where'd Crash get off to?"

Martha passed me a plate, and nibbled on a square of toast. "He walked himself into town this morning."

"He say why he was going?"

She shook her head, russet curls falling across her eyes. "Nope. And I didn't ask. Might be trying to check up on our guests from yesterday. Or he might be puttin' an ear to the ground to make sure them tramps don't sully our good will with the town."

"Alone? Man could get himself killed."

"Ain't you learned a thing about Crash yet, Jim?" Her smile twinkled over me. "No one but the Devil himself will take Crash Haus from this world, and even then he'd probably convince Ol' Scratch to let him stay around for another song or two. He does this from time to time," she assured me. "Wanders off for a night or a week. Always comes back nary a hair missing from his pretty little head."

I looked down at my plate and for the first time in months I wondered if I'd done right, quitting my Pinkerton days and taking up with Sanford Haus and his travelling show.

"Always something new to learn, isn't there?" she asked.

I nodded. "Just when I think I got it all figured out..."

Martha's laughter was light and fresh. "Got the life figgered out? Or him?"

"The life. Him. Myself. Everything."

"Jim Walker, you listen good to me," she said, squeezing my shoulder. "You listening? Cause I'm about to lay the greatest secret on your ears, alright? This secret is so precious that it's been sought after by the crowned heads of the world. Solomon kept this one locked in his deepest tunnels with a stockpile of gold and jewels. You ready? You listening?"

"Yes, ma'am."

She brought her lips to my ear, her breath fluttering over my skin. "No one's got it figgered out, love."

"That so?" I asked.

Martha dipped her forehead. "That's so."

I cast my gaze over the lot, thinking about the score of people I'd met and come to regard as friends. People who'd made room for me. Thrown punches for me. And this woman who held me together when I thought little else would.

"Y'all seem to have some wisdom that common folk don't. And dammit all if you don't seem happy and complete without even raising a finger to try."

"None of us knows what we're doing, Jim. We're living the life because it's the one that accepts us. A dwarf like me wouldn't do well as a townie. Here, the folks don't give a piss about my stature. They smile at me and are grateful when I serve up something hot."

"But Crash..."

"Let me tell you summat about Sanford Haus," she said. It was the first time I'd heard any of the crew call him by his given name. "He came to us a few years back, and though he never said as much to me, it was written plain as paint on his face that he felt like a fish out of water in the *other* world. The one with all the rules and taboos. The world that tells you who you can and cannot be, based on who you was born to, or how your skin looks, or if you measure up to some new meaning of 'normal.' He didn't belong there and it ate at him. Like a poison. Made him sour. Until he did something about it. Sanford stepped off of the ride he was on and Crash jumped into a new one. One where he could decide for himself what kind of man he'd be, and what he'd do with the time given him on this earth.

"Here," she continued, "no one gave a good goddamn if he had money or some high-and-mighty status. Only that he could carry his weight and offer something to the show."

"And what do I offer?" I asked.

"Besides the sweetest ass this side of the Mississippi?" Martha pinched my cheek. "You're a damn fine camp medic, Jim. And you pitch in when you can. Not to mention you've been a good influence on the Boss."

"Really? He seems just as ornery as the day I met him."

"He is at that," she grinned. "But he's happier. I think Crash sees some of himself in you. You come from the same world. While he's made a good spot for himself with us, I think he gets lonesome from time to time. You help him out with that just by being your wonderful self."

I brought her fingers to my lips and laid a whisper of a kiss over them. "You're too good to me, Martha."

"Darlin'," she purred, "I ain't begun being good to you yet."

twelve

I STOPPED INTO my wagon long enough to confirm that Crash had gone walkabout, and to grab a change of clothes before heading back to spend the day with Martha. I'd tried to get a hand in, but Diamond Joe made a very blunt point that while my eagerness was appreciated, I'd likely just get in the way. As I watched 'em go, I realized Joe was too right. Those roustabout boys knew their trade and worked in a rhythm I'd yet to learn. So, after checking in on Mr. Mars again, young Maeve and I played a hand or two of rummy, all the while listening to the clatter coming from the growing carousel.

She soon took off with Phin, the lad I'd seen her with by the fire, and spent time with his family. Good folks, they were. The Tynker clan had a whole passel of kids just her age, give or take. On stage, the group act did acrobatics and juggling with fire. Phin, his brother and two sisters welcomed Maeve to spend time with them. She even tried her own hand at juggling, though she started simply, with a couple of colored balls.

We dined. We sang. We lived good lives and made good times. At the end of the night, there was still no sign of Crash. And the way Martha batted her eyes at me, there was no reason to be going back to my wagon, either.

That's how the days went. Sunup to sundown, people working

or learning, smiling and loving. And though Crash remained off on his sojourn, the rest of the tribe didn't seem bothered, so I took a page from their book and kept on my merry way.

Maeve and the Professor had been with us about two whole weeks by the time the wedding day arrived. The carousel's skeleton rose black and wiry on the edge of the camp, mirrors glinting along its center pole. The wooden floor had been hammered together, the ornate panels around its crown fixed into place. Slaney and Hoss lugged the red-and-white striped tarp that would cover the bones of the galloper's top. All that was left to do was saddle up the horses, and we'd have ourselves a proper merry-go-round.

Before grabbing some grub from the missus' cart, I ambled over to my wagon to find the door ajar. Unease slipped over my skin in a cool, prickling sensation. Carefully, I edged inside 221b.

"Crash?"

Soon as I was inside, I saw the body. Facedown in a crimson puddle, his curls matted and damp. The box of herb was upended on the floor, phials of cocaine emptied. And the revolver glared at me from his limp hand.

"No," I shuddered. "No!"

I knelt beside him and tried to find a pulse in his throat. His skin was cold and waxy. "Fuck!" I screamed. "How long have you been here? Why didn't you come find me, you bastard?"

I rolled over his body and listened to his chest. Nothing but a firmness that spoke of rigor having set in.

"I can't do it, Crash. Not without you here, too. And I sure as hell can't go back. I won't! Dammit!"

I punched him in the heart. One good turn deserved another, after all. *How could... why wouldn't... if I'd come sooner.*

I socked him one again. This time, I thought I heard him cough. Or maybe moan a little. Something, though, came out of him.

"Still there," I said to no one. "You're still there!"

Training took over and I set to work. I'd seen men that appeared more far gone than this sorry bastard come back from the brink of Hell. I'd be damned if I didn't give Sanford Haus the same chance to work a miracle.

Though I couldn't see for the tears welling up in my eyes, I kneeled over him and put both hands to Crash's chest and pumped, pouring my will into each thrust. Begging him to not be dead. After a count of ten, I leaned over and brought my mouth down over his to breathe into him.

I gagged at the taste of paraffin and hauled back. "The bloody blue fuck?"

A thready giggle drew my attention up. Some devious worm had made himself a cocoon of my hammock in the ceiling of the vardo. A cocoon with naught but a curly head that tittered itself purple.

"You son of a thankless, bilge-drinking whore!" I roared.

That sent Crash into a giggle fit. I rose off the floor and grabbed for my cane. Wasn't sure if I wanted to stab him or beat him like a piñata. Between guffaws and chortles, Haus wheezed.

"Something funny?"

Frenzied nodding. Tears—his—fell down and rained on my face. "*No!*" he sang in falsetto. "*I can't go back.* Brilliant!"

I swiped at the cocoon with my cane and managed to knock loose one of his moorings. Haus earned his nickname then as he came crashing to the floor. The wax dummy broke his fall.

"You didn't even have a chance to read my note!" he complained.

"Your note?"

"I slaved over that piece of paper for at least ten whole minutes, Dandy. It's some of my finest work and the least you could've done was given it a glance."

"The gun, Crash. There was a goddamn gun and your bloody head!"

Crash pulled himself to his knees and held his stomach as though it pained him to breathe. With the other hand he picked up the revolver and put the barrel between his teeth. When he tilted his head, the whole barrel bent.

Rubber.

"You bastard," I growled.

Haus tossed the fake gun into the detritus of drugs and parchment littering the floor.

"You bastard, I could kill you myself."

"No, you wouldn't, Dandy. You just said you couldn't do it without me, I don't think you'd go so far as to end my life when we've just had such a heartfelt bonding experience."

"You demented, sick... fuck!"

My fist balled up, tendons popping and ready to fly, but I stayed my hand.

"Damn you, Sanford Haus."

He jerked. "It's all in good fun, Dandy. There's no need to resort to mudslinging."

I shook my head. "You don't get it, do you?" When he gaped at me like an innocent babe, I added, "Of course you wouldn't."

"What's that supposed to mean?"

My heart still raced, but it broke all the same. "Most days it's not so bad, but sometimes... something sets me off. It might be a song, or a smell a little too close to black powder, or finding your ass on the floor..." I turned away from him. I didn't know if I could handle looking someone in the face when I was about to say it out loud. "Sometimes it just takes one little thing to remind me that I'm broken."

The vardo went still. I closed my eyes and counted out the heartbeats to slow them down, listened to the chanting outside. Waited for him to say something.

"Broken? Broken how?"

When I faced him again, he had transformed. Gone was the tittering prankster, replaced with a somber fellow with age lines around his blue eyes that I'd not noticed before. "You ever killed someone, Crash? And I'm talking about really ending a man's life, not just playacting with some rubber gun or plastic knife."

He shook his head.

"Didn't think so. And I pray you keep it that way. It does things to your soul. I went to school so that I could heal people. I went to war to kill them in the name of my country. Can you wrap your head around how that could tear at a man?" I didn't wait for him to respond. The words had started flowing. What I would've poured onto paper now sprang from my mouth and the depths of me in a gush that would not abate.

"I went to war because it's what we thought was right. And I've got medals that say I'm a good man. Stars and ribbons that are supposed to mean I'm brave. I gave my leg, but that's not the only piece of me I lost over in France, Haus. Since then I've... I've been looking to make myself whole again. Searching for a place where I can reconcile that I am both evil and good. That I am a man of honor and a coward who can't stand to think of his past!"

The tears streamed down my face. I wiped at them with the cuff of my sleeve. Crash just stared at me.

"I. Am. Broken," I assured him. "And when something reminds me of it, it scares the devil out of me. Today, I tried to save you. The doctor in me went to action. But the other day when I went to see that hobo fellow down at the boarding house, Crash, it was like I was fighting the damn Boche again. I took him down and held his own knife to his chest, ready to end him just as easy as I killed a couple dozen Krauts during the War.

"I don't know what will come out of me," I said, voice raw. "I don't know which Jim Walker will rise out of the ashes, or if I'll rise at all."

He clapped me on the shoulder, face sober as a corpse. "You already have, Jim. And I know who you are, even if you don't."

"Oh, really? Is that Miss Yvonde talking?"

"It's me. Your friend that you tried to save though he was beyond help. Just like you didn't hesitate to help Mr. Mars, or rush to the aid of Mrs. Hudson."

"Martha," I corrected him.

He smiled. "I've never seen your military awards, Jim. You've never shown them to me. But I don't need to see stars or ribbons to know you for the valorous, caring man you are. You are brave in the face of your fears, and true to your oaths. You are loyal beyond reason. You are not just a good man, Jim Walker, but you are, quite frankly, the best of men."

I had nothing much to say to that. Felt the heat of embarrassment rise to my ears, so I looked down and kicked the dummy on the floor.

"Where'd you find this damn thing, anyway?" I asked.

"Storage. First I remember seeing of it, so it's probably been sitting in there for quite some time. Which would account for the warping and disfiguring on the face." He squatted beside the thing, pulled a handkerchief from his back pocket, and got to smearing the blood off.

Now that I looked proper at the thing, there was no way this could be mistaken for Crash, or any other human being. The face, as he'd said, was scarred by heat, which had pulled one side down into a grotesque cascade of flesh-colored wax. The other half gazed up with a glass eye, expression featureless.

"Just some of the fake stuff we use in the funhouse from time to time," he explained, hefting the handkerchief. With a flourish, he whipped off the dummy's wig and tossed it at me. I threw it right back in his chest. "With a few of my clothes donated to the cause, the scene was perfect."

"Why do it at all?" I asked, not bothering to mask the hurt.

"For a lark. For a test."

"A test?"

"I wanted to see if this piece of wax could be purposed somehow in the show or if it'd be better suited for the bin."

I shook my head. "You tested a hoax on me to see if it would work on the marks?"

"Not on you specifically. How was I to know you'd be the one to find me?"

I shot him an incredulous stare until he squirmed.

"Alright," he admitted. "Probability suggested it would be you. I'm sorry, okay? It was a joke and meant in good fun. If you're really still burned up about it, go ahead and sock me one in the stomach and we'll call it square."

I thought about it. I thought about it long and hard. The invitation to punch him may as well have been written on gold and penned in diamond ink. A rare one, indeed, and not likely to come my way again without a similar insult as its harbinger.

I shoved away from him and stalked out the door. "You're a bastard."

He followed me out into the cold. "Does that mean you're not going to hit me?"

I didn't honor him with an answer.

Outside, Slaney waved. "Howdy, Boss man!"

His yellow grin told me all I needed to know. "You let him in on it?"

"Who do you think hoisted me up into the rafters?"

I grumbled. "So, where the hell have you been?"

"Out and about," he said, mood shifting. His smile turned smug. "Digging up graves and making discoveries."

"Care to tell me? Or was that part of your damn note?"

Slaney and a group of roustabouts approached us, grins on their faces, and Crash waved me to silence. "Later, friend. Later."

"Boss," Slaney said, "she's all ready but for the horses and chariot."

"Alright, so why are we waiting?"

"Wanted to make sure this was gonna happen today. Otherwise, we want to keep the gallopers out of the elements."

"Let's find the bride and groom, then."

Let me tell you, Artemesia didn't take any convincing. If she could've, I think she would've just grabbed Jonny and ridden the carousel without the horses. Mars, however, insisted on "doing it proper." Nothing but the best for his lovely woman.

thirteen

IT'S NOT EVERY wedding that begins with a parade. But then again, it's not every wedding that is presided over by a man who spends half his days in drag pretending he can see the future. The whole camp was roused to help bring the horses out of the storage silo. White Arabians with golden bridles. A black stallion with silver hooves and flame-red eyes, nostrils flared as if he sped from the depths of Hell itself. Palominos and painted ponies without saddles, carved as if they were running free on the back of a prairie wind. Horses with barding as if headed for a knightly joust. Plodding, decorated elephants, a fearsome lion, a pair of stalking tigers, lazy camels. The menagerie made its way to the merry-go-round. Brass poles polished to a gleaming shine, the work was done. Assembled, the carousel presented several tons of art. Sooner than you could hum a tune, the animals were fixed into place, and the steam boiler began to rumble.

Slaney guided Crash through the workings of it and, I'm certain, gave him a little bit of a lesson on what was expected of him as master of this particular ceremony.

The Professor sidled up beside me. The scoundrel was dressed to the nines in his purple tail coat, a black vest with a silver chain dangling from it. He'd waxed his moustache into wide handlebars. He touched the brim of his top hat and, in his own Scottish accent, he asked, "First time at a circus wedding, Dandy?"

I nodded. "I take it this ain't your first."

"Are you kidding?" he scoffed. "Been around the wheel myself a few times. Forwards, backwards. Once three times in the same night!"

I searched his vicinity for the inevitable shadow, but couldn't find her. "Where's Maeve run off to?"

"Why would she be here?"

"You really don't give a care for that girl, do you, McGann?"

"What? Of course I do! I feed her, don't I? Give her a place to live. A winter like this would've probably killed her had I not shared my roof with her."

"There's more to caring," said I, "than a roof and three squares a day."

I didn't bother to waste another breath educating him. Instead I shoved off to the other side of the galloper where a crowd of people were massing up. Crew folk like myself and the roustabouts were in their cleanest duds, but the cast folk—they went all out. Sequins glittered in all the colors God made, sparkling in the afternoon sunlight. Belly dancers jingled and swished as they made their way next to acrobats, clowns and sword swallowers.

And not a one of 'em looked a bit better than Miss Artemesia and her intended as they walked together arm-in-arm. Being as Jonny's costume generally bared more skin than a koochie girl's frock—and being that it was January and he had a right gaping wound in his flank—the strongman wore a respectable suit and wingtips polished just for the occasion. No amount of washing would clean the ash out of the lace gown the bride had hoped to wear, sadly. But Miss Proust held her head high and proud at her man's side, in a blue silk dress that still let others enjoy the artwork drawn on her pale skin.

Crash smiled at them with genuine warmth. "Mr. Mars.

Miss Proust." He bent over her hand and kissed it, ever the gentleman. "I've heard a rumor that the two of you are fond of one another."

A small chuckle spread through the assembly. Artemesia's cheeks blushed pink and Jonny nodded 'til I thought his head would pop off.

"Well, then," Crash continued, "I suppose you wish to do something about it, make it official and all that? And, though the gods can only guess at your questionable taste, you've asked me to do the honors of setting you about it, eh?"

Jonny beamed, his chest heaving to the point I feared he'd bust his stitches. "Aye, Crash. You're family to us."

Some of the cool, cocksure swagger melted off my prodigal roommate at the words. His smile faltered and his eyes became sober. And—write it down in stone for the ages—on that day in January, Sanford "Crash" Haus found himself at an utter loss for words.

Beside me, Martha giggled and squeezed my hand. I put my arm around her and held her to me, cherishing the warmth of her body and the closeness of her spirit. Staring at Jonny and Artemesia, I wondered if this was what the future had in store for me and the missus. No church or courthouse in the land would see a white woman and a negro as fit to wed one another. The law didn't abide by such a union. But here, as Martha'd said, the rules made themselves. Would the woman so many knew as Mrs. Hudson consider taking a ride with me to become Mrs. Walker?

I let out a small chuckle. A few days spent relishing her company and I was already entertaining notions. Time would tell. I turned my attentions back to the wedding at hand just as Crash led the two up to the carousel.

Jonny and Artemesia squeezed into the loveseat together. Well, truth be told, most of it was full of Jonny's bulk, but they managed all the same. Nor did they seem to care about sharing such close quarters. The chariot had been carved to mimic a peacock. Its jewel-bright blue body formed the front, its head curling up sinuously with ornate flourishes of gold and green paint, and its signature tail spread out to form a feathery canopy over the couple.

Beside me, Martha bounced and beamed like a young girl. I smiled down at her. "You're a sight, you know that?"

"Just dreamin'," she said, her round face flushing even pinker.

I gave her a tight squeeze.

The bride and groom settled, Crash moved to the side of the carousel and took a place near the large red boiler. With a heave of a lever, a valve hissed and the gears turned. The horses and elephants and other creatures lurched forward, and a melody wheezed into life. Both were sluggish at first, but soon the contraption gathered a good head of steam and the waltz jangled out into the air. Jonny and Artemesia sat happily as they made their first circuit. On the second pass, they waved merrily. The third time around, Artemesia was in Mars's lap, layin' a whopper of a kiss on her newly minted husband.

A roar went up from the assembled mass, crowing and howling their congratulations. The missus and I just looked at one another like a couple of goofy kids. It was all I could do to stop myself from scooping her up and jumping onto the carousel with her right then.

PROPERLY WED BY the only terms that mattered to them, Mr. and Mrs. Mars descended from their ride and weathered a storm of embraces and hugs. Meanwhile, Slaney took over operation of the merry-go-round so others could have a ride—innocent and carefree, not the betrothing type. Mrs. Hudson scampered back to her cart to dole out the feast, complete with sweet cakes she'd rustled up out of her own pocket money for the bride and groom.

Soon the fires were going, the hooch was flowing, and the evening was awash in sounds. The carousel continued its waltz while the carnies near the fire played their own tunes in a very different key. The cacophony of it was intoxicating as any moonshine, or the scent of Martha's perfume. The music even enticed Maeve out of her den. (Of course I'm saying it's the music, when it easily could've been the promise of time with her young juggling friend.)

Round about sunset, I found Crash standing near the carousel, just watching others ride with a grin on his face.

"I'm going to write to Moira," he said quietly.

"Are you now?"

He nodded. "It's like you said. She's family. I'll put the letter in the post some time tom—" He stopped abruptly, stare fixed at the center of the galloper.

"What is it?"

I may as well have been talking to that damn wax dummy again for all the good it did. Crash gaped, unmoving, the lights and glimmer of the mirrors around the middle of the ride flashing across his features.

He cocked his head to one side. Brought up a hand. Waited.

A heartbeat later, Crash was wearing the persona that fitted him best. Wild eyes widened, his demeanor blazed with a ferocious hunger. This was Crash, the molten core of his whole being.

"That's it!" he snarled. "That's *it!*"

He tore off then and I hustled to keep up with his pace as we made our way back to the wagon. Haus threw open a steamer trunk and rifled through it, tossing out bald caps and suspenders and tubes of greasepaint. He came up with a roll of ticker tape unspooled across his shoulders and a charcoal pencil. Without a word he was off again. He stopped only long enough to grab the Professor by his ear and drag him to the man's own blue vardo.

McGann, of course, sputtered curses and epithets as only a Scot can. Crash heard none of it, so fixated was he on the goal in his mind.

"Crash," I said, "you gonna let someone in on what's going through that head of yours?"

In answer, Haus kicked open the vardo door and threw the Professor in.

"What the devil are you doing, Haus? What's this about? I was only going to have a bit of a poke at the dame, nothing else."

Crash thrust the pencil into McGann's left hand and spread out the ticker tape across the floorboards. "Draw!" he commanded. "Draw the figures in the precise order they appeared."

"All three of them? Crash, you didn't drag me here for this, did you?"

The Professor made to stand up but Crash knocked him back to sitting with an open palm to the chest. "No. They're not the same. There are ten or eleven different drawings just in this wagon. You said it yourself, the first time you showed me, that each of them is different."

"Well, only by a slight angle of the arm or something."

"Draw them. Now."

"All of them?"

"Yes! Draw them all, it's not like I'm asking you to copy a Rembrandt!"

Crash poured his focus into the Professor's shelves, searching the myriad contraptions collecting dust. "No, no, no... come on, I saw it here..."

Eyes on his paper, McGann quietly asked, "What is it you're searching for, Crash?"

"Shut up and keep scribbling. Not this one, where is it? Damn you! Where the hell did you put it?"

"Might help if I knew specifics."

"Ah-ha!"

Crash pulled down a tiny replica of a carousel. Well, sorta.

The carousel itself was a squat wooden cylinder with ornate embellishments and the customary horses and such painted on its slat-like sides. It was attached to a pedestal of polished wood. With a single finger, Crash set the ride to spinning on the pedestal just as easy as the behemoth version out on the lot.

"Alright, Haus," the Professor grumbled. He stood up and offered the ticker tape to Crash. "Now what's this about?"

Without taking the drawings, Haus used two fingers to slowly, reverentially lift the striped roof of the minute merry-go-round, revealing the inside of the contraption. Like our galloper, the center cylinder was a thick pole covered with mirrors. Around the inner face of the carousel itself, however, was nothing but blank white space. With the top off, I could now see the slits cut every inch or so along the wheel.

Crash placed the tent topper down on the nearest surface, then placed the spinning wheel in my hands. He plucked up the ticker tape and spooled it in, tearing it off at the appropriate length, and pinned it into place with tiny metal prongs.

"It's a zoetrope," I said. "I ain't seen one of these since I was a toddlin' babe."

"Aye," McGann intoned, "and that one is older than you by a stone's age, I'd wager. Belonged to one Phineas Taylor Barnum."

Crash shook his head. "No, it didn't."

"It did! He put it in my hands himself."

"Impossible considering he died in ought-eight and the black, vomitous slime that spawned you didn't do so until five years after the fact. Unless you've had congress with the Other Side, or PT Barnum was also a six-or-seven year old child named Maryanne Miller—whose name is inscribed on the bottom of the pedestal—you will shut your lying mouth until I bid you open it again."

The Professor snarled and spat, opening his gob to say something that might offer some satisfaction. But Crash of course wouldn't allow it.

"Now watch," he said.

He set the zoetrope to spinning, and the stick figures began to dance.

"I'll be damned," I muttered.

The Professor stared into the zoetrope, Crash looking ever like the Cheshire cat with a horned-moon grin. Together we three watched the little men. It quickly became apparent that they weren't dancing, they were struggling. Two people, arms locked, punching back and forth until one ended up flat. Over and over the cycle repeated. Punch. Punch. Fall. Punch. Punch. Fall.

"Incredible."

"Coincidence," the Professor countered.

"Coincidence?" Crash glowered at his foe. "You can't possibly be so daft. The evidence is staring you in the face."

"But what does it all mean, Haus? Tell me, if you're so bloody brilliant, what the blasted little pictures mean?"

"It means that..."

Once again his voice trailed into nothing and his eyes fell on something far, far away. When he resurfaced from the depths of his thoughts, he drew in a deep breath.

"Oh. Oh, dear."

"What?" I asked. "What's wrong?"

He clamped the top on the zoetrope and shoved me toward the door. "Dandy, we have to hurry. If we don't set the trap soon, we won't be able to work the miracle."

The Professor's voice oozed with derision. "Miracle? Fishes and loaves again, Crash?"

"Hardly. We're going to solve two mysteries tonight, and you'll be on the road by breakfast."

fourteen

I FOUND CRASH by the campfire with Mrs. Hudson. Crazy and unnecessary as it may have been, I felt a stab of jealousy in the gut to see them looking so chummy. The moment passed, however, the second she looked up and saw me over the flames.

"Crash, what's—"

He shushed me by shoving a flask into my hand. "Never mind, Dandy. You shouldn't be working tonight. None of us should."

I raised an eyebrow. "You're lying."

"Nonsense."

"You're lying or you've done hit some righteous high."

He waved me off. "Honest, Dandy. Look over there."

I followed Crash's gesture and saw Jonathan and Artemesia, snuggled up on a bench together, enjoying their first night as a wedded pair. The smiles were plastered on their faces, along with a dreamy look in their eyes any time they happened to glance at each other.

"Remember what's important," Crash said. "Isn't that what you've been trying to tell me about Moira and such? This is a wedding feast, not an inquisition. Go on. The stick figures will be there tomorrow. Tonight enjoy yourself."

"He's right," Martha said, nudging me in the ribs. Her fingers slipped through mine. "More important things."

Crash clapped me on the shoulder and waded into the crowd. Martha drew me over to the bench that had become our own of late. Darkness fell over our little lot and the party had yet to reach its full swing. Though the carousel continued its jangling waltz in the distance, the campfire attracted a squeezebox, drums and fiddle, like honey draws flies.

The familiar tunes played and the missus and I danced our awkward steps. Stories were swapped and new ones formed. Sooner, rather than later, Crash jumped up on a chair and rose above the crowd. He drew everyone's attention to him with a ripping arpeggio on his violin before handing the instrument down to Slaney.

"Ladies and gents," Crash said, "I wanted to thank you all for the hard work of making Jon and Artemesia's wedding go off with nary a hitch. Mr. Slaney tells me that he and Diamond Joe's gang would tear down the whole carousel tomorrow, but I wanted to let you all know that... well, that won't be the case this time."

A chorus of intrigue went 'round the fire.

"Do tell," Artemesia called.

Crash fixed me with his stare. "I know you didn't want me to announce it yet, Dandy, but... what better time is there than this? Friends, tomorrow Dandy will ride the carousel, and our dear Mrs. Hudson will become Mrs. Walker."

As if the cheers weren't deafening enough, Martha clapped her hands over my ears and pulled my face to her lips in a searing kiss. Then she wrapped her arms around my neck. With her lips against my ear, she whispered, "Just go with it. He's got a plan. Now make it look good, Dandy, and kiss me proper!"

I couldn't very well turn down a request like that. I dipped her low and laid one on her, much to the amusement and joy of the assembled crowd. Before I could catch my breath, it felt like they were all there, pressed in a circle around me and my lady. Drinks were taken, toasts given and congratulations offered for what seemed a god's own time. Truth be told, I started to enjoy the idea. Hell, I'd thought about it already, hadn't I? Why not take her for my wife? Tomorrow was just as good a day as any, right?

When the scrum peeled back, Crash stood thumbing his suspenders. "I couldn't be happier," he bellowed.

I pulled him into a brotherly embrace and asked in his ear, "What the hell are you on about, Crash?"

"Solving mysteries, I told you."

"You also said we wasn't going to bother with that tonight."

We pulled apart and his face was boyish guilt.

"You lied," I confirmed.

"Of course I did."

"And you let him?" I asked Martha.

My faux fiancée bowed. "If it gets a girl what she wants, I don't suppose I'll complain."

I smiled at her. "Is that so, Martha?"

"What can I say? I like it when you call me missus."

We would've kissed if that bastard Haus hadn't pushed me off to the side of the lot where we could speak a little more candidly.

"So, here's the plan... what?"

He'd just noticed me glaring at him.

"What? What is that face?"

"I was going to kiss my fiancée, Crash."

"Don't bury yourself in the part on my account, Dandy, I need to talk to you about... oh; oh, dear. I've gone and bungled things haven't I?"

"You mean other than proposing to Martha on my behalf before I had the chance to do so? For starters, yeah."

His mouth flopped open and shut like a cod's. "You'd... but I didn't think... you haven't even—"

"Do you think I sat in our wagon every night pining for you to come home, Crash?"

"Oh, my. Really?"

I nodded.

"Well, it's about bloody time, then." He hugged me, genuine glee in his smile. "Tomorrow? You'll go through with it tomorrow?"

"Life's too damn short."

"So is she," he countered jovially. "Here I thought you'd never get off your ass and so much as dance with her by the fire!"

"Strange days we're livin' in, Crash. There are more important things than rules and the laws I was brought up with, I suppose."

"Well, here's to more important things," he said soberly.

"Now, you were sayin' something about a plan?"

"Oh, right!" He clapped his hands together and looked about to make sure we weren't overheard. "So, here it is, then..."

Nigh onto three strikes after midnight, the lot was a very different place. The carousel stood still and empty, its lights dim. The campfire long-since doused and the band's last note long gone, the Wonder Show's residents had returned to tents and wagons for warmth and sweet slumber.

Martha and I had taken to her tent at a reasonable hour, but hadn't had the chance to dally. Before long Crash had rolled the old knife wheel up to the rear of the tent. Carefully, quietly, we'd set it up behind Martha's bed.

"Odd sort of headboard," she observed, "but it could have its purposes."

"Really, woman," I said, "you are a wondrous creature."

She pinched me on the rear.

"Later, you two," Crash warned. "It all needs to be in place with you lot out of the tent before the vandal comes."

"You're sure he's going to?"

"Sure as fire burns."

Martha retrieved a dress from one of the steamer trunks at

the foot of the bed. The gown had yellowed over time, but there was no doubt in my mind that it had once been white as starlight. And by the look of it, Martha'd probably shone just as lovely when she wore it on her wedding day. Satin cut just to her unorthodox size, with long sleeves and a veil made of a fabric sheer as a whisper.

Her hand lingered over a velvet box inside the trunk. Beside it was a photo of a handsome fellow barely old enough to call himself a man. He wore the uniform and a new recruit's innocence. She gave the picture a glance, the box a tiny pat, then closed the trunk.

"Here 'tis, Crash," she said, offering him the dress.

"You're sure?" he asked. "I can find something else if this is too much to ask."

She shook her head and stared at me, eyes moist but full of hope and affection. "I'll not wear it again, Sanford. If it turns out unharmed, that's fine, too, but it's just fabric, ain't it?"

He placed a kiss on her forehead. "Remarkable woman."

"Aye, Boss, and don't you forget it."

Once the trap was set, we three dashed out of the rear of the tent and waited out the rest of the night in the storage shed. The missus and I sat on a pile of canvas, enjoying the relative quiet together and the obvious strain on my roommate. By his own reckoning, we had to keep mum as mice for his plan to unfold. It must've pained Crash something fierce to keep silent all that time, what with not hearing the sound of his own voice. He paced and plodded between stacks of wood and towers of metal poles.

Gradually the noise died down, and that's how we found ourselves skulking on the lot at three in the goddamn morning when all sane folks was sleeping off the buzz.

We set up watch from a spot not too far off the circle of tents and wagons, where we could observe Martha's tent unnoticed. Just about the time my leg began to cramp up from taking a knee for so long, a figure moved through the darkness on a course for my lady's home.

Steel glinted in the moonglow. It was the last I saw of the silhouette before he drew back the flap and entered the tent.

I rose to my feet, ready to swoop in and catch the vandal red-handed. Crash stayed me with a hand on the shoulder.

"They've taken the bait," Martha said. "Now what?"

"Bide," Crash answered. "The deed's not yet done. Mrs. Hudson, dear? Would you be so kind as to go rouse the Professor? Tell him I'd love to speak with him at your cart."

She nodded and waddled off toward McGann's vardo.

"She's out of harm's way. Let's go."

"Patience, Dandy. Don't you want to relish this? Savor the suspense a moment longer and let it wash over you before we draw back the curtain and see the gears and cogs at work?"

The thick noise of a blade sinking into wood cut through the night air.

I burned with the idea that, had we not been expecting just such a thing, my beloved might have taken that knife to one of her more tender parts.

"That," I said, "is all the suspense I care to relish. I'm going in."

It was Haus's turn to keep up with me for a change. I ran to the tent and burst through the flap, my flashlight beam catching the vandal in the act of carving a new symbol into the knife-thrower's wheel.

Between the culprit's black clothing and the shadow cast by my light, he looked small and large all at once. Our presence didn't stop him neither. He kept on carving, the only sounds his rapid, feral breathing and the splintering of the wood.

The symbol was a house. Two lines for the walls, two coming together in a point for the roof. Crudely drawn flames sprouted from the top of the sigil.

"What the hell?" I asked.

Startled by my voice, the carver whipped around to stare at me over a shoulder. She regarded me with dark eyes that glittered with malice.

I drew in a quick breath and let it out. "Maeve?"

"Shh!" Crash put a hand to my lips. "Silence," he whispered.

Maeve—staring coldly, her fingers still wrapped tight around the hilt of her knife—swayed where she knelt on the bed. After gazing at us for yawning minutes, she came to some sort of decision and returned to her artwork.

I glanced at Crash uncertainly.

Bringing his mouth to my ear he breathed, "Dangerous to wake a sleepwalker."

This answered the least of my questions. Maeve? The vandal?

We waited, watching her drawing a stick figure in the burning house. In short order, Martha ducked through the flap, the Professor in her wake. A belt around his waist kept his housecoat closed.

"What's this, then, Haus?" he asked, rubbing his eye with the heel of his hand.

Crash tried to quiet him, but Maeve had heard. She whirled at the sound of his voice.

"We've found your vandal, Professor," Haus said, his words quiet as he could make them. "Have a look."

McGann followed the beam of my flashlight to the steely glow in his ward's gaze.

"Maeve? Dammit, girl, explain yourself!" he bellowed.

Without any hint of what switch had been triggered, Maeve wrenched the knife out of the wooden wheel and hurled herself toward her caretaker, blade raised to kill. Though little more than a slip of a girl, she proved to be nimble and scrappy as any threatened critter.

She swiped at McGann. He raised his arm to ward off a nicked face, only to get a torn sleeve for his troubles. Maeve jabbed at him again, aiming for his belly. Fun as it might've been to watch the Professor dance for his life at the hands of a ninety-pound girl, Crash and I did our best to intercede without getting cut up ourselves. I shoved McGann out of the way and Martha edged him along the wall to more open quarters. Crash took the chance to get into Maeve's blind spot. He pounced, wrapping his arms around hers and squeezing hard. I slid down to a knee and pinched her wrist at just the right point to make her fingers go loose. I caught the knife by the hilt before it had a chance to clatter to the floor.

Struggling to get loose, Maeve growled and snarled. You'd have thought Crash had snared a werewolf, the way she carried on.

"Maeve!" the Professor shouted. "What the bloody hell have you done?"

Crash's voice was soothing as a lullaby in comparison to McGann's bellowing. "Opal. Opal, wake up."

"Opal? Have you gone mad, Haus?"

Her grunts turned into tortured sobs. Tears streamed down her face and caught the beam of my flashlight like icy gems.

Ignoring the Professor, he repeated himself. "Opal. Come on. It's time to wake up, Opal."

The girl we'd known as Maeve let out an anguished howl of the purest grief. When her voice was little more than a threadbare trickle at the back of her throat, she went limp, completely spent, in Crash's arms, and the two sank to the ground.

fifteen

"OPAL SKINNER," CRASH announced. "Fourteen years old. Born in Rockford, Illinois."

The girl was tucked into the Professor's warm bed, snoozing away the sleep of the righteous while Haus regaled us with the news. McGann sat on an overturned bucket, head in his hands, eyes rimmed red.

"Her parents died when she was just a babe in arms. Her sister Camilla raised her."

"How did she end up on the street?" I asked.

"Camilla was murdered by her husband on the night of their wedding. Opal was thought dead as well, though they never found her body in the burned ruin of the house she shared with the couple."

McGann's attention shot up to Crash. "Fire? Murdered? Did she...?"

Crash retrieved a letter from his pocket. I recognized Agent Trenet's handwriting on the envelope. "My sources say that the neighbors heard Camilla and her husband arguing. There was a struggle. Someone probably knocked over a lamp in the process, and the whole thing went up. The newlyweds were found in the ashes, both with knife wounds."

"Oh... oh, God Almighty, that poor girl," I said.

Crash nodded. "You have reached the same conclusion I have, Dandy."

"Maeve killed them? Murdered her own sister?" McGann asked, appalled.

"Not her sister. Hearing the struggle, Opal likely went to her sister's aid, whereupon she found Camilla dead, or close enough to it. Her brother-in-law... shall we just say he fell on his own blade? Leave it at that, chaps?"

I shook my head with weary understanding and empathy. "That girl's been carrying that with her. in such a tiny heart."

"So, she ran? And took up with me? Never bothered to tell me this rather important bit of history?"

"She forgot," Crash corrected. "She blotted it from her mind, wiped everything including her true name. The roadmen called her 'Maeve,' their slang for a young girl. So she took that on as her name. And you found her, as you said, living rough."

Denholm McGann dragged his hands through his hair. "But why? Why start up with the carvings and such? Why kill our horse?"

"Tell me, Professor, while you were on your travels, did you happen upon any weddings?"

"No, we did... wait, there was that one in Lexington. And come to think on it, we invited ourselves to a fine reception just outside of Evansville the night before the horse was dirked."

Crash snapped his fingers. "Trigger events, Denholm. Triggers."

I knew all too well what he meant. "Hearing about the weddings. And the sight of our campfire dredged it up in her mind, and when she went to sleep..."

"Her dreams took over the rest," Crash concluded. "She was trying to tell someone. Screaming for help, writing messages in her sleep. You said yourself, Denholm, the first time you were vandalized you found her screaming and sobbing. It wasn't because she was attacked that night, but because she was remembering the attack that made her homeless."

McGann pressed his fingers to his lips, and stared at the girl in his bed like she was an alien creature from the depths of the sea.

"So what do I do now? Eh? What the bloody hell do I do?"

Crash squatted in front of the Professor. "I have a thought on the matter, if you'd be keen to hear it."

"I'm all ears."

"She needs more than you can give her."

I nodded. "She's gonna need people around her who will listen to her, hold her when she cries and accept that she's done deeds she'd rather take back."

McGann regarded me with a sad smirk. "Know where a lot like that can be found, do you, gaucho?"

"As a matter of fact."

Crash smiled. "She needs to stay here with us, Denholm. I hear she's been chummy with clan Tynker over the past few days. They love her like one of their own already. Don't think it would be too farfetched to say they'd give her a bed."

As he stared at his ward, McGann's feelings rose to the surface, stark and raw. He had cared for Maeve in his own way. What was it Crash had said about the Professor being lonely? Bitterness tinged his words. "So you'll keep her here and send me off? Is that it?"

"If that's what you want. Your wind takes you where it will, McGann. If you want to stay here and keep an eye on her, throw in your lot with us again, you can. Assuming you can work for a gaucho like me."

The Professor didn't answer. Just stared up at Crash, weighing his words.

"With or without you, though," Haus added, "Opal stays here with us. If you do decide to leave, you don't do it like a coward in the night. You tell her. Explain it however you like, but the girl's lost enough folk in her days without you going and adding another to the list."

McGann hung his head. "Can I have some time to think about

it? The staying or going part, I mean. First thing tomorrow, once I've slept off this hangover, we'll check with the Tynkers about Mae—Opal," he corrected himself, "taking up with them. As to myself, though... I might like to stay. Then again, I might not. I still don't like you, Haus."

Crash smiled. "Of course you don't. And I despise you right back, you serpent-tongued shitbag."

"Now get the hell out of my home, you've darkened my doorstep enough tonight," McGann said with a smile. "Oh, and when you do set her up with the Tynkers, tell Elijah and them to keep her away from sharp objects." He held up his slashed sleeve as evidence.

I grinned. "Keep her away? Hell, they'll just teach her to juggle 'em."

THE SUNRISE WAS a grey line on the horizon when Crash and I left McGann's vardo. As we shambled around the back end of the wagon, Haus pulled up short. I looked to see what caught his attention, and frankly it stopped my steps, too.

A pair of headlights blazed across the lot, casting twin beams on 221b. A tall, thin figure stood in the light, waiting at the foot of the stairs.

"What do you suppose that's about?" I asked.

Crash evidently already had ideas, and his mouth hung open wide as a barn door. His eyes were haunted.

"Why?" he said, the word barely a puff of air in the chilly dawn. "Why are you here?"

Like a man walking to the gallows, Haus lurched silently toward his ramshackle home. Something quickened his pace until I found myself lagging behind my running roommate once again.

"Why are you here?" Crash shouted.

As we closed in, I could see the man waiting for us. Tall as

Crash, with the same auburn hair, although unlike my friend's unruly curls, he kept his close-cropped and smoothed with grease. His moustache was combed and clipped to precision. He wore a suit beneath the winter coat—the cost of which I didn't even want to ponder. He held one hand behind his back. The other gripped the handle of a black umbrella.

"Director Haus?" I puffed.

Crash skidded to a stop, nearly losing his footing in the mud. "Leland. Why are you...?"

The elder Haus was dour and stern as a nun, and his jaw was rigid. He glared at his wayward sibling with a mixture of contempt and the same haunted anguish I'd seen in Maeve only an hour ago.

"Leland," Crash pleaded. "What has happened?"

"Moira," Leland croaked. "Sanford, my daughter is dead."

Crash's face wrinkled with confusion, a child's lack of understanding. "What? No, that's... I was just writing to her. She was..." He choked on a sob, brought a hand to his mouth as if he might vomit.

"How?" I asked.

Leland said nothing. Didn't take his eyes off of his brother's as he swung his hidden arm around and dropped something at Crash's feet. The coffee can hit the ground with a clang, too loud in the pastoral morning.

It took me a moment too long to recognize the coffee can. Yellow, rusty.

Just like the others.

Crash staggered back and I caught him, held him upright. "Steady. Steady now."

"No," he sobbed. "No! Not my niece!"

Sanford Haus swiped at me, shoved me away and fell to his knees in front of his brother. He took up the coffee can, opened it. I couldn't see, his body blocked my view. But I heard paper. I heard something rattling about in the old tin cylinder.

I heard shaking breaths as he wept. One word soon became audible.

Moriarty.

all the
single ladies

GINI KOCH

"I'm sorry," Mrs. Hudson said, sticking her head into my office. "But these detectives insist they need to speak to you, Doctor." She looked worried. I couldn't blame her. A visit from the police is rarely a good thing.

As I slid the file I'd been perusing into the top drawer of my desk, three people entered my office: two men and a woman. One man was at least a half a foot taller than the other, but the shorter man was the one who stepped forward. He had dark hair and eyes, with sharp features that reminded me just a bit of a rodent.

"Dr. John Watson?"

"Yes. What's this about?"

"I'm Detective Straude. This is Detective Saunders." He indicated the taller man, who was fair to Straude's dark, and who also looked as if he'd played football in school. "The lady is Sherlock Holmes. She's with us."

Holmes was between the two men in height; tall for a woman. Slender, but clearly well-muscled, with long, dark hair pulled back into a severe ponytail. She wore a grey turtleneck sweater, grey slacks and grey high-heeled boots, and had a grey wool coat draped over her arm. Apparently, grey was her color.

Holmes was what, about a hundred years ago, would have been called a *handsome* woman—not pretty, certainly not beautiful, but not unattractive, either. Like Straude, she had sharper features, but unlike him, she didn't resemble a rodent in any way. She reminded me more of an eagle, or even a wolf—a solitary, noble predator.

"Clearly, seeing as she came in with you." I tried to keep the sarcasm out of my tone, but didn't feel I'd been too successful.

Holmes hadn't been looking at me—she'd been examining the room, looking everywhere with seemingly great interest. I had no idea why—mine was a typically small office, with the standard diplomas and certificates on the walls. I didn't go in for much clutter, so the bookcases were filled with books helpful to my practice and some few mementos displayed on top. Otherwise, there wasn't much to see.

However, my sarcasm caught her attention. She turned to me and I realized why she was so committed to one color—her eyes were a piercing grey, and they radiated intelligence, more than I'd ever seen before, from anyone, man or woman. The resemblance to an eagle was even more pronounced.

She turned those eyes onto me and her lips quirked. "What a feat of deduction. Forgive Lee. He's the master of stating the obvious." She had an English accent, and a husky voice. She could make a fortune as a phone sex operator, but I knew without asking she wasn't interested in that kind of work.

"Sherlock, please," Straude said tiredly. "Not now."

"You're wasting your time," she said. Then turned away and went back to examining my unexciting office.

"Can I help you, detectives? And Mrs. Holmes?"

"Miz," she said, without turning towards me. "Not married, not divorced, not a sweet young thing, not looking, not interested, in you, your brother, or your sister."

"I see."

"I doubt it."

"Possibly you can help us, Dr. Watson," Straude said quickly. "I understand you're the school physician at New London College."

"Yes." New London was a small, private women's college, dedicated to the idea that young women learned better without the distraction of young men. That there were several other colleges and universities nearby, loaded with all those young men, and that much of the staff were male, never seemed to enter into consideration. "I see you're still set on stating the obvious, since the Dean's secretary brought you in, after all. To my office. On campus. Where I've answered questions from uniformed officers at least four times." I gave up on trying not to sound sarcastic.

Holmes was in profile to me and her lips quirked. She began moving through my office, taking special interest in the bookcases, but still giving the rest of my place a closer look as well.

"Where do you live, Dr. Watson?" Straude went on without any reaction.

"I'm between residences at the moment. I'm sleeping here, on campus, in the visiting professor's dorm room attached to the artist's wing."

"Why's that?" Saunders asked.

"Private colleges don't pay as well as rumor has it. And I'm not financially able to start my own practice, let alone afford any place close." I had no car. And in Southern California, that meant I had to live within walking distance of my job, because the bus system was deplorable at best. New London was in the Brentwood hills, meaning I couldn't afford to rent someone's tool shed, let alone a room or apartment.

"No friends to stay with?" Straude asked.

"Not any I want to burden, no."

"No family?"

"Not nearby."

"Where were you last night between nine p.m. and midnight?"

"Here, doing paperwork, and then in my room, watching TV."

"*Campus Queen* was on," Holmes said.

"Yes, it was. I don't care for reality TV, though. I watched an old movie, *Death Wish*."

"It's the number one reality show right now. *Campus Queen* is filming at New London this school year, isn't it?" Holmes asked.

"Since you appear to follow the show, why are you asking me? Yes, we have film crews here all the time. They practically live here." Some of them *were* living here, camped out to capture nighttime footage. Unlike me, they were allowed to be in the dorms, and didn't have to troop halfway down the high hill to get to their beds. Unlike them, I actually had some hope of sleeping in peace and quiet.

"Do you know why we're here?" Straude asked.

"I have no idea." This was a lie. By now, I had a very good idea. Bad news traveled fast, and until I'd taken this job, the police had never visited me before. At least not in America.

"Fifth rape and murder of one of the New London students in as many months and you don't know why we're here?" Saunders' tone was definitely snide.

"I do know that another one of our students was brutally murdered. I have no idea why you're here with me, however, unless it's to express condolences and assure me, as one of the many who work here, that you're doing all you can to find the murderer and bring him to justice."

"How is *Campus Queen* working the murders in?" Saunders asked. Straude shot Holmes a *why-me?* look. She looked like she was trying not to laugh.

"How would I know? I'm not part of the show, and I don't expect to get a 'secret letter announcing my potential royalty' any time soon."

Holmes was definitely trying not to laugh. "I thought you said you didn't watch the show."

"I work here. Some days it's all the girls talk about. It's good for the school, though." Hollywood on campus meant money coming into the school, plus the notoriety of being one of the colleges deemed worthy to have the next *Campus Queen* crowned. From what Mrs. Hudson had told me, applications for the next school year were up from the past five years, solely due to the show. I might hate *Campus Queen*, but it was helping my employer continue to employ me.

"Can anyone confirm your alibi?" Straude asked.

"Shockingly, I was alone, seeing as it's not exactly appealing to women to bring them back to a tiny room at an all-girl's school for a nightcap, reality TV show filming there or not. And before you ask, no, I didn't have a date last night, I was being sarcastic."

"Again," Saunders said.

"Sarcasm in the face of danger," Holmes said with a chuckle.

"Are the police dangerous to me?" I asked as mildly as possible.

Holmes looked at me over her shoulder. "Only if you're innocent."

I managed to control myself from laughing, and only achieved this because both detectives were glaring at me.

"Molly Parker saw you just last week, didn't she?" Straude asked.

"She did. I saw her the month before, too. Over the course of the school year, I'll end up seeing most of the student body, many of them more than once."

"Justine Clarke, Ramona Hernandez, Quannah Wells, and Susan Lewis all were your patients as well, were they not?" Straude asked.

"I've seen all of them, yes." I had. They were all nice girls. All different from each other. All dead now. Bright futures cut short. I tried not to think about it. Thinking about it created anger for which I had no safe outlet. "New London has a heavy emphasis on wellness and preventative care."

"Who was the doctor before you?" Holmes asked, as she examined the small statuettes of St. George slaying a dragon and

St. Rita with a thorn in her forehead and a grapevine wrapped around her, both gifted to me by an old friend.

"I honestly have no idea. He or she left no notes or files. I'm sure Mrs. Hudson would know. Why am I being questioned?"

Straude opened his mouth but Holmes spoke before he could. "Save your breath, Lee." She was still looking at the statuettes. "Despite having gone to Oxford for medical school, which is both impressive and explains why he speaks properly, medicine is not Dr. Watson's life's calling, although he enjoys it. He's a veteran of Operation Enduring Freedom in Afghanistan and the War on Terror in Iraq, with his time in Iraq sandwiched between tours in Afghanistan. He hated war, but was a good soldier. He was wounded in battle, taking damage in his left shoulder and right hip. He's fully recovered, though wet weather makes him ache, hence why he moved to the Southwest instead of returning home to the Northeast, which is a wonderful excuse he uses for why he rarely visits his parents or siblings, whom he loves but doesn't really like. While he received an honorable discharge, that was because he was popular with his superior officers, since he killed a man in a protective rage. He does fit the profile, since he's highly intelligent, underachieving, and a loner. Sadly for you, Detectives, he's not our killer. However, once we find that man, should he be killed before trial, our good doctor should ensure he has an airtight alibi."

"None of that says he isn't our man," Saunders pointed out.

"True enough," Holmes said. "Regarding the man you killed in Afghanistan, how old was the woman he was attacking?"

"You seem to know so much about me; why don't you tell me why you've been investigating me and answer your own question at the same time?"

"Oh, Lee hates it when I do that." Holmes turned around and crossed her arms over her chest. "But it does save time." She looked at Straude.

Who shrugged. "I didn't ask you to come out from New York

just for the weather. I'll let you work as you want, Sherlock."

"Fine. First off, I haven't investigated you, other than the time spent in this room. I was called to meet Lee and Will while they were en route to the college."

"You're saying you know all that about me from having been in this room ten minutes?"

"It's been nine minutes, but, yes."

"How?"

She shrugged. "You have your service medals framed and hung, but they sit on a side wall, meaning you have to stand where I am in order to see them—you're proud of them, but don't want to be reminded of your service. Presumably it's because you felt the horrors of war deeply and regret all you did there."

"That's quite true, yes. What about medicine? You insinuated I'm not happy being a doctor?"

"No, I said you enjoyed it but it wasn't where your heart lay. All your diplomas and certificates fill the wall behind you, but they're quite dusty. They need to be up and displayed to prove you're allowed to practice medicine, but you rarely think of them, meaning this wasn't your choice for a career. Before we joined you I verified with Mrs. Hudson that the medical practice is off limits to the regular cleaning staff. There's a service that picks up any hazardous materials, but otherwise, you're responsible for keeping the offices clean. It's part of your arrangement for living on campus."

There was a knock at the door, and Mrs. Hudson looked in. "Terribly sorry to interrupt, but Howard is here to collect your hazardous wastes."

"Speak of the devil. This needs to be done," I said to the police. Straude nodded and I went and opened the door all the way as Mrs. Hudson headed back to her desk.

Howard rolled his dolly in. He was a big man, not the sharpest knife in the drawer, but pleasant, thorough, and punctual.

"Afternoon, Doctor," he said. He gave the detectives a nod, and Holmes a wide smile. "Miss, excuse me, don't want to run over your toes."

Holmes gave him an amused smile and moved out of his way. Howard collected the two hazardous bins and left two others in their places. "See you next month, Doctor." He shot Holmes another smile. "Hope to see you next month, too."

"You never know," Holmes said. Howard grinned, then left.

I shut the door behind him. "Sorry about that. Now, you were telling us how you know medicine isn't my heart's desire while rating my cleaning skills."

She lifted one of the statuettes. "There's no dust under these statuettes, nor on the bookcases. You're very thorough. And yet you rarely, if ever, think to dust your diplomas. But you haven't turned your hand to anything else. Meaning you enjoy it well enough, but it's not what you wanted to do, not really."

"I suppose you're right."

"Why did you go to school in England, when there are plenty of good medical universities in the States?"

"Family tradition. My parents immigrated here before they had children, and I'm the fifth in my line to graduate from Oxford in medicine. Huge point of pride for my family. Speaking of whom, why do you think I don't like them?"

"The picture of your family is low on a wall you can't see—you love them enough to have their picture up, but you don't like them, which is why the picture isn't where you can see it easily. It also clearly shows architecture and landscape that's typical of the Northeastern United States. And I can understand the resentment, being forced into a role you do well with but didn't actually want. Why did you join the Army?"

"It seemed like... the right thing to do."

"Yes, and for at least one person, it made all the difference in the world. Which is why you went—to make a difference."

"How do you mean?"

"Your statuettes—they're cheaply made and inexpensive, yet you have them in a place of honor, where you can see them any time you look up from your desk. Saint George slew the dragon, Saint Rita is the patron saint of those wounded in battle. I doubt you bought those for yourself. They strike me as being gifted to you by the young woman whom you rescued."

"How do you know I saved a young woman?"

Holmes took a picture off the small wall opposite the one my medals hung upon. "She's about fourteen, based on her face, and Afghan, based on her clothing and location—somewhere in Kabul, if I'm any judge." She handed the picture to Straude. "She's also holding a sign that says 'to my hero' in Pashto, with a simple drawing of a man with blood on his left shoulder and right hip and a crown on his head. The photo is wrinkled, but you framed it anyway. It came with the Saint Rita statuette. You were injured after you rescued her. The Saint George statuette is older and shows signs of wear—she gave that to you before your injury and you kept it with you."

"Yes. To all of it. And she was being attacked by three men, one of whom was a relative of hers. I killed them all. They were insurgents, so my superior officers didn't mind. Her name is Anoosheh, it means—"

"Lucky," Holmes interrupted. "Or happy. And she was both, thanks to you." She took the photo back from Straude and hung it back up. "It's a rare thing for a man to save one girl from a brutal attack, in a situation where the authorities are unlikely to ever be involved, only to rape and murder five others in a country where the police are far more concerned, Lee."

Straude sighed. "We need to look at every possibility, Sherlock."

"I'll happily provide DNA if that's helpful."

"The killer uses a condom," Holmes said. "And he's very good about leaving nothing much for forensics to work with."

"Almost as if he's medically trained." Saunders shot me a look that said I was definitely still his favorite suspect. "He needs to be stopped. Whoever it is. It's why we called you in, Holmes."

"Four months too late," Holmes snapped.

Straude shrugged. "It took some convincing, Sherlock. You know I'd have had you out sooner if I could have."

Holmes didn't look appeased, but before anyone else could speak, there was a knock at my door and Mrs. Hudson stuck her head in. "I'm so sorry to interrupt yet again, but you're running late now, Doctor. Mr. Corey is here for your weekly order, and Alisa Brewer is waiting for her appointment as well. They've been chatting with me for a good ten minutes now, and Mr. Corey said he has to be off soon, and I know you don't like to miss him. And Alisa has a class starting at the top of the hour."

Straude and Saunders didn't look happy. "You two go to our next obvious suspects," Holmes said. "I'll stay here with the good doctor."

Straude heaved a sigh. "Fine, Sherlock. Meet up with us before you chase anything down, would you? Dr. Watson, don't leave town." With that, the two detectives left. The tension in the office went down to something normal.

"I'll see David first, Mrs. Hudson. Tell Alisa it'll just be a couple of minutes."

She ushered in my preferred pharmaceutical sales representative. Corey was a pleasant, unassuming man about my height, slender, with thinning blond hair, even though he wasn't quite out of his twenties. He shoved his glasses up as he came in, shot a shy look towards Holmes, then gave me a wry smile. "Guess I can't say you have the best job in the world today, can I, John?"

"I'll leave you to it," Holmes said as she stepped into the examining room. She closed the door, but not all the way.

Corey shook his head. "I heard about the latest. Terrible thing, John. I suppose drinks tonight is out. How are you holding up?"

"As well as can be expected. It wasn't my daughters who were raped and murdered, after all."

Corey shuddered. "Still, it's awful, and they were all your patients."

"True enough. And yes, I think our regular meet-up is out for this week. "

Corey dropped his voice. "John, I spoke to Howard on my way up. He said you had police in here, and those were police detectives I saw leaving. Are you... alright?"

"Hope so. Did the police question you?"

"No, and I don't think they've questioned Howard, either. I don't think we're here enough for them to care about us." He shot me a reassuring smile. "Well, for what it's worth, I know you didn't do it. Because there's no way my favorite customer is a lunatic." We both managed a chuckle, Corey gave me some new samples and I gave him my order. "John, I know your living arrangement isn't... ideal. I'm looking for a roommate. If you'd be interested, I'd like to offer it to you."

"Thank you, David, I appreciate that. Get me the information and I'll see if I can make it work."

Before Corey could leave, I heard raised voices from the hall, and my least favorite colleague burst into the room. My office was rarely this popular except during fraternity rush week, when all the girls came for help with 'difficult menstruation issues,' which was the nice girl code for wanting to get on birth control pills without upsetting their parents.

The head of the Physical Fitness Department, Frank LaBonte, slammed my door shut. "You little weasel, what have you done to my girls?" he roared at me. He was a big, muscular man, with a full head of thick hair and a walrus moustache. He seemed a century or so out of date, as if he belonged in the 1890s or 1920s, not now.

"What the hell are you talking about?"

"The police were here, questioning you. They know it was you who took my girls. I won't let you get Alisa, too!"

The one commonality the murdered girls had, in addition to

being New London students, was that they were all on New London's track team. But this was close to the same as being a student, since track was the only competitive sport the college had, meaning any girl who had an ounce of athleticism in her was drafted onto the team. But it was a good program, and the team routinely medaled. That said, I didn't like how LaBonte claimed ownership of all the girls.

"Alisa's here to see her school physician," I said coldly. "And you're interrupting a business meeting."

"He undoubtedly wants the sick bastard doing this brought to justice. As in you, arrested."

Corey edged towards the door. "That's alright, John. I was just leaving. Sorry again about your loss. And, ah, Coach LaBonte, great job with the team. Hope one of them wins *Campus Queen*."

Corey fled. I couldn't blame him.

LaBonte glared at me. "You killed them."

"Hardly. You have more access to the girls than I do. You have them run through the trails in the hills behind the school. You're in a position of authority over them."

His face turned an interested shade of purple. "You're accusing *me* of hurting one of my girls? Of hurting *five* of them?"

"Oh, stop blustering." Holmes stepped out of the examination room. "I see Detectives Straude and Saunders have finished questioning you."

"For the fifth time," LaBonte shouted. "And yet they're no closer to finding the truth." He stabbed a thick finger at me. "He's the rapist, why isn't he under arrest?"

"I've heard that this country still enjoys little things like evidence and proof." Holmes got right up into LaBonte's face. "I said to stop blustering. You can calm down and leave, or I can make you leave. Your choice."

LaBonte glared at her. "Who the hell are you," he shook his finger at her, "to try to tell me—"

Holmes interrupted him with a lightning-fast jab to his throat, which shut him up. Then she grabbed the finger he'd waved in her face and bent it backwards. LaBonte was gasping and grimacing in pain, as well as on his knees on the floor in a moment. "I am Sherlock Holmes. I'm here, consulting for the L.A.P.D. I'm also adept in several forms of martial arts and am an excellent shot. And before you ask, I have a gun with me, and I'm truly not afraid to use it. Now, when I let you go, you'll have two choices. You can get up and leave, quietly, or I can beat the bloody crap out of you and you can leave on a stretcher. Choose wisely. If you're capable."

"I'd also apologize to her," I added. "Because you were extremely rude. I'm used to it, but Ms. Holmes is a visitor and you should represent New London better than you have so far."

To his credit, LaBonte stopped struggling. "I... apologize."

Holmes let him up and LaBonte stalked out of the room. "He's my top suspect," I said as Alisa peeked her head in.

"Maybe," Holmes said absently. "However, you'd do well to remember that just because you find someone reprehensible, it doesn't mean they're guilty. And the opposite is true as well." She looked Alisa over. "Why are any of you girls going out alone?"

Alisa blinked. "Excuse me?"

"Since the second murder, the police have installed officers on campus, so it's presumably safe here. However, the five victims—they were all alone. None taken from their rooms, and their bodies weren't found on campus. Those with cars didn't drive them off school grounds, and all the girls were seen in the cafeteria at dinner the nights they were killed. As far as it's been determined, they left campus alone and were never seen alive again. Why, after the second murder, are any of you going out alone?"

"Most of us aren't. But some of the girls have jobs off-campus."

"None of the murdered girls, however." Holmes gave Alisa another piercing look. "Why, for instance, do you plan to go out tonight?"

"It's Friday night, and I'm done with homework and studying. Why shouldn't I go out? Molly was killed last night, and that's awful, but we weren't friends. The only thing we have in common is the track team, and we aren't in the same events. So I'm sorry, but..." She shrugged. "Besides, if it's a pattern, that means we're all safe for another month anyway."

"It's not been quite that regular," I said.

"Pretty close, though," Alisa argued. "Besides, I get the *Campus Queen* crew with me tonight, so what do I have to worry about?"

Holmes stared at her. "An excellent point. Are you a chosen contestant?"

"Not yet, but here's hoping."

"Indeed." Holmes nodded to me. "Go ahead and do your doctor-patient thing. I need to see your appointment book."

I handed it to her and took Alisa into the examination room. "She's strange," Alisa said.

"She's on to something." Although I had no idea of what.

ALISA TAKEN CARE of, I sent her on her way and rejoined Holmes. "What did you find?"

"It depends." She gave me a long look. "Did you know that the medical examiner has found steroids in all of the victims so far? Molly included."

"They weren't prescribed by me! But LaBonte likes winning. It wouldn't surprise me if he's encouraged the girls to dope themselves."

"How much of that statement is based on observation, or blood work you've done on the girls, and how much on the fact that the two of you obviously don't get along?"

"Honestly? I don't know."

"That's fair."

"I don't have blood work on all of them, but I did on Quannah and Molly. There were no steroids in their blood. So if Molly had steroids in her system, she started taking them after her appointment with me the month before last."

"The second-to-last appointment she had with you?"

"Yes. I drew no blood at her last visit."

"Interesting. Watch your back."

"Why?"

"You're the point of origin." Then she turned and left.

"That was abrupt," I said to the closed door. I waited a few seconds, then I left my office. Mrs. Hudson was able to act as my receptionist because the medical offices were on the main Administration floor, next door to the Dean's office. None of the police were there, and Holmes was walking down the long hallway. I nodded to Mrs. Hudson, then followed Holmes.

She didn't look behind her, just left the building. The school was quite beautiful and picturesque, and sat high on its hill, surrounded by foliage, mountains, and not much else. The visitors' level had a circular drive from which the main buildings radiated. The *Campus Queen* crew had taken over most of this area, using it for equipment storage and craft services. They let the girls and school staff eat from craft services, though I refused to on principle. I was, as far as I knew, the only person on campus who hadn't snuck at least a chocolate croissant and a latte.

I stopped at the main doors and looked out. Holmes was standing with Straude and Saunders and the men I knew to be the show's producer, director, and casting director—Tony Antonelli, Cliff Camden, and Joey Jackson—or, as I thought of them, the Unholy Three. Despite dressing in typically casual Southern California style, they gave off Mob vibes, but they were hugely successful in this realm. In addition to *Campus Queen*, they ran *Campus King*, *High School Confidential*, *The*

Real Families of Suburbia, and *The Real Families of SoCal*. As moguls went, they were laid back, generous in many ways, and smarmy beyond belief.

Antonelli and Camden were having an animated conversation with the detectives, but Jackson was talking to Holmes. I got the impression he was suggesting that she try out for *Campus Queen*. Sometimes they asked faculty or staff to participate, to mix things up and keep the ratings high.

I wandered out. Beyonce's 'All the Single Ladies' was playing, courtesy of the show. It was the theme song for *Campus Queen* and, as such, seemed to be on constant repeat everywhere. Once, the first time I'd heard it, I'd enjoyed the song. Now I wondered if we were under some form of aural torture. As I neared them, Jackson shook his head. "Can't tell you that. It'll ruin the show."

"Oh, please?" Holmes asked, voice sweet as honey. "I'm such a big fan. And the soul of discretion, I promise you." She gave him a beaming smile.

Jackson smiled back. "Let me sleep on it."

Holmes winked at him, handed him what I thought was her card, nodded to the detectives, then got into a silver sports car parked nearby and drove off. The detectives got into their far less interesting sedan and left as well, and two of the Unholy Three went back to whatever it was they did on our campus.

Jackson waved me over. "You're the school doctor, right? The one all the girls have a crush on?"

"Excuse me? I'm the doctor, but no one has a crush on me that I know of."

Jackson laughed. "Don't be coy. You're a war hero, young, good-looking, a doctor. You're catnip for the kittens."

"I'm not that young, and I don't date students."

"Then you have a baby face, which goes over well with the viewers. You could meet us down in Westwood. Alisa will be there—she's already told us she thinks you're hot. You two could casually knock into each other and spend the night getting to know each other off-campus."

"She's only nineteen." And now I was guaranteed to feel awkward the next time she needed medical attention.

"Okay, we'll find an older girl for you. But no problem if you don't want to show off your Casanova reputation on this show. We're going to be branching out—*Know Your Soldier*. More of a meaningful-month-in-the-life-of-a-returned-hero sort of thing." He nudged me. "You know, keeping the image up and giving some of the more patriotic something to be proud to watch."

"Good luck."

"Take my card." Jackson shoved his card at me.

I took it and backed away. "Thanks."

"Call me," he shouted, as I spun around and headed back into the Administration building. "We'll do lunch or have drinks."

I returned to my office and pulled out the file I'd been looking through when Holmes and the others arrived. For all her observational skills, it appeared she'd missed my slipping it away.

Or so I thought. As I opened the file, I saw a note, written in an unfamiliar hand. *You have a good case file started here. You're also making it very easy for the real culprit to incriminate you. Call me if you think of anything, or if anything out of the ordinary happens. And watch the show.* There was a card underneath this. The only thing printed on it was *Sherlock Holmes*, but there was a New York phone number written on the back in the same hand as the note. I slipped the card into my wallet.

NOTHING UNTOWARD HAPPENED for the next three and a half weeks. The entire campus was on edge, and some of the girls had been brought home by their parents, though none of the girls so far selected for *Campus Queen*. But no one else was attacked.

In addition to seeing patients and participating in what seemed like endless safety preparedness lectures for faculty, staff, and students, I did my best to avoid LaBonte, who glowered at me any time we were within eyeshot of each other.

It was impossible to avoid the Unholy Three, and apparently Jackson had shared his desire to 'cast' me with the other two, because they also spent time badgering me to 'bump into' various girls in various spots. I drew the line at their cameras entering the medical offices, but there were several times I was ambushed by some of the girls with cameras rolling.

Holmes was on campus frequently, as were Straude and Saunders, though she didn't drop in to see me. I tried not to allow it to hurt my feelings, with limited success. Why it bothered me I couldn't say, especially since she was cordial when we ran into each other in the halls. She spent quite a lot of time with Mrs. Hudson; they went to lunch together frequently.

Other than a couple of pleasant and unremarkable nights out with Corey, wherein, despite the protests of the Unholy Three to the contrary, we got no women to pay us any mind but did get to make each other laugh, I spent my spare time looking at my file and my appointment book. Holmes had seen something in them that had set her off and I wanted to figure out what.

Per the papers and my own experience, literally every New London student, member of the faculty and staff, including groundskeepers, delivery people, and all of the *Campus Queen* crew, had been questioned by now, not just by uniformed officers but the detectives in charge of the case. Some, like LeBonte, several times. Nothing.

The usual suspects at the other colleges and universities in the general area—the fraternities and similar groups—had also been investigated. After the second murder, the police had expanded to include all the colleges in the Los Angeles basin, of which there were many. But nothing had popped, and as near as forensics could tell, none of the murdered girls had gone too far from New London when they'd been taken.

LaBonte was still my number one suspect. The girls would trust him implicitly, meaning he could get them to leave campus alone to meet him somewhere. He was certainly strong enough to overpower them. And if drugs were involved in some way, they'd all be more likely to take them from their coach than anyone else.

I also, per Holmes' odd request, watched *Campus Queen*. The premise was that the show's staff spent time at a lucky college chosen at random. Their goal was to choose a set of 'beauties of all kinds' via an overly wrought Secret Invitation process which required total secrecy on the part of the recipient and bizarre stunts just this side of hazing in order to pass the show's approval stage. All filmed for the entertainment of the viewing public.

Once the girls had accepted the offer, and presumably signed all the consent forms, they were put into a competition with each other to see who would earn the title of Queen and a dream week in an exotic location with an attractive male celebrity chosen probably because he had a movie coming out.

Because the most popular portion of the show was the selection process, the crew followed more than just the girls given invitations, which was why there were on campus so much, capturing 'live' footage. They'd been at a college in New York prior to ours, and that was what this season was featuring. Other than making me hate everything about reality TV, there was nothing much of interest.

Corey and I had had drinks and dinner earlier, but he'd taken me back so he could get home in time to watch *Campus Queen*. He claimed to enjoy the show, which was the only thing about him I didn't like. But it allowed me to watch my assigned homework. This week's episode finally ended and, as I turned off the TV, my phone rang. The number had a New York prefix. "Hello, is this Sherlock?"

"Yes. Watson, your hazardous materials pickup is tomorrow, correct?"

"Ah, yes, I believe so. Why? And how did you get my number?"

"You believe or you know? I got your number from Lee. And, where are you?"

"I know. It's always the first Friday of the month. I'll complain about the police's invasion of my privacy later. And I'm at home. Just finished watching that Godawful program you told me to, though I have no idea why. Either why I'm watching or why you told me to. Or why you care about my wastes pickup."

"You're alone?"

"Yes. Why?"

She heaved an exasperated sigh. "Why do you think? The game's afoot and our serial killer is going to strike again. Tonight. If you have a gun, get it ready, and ensure you're in dark clothing. I'll be with you in ten minutes or less." She hung up before I could say anything and without answering any of my questions.

Wondering why I was doing what this woman told me to, I got my gun, ensured it had a full clip, shoved a few other clips into my jacket pocket and clipped my holster onto my waistband. There was a soft sound behind me just as I did so.

I spun around to see Holmes standing there, in a dark grey sweater and jeans, woman's pea coat—dark grey, of course— hair again pulled back into a ponytail. Like me, she had a gun clipped to the waist of her jeans. Unlike me, she seemed intent, almost excited. I managed not to jump or shout, but just barely. "How did you get in here?"

"Through the window. Which is how we're also going out. Lock up, but leave your lights on, as if you're home and having one of your many sleepless nights." She handed me a pair of goggles. "Night vision. Oh, and please assume we're in enemy territory and trying to avoid being captured."

"What? You literally don't speak to me for over three weeks and then just assume I'm going to head out on some weird adventure with you?" She put a pair of goggles on and I followed suit.

"So sensitive. I'll remember that. And I'm sorry I wounded your feelings. I was working, as were you. Unlike some people, I don't feel the need to see someone every waking moment to reassure myself of affinity." We crawled out the way she'd come in.

"How do you know I have insomnia? And yes, fine, I'll be stealthy. And stop complaining."

"Good. I could explain my cleverness," she said in a low voice, "but I know because I've been watching the school at night for the past three weeks. None of you has the first idea of what security actually means. There are twenty uniformed officers stationed all over, and yet the entire student body, all of the *Campus Queen* crew, and half of the staff are doing their level best to ensure that the police never see them coming or going. It's as if everyone *wants* to be the next victim."

"Well, you're having us avoid them, too; at least, I assume that's why we left via my rear window."

We were walking up the hill, towards the dorms, though we were off the paths or main road, moving through the foliage. I'd been trained in how to move without making noise or being seen, as well as how to speak softly enough to be heard by those right next to me and no one else, and I was good at it. The night vision goggles helped tremendously, of course, but if I was good, Holmes was a master. Barring us setting off a motion detector or stepping on an animal, no one would know we were around.

"I'm working *for* the police, and I'm trying to catch a killer. It's a tad different."

"Why are you having me back you up? I mean, I assume that's why I'm here."

"Why do you think?"

"The only thing I can come up with is that you trust me. While I appreciate that, I have no idea why you do."

She sighed. "You see, but you don't observe. That's the problem with most people, honestly. However, despite what you may think, we have a lot in common, you and I. We're both avoiding family we love but don't like, we're both loners who don't actually like being alone, and we're both protectors. Plus, you speak English properly and you have *no* idea how refreshing that is."

We reached the point where we should have turned to get to the dorms, but Holmes kept on going, towards the back of the school.

"Ah. Well, alright then. Speaking of which, shouldn't we be trying to protect whomever you think is the next intended victim? As in going into the dorms?"

"No. The idiot will come directly to him. By personal invitation."

"Then why are we skulking about?"

"Because I need our killer to firmly believe I'm nowhere around and that you're sitting home alone, making yourself the perfect patsy. You need a roommate."

"David's already suggested it. I don't have a car, however. And you think the killer is trying to frame me? Why?"

"I don't think, I know. And as for why? Because the killer is doing all of this to hurt *you*."

"That's insane."

"Most serial killers are."

"Why would you even think that?"

"Because after we remove the obvious connections of school and athletics, the only thing that the murdered girls have in common is that they all visited you and died a month later."

"If you know who it is, why isn't he under arrest?"

"Knowing and proving, Watson, are not the same thing. I've already searched and found nothing definitive. If I couldn't find it, the police won't, either, and a search warrant would just mean he goes to ground. Right now the only advantage we have is that he doesn't know that I suspect him."

"But you said you searched his home or wherever."

"I did. When I search, you don't know I've done so unless I want you to know."

"Ah. You've searched my rooms, haven't you?"

"Invading your privacy, one day at a time."

We reached the main trail that connected the school to the mountains behind. It was there for the fire department, and truly more of a dirt road. There was a main dump about a mile away, and those trucks occasionally used this part of the trail road as well. Sometimes hunters also accessed it. But mostly it was used by our track team for training.

"Are you going to tell me who you suspect?" I whispered, as Holmes once again kept us off the main track and in the foliage.

"I was rather hoping you'd figured it out," she replied in kind. "You have all the information I do. More, really."

"I haven't the faintest idea."

"Well, maybe that's not a surprise. He's a clever one, Watson, make no mistake. As clever as he is punctual. But we're going to be more clever."

Before I could respond to this, Holmes put her finger to her lips and pulled me down. I heard the sound of someone running. A girl jogged right past us on the path. She had something white in her hand.

I put my mouth to Holmes' ear. "That's Alisa."

She nodded, then nudged me. We followed Alisa, still staying off the main road. The trail forked and she went to the left, meaning she was heading for the dump. The goggles were a blessing—we were having to move quickly to keep her in view, and we wanted to remain unseen.

Alisa wasn't trying to go too fast, and we reached the dump in about six minutes. As she neared the entrance, car headlights flashed three times. Alisa headed for them.

"Hurry, Watson," Holmes said, as she took off running.

I'd been fine with all the exertion and the slow jog we'd been at. But my injury didn't allow me to sprint with ease. And Holmes was absolutely sprinting. If LaBonte wasn't the killer, he'd want to see if she'd be willing to take a course as a returning student just to get her onto the team.

I lost sight of Holmes, but could still see Alisa and the car she was heading for. The car door opened and someone got out, but he stayed behind the door and I couldn't tell who it was, only that, judging by his build, this wasn't LaBonte.

Alisa ran over to him and handed him the white thing she was holding. He stepped around the back of the car, went to the other side, and opened the passenger door. This side was near a pile of garbage that had what looked like a tarp against it.

As Alisa was between the door and the garbage, he grabbed her. I still couldn't tell who he was. Alisa's mouth opened to scream, but he stuffed something in it, backhanded her face, and shoved her down, hard, onto the tarp. He was on her in a moment.

And then Holmes was on him.

She body-slammed him off Alisa and they rolled, which put them into the glow of the car's headlights. They struggled for what seemed like forever, while I ran in what truly seemed like slow motion. He landed some good hits, but Holmes landed more, and she was clearly the more experienced grappler. He tried to hold onto her, but Holmes was able to shove him off and away. She scrambled to her feet and managed a good roundhouse to his head as he tried to stand up. He went down, but got back up again. And he had a gun in his hand. I looked— it was Holmes'.

I had no time to be shocked that she'd let her gun be taken away. I was too busy being shocked by who was in front of me.

There was no time to think, really. He wasn't going to grandstand. He was going to shoot Holmes dead with her own gun, wipe it, and then still rape and murder Alisa. So I didn't think. I did what I'd done before, in Afghanistan. I emptied the clip into him.

"NICELY DONE, WATSON, thank you," Holmes said a little breathlessly, as I reached them and she shoved her gun away from his hand and then retrieved it. "Can you please check on Alisa? I don't think he had time to drug her, but he did have time to hit her."

"I'm okay," Alisa said, sounding shaky, as she joined us. "I thought..."

"That you were the next *Campus Queen* contestant," Holmes said. "Yes, I know. You've had that invitation for a week, haven't you?"

Alisa nodded. "I got it last Friday."

"And you managed not to tell anyone, because if you had, it was goodbye to your shot on *Campus Queen*. It was brilliant, really. A *tour de force* example of utilizing all the elements available to you."

"He's a murdering rapist," Alisa snapped.

"Always appreciate intelligence, young lady. It will help you, in your later life. Which you're lucky to be able to look forward to having. And strictly speaking, he *was* a murdering rapist; now, he's a dead monster."

I flipped the man over, to be sure. I stared, still shocked. David Corey's glassy eyes stared back at me. "David? But... why? And how?"

Holmes was on her phone. "Yes. Yes, the pharmaceuticals rep. Right, the dump. Yes, thank you, the sooner the better." She hung up. "Lee's on his way. *Why* is simple, Watson. I already told you. He was doing this to hurt you."

"Why me?"

"You had what he wanted. A medical degree from an extremely impressive university, a job with all those lovely single ladies—

none of whom were giving him the time of day, other than when they were waiting to see you—and a hero's reputation."

"But... he was my friend. He wanted to room together."

"No, he was a psychopath who'd created a dangerous and unnatural fixation on you. He *wanted* to ensure you didn't somehow take a roommate before he could complete his killing spree and frame-up, because you having an alibi would ruin his plans. Per Mrs. Hudson, Mr. Corey had applied for the position you ended up filling, but since his degree in medicine was from an unaccredited college, New London refused his application."

"He always visited me the day of my hazardous wastes pickup."

"Yes, and always took the time to speak to Howard, who is a nice man, though not a very observant one. The used condoms were therefore tossed into a hazardous waste bin, meaning they weren't going to be found."

"Did he bring all the girls to the dump to attack them?"

"Most likely. Because of *Campus Queen*, all the girls were prepared to get bizarre and highly suspicious invitations to go someplace remarkably dangerous alone and, also because of the show's secrecy policy, without telling a single living soul about it. In other words, he had an open field of choices and an easy way to fool them. Rape and murder her at the dump on a clean tarp, wrap her in heavy duty plastic when done, dispose of the tarp somewhere at the next dump area, transport the girl's dead body to a random site, and move on to the next."

"So forensics would only find the tarp traces, nothing else. What about the steroids?"

"That was done to implicate you and LaBonte both, just in case you had a clear alibi. LaBonte wants to win, and all the girls know it. It wouldn't take a lot to suspect he'd had them juicing, or used it as a way to get them to a secluded place alone. Corey here had access to drugs." She shrugged. "And for all we know, framing LaBonte was his backup plan. I'm sure he had one. At least one."

"This car, it isn't his."

"He only came to New London in his company car. This one is his personal car that he kept in a garage nowhere near his house. A garage that doesn't require a code for entry, by the way, just a key. And has no video surveillance."

"How did you find all this out? You'd had to have had suspicions earlier than today."

"I knew he was the killer when I met you," Holmes said. "Howard was a possibility, of course. Only those two were here only at the day and time when one of the murdered girls visited you. You pointed that out to me," she said to Alisa, as the sound of police sirens reached us. "So thank you."

"Oh, my God; no, thank *you*." Alisa heaved a shuddering sigh. "So, I'm not a *Campus Queen* candidate after all, am I?"

"You will be," Holmes said. "I've already arranged it. Under the circumstances, I can guarantee that Mister Jackson will have you."

"You have? Why?" Alisa sounded as shocked as I felt.

Holmes shrugged. "I'm something of a reality TV addict. You gave me the one clue I needed. I'd like to both thank you for that, and have someone I know personally to root for."

Alisa gaped, then flung her arms around Holmes. "You're so awesome!"

As they hugged, Holmes caught my eye. She was once again trying not to laugh. "Happier about landing a spot on the show than being alive. Ah, Southern California."

The police arrived before I could comment.

"Now what?" I asked Holmes, once we were done briefing Straude and a rather disappointed Saunders on what had happened. "I mean, when are you going back to New York or London?"

She looked around. "I rather like it here. Lee's convinced

his superiors that I'm an asset the L.A.P.D. should be holding onto, and they've offered a very generous retainer while also allowing me to pursue cases on my own, which is better than the arrangement I had in New York. Did you know that Mrs. Hudson owns a duplex in Santa Monica? She lives in one half and rents the other. Each side has two bedrooms and two bathrooms, with shared kitchen, dining, and living rooms. On Baker Street. Nice little neighborhood, close to everything, but still private."

"No, I didn't. Santa Monica is rent-controlled. The waiting list must be extreme."

Holmes shrugged. "It depends on who you are. I quite like her, and she appears to have taken a shine to me, just as she has to you." She looked at me. "I can afford to rent it by myself, but I don't enjoy living alone. I lived with my brother in London, which is why I moved to New York. My... roommate in New York didn't work out, for a variety of reasons. However, I've never actually tried living with a friend. That's how most people do it, isn't it?"

"If I'm understanding your insinuation correctly, you realize I don't have a job anymore, don't you? I can't possibly stay here, not after all of this. The moment it comes out that David was doing this to harm me, I'll be asked to leave for the safety of the girls, just in case another lunatic fixates on me. I'll be the scapegoat to make New London safe for its students again. And the notoriety isn't going to help me land another position any time soon."

"That depends on what position you're looking for. And I think you're selling a campus that gleefully welcomed a reality TV show short." She shrugged. "However, you're open to leaving without a fight because you don't love medicine, Watson. People who love medicine don't keep files on murders and try to solve them, nor do they enthusiastically participate in the pursuit and capture of a dangerous serial killer."

"I suppose not."

"However, there are people who do that on a regular basis. We call them *detectives*." She smiled. It looked good on her. "And I'd like to offer you the position of partner. From what Lee tells me, I'm going to be very busy here. Your military and medical background will be most helpful to me. And... it's always good to have someone I can trust watching my back. Plus, it's just such a relief to hear someone, anyone, who doesn't murder the Queen's English every other sentence."

I couldn't help myself, I grinned. "Then, I'm your man."

"And, as you'll learn, Watson, I always get my man."

a study
in starlets

GINI KOCH

My FRIEND AND roommate, Sherlock Holmes, looked out our front window and heaved a sigh. "The mail's here," she said in a voice of total doom. "Can you fetch it, Watson?"

"What are you expecting that's got you so depressed?" I asked, standing to accommodate her request.

"Nothing. Not one single solitary thing of interest."

"Ah. Well, perhaps you're wrong this time."

"When, truly, am I ever wrong?"

She had a point. We hadn't known each other all that long, but in the time we had, Sherlock had never been mistaken. If I didn't admire her so, it would have been extremely annoying.

Sherlock was a consultant for the L.A.P.D. From the way she was acting, you'd have thought the entire Los Angeles basin had given up crime. On the contrary, business, in that sense, was booming.

But the cases weren't challenging for her. For the police and the rest of us, yes, they were complex. For a mind like Sherlock's they were mundane, and quickly solved. So she'd been bored, but at least occupied. But this week we hadn't had a single case that needed her—not even an easy one.

Some people would straighten the house, go shopping, get caught up on their reading, even just lounge about. Sherlock was a reality TV addict—emphasis on *addict*. She watched reality

TV the same way cokeheads snorted down lines. She recorded every show on every channel, even the ones with no budgets or sets of any kind. She even watched all the commercials; a different sort of madness, in my opinion.

I found every single show appalling in some way, and the less said about the commercials the better, but she said they showed her a tremendous amount about human nature as well as theatrical artifice. And she found the commercials entertaining.

So she'd spent these quiet days in front of the TV watching what felt like every single reality show in existence, muttering about the lack of mental stimulation and cursing the criminal classes all the while. No one was hoping for an interesting case to turn up—of any kind—more than I was.

I went down the walk to the mailbox, doing my best to both take my time and observe all that was going on around me. We shared a duplex with our landlady, Mrs. Hudson, who worked at New London, an all-girls' college. I'd worked at New London, too, as the school's physician, until the case where Sherlock and I had met.

Baker Street was a nice, quiet, tree-lined street in Santa Monica. Sherlock enjoyed living here, most of the time, but sometimes I wondered if she missed London and New York, simply because they were so much more manic. She thrived on levels of stimulation that would make others go mad, and this part of Santa Monica tended to be serene. I loved it, but then again, after combat, serenity was a blessing.

As predicted, there was nothing in our mail other than bills and promotional flyers. As a courtesy, I always brought Mrs. Hudson's mail up to her screen door. She told me she appreciated not having to take the extra steps down to the mailbox after a long day of listening to the Dean complain about the student body and the student body complain about everything, particularly how far away from young men they were.

I perused Mrs. Hudson's mail, just in case. Nothing of note there, either. Sherlock was going to go into a sulk for certain.

I tucked Mrs. Hudson's mail into the wrought iron on her screen door, right in between the 221 and A, then took one last look around before I went inside 221B and faced the whining.

As I did so, something caught my eye. A car. Not that cars were a rarity in Southern California—*I* was the rarity, in that I didn't possess one. But this car didn't fit our street. We rarely saw limousines on Baker Street.

The limo pulled up in front of our duplex, filling the curb space in between the two driveways. The driver got out—he was dressed as I'd seen limo drivers on TV dressed, complete with cap. I'd taken a few limos from the airport now, thanks to working with Sherlock, and none of those drivers wore caps or three piece suits. Either the person in the back had money or they wanted everyone to think they did.

The driver opened the curbside door and the passenger stuck a leg out—a slim, pale, incredibly attractive leg wearing a black platform stiletto. The rest of the body that followed it was also quite attractive.

The woman was a brunette, with her hair piled up in a way that looked casual but which I knew took time to do. She was in a red and gold short-sleeved kimono dress that went to mid-thigh and had slits on each side. She wore bracelets on both wrists that glittered in the sun and carried a black clutch.

She was, quite frankly, possibly the most attractive woman I'd ever seen.

She sashayed up our walk. "Mister Sherlock Holmes?" Her voice was like honey.

"Ah, no. No, I'm sorry, I'm not. I'm Doctor John Watson. I work with Sherlock." She had perfect features. She was also vaguely familiar. Maybe I'd seen her in a dream.

"Ah." She smiled. "Is he in?"

"What? Oh, yes." I opened the door and ushered her inside. "However, he is—"

"Not a 'he,'" Sherlock said. She was leaning against the frame where the hallway opened up into our living room. She was a tall woman and, even around the house, she tended to wear shoes that made her just a bit taller. "Which I'm certain you already knew."

Sherlock was dressed in all grey, as was her fashion. She never admitted it, but I knew it was to bring out her eyes, which were a piercing grey, through which her great intellect blazed.

Under normal circumstances. Right now, all I saw blazing was disdain and dislike. And I had no idea why.

The woman's lips quirked. "No, I didn't."

"You don't lie exceptionally well. Somewhat a problem in your profession, isn't it?"

The woman laughed, one of those tinkling laughs that we men tended to like. I certainly did. "I only lie onscreen, Missus Holmes."

"Miz. And you are?"

I had the distinct impression Sherlock already knew who the woman was. I didn't, however, though the word 'onscreen' was a clue. I made a mental note to find all of her films.

"*Miss* Irene Adler." She smiled at me. "I'm very single and not afraid to admit it."

"Can't imagine why." I felt myself flush—I hadn't intended to speak aloud.

She tinkled another laugh. "Aren't you charming? Please, call me Irene."

Sherlock rolled her eyes. "So, what can we do for you, *Miss* Adler?"

"I've lost something quite valuable. Excuse me, but would it be alright if we sat down somewhere? Or do you do all your consultations in your hallway?"

"The ones I'm uninterested in, yes."

Irene's eyes opened wider. "But... you haven't heard what I've lost. And I'm willing to pay you very well."

"I'm sure you are, at least based on your grand entrance. However, I'm not interested in anything you have to say."

Irene's lower lip trembled. "They said you were the best. And I need the best."

"How nice of 'them.' They're right, and I'm sure you feel you do. Since you're not able to go to the police, a standard private investigator should be able to help you find whatever you've lost."

Irene gaped at her. "How did you know I don't want police involvement?"

"Because you said 'they' referred you to me. Had you gone to the police, you'd have led with that, not a vague pronoun. Good day, *Miss* Adler. John, please escort the lady back to her limousine. I'm sure the rental is costing her a fortune."

Irene stood there for a moment. Then her demeanor changed. The grand airs were gone—the woman standing there, while still beautiful, suddenly appeared far less ethereal and far more real. "Look... I need your help. Please. I borrowed... something and it's been stolen. I can't afford to pay for it, and I'm going to lose everything if it's not returned."

"Especially since you'll be assumed to have stolen it, since you had it at your home, and your home shows no signs of forced entry. Again, hire a private investigator."

"How did you know *that?*" Irene asked. I was curious myself. Sherlock rolled her eyes. "You haven't gone to the police. If there was a break-in or a robbery, then you wouldn't be bothering me, you'd be batting your eyelashes at someone in uniform. That you're here, speaking about something 'lost,' indicates that there's no evidence of theft, meaning you'll be accused."

"But how did you know I had it at my home?"

"Because anywhere else would mean other potential perpetrators. You're single, as you made quite clear. There's no one but you to look to as the likely thief of whatever 'it' is."

"That's right, all of it."

"What a surprise. I know. Again, a private investigator would be, I'm sure, thrilled to have your case."

"Why won't you help me?" Irene asked rather pitifully.

Sherlock shot her an icy look. "I don't work for people I don't like."

"That was the show! I was *supposed* to be the villain! I'm not like that in real life."

"Ah, I hate to sound uninformed," I interjected, before Sherlock could give the scathing reply I could literally *see* forming, "but what show is this?"

"*Campus Queen: Tulane*," Irene replied.

"The first season of the show," Sherlock added. "Miss Adler there spent much of her time sneaking around destroying other contestants' clothes. She also went so far as to steal someone's invitation."

"They asked me to," Irene said, somewhat desperately. "The show wasn't working, there wasn't enough drama. Cliff came to me and said that I had the most onscreen personality. He begged me to do all that. It helped, too."

"Yes," Sherlock said. "It did. You also destroyed the school careers of not one, but two other girls."

"They were compensated by the show."

"Not enough. But you turned all that into a career. Good for you. You were happy to drop out. Those other girls were not. Good day, Miss Adler." With that, Sherlock spun on her heel and stalked into the living room.

Irene looked at me. "Can't you do something, anything, Dr. Watson? Cliff, Tony, and Joey all said that she was brilliant and would be able to help."

Based on everything that had just transpired, I couldn't feel brilliant for realizing that she was speaking of Cliff Camden, Tony Antonelli, and Joey Jackson or, as I thought of them, the Unholy Three. They were the creative force behind not only *Campus Queen*, but a host of other reality TV shows. I found them repulsive, though Sherlock got along with them.

"So whatever has been... lost, it's not something one of them gave you?"

"No."

"What is this thing? I might be able to convince Sherlock to at least hear you out, but not based on anything so nebulous. She'll want details."

Irene bit her lip. It was incredibly sexy. I knew she knew it, too. But that didn't stop me from being attracted to her a little bit more because of it.

"I borrowed some jewelry for a gala. I wore it to the gala, and also when I went out during the weekend. I was very careful with it and put it into the wall safe in my house. But yesterday when I went to return it, it was gone. No one but me knows the combination to the safe, and there were no signs that anyone had been in my home, let alone tried to open the safe."

"What's the value on the jewelry, and what specific pieces? And their description. Sherlock will want to know."

"No she won't," Sherlock called from the living room. I could hear her typing on her laptop.

I pressed on anyway. "The value?"

"Millions of dollars. Necklace, bracelet, and earrings. Chunky black jet, obsidian, and black diamonds."

"What event did you attend?"

"The Gala for Everything."

"Excuse me?"

"It's a charity function run by the Odessa Foundation. We raise money for a variety of worthy causes."

I heard Sherlock snort, but forged on. "Is that well-attended?"

"Yes, it's something that brings out most of Hollywood. I was photographed, of course."

"Of course." Now I was sure I heard Sherlock making quiet gagging sounds. "So anyone who attended the event or saw photos of you at it would have seen the jewelry?"

"Yes. It's not unusual to showcase people's jewels or dresses, of course. It's a given that whatever most of us are wearing is borrowed." She bit her lip again. It was still sexy, but this time it seemed less affected. "I haven't heard that anyone else has lost anything."

"Well, if I can convince Sherlock, we'll check that out. I'll need a way to contact you." I pulled out my cell phone.

Irene gave that tinkling laugh again, took my phone from me, and entered her number into my address book. "You think you can bring her around?" she asked, softly.

"I can't promise, but I'll do my best."

She smiled and handed the phone back to me. "Call me either way." She leaned over and kissed my cheek. "Definitely call me," she whispered, and in a louder voice, "I'll see myself out."

She turned to the door, opened it, looked over her shoulder at me with a move I knew she had to have practiced many times in the mirror, and gave me a slow smile. Just then, it didn't matter that it was an affectation. It was still sexy and fetching "Goodbye for now... John."

And then she was gone.

I GATHERED MYSELF for a few moments, then went into the living room. Sherlock was studiously staring at her laptop.

"I don't understand why you won't help her."

Sherlock heaved a sigh. "Watson, you know why I watch reality television, correct?"

"Yes. Because it gives you insights into human nature. But it's still pretence."

"Yes, it is. And yes, she's an actress. However, personality traits are truly revealed during these reality shows, in part because most of the participants aren't trained actors—they may aspire to be, may hope to use the show as a launching pad as your *Miss* Adler did, may hope to use the fame and notoriety in some way, large or small—but what they are not is good actors. At least, not on those programs."

"You feel that because Irene was asked to play the villain when she was a younger woman that she's a villain now."

"I don't think it, I know it." Sherlock looked at me and heaved another sigh. "And yet you're already smitten and anything I say will be ignored. Fine. For you, I'll look into whatever con she's perpetrating."

"Why do you assume she's conning us?"

Sherlock turned her laptop towards me. There was a picture of Irene on the screen, clearly at an event of some kind. "This was taken at the Gala for Everything. Please describe what you see."

"Irene posing. She's in a tight, glittery, low-cut red dress with a slit up the side showing off quite a bit of her excellent legs."

"I've noted that you're smitten. I'll try and hold off gagging for later."

"Heard you gagging earlier. Anyway, she's in the same shoes as she wore here today—black stiletto pumps."

"Interesting that you noted that, Watson, I'm impressed. What else?"

"Her hair's up the same way it was today. And she looks amazing."

"Duly noted. Feel free to ask her out to dinner—I'm certain she'll be willing to pick you up in her rented limo."

"How do you know it's not hers? Or from the studio?"

"Honestly, Watson, you see and yet you do not observe. Rental limousines have numbers on them to allow them to be traced back to whoever owns and manages their fleet. They also have license plates, and I ran *Miss* Adler's while you and she were chatting. It's a rental."

"Stop calling her that," I said mildly.

"As you wish. Anyway, what else do you see in the picture of The Woman?"

"'The Woman'?"

"You've asked that I change how I refer to her. For now and ever after she will be The Woman as far as I'm concerned."

I decided that arguing this wasn't going to improve Sherlock's mood or my chances of her truly helping Irene. So I turned back to the picture. "Maybe she doesn't know how to drive or have a car."

"She knows how to drive, and I'm certain she has a car. However, I'm also certain The Woman likes to make an entrance."

This was a point I couldn't argue with, so I didn't. "I don't see anything much else of interest in this photo."

"Because you're a straight male and what you're staring at are her breasts and her legs. Look up just a tad from the breasts. Now what do you see?"

"Uh, creamy skin?" That I'd like to run my mouth over...

"Truly, ask her out. If only so I don't have to see you panting over her, at least for the time you'll be gone. But *nothing* is the key, Watson. The Woman is not wearing jewelry of any kind. And if she's not wearing it at the very event she said she was, then it's unlikely to either exist, much less to be lost and/or stolen."

I stared at the picture. "Perhaps she took it off? For some insane reason?"

Sherlock scrolled through the rest of the pictures of Irene at the event. No jewelry was in evidence. "She took nothing off because she had nothing on. And she had to know I'd check immediately."

"But why lie to you?"

"The question, Watson, is not why The Woman lied. The question is why did she go through this ridiculous charade in *order* to lie to us?"

I GAVE THE question serious thought.

"My normal answer would be 'to case the house,' or 'to see you when you're at home.'" I didn't like my normal answer, but appealing as Irene was, Sherlock had enemies, and those enemies would certainly have the money to hire Irene to infiltrate our home.

"Possibly." She patted my hand. "I'm touched, Watson, thank you."

"Excuse me?"

She chuckled. "You went from slavering man-beast to protective, worried friend in a moment. Your entire demeanor changed. And I appreciate it, truly. Yes, it's very possible The Woman has been hired by an enemy—don't ask, it's an obvious concern—however, I tend to doubt it. It shouldn't be ruled out, and we should sleep with one eye open and keep that eye on Mrs. Hudson as well. But I think The Woman is playing a game. Whether that game is dangerous to us or not is the question."

"How do we determine the answer?"

Sherlock shrugged. "Do what you wanted to anyway. Call her up and ask her out."

I was about to ask if this was really the wisest course when the house phone rang. Mrs. Hudson insisted we have a landline, for safety reasons, and Sherlock liked it because we could ignore it and allow the calls to go to voicemail if she wasn't in any mood to interact. While she could and sometimes did do the same with her cell, she felt that not answering her cell was rude. I could never fathom the difference.

Sherlock had wanted an old-fashioned rotary phone, but not only were they almost impossible to find and exorbitant in cost, they were hugely inconvenient. I'd put my foot down and we had a nice cordless set with five different handsets, meaning I didn't have to run from one room to another to answer the phone. Sherlock never, ever answered the landline unless she point-blank expected a call from Mrs. Hudson. Everyone else used her cell, myself included.

We both stared at the phone on the side table for a moment. "Any guesses?" I asked as I lurched into action and went to the phone to do the main portion of my job in our partnership—running interference.

"The Woman is going to wait for you to call her. At least for a few days. We're paid up on all our bills. I remain blissfully unattached to man, woman, or beast, and you're between romantic liaisons, at least until you and The Woman make a date. We can hope it's a real case, but I wouldn't count on it."

I answered. "This is the office of Sherlock Holmes, private consulting detective. How may we help you?"

"Doctor Watson?" The man's voice was familiar, but I couldn't place it. It definitely wasn't any of the people at the L.A.P.D. who normally called.

"Yes. Who's calling?"

"Is Her Nibs in?"

"Excuse me? Who is this?"

The man chuckled. "Still a joker, I see."

"Not really." Not now or ever, really. "I'm sorry if you think I've recognized your voice, but I haven't."

"And you don't know you're catnip for the kittens either, right, Johnny Boy?"

No one had ever called me Johnny Boy, and this was a lack I hadn't even realized I cherished until this exact moment. However, I now had an excellent guess for who was calling. "This wouldn't be the infamous Joey Jackson, would it?"

"It would! And you'd be the only American who sounds like a Brit without the accent who isn't on TV or in the movies. You really need to give it a try—you have the face for it."

"So you love to insist. Why are you calling?"

"I need to speak with Her Nibs."

"I can practically guarantee that she won't like that nickname."

He chuckled again. "I can guarantee that she loves it. Anyway, is she around? We need to hire her."

"Hold please." I put the phone on mute. "The most obnoxious of the Unholy Three would like to speak to Her Nibs about a job."

Sherlock laughed. "Thanks for being offended on my behalf, but 'Her Nibs' honestly doesn't bother me."

"Why on Earth not? He called me *Johnny Boy*." I tried not to sound offended and failed, judging by Sherlock's effort not to laugh. "I don't like the name," I muttered.

She shrugged. "He doesn't matter enough for me to care what he calls me." She reached for the phone, then stopped. "Put it on speaker, would you, Watson?"

I did as requested. "You're on live with Ms. Holmes."

"Johnny Boy's the best secretary around. How are you, Sherlock?"

"*John* is not my secretary, Joey. He's my partner. And I'm in good health, thanks for asking. Why are you calling out of the blue?"

"Wanted to make sure you were at home, honestly. We'll be there in a few minutes and we'll explain it all then." And with that he hung up.

"I hate him. I really, really *hate* him." I punched the speaker button off for emphasis.

Sherlock's eyes were narrowed as she leaned back in her chair.

"What?" I asked after a few moments of silence.

"Doesn't it seem the height of coincidence, Watson, that The Woman—who got her start with Andenson Productions—would come here with a bogus 'case,' and then, not fifteen minutes after she's gone, Joey would call to hire us?"

"Yes, I have to admit that it does. However, he said *they'll* be here, so I assume all three of the Unholies are coming. Please tell me you don't want to offer them tea."

"That," Sherlock said, as she gazed out our front window, "will depend entirely on what it is they're here to try to hire me to do."

TEN MINUTES LATER, another limousine pulled up in front of our home. We hadn't lived here long, but I was willing to wager that Baker Street never saw this many limos outside of prom season.

Tony Antonelli and Joey Jackson got out, unassisted by their driver, who remained at the wheel, though the car was turned off. Jackson closed the door behind him. If Cliff Camden was along, he was staying in the limo.

They were both dressed as I was used to—laid back California business casual—khakis and polo shirts, Antonelli in Ralph Lauren, Jackson in Tommy Hilfiger. Despite their both being well-groomed and dressed, they still gave me an oily feeling. I remained certain they were both in the Mob. They certainly looked it, just West Coast style.

"Interesting," Sherlock said, as the two men approached our door. "Do me a favor, Watson—don't ask them where Cliff is and definitely don't mention that The Woman has been here."

"As you wish." I hurried to the door and opened it just as Jackson was starting to knock. I'd anticipated this—in fact, I'd hurried to ensure this would happen—so didn't get punched in the face. He lost his balance momentarily, which I'd hoped for and confess to enjoying far more than I should have.

"Ah, John, great timing," Jackson said, as he regained his balance.

I gave him points for registering Sherlock didn't want him calling me Johnny Boy, though I still didn't feel sorry for the little slapstick moment. "We do our best. She's waiting for you."

Antonelli grunted at me as they walked past. Unsurprisingly, they didn't wait for me to escort them into our home. Whatever their problem was, a large paycheck needed to be attached to it before I'd willingly help Sherlock with their case. I closed and locked the door, then followed them into the living room.

"Sherlock," Antonelli was now beaming, as he opened his arms wide. "It's great to see you. You look as amazing as the last time we saw you. How are you doing?"

Sherlock wasn't pretty or beautiful, but she wasn't unattractive, either. She was what, a hundred or so years ago, would have been called a handsome woman. Her features were somewhat sharp and, especially when she was involved with a case, she reminded me of a noble predator, an eagle or a wolf. She looked like that now. Considering her boredom just a little earlier, I hoped whatever the Unholies had for us was going to be worthwhile.

She stood and allowed Antonelli and Jackson both to hug her. "I'm well, Tony," she said after they'd done the fake Hollywood thing. She cocked her head and examined the men. "But you're not." She reseated herself, leaned her elbows on the chair's armrests, and steepled her fingers. "Tell me what's happened to Cliff, and be sure to leave nothing out."

Both men looked surprised. "There's no fooling Her Nibs," Jackson said. "Ever."

"A track record I hope to continue. Again, details, gentlemen. I can't work without them."

Antonelli seated himself on the sofa, but Jackson stayed on his feet, so I did as well. "We don't *know* what's happened, Sherlock," Antonelli said. "That's the problem."

"Start from the beginning," Sherlock said, as I turned on my pocket recorder and got my notebook and pen, sitting in my chair next to hers but set back a bit—so that the clients focused on Sherlock, not on me recording them. "From when you first think something might have been off."

Antonelli and Jackson looked at each other. "A couple days ago?" Jackson asked.

Antonelli nodded. "We're filming our first fully scripted show. *Glitterazzi*. A telenovela-style show. Lots of drama, lots of sex, lots of action."

"Sounds interesting," Sherlock said noncommittally. She rarely watched scripted television.

"It will be," Jackson said. "Cliff's the director, of course. And I've cast some of our former reality show contestants as well. We have a large pool to draw from, and we think it'll give fans of our other programming a reason to tune in."

It took all my self-control not to ask if one of those cast was

Irene Adler. But Sherlock's admonition was still in my head and I studiously kept my mouth shut.

"Such as?" Sherlock asked.

"Sarah Foster, Elizabeth Gale, Amanda Rice, George Benning, Julianna Whitesmith, and Irene Adler, for starters," Jackson rattled off. I was scribbling, so looking at my notepad and hopefully not giving anything away.

"From *Campus Queen: Berkeley*, *Campus Queen: Notre Dame*, *High School Confidential: Alhambra High School*, *Campus King: Ohio State*, *The Real Families of SoCal* season three, and *Campus Queen: Tulane*, respectively," Sherlock added, presumably for my benefit, or the benefit of our recording.

"Don't forget Anna Wooten and Kara Rieke," Antonelli added. "From *Real Families of Suburbia* seasons one and two. Two of my favorite seasons."

"Mine, too," Sherlock said. Whether this was true or not I had no idea. I'd find out sooner or later, probably sooner.

"We did a talent search outside of our stable for the ingénue, though," Jackson added. "Dawn Niles is just starting out, but that girl has star power like you wouldn't believe."

Antonelli nodded. "We expect her to be the breakout, and we have her signed to a seven-year contract. She'll help us get to the next level."

"A noble goal. However, I'm failing to see any issues, unless you want to film in front of a live studio audience and want Watson and myself in attendance."

"We had no problems until a couple of days ago," Jackson said. "That's when Cliff disappeared."

Sherlock's eyebrow raised. "Excuse me? A disappearance should be a police matter."

"We tried," Antonelli said. "We called Detective Straude. He sent some uniforms, they did a cursory investigation, and found nothing. The police think Cliff's off on a drunk somewhere."

"Is he a drinker?" Sherlock asked. I hadn't seen any evidence of that when *Campus Queen* was filming at New London College, and from Sherlock's expression, she hadn't either.

"Well, he's not a saint," Jackson said. "But he's not an alcoholic, either."

"He's been drinking more since we started production on *Glitterazzi*," Antonelli admitted. "There are different stresses with this kind of show, especially for the director."

"Drugs?" I asked.

Both men shrugged. "Nothing major," Jackson said. "Here and there, but Cliff's not a big user. None of us are. Better ways to spend our money, you know?"

"So, Cliff didn't show up for work two days ago?" Sherlock asked.

"No, he showed," Antonelli said. "We filmed a bit, then there were some costuming issues, some minor script arguments, and Cliff went to take an early lunch." He sounded casual, but he didn't make eye contact with Sherlock.

She sighed. "Tony, Joey, if you want my help, you need to give me all the information. I don't pass judgment on, in the vernacular, who's zooming who."

Both men again looked surprised. "How did you know?" Jackson asked.

She rolled her eyes. "He doesn't have an issue with drinking or drugs. If he had gambling debts you'd be talking about those right off the bat. So he's sleeping with someone, or several someones, that he shouldn't be. And I need that information. I must stress that details and a coherent storyline matter for detective work as well as television shows."

Jackson looked at Antonelli, who nodded. Jackson turned back to Sherlock. "Okay, well, Cliff's got an eye for the ladies."

"All the ladies," Antonelli added.

Jackson shrugged. "Yeah, he's not picky, and since his wife left him he's been a little out of control. Sleeping with anyone he can get."

"As a director for a successful production company, I'd imagine he can get a lot," Sherlock said, sarcasm dripping.

"He can, and he does," Jackson confirmed. "But since we cast Dawn..."

"He's taken up solely with your ingénue?" she asked.

"Yeah, he has. Nothing forced," Jackson added quickly. "Cliff's all about mutual consent."

"Which is so gentlemanly, since he can offer these women a chance for stardom," I muttered.

"We're familiar with the casting couch," Sherlock agreed.

"It's not like that," Antonelli said. "We have a reputation to maintain. Half of our reality stars are underage. Andenson Productions has a strict sexual harassment policy, and Cliff's always stayed well within it."

"He's a good-looking guy with charisma and a great career," Jackson said. "All three of us have no trouble attracting women, without offering them jobs."

I could feel Sherlock mentally telling me to keep my mouth shut, so I did. Money and power were aphrodisiacs; Jackson probably wasn't actually bragging.

"We don't want actresses, amateur or real, who think they have a right to be on our shows," Antonelli added. "We *make* stars. They're beholden to *us*, not the other way around."

"And not in the sexual favors kind of way," Jackson added quickly.

I wondered if Irene agreed with this statement. Perhaps I'd ask her if she said yes to dinner.

Sherlock heaved a dramatic sigh. "Gentlemen. Stop making me drag the facts out of you. Stop worrying that I'm going to pass judgment on your lifestyles. I want to know why you're here, why you think something's happened to Cliff, and so forth, and I want to know it immediately. Or else, as much as I enjoy your shows and your company, I'm going to have to ask you to leave so I can get back to real work."

I didn't need to point out she *had* no real work. Besides, I shared her desire to make these two cut to the chase.

"Fine," Antonelli said. "Cliff and Dawn went to lunch. For a tryst. She came back. He didn't."

"And has your young ingénue been questioned?" Sherlock asked, interest back.

"Yes, of course," Jackson said. "At least, by us. Not so sure the police asked her more than her name. Anyway, Dawn says that Cliff told her to head back after… uh, because he had a meeting she couldn't attend. It wasn't an unusual request—they usually leave and return separately."

"So the rest of the cast doesn't know they're sleeping together?"

"More so the rest of the cast can't prove it," Antonelli said. "We're about to start filming *Glitterazzi*'s pilot. This is literally the most important week in our company's history, and my director and half of my screenwriting team has disappeared. And no one but us seems to care."

"Cliff also writes the scripts?"

"Yeah, he's used to it, he does most of the scripting for our reality shows already. He was a theater arts major, which is also why he's the director—he knows what actors need." Jackson shrugged. "We're very hands-on. It's been the three of us from day one, and we're doing our best to keep it that way. Less people to share the profits with," he added with a grin.

"Joey and I write the rest of the reality scripts following Cliff's formula for each show," Antonelli said. "But we did bring in a professional to work with Cliff on *Glitterazzi*, Collin Toohey."

"And what does Mr. Toohey have to say about all of this?"

"He's freaked out because Cliff has the revised script for the pilot," Jackson replied. "The only one. The actors' scripts were pulled because Cliff and Collin weren't happy and made a lot of changes over the past few days. Cliff was getting the new script copied."

"You don't have people for that?" I asked.

"We do," Antonelli said, "but you have no idea what scrutiny we're under. We have a lot of people desperate to get a hold of the script so they can tear it to shreds, do some kind of big reveal, or whatever lunacy the losers who live on the internet do for fun these days."

"Was he going to make the copies when he sent Dawn back to the set?" Sherlock asked.

"Not sure," Jackson replied. "But it would make sense. She's not allowed to get her script any earlier than anyone else."

"Did the police consider the idea that Cliff might have been taken because of this script?"

"For about two seconds." Antonelli shook his head. "Sherlock, I'm begging you—come to the set and see what you can figure out. But please, do it soon. We have the potential to be ruined if this pilot doesn't get filmed. If the show isn't picked up, we'll deal. But if we don't even *have* a product to show the studios we've been talking to, we'll be done in this town."

"That seems extreme," I pointed out.

"They're right, actually, Watson," Sherlock said. "Reality TV and scripted are in the midst of a sort of war, if you will. And those in the industry who despise reality TV—and they are legion—would be overjoyed to have the opportunity to point to the fact that one of the top reality TV production companies can't get their act together enough to handle one pilot. It could indeed mean ruination for Andenson Productions."

"Exactly," Antonelli said. "Sherlock, are you in or out?"

She stood. "We're in, Tony. Give the address and directions for where we're heading to Watson. We need to finish up some things here, so we'll be on set first thing tomorrow."

Antonelli stood as well, both men hugged Sherlock, Jackson gave me a business card and a parking pass with a map on the back, and I escorted them out.

I ensured the door was securely locked again and returned to Sherlock. "What do you think?"

"That I still appreciate your concern for my safety. Truly, Watson, it's quite touching."

"How do you mean?"

"You've taken care to lock all three locks—regular, chain, and deadbolt—in the middle of the day, and only since the thought that The Woman might have come in order to determine how to do me harm." She smiled. "As for the case, it's probably nothing. But visiting the set should be of at least a few minutes' interest, and while you loathe them, I rather like the Unholy Three. If it makes them feel better that I take this seriously, so be it."

"You think Cliff's off on a bender?"

"The possibility exists that Cliff met another young lady of wild character and is off on another kind of a bender. However, the game could be afoot, so let's have you arrange for your date with The Woman. Then I'd like us to do a bit of prep before we head to the set of *Glitterazzi* and see what we shall see."

Making a date with Irene had been nerve-wracking for all the time I was dialing and then the easiest thing in the world once she answered. Per Sherlock's advice, I asked for our dinner date to happen two evenings hence, and Irene accepted with evident delight.

I didn't own a car, which made me a pauper by Southern Californian standards. However, Mrs. Hudson had two cars—her small commuter SmartCar and a far nicer Mazda3 sedan. I was allowed to borrow either car whenever I might need, which was rarely. But Sherlock had checked with Mrs. Hudson before I arranged my big date and the Mazda3 was mine for the night.

The rest of the afternoon and evening was spent with Sherlock researching Andenson Productions and Irene. She tried to force me to watch selected episodes from the various reality shows featuring the cast of *Glitterazzi* as we knew it, but I flatly refused. So, instead, she made me research everything on Cliff Camden I could find, which wasn't all that much.

My researched matched what Sherlock found—Andenson Productions were hugely successful, with little to no controversy over the years. They were highly respected in the reality industry, but weren't so popular among the rest of Hollywood. But they delivered hit series after hit series, and that meant that they had a tremendous amount of clout. They were, point of fact, a major player.

Antonelli had been married to the same woman for thirty years, Jackson was a confirmed bachelor, and Camden was, as we already knew, divorced from his first wife. He'd been linked romantically to a variety of women, behind the camera and in front of it, but no names stood out. Unless you counted every single starlet in *Glitterazzi*.

Cliff had apparently been involved with every one of them at one time or another, though all reports said things had ended in a friendly way each time. There were no scandals associated with any of these matchups—Cliff was just known for dating women from their reality shows, loving them, leaving them, and also apparently continuing to employ them.

Andenson Productions appeared to have no real enemies other than their business rivals. Sadly, and despite my best efforts, I couldn't link them to organized crime. Clearly I needed to hone my research skills.

Irene had worked steadily since her time on *Campus Queen*—which, somehow, she had not won—but it was all guest appearances or small parts on pilots that didn't get picked up. She hadn't yet had her big break.

She had a profile, but it was low by Hollywood standards. As near as Sherlock could tell, Irene had been invited to the Gala for Everything because she was friends with the promoters.

"Why the ruse?" Sherlock asked, more to herself than me.

"She wanted to be sure you took the Andenson case?" I suggested without a lot of enthusiasm.

"Perhaps, but in that case, why not tell me that her employers were in trouble? Why lie about something specific? Why have me looking at the photos of the Gala for Everything if..." Sherlock's voice trailed off and she was suddenly intent, tapping at her computer like mad.

"What is it?" I went over to see what she was looking at. "More pictures of the event?"

"Yes. That's the only logical answer, Watson. There's something here, in the pictures that are available from the event, that The Woman wants us to see."

We perused the photographs on every website for the rest of the night, but if there was something we needed to catch, it escaped both of us.

Sherlock yawned. "Perhaps we'll see the connection tomorrow, Watson, when we're on the set."

"Truly, I cannot wait."

"The doom in your tone speaks otherwise. Look at it as another opportunity to broaden your horizons."

"They're broad enough already, thank you."

Sherlock laughed. "Never think you have nothing left to learn or experience. Fate always lurks around the corner, waiting to prove to you that you haven't seen anything yet."

THE MORNING DAWNED bright and early and we headed out in Sherlock's sleek, silver Aston Martin DB9 convertible sports car. It was an older model, but you'd never know to look at or drive in it. There was a story behind the car—it had been gifted to her by a thankful client so that she'd have good transportation when she came to the States—but so far I'd been unable to get the details out of her.

Sherlock kept two leather duffle bags that contained the same equipment in each—a magnifying glass; a jeweler's loop; fingerprint dusting kit; a variety of other kits that tested blood, saliva, and more; plastic gloves; rope; duct tape; a voice recorder; a notebook and several pens; a black light; and some things I couldn't identify and hadn't yet seen her use. One bag remained in the trunk of her car, one was in our home.

Even though one of the bags remained in the car, she always verified that it was there and that the contents were secure before we left the garage. "Better to take the minute and a half to be certain, than to arrive and discover I'm missing something key," was her reply when I'd asked why she bothered.

As we headed out of our neighborhood and up Wilshire, top down and wind in our hair, Sherlock had me call Detective Straude.

"John, what can I do for you—and, I assume, Sherlock?" he asked when he came to the phone.

"Putting you onto speaker, Lee. We want to find out any information you had on the situation over at Andenson Productions."

"It's nothing." Straude heaved a sigh. "They hired you to look into this?"

"Yes."

"Lee," Sherlock said, "we're on the way over. Just in case, why don't you meet us there?"

"Sherlock, we've investigated. There's no proof of foul play."

"It's a missing person case at the least," I pointed out.

"True enough, but it's not a homicide, so my being involved is a ridiculous waste of time."

Sherlock pursed her lips. "Lee... humor me. And them. They'll quiet down if I don't find anything. And, if I happen to, then you'll be there, all ready to leap into action by doing exactly what I say."

Straude snorted. "I'd be offended, but it's the truth."

"That's why I enjoy working with you—you accept reality. By the way, I don't really expect to find anything, but let's ensure that a company that has myriad opportunities to run down the L.A.P.D. isn't given a reason to do so."

"You do look out for us, don't you, Sherlock?"

"I consider that part of my job, Lee."

"Really?" he chuckled. "Scotland Yard would say differently."

"As would the N.Y.P.D. Which is why I'm so happily settled out here in the City of Liars enjoying the constant, unbearable sunshine."

"Some people enjoy it, you know. Though I can't argue with you about it being the 'City of Liars.'"

"I just look at it as ensuring that I never have to contend with the elements at outdoor crime scenes."

"Whatever makes you happy, Sherlock."

"Luckily for you, it's solving crimes. We'll see you there?"

"Oh yes, I'm ever your obedient servant."

"I'd laugh my head off at that, Lee, but I'm driving and don't want to take my eyes off the road."

"Good. We at the L.A.P.D. appreciate good driving habits."

We hung up and drove on in the sunshine. *Glitterazzi* was filming on the Paramount lot, so we stayed on the surface streets. Sherlock was quiet, which wasn't unusual. I spent the time thinking about Irene. I wondered if she was involved and, if so, how. And if she wasn't involved, why had she come with a bogus case? I had no answers, but I had a date with her and perhaps I'd find the answers then.

We flashed the parking pass at the Paramount main gate and were allowed inside. The map that Jackson had given us was easy to follow, and we soon reached the parking area for Soundstage 12. We had to walk a ways to get to the actual stage, but Sherlock didn't seem to mind. In fact, after she pulled out the duffel bag, handed it to me, and locked her car, she examined the parking area.

"Why?" I asked her, as she strolled through the parking spaces, most of which were filled.

"Andenson Productions has three assigned parking spaces—which isn't a surprise, seeing as the studio also has an interest in the majority of their reality shows. However, the spaces are assigned to the production company itself, not to anyone in particular."

"Is that relevant to the case?"

"Maybe."

"Why?"

"All three spaces have cars in them."

I considered this. "And you think that this indicates that someone other than Cliff is using his space?"

"I don't possess enough facts to formulate a hypothesis, Watson. It's simply something to note for now, and investigate when we take stock of who's here. And who isn't."

"You think we'll find someone missing other than Cliff?"

Sherlock sighed. "Watson, I have no idea. I'm pointedly not coming up with potential scenarios, because by doing that I would focus on my theories, not on the facts and clues themselves. Instead of seeing what *is* I would focus on how the details fit what I *want* them to. Going in with my mind blank, so to speak, means that I'll see what's there, clearly and without prejudice."

"Why were you prejudiced against Irene, then?"

"The Woman comes with existing baggage. If you see a viper, you know that vipers can and will bite. You don't need to ask if this particular viper might not bite—you go in knowing that it can and probably will. Therefore, you approach it cautiously, ready to run or shoot."

"Should I be ready to run or shoot tomorrow night?"

"Always be prepared and ready, Watson. Always."

Reaching the security checkpoint for the soundstage ended this particularly cheery conversation. We were quickly ushered in to see something I hadn't been prepared for—utter chaos.

"First time on a set, Watson?" Sherlock asked me as she strode in amongst the myriad people scurrying here and there, some carrying equipment or building materials, many talking or shouting at each other.

I closed my jaw. "The very first. Has something happened?"

"No, other than they're prepping for shooting. This is tame." She headed in the direction the person who'd let us in had indicated, and I followed after.

There were a variety of people on what I realized was the stage area, mostly because they were surrounded by cameras and people doing last minute hair and makeup fixes.

We skirted them and reached a table laden with food. Sherlock stopped. "Nice to see you again, Henry—Maddie—Sharon," she said to the people handling the food service.

The man and two women all smiled at her with recognition. "Here to watch the filming?" the man I assumed was Henry asked.

"Yes. So exciting!"

"Have something to snack on, Sherlock," Henry said. "Baked goods are all fresh—this is a heavy carbs crowd."

"Really? I'd think that they'd all be eating nothing but lima beans."

"The crew," Henry said with a laugh. "You're right about all the talent eating next to nothing."

"Where's Frank?"

Henry grimaced. "No idea. Left for a smoke break the other day and never came back. Maddie called, but he hasn't answered. Guess he found another job."

"Perhaps." Sherlock took a croissant, nodded to Henry and the two women, then walked on.

"Why did you take their food?"

"Craft services, Watson. You saw it at New London when we met. This very team, to be precise."

"Yes, but I didn't ever partake."

"Bully for you."

"Apparently you partook enough to be on a first name basis with all of them."

"I have no objection to eating well, Watson, especially if no one's losing out from it, and I confess to enjoying not having to pay." She bit into the croissant and looked disappointed. "I can tell that Frank's not here. He's the main baker, and, while delicious, this doesn't have his touch."

"Why does it matter?"

"I don't know. Yet. Anyway, craft services are here for everyone working on the picture, and that now includes us. If you're peckish, go back and grab something. Believe me, our employers won't mind and Henry's team are culinary geniuses. And you certainly *sound* peckish."

I was about to mutter that I didn't want to take anything from the Unholy Three when Jackson bounded through a closed door I'd thought was part of the set. "Sherlock!" he boomed, as he embraced her. "So glad you could come visit!"

"Thanks for inviting us," she said, without missing a beat. "Watson's never been on an actual soundstage before, so he's quite thrilled."

I'd learned to keep my mouth shut and my expression neutral whenever Sherlock said something I wasn't prepared for, so I merely smiled and nodded.

"Wonderful," Jackson said. "Let me show you around. Get something from craft services, why don't you?"

"Oh, I grabbed something already"—she waved the remains of the croissant at him—"but Watson's concerned that there won't be enough for the cast and crew if he indulges."

"Nonsense!" Jackson headed us back to the craft services table. "These are some friends of mine," he said to Henry and his team. "Let's show them how great your food is. How do you like your lattes?" he asked the two of us.

Now clearly wasn't the time to resist. "I prefer cappuccino."

"I'll take a coffee black," Sherlock said. She shot Jackson a sideways glance. "Just like my men."

I'd never heard Sherlock make any kind of sexual joke before, and I knew for a fact she had no interest in romance, but Jackson loved it. "That's my girl. I'll take a latte, though, Henry." Henry nodded and the women turned and went to make the drinks. None of them mentioned that they already knew Sherlock.

"Are you ready to start shooting?" Sherlock asked while we waited and I broke down and took a scone. It was delicious; I found myself wondering if Sherlock had said yes to this case only for the food. I also wondered if the scone would have been even better if this Frank had baked it, then reminded myself we were here because a man was missing.

"Just about," Jackson replied. "Still getting a few things in place."

"Ah."

I took this to mean that Camden hadn't shown up yet. Though how anyone would notice that he wasn't here amidst all the people and activity I couldn't fathom.

While we waited, Jackson explained how filming on set was different from what I'd seen before, when they were filming *Campus Queen* at New London. That was a location shoot and also reality, so they used mostly handheld cameras and had less emphasis on makeup and wardrobe. Lighting had mattered, but because they'd been filming on an existing college campus, no sets had been needed.

Glitterazzi, on the other hand, required sets and a soundstage, stationary cameras, extensive lighting, and a heavy emphasis on hair, makeup, and wardrobe. Most of the people racing around were crew, both those who'd been with Andenson Productions from the start and at least twice again as many who'd been hired on for the new show. Between the cast and crew, there were easily a hundred and fifty people on the set at any one time.

In some ways I was amazed—it was eight in the morning but most of these people had been here for hours already and would be here for many hours more. This was not a nine-to-five endeavor. The need to keep everyone fed and watered seemed more explainable all of a sudden.

I tried to keep everyone straight, but there were so many people I found it difficult. Sherlock's eyes were darting everywhere, though she kept up a steady stream of casual conversation with Jackson.

Coffees in hand, we finally headed back towards the door Jackson had come through, which led to a corridor with many other doors. "Cast's dressing rooms, makeup, hair, and wardrobe, our offices, and so on," Jackson said as we walked past. The last door at the end of the corridor was the one we entered. "And here's the writers' room."

An oval table with twelve chairs around it sat in a room that had more whiteboards and bulletin boards than I thought necessary for any sane place. The boards were filled with scribbles, papers tacked up, spare pushpins, and whiteboard markers. The table had stacks of pages on it, along with pencils, pens, and more markers. This was a busy-looking room, for having no one in it before we'd arrived.

"Where are the erasers?" Sherlock asked as soon as the door closed.

"Huh?" Jackson looked around. "Somewhere, I'm sure. Why does that matter?"

She shrugged. "They're something missing from a room where they belong. That's all."

"Well, what's missing is our head writer and director, and I'm a lot more worried about Cliff than the erasers."

"Still no word?" I asked.

"None."

Sherlock nodded. "The L.A.P.D. are on their way. It's clear that you didn't want the cast and crew panicked, but they'll be here soon. I'd like to talk to the actress Cliff is romantically attached to—Dawn Niles, I believe you said her name was— before Lee and his people arrive."

"She's probably in her dressing room. All the names are on the doors and the chorus and background people's rooms are also marked. Don't you want to question anyone else?" Jackson sounded worried.

"Not yet. They all know something's wrong. You've had uniformed officers out already, their director isn't here, and you haven't assigned the assistant director to take over."

Jackson sighed. "I'm the AD on this. I'm trying not to take over until I have to."

"That seems out of your bailiwick," I mentioned.

"It is. We had a falling out with the AD we'd hired and had to fire him. The ADs we use for our reality shows are all directing those shows. We can't pull anyone from one of them, or we'll watch our empire start to crumble, brick by brick."

"I'd like the information on the person you fired," Sherlock said. "Sooner rather than later. I'd like information on anyone you've let go from the production company within the last year, actually. As well as any actors who made it through the casting process but weren't chosen."

"You're thinking someone might be taking revenge on us?" Jackson genuinely sounded like it hadn't occurred to him.

"I believe that revenge is always a strong motivator. And don't be naïve, Joey. You know it's a motive, just as money, fame, and power are motives. Do you have the personnel records here?"

"You're right, of course. And, yeah, we've set up a satellite office here, so I have access to everything that we have at our main site. It'll take me a few minutes to pull up."

"Go ahead. We'll be here or wandering. I'm sure you'll be able to find us."

Jackson trotted off and I looked at Sherlock. She was reading the whiteboards. "Why didn't you have him introduce us to the actress?"

"Because I have you with me, Watson. A handsome man is always a wonderful calling card with most women."

I felt my cheeks get hot. "I'm not that handsome."

"Oh, Watson, let's stop this. False modesty helps no one, least of all me. I'm brilliant, you're handsome. Accept your strengths, and your weaknesses—utilize and work on them, respectively. You're appealing, and I'd like to wield that appeal with more people here than just The Woman."

"Fine. Let me stop blushing before we go, though."

She chuckled. "As you wish. I need to finish reading the boards anyway."

I took another glance. *This Scene Stays No Matter What* was the headline on one board, but the scribbles weren't worth deciphering. "It's just gibberish about the shows."

"Yes, and if this case is nothing, then all this gibberish doesn't matter and we'll just enjoy spending time on the set and eating well. If, however, this case is something—and a lack of whiteboard erasers and a missing craft services baker indicates that it might be—then the gibberish becomes clues."

"Seriously, Sherlock, why does a lack of erasers indicate anything other than forgetfulness? And why does someone wandering off merit attention?"

"Frank being MIA is significant because Cliff is as well, and they disappeared on the same day and roughly at the same time. Things that should be somewhere but aren't are always indicative, Watson. I earned my car by noticing something lacking."

"What?"

"Noise. Specifically a dog that should have been barking but wasn't. No"—she turned back to the boards, eyes narrowed, as she pulled out her phone—"there's potentially much more here than meets the eye."

SHERLOCK PHOTOGRAPHED ALL the boards carefully, and had me do the same with the pages on the table, from a variety of angles. I chose to stop asking why we were wasting time and instead did what she wanted as quickly as possible.

We were done before Jackson was back, so we headed out and to the door marked *Dawn Niles*. It was next to the doors marked *Production Suite*; Camden was keeping his paramour close. I heard the sound of a printer going, so presumably Jackson was printing out everything Sherlock had requested, and apparently that was a lot of data. It came as no surprise to me that the Unholy Three might have made enemies—I certainly didn't care for them and I barely knew them.

Sherlock knocked and I heard an audible sniffle from inside. "Just a minute," a female voice called. Not as sultry and enticing as Irene's, but sweet and compelling nonetheless.

The door opened to reveal a small, brown-haired, blue-eyed girl, with a light smattering of freckles. She was pretty, but I saw no future big star in her. She was wrapped in a cornflower blue dressing gown and her eyes were slightly red, as if she'd been crying. Hence the sniffling.

"Can I help you?" she asked nicely.

Sherlock nudged my foot with hers. I had no idea what she wanted me to do, so I went for 'professional detective.' "Dawn Niles?" I asked with a smile.

She smiled back. It was wide, wholesome, and lovely. And still nowhere near as enticing as Irene's smiles. "Yes, that's me."

"Excellent," Sherlock said pleasantly. "Joey suggested we have a sit down with you."

"What about?"

"Doing a piece for the *Times*," Sherlock said without missing a beat. Once again I was glad I'd spent time learning how to keep my expression neutral.

The girl brightened. "Oh, come right in."

The dressing room wasn't overly large but it had a changing screen with a variety of clothes tossed over it, a rather old-fashioned vanity with a three-way mirror and chair that matched, a loveseat and two chairs, all black leather, and a sleek black glass coffee table. The changing screen and vanity set went together, but they didn't fit at all with the loveseat, coffee table, and chairs.

"Please, sit," Dawn indicated the chairs as she settled onto the loveseat. "What can I tell you about?"

"Where did the changing screen come from?" Sherlock asked as I got out my pad and pen to take notes, both for Sherlock and to keep our cover from being blown.

Dawn dimpled. "My grandmother. The vanity set is hers, too. She was a stage actress in the 'forties."

"Anyone we'd know?" Sherlock sounded fascinated.

Dawn shook her head. "I don't think so. Mary Niles. She was never a headliner, she was usually chorus. The best she ever got was a role as the first murder victim in *Murder Most Foul* in an off-Broadway run. But"—she shrugged—"it's in my blood, and my grandmother paid for me to take acting lessons when I was little, so I like having something of hers with me."

"The murder victim in that was hanged, wasn't she?" Sherlock asked.

Dawn nodded. "But in the stage play, my grandmother actually had some lines. She got a lot of praise, but then she got pregnant with my dad and the rest is kind of history."

"She's passed on?" Sherlock asked, sounding sympathetic.

Dawn nodded again. "A few years ago. I miss her. But I have her things that she used when she was on stage. Hopefully they'll bring me luck."

"Let's hope so," I said, which earned me a smile from Dawn and the 'hush up' look from Sherlock. I went back to taking notes.

"Why do you think you were cast as the lead ingénue in this production?" was Sherlock's next question.

"Cliff—Mr. Camden—said that I have screen presence. Mr. Jackson and Mr. Antonelli agreed."

"I'm sure you do," Sherlock said.

Dawn smiled. "That's sweet of you to say, but honestly, I didn't think I did until Mr. Camden showed me my screen test.

When I saw myself on film, all of a sudden I realized that I maybe *could* make it."

"Any chance we can see your screen test, perhaps?" Sherlock asked. "It would make a nice addition to the piece."

"Sure. Give me a moment and I'll take you over." Dawn got up and trotted behind her dressing screen. "It's exciting to finally have someone notice that I'm in the cast."

"Oh?" Sherlock's tone was just right—leading without appearing to be leading. She had her phone out and was taking pictures of everything on or around the vanity, including the gigantic stack of bound scripts. Based on a fast count, the scripts had changed at least twenty times, which seemed extreme.

"Well, everyone else is an established reality star. And they're kind of typecast."

"How so?" Sherlock was finally done with the vanity and had turned around to get the rest of the room.

"Well, if you were a villain on your reality show, you're one on *Glitterazzi*. If you were the winner, same here, your character is a success. Nice people are nice. And so on. At least at the start. Mr. Camden said that he was going to switch some things around pretty quickly."

"Why is that?" Sherlock had cocked her head at Dawn's last statement, but she sounded just interested enough to keep the girl talking, but not so interested that Dawn might clam up.

"He said that while some were exactly as they'd been in their reality shows, there were some distinct differences in the real reality of life. I think he kind of regrets a couple of my co-stars."

"Who?" Sherlock finished snapping photos and put her phone away, just in time.

Dawn sighed as she left the changing screen. She was dressed in a summery dress that looked incredibly expensive. I assumed this was her costume for whatever scene she was supposed to be shooting. The dress was multicolored, but her fingernails and toenails matched the main color, which was fuchsia.

"He wouldn't tell me. Said he didn't want my experiences colored by his prejudices. I assume it's one or two of the other girls—he's dated most of them before." She smiled. "He's very sweet, and very protective, too. I'm lucky to have him as my... director."

The pause was slight, but it was there. Sherlock ignored it, however. "I'm sure you are. A lot's riding on this show, isn't it?"

"Yes. My career, Andenson Production's credibility, ad revenues, probably more. It's kind of daunting, but Mr. Camden, Mr. Jackson, and Mr. Antonelli keep telling me I'm up to the task."

"Then I'm sure they're right." Sherlock stood. "Ready for us to see you on film?"

"I am!" Dawn led us out of her dressing room. I'd expected to go to the room Jackson was in, but she went right past it—the sound of printing ongoing behind the door—and led us out of this area.

We were back on the set, and it remained chaotic. I spotted Irene talking with several people, all of whom looked like they were actors, but didn't try to catch her attention.

We passed craft services and Dawn waved to the people working it. They all waved back. The crew we passed all seemed agitated, but when Dawn came by they all stopped and said hello to her, waved, or similar. Clearly she was popular on the set. This was interesting, since Camden wasn't around and there was no reason for them to pretend.

We reached a camera that was off to the side. The man sitting there looked incredibly bored.

"Hi, Dennis," Dawn said. "These are reporters from the *Times*, and they'd like to see some of my screen test."

"Sure, Dawnie." Dennis stood up. "Come with me, folks."

We walked around behind the set and to a different set of rooms. There were fewer rooms here, but they were clearly important—*Sound and Effects*, *Editing Bay*, and *Computer Room*. All three had red lights above their doors and signs that said *No entry when red light is on*.

All the red lights were off and we entered the editing bay,

which had a lot of computerized equipment and a big screen. Dennis sat down, fiddled with some knobs, and suddenly Dawn was on the screen.

She was still wholesome and lovely, but now I could see the star power. The camera loved her, and made everything she did or said seem better—funnier, sadder, more romantic.

"Amazing," Sherlock said quietly. "I believe Andenson Productions is right. You're going to be a big star."

"Aw, thank you," Dawn said. It was dark in here, but I could see her blushing. "You know that's for the public to decide. Sometimes you can think you're going to be a star and all you are is a great wife, mother, and grandmother."

"Your grandmother sounds like a wise woman," Sherlock said kindly, "but having seen this, I think you can plan for something a tad more exciting."

Before I could chip in or Dawn could say anything else, the door opened and a man I'd seen on the set stuck his head in. "Dennis and Dawn, there you are. Great. Miraculously, we're going to start filming."

"Cliff's back?" Dawn asked eagerly.

The man shook his head. "Sorry, sweetie, he's not. But Joey's going to give it a shot."

Dennis groaned quietly. "This should be hell. Thanks, Mitch, we'll be right there." Mitch nodded and shut the door, and Dennis eyed us. "Dawn, you run along. It'll take longer for them to set you up than me."

"Okay. See you on the set," she said to us, then trotted off as she'd been told.

Once the door was closed again, Dennis crossed his arms over his chest and glared at us. "You're not reporters."

"In fact," Dennis went on, "I know exactly who you are. So, why are you here and why are you lying to Dawn?"

"Who do you think we are?" Sherlock asked, unruffled.

"I don't think, I know. You're Sherlock Holmes, the British detective out of New York." He looked at me. "And you're Doctor Watson. From New London College. You think any of us who were working that season of *Campus Queen* wouldn't know you both on sight?"

"No, and we weren't trying to fool anyone," Sherlock said soothingly.

"Other than Dawn." Dennis sounded extremely protective.

"Only to get honest answers." Sherlock cocked her head a bit. "You all seem very fond of her."

"She's just a kid, a sweet kid, who's not into drugs or booze or partying or all that other crap." He looked quietly upset.

"Just into sleeping with the director." Sherlock spoke evenly.

Dennis shrugged. "The heart wants what it wants. Sure, he's slept with every woman on this set, but it's different with Dawn. Cliff's in love with her, it's really obvious. Maybe not to him, Joey, or Tony, but it's easier to see if you're a little removed. And *she's* head over heels for him. So, that's really not the problem. She's twenty, she's old enough to make her own choices."

"Really?" I blurted out before I could stop myself. "She looks sixteen."

"That's why she's the lead," Dennis replied.

"So," Sherlock said, "what is it that you're upset about, then?"

"Nothing. Other than you two lying to her."

"And now you're lying to us, and obviously. Please don't."

Dennis eyed Sherlock. "You're here investigating what's happened to Cliff, aren't you?"

"We are."

"Well, take a look at Andenson's financials. Because I think Cliff's run off with the company's money."

"Why on Earth would you think that?" I asked, again before I could stop myself.

Dennis sighed as he stood up and headed for the door. "Because none of us have been paid for two weeks and counting."

WE FOLLOWED DENNIS out of the editing bay and back into the chaos, which was getting markedly louder and more chaotic. I had no idea how anyone worked successfully in this kind of atmosphere. The entire *Campus Queen* experience at New London, murders included, had been less frenetic than five minutes on this soundstage.

Adding to it all, Detective Straude and his partner, Detective Saunders, had finally arrived. While I got along just fine with Straude, Saunders and I had never gotten on. If Sherlock or the police found any evidence of a real crime, I half expected Saunders to accuse me of being the perpetrator.

Several people approached us. "We hear you're from the *Times*," said a normal-looking woman in her mid-forties.

To his credit, Dennis didn't say anything. He just grunted and hurried off, back to where Dawn had found him.

"John, this is Kara Rieke," Sherlock said. "That's Julianna Whitesmith." She pointed to another woman who also looked mid-forties. She was taller and blonder than the first woman, but they both had a certain look about them.

"And I'm Anna Wooten," the third one said, shoving in so that the three of them formed a semicircle around us. She looked late thirties and was a brunette. But otherwise, she reminded me of the two blondes. There was something overly fake about them, an air of trying just a bit too hard.

I quickly perused my notes to avoid Sherlock's *if-you'd-but-done-as-I-said-you'd-know-this-already* look. "Ah, Kara and Anna from the *Real Families of Suburbia* and Julianna from the *Real Families of SoCal*, correct?"

The three women beamed. "That's us," Julianna said. "And we'd love to do an interview with you, if you have the time."

"They want Dawn, girls, just like everyone else," a bored male voice said. A beefy young man who looked a few years older than Dawn joined us. He flashed us a sympathetic smile. "You know us reality whores—we'll do anything to get our names in the papers."

"Speak for yourself, though apparently you'll do anything for a photo op, George," Anna snapped.

"Bros before hos, babe," George said with a smirk. "Especially you hos."

I risked another look at my notes. This would be George Benning, late of *Campus King: Ohio State*. He was a good-looking man, but visibly disgusted, with himself and everything around him. I figured him for the show's male villain. He also looked vaguely familiar, but I couldn't say why.

"Of course, if you stopped trying to drag girls off into dark corners against their will," Julianna said, "you might have better shots taken."

"Not in front of the nice people from the *Times*," Kara said with an extremely fake smile I assumed she thought was fooling everyone. "That's all in the past, isn't it, girls?"

"Oh, we're not that nice," Sherlock said. All four of them tittered, but I was quite aware that Sherlock wasn't actually making a joke.

We were spotted and three more women raced over. "Yoo-hoo," another blonde who looked mid-twenties called. "What are we missing?"

George rolled his eyes. "Oh, good. The party's complete."

"This isn't the entire cast, is it?" I asked him as she and the other two women shoved in. Sherlock and I were literally surrounded.

"No. A few have managed not to run over here salivating. Don't expect it to last."

Risked a look around. Irene was nearby, between us and the stage. I caught her eye by accident. She smiled slowly, winked, and sashayed off. I felt the heat rising in my face and looked back to the new arrivals.

"Sarah Foster," Sherlock said, pointing to the newest blonde. "*Campus Queen: Berkeley*. Along with Elizabeth Gale, *Campus Queen: Notre Dame*, and Amanda Rice, *High School Confidential: Alabama*."

Elizabeth had red hair and looked late-twenties, or possibly early-thirties. Amanda looked early twenties and was a brunette. They were all conventionally attractive. And, unlike the first three women, didn't reek of the same desperation. It was still there, but not as strong.

All of them were looking at me expectantly. "Ah, it's a pleasure to meet you," I managed.

"I think he's a new male lead," Julianna said to the new arrivals. "Far too handsome to just be a reporter." The other women nodded in agreement. My face felt even hotter. George laughed and winked at me.

"I'm with the *Times*," I muttered.

"I have headshots if you'd like an autograph," Amanda said.

"I do, too," Elizabeth added quickly.

"Oh, I'm sure we'll take our own photos," Sherlock said. "I was wondering, though—how do all of you feel about the situation?"

"Which one?" Elizabeth asked with a short laugh.

"There's more than one?" Sherlock asked ingenuously.

"Oh, good lord, you can take your pick," Anna replied. "We have no scripts, our director's AWOL, roles are being reassigned as we speak—still without a script again, let me remind you—and the crew keeps losing things."

"What kinds of things?" Sherlock asked.

"You name it," Julianna said, "and it's gone. Props, costumes, personal items. We either have thieves or we have raccoons."

"I haven't seen any woodland creatures," George said. "Present company excluded."

"We hate you, too, George," Kara snapped. "Even Dawn hates you, and that's saying a lot."

"Dawn loves me," George said with a laugh.

"Really?" Sarah said. "That's why she won't be alone with you and makes one of us come with her if she has to be?"

George opened his mouth, but Elizabeth put up her hand. "The reporters aren't interested in this little on-set friction. But Julianna's right. They tell you it's so much more professional in the big leagues, but you can't prove it by this crew."

"Well," Sarah said, "the crew members we're used to are all great. It's just the new ones that are problematic."

The others nodded. "True enough," Amanda agreed. "Anyway, it's a madhouse here."

There was nothing I could see that actually dispelled any of their complaints, so I merely nodded and continued to take notes.

"Could you go into detail about what's been taken or gone missing?" Sherlock asked.

Mouths opened, but before any of them could talk, a man's voice rang out. "All principals to the set!"

The actors' mouths closed. "Back soon," Amanda said.

"Wait around for us," Kara added.

"Oh, we will," Sherlock said, as they all trotted off.

We wandered back over to craft services, in part because that would keep us out of the way, and in part because apparently Sherlock was quite the fan of free food. I'd not known this about her before today, but added it to my List of Sherlock's Idiosyncrasies.

A young man shorter than me rushed over to us. "Excuse me, Ms. Holmes, but Joey asked me to tell that he left what you wanted in the production office."

"Thanks, Avery," Sherlock said. "How are you enjoying being the main production assistant?" To me, she added, "Avery's been with Andenson since *Campus King: Ohio State*."

Avery managed a weak smile. "It's not all the glamour you hear about, I'll say that."

"So you know George, then?" I asked.

"Yeah. Good guy. A little too into the girls, but he's always got your back." Someone shouted his name and Avery sighed. "Duty calls. See you around. Have a latte." He raced off. It was starting to feel like we were being given the party line. And they were way into their coffee around here.

Straude and Saunders wandered over to us. They both nodded to the caterers, who remembered them from New London as well. Lattes and fresh donuts were handed out immediately, earning the catering crew a beaming smile from Saunders, a quiet grunt of thanks from Straude, and a wink from Sherlock. I gave up and accepted a maple bar and another coffee; by now it seemed expected and I didn't want to be rude. The fact that the coffee and foodstuffs were quite delicious had nothing to do with it.

More chaos, rushed and random milling about, and shouting ensued. But, at long last, Jackson was in the director's chair, so that was progress of a sort. Everyone was in their places, except for one. "Where the hell is Dawn?" Jackson shouted. "I need my leading lady."

Sherlock stiffened, and put her food and drink down onto the table. "Watson, quickly."

"What is it?" I asked as I followed suit. Sherlock strode towards the dressing rooms, almost running, and the detectives and I followed. Saunders was also tall and a fast walker, but Straude and I were both jogging to keep up.

"The most professional actor on this set is Dawn Niles. She was told to get to the set and she left us to go to the set. Therefore, the last person I'd expect to be missing from said set is Dawn. I hadn't seen her, but I assumed she was behind something waiting to make an entrance. Clearly that isn't the case."

We reached Dawn's dressing room and Sherlock flung the door open without knocking. The room was devoid of anyone, Dawn in particular, and it looked just as it had when we'd left it.

Sherlock spun and headed off towards the back of the stage. Then a woman's scream rang out and Sherlock broke into a run.

WE REACHED THE area behind the main set, where the rigging was. A web of metal catwalks—laden with ropes and pulleys, sandbags, light bars, and other things I couldn't identify—arched overhead.

The screamer turned out to be Irene. She looked white and was shaking. And she was pointing up.

A pair of bare feet were just visible in the middle of a particularly clustered group of ropes hanging from the highest part of the rigging.

"Get someone up there immediately," Straude barked. Mitch and a couple other men were scrambling up even before he'd given the order.

"From the way the feet are hanging, whoever's up there is unlikely to be alive," I said quietly. "Though I'll do my best."

"I know you will, Watson, but I fear we're too late." Sherlock sounded angry and upset.

"You think it's Dawn?"

"I know it is. Note the toenail polish."

I did, now that she mentioned it. It was fuchsia.

"Watson, we need some evidence gloves," Sherlock said quietly. I dug through the duffel and pulled out a pair for her and for me.

The body was lowered to the ground, laid out by Straude and Saunders, and confirmed as Dawn Niles. I leaped to her, but the angle of her neck and her open, staring eyes told me that there was going to be nothing I could do. Even so, I checked her vitals and tried CPR.

I closed her eyes gently. "It's no good. She's dead."

"Nice to see that required an Oxford education to determine," Saunders said under his breath. "My own damn eyes wouldn't be good enough." I ignored him.

"Any guess as to how long?" Straude asked, flashing Saunders a dark look.

"Less than thirty minutes," Sherlock replied. "That's the last time we saw her alive." She looked around and up. "You there! Leave things alone. Touch nothing and get the hell down here." Her voice radiated authority, more than Straude's had, and the men on the catwalk hurried down.

Everyone else had gathered around by now. Jackson stared dumbly at Dawn's lifeless body. Irene hugged herself. Some of the female crew members cried quietly; some of the male ones, too. The rest of the actors seemed unsure as to what expressions they should be wearing, though Amanda gave Joey a calculating look. She was the youngest-looking of the reality stars and it didn't take Sherlock's genius to guess that she was hoping she'd be the one to step into Dawn's role.

I heard the sound of a man running, then the sounds of someone shoving through a lot of people. Antonelli reached us and stopped dead. "How did this happen?" he asked.

"I don't know why she'd have been up there," Mitch said. "There was no reason for it. But it looks like she was and she slipped and fell."

"She didn't slip, she didn't fall, and this wasn't an accident," Sherlock said briskly. "Lock down this set," she said to Saunders, who nodded and stepped away to call in reinforcements. "Lee, make sure no one leaves and no one disturbs anything. Watson, with me."

Sherlock headed for the catwalks and started to climb up. I followed suit, hoping that the gloves we were wearing to keep from contaminating the crime scene wouldn't cause us to actually slip and fall to our deaths.

It was a little dicey in a couple of places, but we made it up without too much trouble. Sherlock pulled the magnifying glass out of the duffel and began to examine everything. It was fairly dark up here, so I got one of our flashlights out to give her light. We worked our way across the entire thing fairly quickly.

Then Sherlock went back to the general area Dawn would have had to have been in order to have landed in the ropes as she had.

"Her neck was broken elsewhere and she was brought up here, then dumped into the rigging. Possibly tied and swung in."

"You're sure?"

"There's no sign of a struggle, no flecks of nail polish, no cloth fibers caught on the metal, no blood. Falling people tend to scream, Watson, and the only scream was from The Woman." She cocked her head. "Please call for Mitch to come up here, would you? And make sure he's got on evidence gloves."

"Why me?"

"You're being the nice one now."

"I'd ask why either one of us is playing good cop or bad cop when we have Lee and my best friend down there, but I've learned not to question." I leaned over a bit. "Mitch, I'm sorry, but could you come back up? Wearing evidence gloves, too, please and thank you." He stared at me as Straude handed him a pair, but he started for the ladder while pulling the gloves on, so I presumed this meant yes. "Is he a suspect?"

"Everyone's a suspect, Watson. Other than you and me, and I'm sure we can exclude Lee and William, too."

"Saunders will accuse me, you know."

"Oh, you're so sensitive." She looked at me. "It's a good quality most of the time."

"Thanks. Dennis isn't a suspect, is he?"

"He was out of our sight during the window of opportunity, so yes, he is. The other actors are, as well. Dawn was a small girl—any one of these people could have attacked her and broken her neck."

"Neck breaking isn't as easy as the movies would have you believe, Sherlock."

"True enough. The medical examiner will have to tell us if her neck was broken after she was dead."

"You think it broke from the drop, not from whatever the attack was?"

"It's very possible. The ME will make that determination. Our job is to find the murderer."

Mitch reached us now. "Look, I'm not going to give you a statement—"

"Oh, stuff it, man," Sherlock snapped. "We're not reporters, we're detectives. Hired by both Andenson and the L.A.P.D. So you will, in fact, give us any and all statements we want. However, what I need to know right now is if that black bag hanging there is supposed to be there."

She pointed and I could see the one she meant. It wasn't filled, like most of the bags I could see hanging around; it also looked larger than any of them.

"No, and I didn't see it before, either. But then, it's kind of in a dark spot, isn't it?"

"It is. I need you to retrieve it, please. Use that gaff pole."

"That'll mean I have to touch and move things," Mitch said, a little snidely.

"Yes, you will. Hence why you're wearing those gloves. Just think—I *could* have asked you to climb into the rigging in those gloves, to retrieve the evidence by hand."

Mitch sighed. "Noted. Don't be sarcastic to the lady detective."

"Or she'll kick your ass, yes."

Mitch stared at Sherlock for a moment, then he chuckled. "Got it. Ma'am."

It took some maneuvering, but Mitch was able to use the tool she'd pointed out—a long stick with a hook at the end—to snag the bag. He managed not to drop it and brought it back to Sherlock.

"Impressive, thank you." She motioned for me to shine the light on the bag, which I did. She once again used the magnifying glass to look it over. "Aha." She pointed to something inside the bag.

Mitch and I both looked where she was pointing. "Ah... hairs?" he asked finally.

"Yes, and also makeup smears. The lab will have to make the definitive tests, but it certainly looks like the makeup Dawn was wearing."

"So, someone attacked her, tossed her into this bag, climbed up here, dumped her out of the bag, and then got back down?" I asked. "All without being noticed?"

"No. Someone killed her, tossed her into this bag, climbed up here with her over his or her shoulder, tied a rope tightly around her neck, tossed her over hard enough that her neck broke, tossed the bag into a spot where it would be hard to see, and then climbed back down. Presumably without being noticed."

"Oh, well, when you put it that way, piece of cake," Mitch said. "Who would want to hurt Dawn, let alone kill her?" He looked down. "You know, other than the rest of the cast, I mean."

"I'm not certain this is about Dawn, and I'm not certain that it *isn't*. But I need a listing of anyone who would have been up here today, anyone who could have been up here *legitimately* today, and a full listing of the cast and crew who were on the set today."

Mitch sighed. "You'll get that from me. I'm the key grip. I have the full crew roster, and I can get you the cast, too. Do we have to keep these gloves on?"

"Yes, we do. In case there are fingerprints up here. Other than the entire crew's, that is."

"Yeah, though if we find any of the actors' fingerprints that would be unusual."

"We should be so lucky, Mitch," Sherlock said, as we started down the ladder.

It was harder going down, in part because of the gloves, but mostly because it was dark and the ladders, while sturdy enough, weren't something I'd want to spend my career on. Mitch seemed to have no issues, nor did Sherlock.

The duffel bag and I went down last. The bag caught on something and I lost my footing. As I slid around and managed to keep myself on the ladder and the duffel still in my possession, I caught a different view, and a flash of light.

"Sherlock, there's something to my left."

"Do you need assistance?"

"No, I've got it. I can direct you to what I'm seeing, though."

She nodded and I did so. It took several minutes, during which I remained hanging somewhat so I wouldn't lose sight of whatever I was seeing.

Once Sherlock found it, though, it made things worse, not better.

It TURNED OUT that what I'd spotted was a door leading outside. The flash of light I'd seen was from the bottom, where the sun shone through just right.

Once I was down and had joined Sherlock, Straude, Antonelli, and Jackson, I got to witness her cursing quietly as she searched the area for clues. The men looked no happier.

"This only makes things more complex, but well spotted, Watson." Sherlock crouched down to examine the bottom of the doorway.

"Consider me happy to have almost fallen, then. Was the door locked?"

"No, it was not," Straude said unhappily. "The murderer could have easily come and gone through this door."

Jackson nodded morosely. "We don't think about that door. It's supposed to be for trash pickup, but there's another door for that which is nearer to the craft services area, and we all use that."

"And it's behind the stage so we've just told everyone to keep it closed and forget it's there," Antonelli added.

"There's yet *another* door in and out no one's bothered to mention?" Sherlock asked, as she looked up. "It's as if you all *want* the murderer to succeed." Everyone seemed ready to lose their cool, even and perhaps especially Sherlock.

"Just like during *Campus Queen*," I pointed out. "Keeps things exciting for you."

This got me glares from the three men, but Sherlock burst out laughing. "Good point, Watson. A very good point." She stood up. "There's nothing here, unfortunately, but Lee, you should have your men check the trash bins just in case."

She looked around as Straude spoke quietly into a walkie-talkie.

"See anything of interest?" I asked. I saw nothing. The doorway let out into an alleyway loaded with large trash cans: eleven on our side, twelve on the other. There were doors to other soundstages scattered about. One of the doors farther down had a couple of folding chairs next to it.

She cocked her head. "Possibly. Lee, keep everyone in. Watson, with me, please."

She strode off towards the door next to the chairs and I followed. "What are you thinking?"

"Chairs means someone comes out here and sits, frequently enough to leave something to sit on."

We reached the chairs. There was nothing exciting about them. "Whoever's out here, they're slobs." The ground was littered with cigarette butts.

"God bless nicotine addiction," Sherlock said happily, as she knocked quietly on the door.

It was opened rather quickly by a middle-aged black man. "Can I help you?"

"I hope so," Sherlock replied. "I'd dearly love to speak to anyone who was out here for a smoke break, or just hanging out with the smokers, over the past couple of hours."

He rolled his eyes. "We aren't hurting anything inside the stage. And we sweep the butts up every night. I'm about ready to complain about discrimination; this is the only place we can smoke in this whole corner of the lot."

"I couldn't care less if the entire cast and crew smokes four packs a day each. We're not here to berate anyone about their lifestyle and addiction choices, nor their cleanliness habits. We've had a situation on another stage and I'm hoping one or more of you might have noticed anything."

The man looked more interested. "Really? What happened?"

"Someone made off with some prop jewelry that, sadly, wasn't fake. Of course the crew are getting blamed for carelessness, and we're just hoping to get any idea of who might have done it."

Again I was glad I was becoming prepared for Sherlock to literally say anything at any time to anyone. Though things *had* been going missing, so it wasn't a complete lie. "We're trying to figure if it was an inside job or not," I added.

Sherlock nodded and neither kicked me nor gave me the *shut up* look. I managed not to congratulate myself. Too much.

The man's eyes narrowed. "Hate it when that happens. It's usually some stupid kid's boyfriend trying to support a drug habit, but if they're hitting your stage they might try ours, too. Sure, let me round up everyone. Give me a couple of minutes."

He disappeared outside and we waited. "You really think someone might have seen something?"

"The chance is good, Watson, so yes. We have nothing else to go on, since I can guarantee that the majority of the cast and crew are going to alibi each other out. And in case you're wondering, theft is far less exciting than murder. Everyone wants to have seen something regarding a murderer. Someone doing a snatch and grab? Much less thrilling, so we're more likely to get truth. Or a version of it."

Another minute or so and the door opened again and several

people exited. All ages, both sexes, some in heavy makeup, some clearly crew.

Sherlock spun her story again and appealed to them to try to remember anything they might have spotted. While every one of them took the opportunity to light up, most didn't remember anything.

One of the older actresses and two younger men who were grips had been on a smoke break together roughly about the time we thought Dawn had been killed. Sherlock sent all the others back inside so we could question these three alone.

The woman took a long drag on her cigarette, clearly thinking. "You know... I think I saw someone come out of there. A man? Around Harry's age." She indicated one of the grips.

Harry scrunched up his face. "I don't really remember. Sorry."

The other man looked thoughtful. "No, wait, we mentioned it, remember? Because he came out and started towards us, then stopped, turned around, and went the other way. Beverly, you said he must have been really anti-smoking."

"Oh, right," Harry said. "I remember now."

"Can you describe him?" Sherlock asked.

"About Harry's age is all I have," Beverly said. The men nodded. This would have put him in his late twenties to late thirties. This wasn't a help.

"White or black?" Sherlock asked.

"White," Beverly said with conviction. The men nodded.

"Light brown hair," Harry said. "I think."

"Looked blond to me," Beverly said.

"I honestly don't remember," the other man said. "He turned to the right, I do remember that, though."

"Well, it's something," Sherlock said with a sigh.

"Did he remind you of any character you might have played or played against?" I asked. Sherlock shot me an approving glance.

"You know... yeah," Beverly said slowly. "He looked like a student."

"A student?" Sherlock asked. "Why? Something he was wearing or carrying?"

"A backpack," she said. "Bill, you saw it, too, didn't you?"

"Yeah. I remember thinking it seemed kind of weird."

"How so?" Sherlock asked him patiently.

"It was a Spider-Man backpack. Seemed too young for him."

"Oh, yeah," Harry said. "I just figured he'd worked on one of the movies and it was a gift."

"No," Bill said. "I have a friend who worked on all of the movies, originals and reboots. I've seen all the cast and crew swag and that wasn't something from any of the productions. It looked more like what a kid would pick up at the drugstore for school."

"Probably stole it," Beverly said. "Just like he stole from them." She nodded her head at us. "Say, what production are you with again?"

"*Glitterazzi*," Sherlock replied. "Andenson Productions."

"Oh, them." Beverly didn't sound impressed. "Sorry you're stuck working for that outfit."

"We just started," I said. "What should we know about?"

"Don't expect to get paid," Harry said. "I have a couple buddies who took jobs there. It's a mess. Half the crew's ready to quit, but they're sticking it out because their contracts all allow for the production to be late on payments twice within a calendar year without causing any breach."

"That seems to be an odd clause," Sherlock said.

Bill nodded. "It is, but it's typical for them, honestly. Stolen props would be the least of it. Talk on the lot is that they're in over their heads, financially *and* creatively." He lowered his voice. "We heard the director ran off with all the money."

"They cast reality 'stars,'" Beverly said, making air quotes. "There's not a professional actor on that set. Of course they're a mess. And if their director ran off it just shows he's the only one with a clue."

"They told us several of the cast were professional actors," Sherlock said, sounding worried.

"Oh, honey, they lied," Beverly said sympathetically. "They have some new kid who's supposed to be good, but other than her and their stable of overacting losers, they have a handful of D-list character actors, and that's it."

"You forgot the diva," Bill said.

"Oh, yes," Beverly said dramatically. "The *act*-tress. Or, as we call her on our set, the casting couch queen."

"She's unattractive?" Sherlock asked.

"No, she's pretty enough," Beverly admitted. "But she's too full of herself. Thinks she should be the star of everything. And from what I've heard, she's willing to do anything she has to, too. Sleep with anyone, blackmail anyone, beg, borrow, or steal from anyone."

Harry nodded. "Anyone turns up dead, she's who I'd look at first."

"Really?" I asked.

Bill shrugged. "She guest starred on our show. She was a nightmare from start to finish. We almost lost a makeup team, hair dresser, a director, *and* two supporting actors because of her. She's poison to a set."

"Who should we be avoiding?" Sherlock asked.

Beverly shrugged. "My money's on you already knowing, even if you've only been there five minutes. Irene Adler."

SHERLOCK GAVE THE three of them her card in case they remembered anything else. Not the one that said *Private Consulting Detective*; the one that just had her name and number on it.

Then we headed down the alleyway in the direction the man with the Spider-Man backpack had gone.

"You can say it," I said to Sherlock as we passed the Andenson door.

"Who me? Say what?"

"That you're right about Irene."

"Watson, rumors are just that—rumors. And while I feel that their assessment of The Woman's character is likely spot on, the person who was seen leaving was a man. A man who went out of his way to not be seen by the only people around *to* see him. Which is far more suspicious than The Woman's well-deserved if possibly overstated reputation."

"In other words, you want me to keep my date and see what I can get out of her."

"Watson, sometimes we're so in sync it just warms my heart."

We reached the end of the alley and looked both ways. We were at a T-intersection with another alleyway. There was a lone trash can far off to the left, but since Bill had said our quarry had gone right, we did as well. "Do you think we're going to get paid?" I asked as we walked slowly along and Sherlock looked for anything that might be a clue.

If we'd been on dirt she'd have found a plethora of data, of that I was sure. She'd done entire studies on shoe, tire, foot, and paw prints. Unfortunately, the lot was all concrete and wasn't giving her much to work with.

"Getting paid is my least consideration, Watson. However, your question is a good one in general. I think that having the set's financial situation confirmed by reasonably uninterested bystanders says that there's far more going on than we've been told by our clients."

"Do you think it's as simple as Cliff ran off with the money?"

"And the new script, but not Dawn? You met her, and word on the set was that Cliff was in love with her. *Is* in love with her, if we assume he's still alive and doesn't know she's dead. And I find it hard to believe that a man who's landed such a lovely young thing, who's in love with him in return, would just leave her and run off. Especially since he could have run off *with* her by simply not having her go back to the set after lunch."

"So, are we at the point of suspecting someone yet?"

"Everyone, Watson. The only person I don't suspect of her murder is Dawn herself."

I considered this as we walked on down this alleyway. "Do you suspect Dawn of something other than her murder?"

"I do love it when you learn. Yes, though in the same way that I suspect the others."

We reached the end of the alley. It opened up to a parking lot. "This is the lot where we parked, isn't it?"

"Yes, but we're at the other end. It's a large lot, but it's a good bet that our quarry got into a car and drove away."

"Will we be able to narrow that down to anything useful?"

"We can but try, Watson. We can but try."

SHERLOCK HAD US walk through the parking lot; she wanted to see what cars were in the three Andenson spots. She'd expected to find one empty, but that wasn't the case. I took shots of all three cars, just in case it mattered down the road.

Straude and Saunders sent uniformed officers over to the various gate exits that covered this section of the lot. Fortunately the exits and entrances all had security cameras, so there was footage to review. Sherlock demanded and got the tapes first.

Now that there was an actual murder to investigate, Straude was no longer reluctant to be here. Though I could tell it was taking everything Jackson, Antonelli, and Sherlock had not to mention that they'd all told him so.

Sherlock also requested a full listing of whatever anyone on cast or crew said was missing, personnel as well as lost or stolen items. Then we went back to search Dawn's dressing room.

To find it in a state of utter chaos.

Sherlock walked in slowly, looking everywhere. She seemed excited.

"Sorry, but I'm confused," I said as I joined her, being careful where I stepped. "This room has obviously been searched since we were last in it. And this is the happiest I've seen you. What is this room telling you that I'm missing?"

"You're seeing all that I am, Watson. You have the same information as I do."

"Yes, I know. And I'm saying that I don't understand why you're suddenly pleased. And I can tell you're pleased—you're humming 'Bad Boys,' the theme from *Cops*. And you only do that when you're truly on the scent."

"*What'cha gonna do when I come for you?* Right you are, Watson. You can note that, and yet are missing the glaringly obvious."

"Enlighten me."

"Whoever left through the back door is not the one who tossed this room. Meaning that we either have accomplices—always a possibility—or there's even more going on than a mysterious disappearance and a murder."

"Alright, that makes sense. So, whoever searched this room in this way was looking for something."

"Presumably. They also didn't know we'd been in this room with the police already."

"Or they did and it's all being done to throw you off the scent."

"I'd agree with that, only the risk of getting caught was quite high—the police were here and already searching for a murderer within three minutes of our leaving this room."

"So someone took the opportunity to search Dawn's room for a mysterious something and then... what? Went back outside to be questioned? Ran away?"

"We'll know if anyone's missing soon. But this is where the cast dressing rooms are, as well as the production office and writers' room. I believe a thorough search is in order."

We went through every room carefully, but it was the writers' room where Sherlock found what she was looking for. "Watson, we need to compare the pictures we took with what we see in here."

"I see exactly what we saw before." I dutifully pulled my phone out.

She swiped through my pictures quickly and stopped at one. "Ha. No, this stack is shorter." She thumbed through the stack quickly. "We're missing a script. An older one, based on where it was taken from."

"You can tell that from the picture?"

"Yes. And from examining the room and its contents before." She looked around. "The information on the whiteboards hasn't been tampered with..." She was staring at the *This Stays In* board.

"Should it have been?"

"Possibly." She was quiet for a long minute, and I didn't disturb her. Her mind was sifting through all we'd seen, looking for connections, making leaps others might not, searching for what connected all of these things together.

I looked at the whiteboard she was staring at. From what I could tell, it was a dramatic scene where one actress was being threatened by another. From the little I'd seen on this set so far, it could easily have been taken verbatim from real life.

But finally Sherlock nodded, and headed out of the room, me following after like the tail to her comet.

She found Straude as quickly as possible. He was interviewing the cast and looking as if he'd wished he'd been the one hanged instead of Dawn.

"Lee," Sherlock pulled him away without preamble or apology. "Where is Collin Toohey, the other writer on the show?"

"Not here. Not missing, either, in case you were worried. He was off the lot today."

"Why?"

Straude shrugged. "Hasn't been on set since Camden's

disappearance. Reason given was that he's trying to recreate the missing script and will work better at home."

"Having seen what this place was like when we got here, I can't argue with that."

Sherlock nodded, spun on her heel, and looked around. She headed for Jackson, who was talking to the craft services people. "Joey, I need a full description of Collin Toohey and his address and phone number. Oh, and the same on the AD you fired."

"Andy Pfeiffer, and sure. Do you want all the paperwork I printed out, too? Unless you got it already, it's waiting for you in the office."

We hadn't, and she did, so we headed for the production office. Jackson jotted Toohey's information down and gave that to me, then he opened a box on the floor by the printer. We'd both noted it when we'd searched the office a short while ago, but Sherlock had been intent and, after a quick glance inside, I'd put the lid back on and we'd carried on.

Jackson stared inside. "It's all gone." A quick look showed that the box was indeed empty.

"Now, who would take all that paper and leave the vessel holding it, which would make carrying said paper far easier?" Sherlock mused.

"Someone who didn't want us to realize they'd taken it?" I suggested.

"Yes. The plot thickens. Joey, once you verify that your files are intact on the main system, send them to me electronically. I'd prefer the paper, but since you've already lost confidential information once today, we won't chance it again." She turned to go. "By the way, what pages were you using for filming today? I understood your other writer wasn't around."

"Collin isn't here, he's at home. And I was using the original script, the first one we drafted. Why?"

"Did you take that from the conference room, by any chance?" I asked.

Jackson shook his head. "No, we all have it. Everyone saved their original first drafts, just because. Souvenirs and all that."

"Why revert to the original?" Sherlock asked.

Jackson shrugged. "The scenes we were going to film are the only ones that haven't changed from any version. The introduction to Dawn's character."

"The scene on the whiteboard?"

"Yeah, that's the one." He swallowed hard. "I honestly can't believe she's dead."

"Have to cast the role all over again?" I asked, perhaps a tad too snidely.

Jackson glared at me. "You're a callous bastard, aren't you? Of course we will, but that's not why I'm upset. A beautiful, talented young girl's been murdered on our set. She had such a bright future ahead of her, and now she's gone. And for all I know, Cliff's gone, too."

"With all the production money?" Sherlock asked.

"No. I've heard those rumors and they're bullshit, Sherlock. We aren't broke and our money isn't embezzled, but we're having to float this cast and crew while we can contractually, because we had some other big expenses hit out of the blue. We'll be fine." He shook his head. "Better than Dawn will ever be, at least."

"Will you recast from your existing talent pool?" I asked. Sherlock and I hadn't found anything to indicate that Jackson was lying about their financials.

"You're really on about that, aren't you?" Jackson replied. "Yes, probably."

"I have my top suspect, then," I said to Sherlock.

"Amanda. Yes, she's the youngest and youngest-looking. Joey, would you move her into Dawn's role?"

"Doubtful. She doesn't have what we need. Though she might think she does. But killer? I don't see that in her." He sighed. "Of the others, the only one with the right screen presence is Irene."

"Irene Adler?" I spoke without meaning to.

"Yes. We're in rewrites anyway, we'll just change the show to focus on an older star who's trying to defend her position, rather than a new star fighting to get to the top."

"What role was she assigned already?" Sherlock asked.

"She's the villain, the faded star trying to get rid of the young starlet who's taking her place. Dawn was the heroine, of course. The other women are all rivals of the heroine's or friends of the villain's, trying to help her bring the young ingénue down."

"So they're playing to type," Sherlock said dryly.

Jackson managed a grin. "Yeah. George is the hero. He's the bad boy love interest who's trying to protect the young starlet while still supporting his mother, the fading star."

"Irene is cast as George's mother? She's not that much older than he is." I was surprised; he didn't strike me as hero material. But then again, if I was surrounded by all those starlets—to use the term loosely—I'd probably be jaded and cynical, too.

This earned me a *really?* look from Jackson. "Yes. It's called movie magic. Happens all the time."

"He's right, Watson. Joey, we'll be in touch." With that, Sherlock left the production office and headed back to craft services. She asked Henry for a description and contact information for Frank, the missing pastry chef.

She collected the surveillance tapes from Saunders, reminded him that she wanted the list of anything and anyone missing from the set, then we headed back to the car.

Sherlock checked the car carefully. "You thinking it's been tampered with?" I asked her, as she popped the trunk for me.

"Always possible, even probable. Especially under the circumstances."

"Ah, Sherlock?" I stared into the trunk. "We have something in here that confirms tampering. And then some."

* * *

WHAT WE HAD was a box's worth of paper that hadn't been in here before.

"Well, at least it's not a dead body," Sherlock said, as she examined the trunk's lid. "Whoever did this is an expert, or got my car fob somehow, because there's no indication that the trunk, or any other part of the car, has been tampered with." She looked thoughtful again.

"What is it? Do you think someone lifted your keys and then, somehow, put them back, all without you noticing?"

"It could be done, Watson. I'm capable of it, and I'm sure that others are as well."

"Why do that?"

"To steal incriminating information in such a way that it will take time to determine what was stolen."

"You've lost me. Why not just keep all the information? That makes the job just as hard."

"Not really. We'll now have to compare every record here with what Joey has on his mainframe. That's meticulous work, Watson." She pursed her lips. "I have a feeling that whoever's done this knows my methods."

"You think it's Irene, don't you?"

"I think the evidence, all of which is circumstantial, points in her favor, yes. And there's the fact that she was in our home and we hang our keys right by the doorway. She could have cloned it with something in her purse."

"I was watching her, Sherlock. And so were you."

"I wasn't watching for most of the time she was in our home, actually. And someone skilled could do it quickly, Watson. Technology is always advancing; she might not have needed to even *touch* the fob to clone it. She was in the hallway long enough, I'm sure. That said, I'm not allowing my active dislike of The Woman to cloud my judgment. You, on the other hand, should. Call her up and move your date to tonight."

"Excuse me?"

"Time is of the essence, Watson. Make the change. She'll go for it, I'm sure. Just use Dawn's death as the excuse."

I heaved a sigh but did as requested. Irene's voice sounded shaky, but she seemed genuinely happy about moving our date up. "Thank you, John," she said as we were getting off. "I just... I don't want to be alone tonight and I can't tell you what it means to me that you realized that. I'll see you at seven."

"Better make it eight. I imagine you'll be on the set a while longer than anticipated now."

She trilled a laugh. "Alright. I'll call you if I escape any earlier."

We hung up and Sherlock shook her head. "Watson, just a gentle reminder that she's now a suspect in several ongoing investigations."

"You're the one pushing me to take her out."

"I am indeed," she said quietly. "And I do wish it wasn't necessary."

Once the car was deemed safe enough, we put everything else we had into the trunk and headed back to Baker Street. After all the chaos and stress, it was a relief to get home to our quiet little neighborhood.

We got right to work. While we studied the surveillance footage, Sherlock reviewed the descriptions of the three men. "All three of them resemble each other," she said, as I paused the tape for a promising exiter.

"You said they were all of average height and weight, light brown hair, and nothing remarkable about their features. What does that mean?"

"No idea yet. But I believe you've found our backdoor sneak."

The car in the frame was an older, late model sedan. It was dirty, and the license plate was covered with mud. "No one would take that car off-road," I pointed out. "That's why I stopped the tape here."

"Well done. Yes, from behind, this man does look like who Beverly and the others described. Of course, he's fairly nondescript."

"You think it was one of the three men? The pastry chef, the writer, or the fired assistant director?"

"The probability is high."

"Beverly thought he was a blond, the man she saw. "

"Yes, and Harry thought he had light brown hair, and Bill hadn't paid attention. It's a bright, sunny day, and that alleyway would have been in direct sunlight when our sneak left, meaning he could have easily looked blond."

"Well, if this is him, we're going to get nothing. The license plate is illegible."

"We don't need that. He's stopped to check out. We just need to speak to whoever's working the gate kiosk."

She made a fast call to Straude and then, five minutes later, an email arrived, which I printed out: a listing of everyone who'd left via the winning kiosk in the time window Sherlock gave for when our quarry left the lot.

"No luck. None of our three names are here. None of the names related to the case are here, for that matter."

Sherlock took the list from me. "Hmmm, no obvious anagrams... he must have used someone else's name or pass." She stared at the list some more and started to laugh.

"What is it?"

"Whoever he is, he has a sense of humor. And I think I know who our mystery man is." She handed the list and pointed to a name—Alan Smithee.

"Who is that?"

"That, Watson, is a name used by people in Hollywood who wish to disown themselves from a project." She stood. "Back to the car. We're going to visit Mister Smithee."

*　　*　　*

WE HEADED TO Venice, the weird sister in between lovely Santa Monica and ritzy Marina Del Rey. Supposedly the arty types lived here, but if that was the case, I was doomed to stay pedestrian and dull, because I loathed every inch of Venice.

Sherlock, on the other hand, loved it. Apparently Venice reminded her of parts of London and New York she missed, and she found Venice Beach to be as entertaining as any reality show on TV.

The apartment we were headed for wasn't on the beach, but that didn't mean parking was easily found. Sherlock didn't seem to mind, however. "If we park a ways away and walk, he might not be prepared."

As we circled the block, a man who fit the nondescript description we had was leaving the apartment building. He didn't seem concerned, though he had something stuffed into his jacket pocket and his hand was inside it. He turned away from us out the door and walked off.

"That's him," Sherlock said softly.

"Think that's a gun in his pocket?"

"No idea, but caution should be our watchword."

She drove slowly up to the man. He was on our side of the street. He turned as we pulled level with him, and his expression told me all I needed to know—he looked shocked, panicked, and more than a little guilty.

Of course, his taking off running was something of a clue, as well.

While cars are faster and can be used as weapons, someone on foot, especially among small, dense streets, has the advantage. Our quarry turned down an alleyway made only for pedestrians. Old war injury be damned—we were *not* going to lose him.

I jumped out of the car and ran after him. I heard the screech of tires, so presumed Sherlock was driving to head him off somewhere.

He zigged and zagged where he could, but the buildings here

were all basic rectangles. He was faster than me, but I kept him in sight, and eventually he headed for a street.

Sherlock pulled up in front of him, and he spun around and ran back towards me. I decided I'd had enough and tackled him. There was a brief struggle, but I was a combat trained veteran and he, clearly, was not. I flipped him onto his stomach and pulled his hands back behind him, keeping my knee in the small of his back.

"Let me go!" the man shouted.

"I'm sorry, Mister Smithee," Sherlock said, as she ran up to us and handed me a set of handcuffs. "Or shall we use your real name, Andrew Pfeiffer? Either way, you're wanted for questioning regarding the murder of Dawn Niles."

"What?" Pfeiffer shouted. "What do you mean, Dawn's dead?"

"As if you didn't know," I snarled at him as I slapped the cuffs on him. My leg hurt from the chase, and I leaned on him a bit more.

"Get him off me! I'm not a murderer!"

"Then what's in your pocket?" I reached in and pulled out the contents. "Plastic bags?"

"I was going to the market."

"Maybe you were. However, innocent people don't run, Mister Pfeiffer," Sherlock said. "And the only reason you'd have to recognize my car is that you'd broken into it earlier today."

"Look, it's not what you think. I didn't murder anyone. Are you serious that Dawn is dead?"

"Dead serious," I snarled.

He stopped struggling. "You're not cops. Look, let me get up and I'll tell you what I did."

"Why should we listen?" I asked.

"Because if Dawn's dead, I know who killed her."

* * *

SHERLOCK HAD ACTUALLY found a decent parking place, which put her in a good mood for some reason. Then she'd examined his car. It was definitely the car from the surveillance tape, right down to the muddy license plates.

Now we were in Andy Pfeiffer's small studio apartment. It was tidy and didn't smell, but otherwise, I wouldn't want to live in it. It was so small as to make me nostalgic for my visiting professor's room at New London.

"It's all I can afford," he said defensively, as I cuffed him to his chair, arms still behind him. Apparently my dislike had shown on my face. Meaning I'd let my guard down. That had to stop. "I need to be close to the studios."

"Why? You were fired from *Glitterazzi*," Sherlock pointed out.

"Wrongfully. And that's why..."

"Why you killed Dawn?" I asked, snarling a tad more than I'd intended.

"No! I keep on telling you, I didn't kill anyone." He heaved a sigh. "I took stuff, okay? To sell."

"You mean you stole props?" Sherlock didn't sound surprised.

He nodded. "Props, clothes, set stuff. You'd be amazed at what crap like that sells for on eBay."

"Not really. The need for the public to have a piece of their idols isn't an unknown phenomenon. How in the world did you think you wouldn't be caught?"

He shrugged. "They're badly run. No one has a clear idea of how much of anything they have."

"That makes no sense," I said as Sherlock showed me an eBay page on her phone. Pfeiffer wasn't trying to hide that he had *Glitterazzi* items for sale, though the seller was listed as Mr. Hollywood. And he had a high approval rating. My bet was that this wasn't the first set he'd stolen from. "They run a huge number of successful shows. You don't become successful by not keeping track of your inventory."

"Some do, but you're right. On the *reality* shows, they're on top of things. They're really out of their element with *Glitterazzi*, though. And they know it, so it's made them all defensive and a lot less careful about little details. I got fired because I was trying to explain to Cliff that you can't direct the actors in the same way on a scripted show as you do on reality."

"He wanted to let them leave the script?" Sherlock asked.

"Sometimes. He wanted too much of their input, though, all the time. And not just Dawn's. All of them. He wanted a collaborative show. But scripted TV doesn't work like that. For an occasional movie? Sure, if your name is Robert Altman. But otherwise? It's a terrible idea. But Cliff was set on it. That's what we fought about, daily. That and the terrible script."

"The script was getting rewritten," I pointed out.

"Yes, and every version was *worse*. Collin was doing all he could, but Cliff and the others wanted to keep their stamp on it."

"Was the original script poor?" Sherlock asked.

Pfeiffer shrugged. "It was okay. I can see why you'd look at it and think it could be turned into something good. The overall plotline was strong. But they tried to rewrite it for their cast, instead of finding the cast to fit the script."

"According to everyone, they had a brand new script that's disappeared," Sherlock said. "It was supposed to be far better."

"If that's the case then they must have let Collin do what he wanted."

"What was that?" I asked.

"Bring on another writer," Pfeiffer replied. "Collin said he had someone who could fix things up fast."

"Who?" Sherlock asked.

"No idea. I was fired, remember?"

"And yet you know all of this, and you've been sneaking onto that set regularly to steal things," Sherlock pointed out. "Here's a script for you—a disgruntled employee steals from his former employer. One day he's caught by a young actress.

Rather than face the charges he knows his former employer will bring against him, he murders the actress; then runs off."

"I didn't kill anyone, least of all Dawn!"

"You were spotted leaving the set right after she was murdered," Sherlock said as she pointed to the Spider-Man backpack sitting on his bed. "You have motive, means, and opportunity. The police are going to love you."

I put evidence gloves on again, thankful that we carried a large box of them, and opened the backpack. It was stuffed with what truly looked like junk. "Should I empty it out?" I asked. Sherlock nodded.

"I didn't kill Dawn," Pfeiffer said again. "You have to believe me. Besides, I have an alibi."

"How so?"

"I don't work alone. I have someone on the inside who lets me know when to come and covers for me while I'm there. That's who tells me what's going on as well."

"We need a name," Sherlock said

As I looked at a set of jewelry I'd already had described to me today—a set made of chunky black jet, obsidian, and black diamonds—I knew who Pfeiffer was going to name before he said it.

"Avery Parker."

I LOOKED UP. This wasn't the name I was expecting. I pointed to the jewelry, Sherlock nodded.

"So, why would Avery help you steal from the set?" she asked.

Pfeiffer sighed. "He's my friend, and he knew I was wrongfully terminated. He also knew that this was a win-win. The production company is covered for a certain level of theft. Avery would tell me what to take, who'd worn it or used it, and so forth. I'd sneak in when he told me to, take what he'd identified, and then sell it."

"And no one from the production company or the insurance company noticed this?" I asked. I pulled out the jeweler's loop and looked at the diamonds in the jewelry. I wasn't as good as Sherlock, but I was fairly sure they were fakes.

"No, not yet. They haven't had time to really inventory, because of all the scripting issues. By the time they noticed, I'd have closed that eBay account and the amount I've taken is just small enough that they won't care enough to pursue with the police. The insurance company pays them for theft, I get what I should have in terms of salary, and Andenson gets to feel like they're not cheating assholes."

I managed not to say that it sounded like he'd done this before.

"People get fired all the time," Sherlock pointed out.

"You're not supposed to get fired for doing your job."

"They've barely done any filming, too," I said. "So sooner rather than later someone was going to notice what you'd taken."

"No. They've filmed a lot."

"We were told they were to begin filming today," Sherlock said.

"The new script, yeah, that was the plan. Trust me, there's been plenty of film wasted. But they're not using any of the footage because they keep on changing the script. So, what I've taken has been removed from the scripts and won't be used, and yes, that includes clothing and props. Besides, it didn't have to last much longer. I've almost made enough to match what my promised salary would have been through the end of pilot season. That's all I wanted."

"Speaking of the missing script," Sherlock said, "did you happen to lift one?"

"I took one of every iteration everyone got, yeah. They're worth a hell of a lot. But I don't have any of them up for sale yet. It's too soon for scripts."

"Even the most recent one? The one that was supposed to be good? Did you take that one as well?"

I looked up to see his expression. He was grinning. "Yeah, I did. When Avery told me it was the only one they had, I was going to offer it back to Collin, so that he could be the hero, but he hasn't returned my calls."

"You weren't planning to sell it to the highest bidder on eBay or elsewhere?" Sherlock asked.

"No, not once I realized that I'd taken the only copy. That kind of thing can blow back on you."

"So, where is it?" I asked, refraining from comment about blowback and how Pfeiffer was probably about to learn what that was really like.

"I put it somewhere safe."

"Where?" Sherlock asked.

He shook his head. "That may be the only thing I have to offer to get Andenson to drop charges. I'll tell you anything else, but not that."

"Fine. You said you knew who'd murdered Dawn," Sherlock reminded him. "Let's see who you're going to suggest."

"I was supposed to grab a couple things from her dressing room the afternoon that Cliff disappeared. I went over, but I guess because Cliff hadn't come back, she was still in her dressing room instead of on set. And I didn't get caught by her because she was fighting with someone and I heard them before I opened the door."

"Fighting with whom?"

"A man. His voice was sorta familiar; I'm sure I've heard it before, but I couldn't say who it was. The door muffled things a bit—I wouldn't have been sure it was Dawn if he hadn't used her name. But he was threatening her. He said that if she told anyone, they'd make her pay."

"They? They who?" Sherlock didn't sound like she was buying this story.

"He didn't say. Dawn was crying. Whoever the man was, he's someone on the set, because Dawn said that she'd just get Cliff to fire him. And then he laughed and said he didn't think Cliff was going to be a problem."

"Alright," Sherlock said slowly. "Let's say that I believe you. Tell me what your relationship with Irene Adler is."

"Irene?" Pfeiffer seemed thrown. "Ah, I have no relationship with her."

"That's not true," Sherlock purred. "You were the production assistant on not one but two of the failed pilots she was in. You know her."

"Well, sure, of course I *know* her, but I don't have a *relationship* with her. Besides, I've worked with a lot of the same people, some of whom, like Avery, are working on *Glitterazzi*. It's not as big an industry as everyone thinks."

"So, how long have you and she been dating?"

"Not at all. I don't have enough money for her. She's got her sights set on landing a producer of some kind, more power to her."

I kept my face turned, looking at the things Pfeiffer had stolen. So what if Irene was aiming for someone with money? That didn't mean she wasn't still interested in me.

"What about Collin Toohey? What's your relationship with him?"

"Collin I'd heard of but I only met him on this set. I liked him, that's why I was going to offer the script to him. He's pretty new in town, but he's got a good reputation as a script fixer. It wasn't really working for *Glitterazzi*, though. Honestly, from what I've heard about him, Collin should have fixed everything up in the first week."

"He's that good?" Sherlock asked.

"That's what they say. Nice enough guy. A little jumpy and not someone who wants to socialize with anyone on or off the set, but otherwise, fine."

"What about Frank Lawson?"

"Who?"

"From craft services."

"Oh, that Frank. He makes great baked stuff."

"Your relationship with him is?"

"Limited to eating his food."

"Has he caught you sneaking in or out?"

"Not that I know of. What does he have to do with any of this? Was Dawn poisoned?"

"Not that we know of, but cause of death is still being determined."

"Well, the guy said that they was going to end her just like her grandmother, which makes no sense because Dawn's grandmother died of a stroke at ninety or something."

Sherlock and I exchanged a look. "Did he say anything else you can recall?" she asked.

Pfeiffer's brow furrowed. "Yeah. One other thing I heard before I got out of there—I think he was heading for the door when he said it, which is why I took off. He said that starlets were a dime a dozen, but true stars were made, not born. It was a weird thing to end on, really, considering."

There seemed to be nothing to say to this. But there was one question we hadn't asked. "Why did you steal those papers and put them into Sherlock's car?"

"Ah..." Now Pfeiffer looked guilty.

"Who asked you to do it?" Sherlock asked. "Right now, the *best* you're looking at is a long stint in prison for theft and possibly going down for a murder rap, so I truly recommend you share everything in the hopes that it gives me enough to work on to find the real killers."

"You believe me?"

"More than I believe some people. Again, who asked you to take those papers and put them in my car?"

He looked down. "Irene. She caught me sneaking in today and put two and two together. Accused me of the thefts. I was caught red-handed with some jewelry she'd worn the week prior, so it wasn't like I could lie my way out of it. She thought it was funny, honestly, that I was doing this and that Avery was helping me. She said she wanted to prank Joey and my helping her would be my payment for her silence. Told me to take the papers and put them into your car."

"How did you know it was Sherlock's car?"

"I didn't. Irene told me it was hers. She gave me a key to use and everything."

"Did you remove anything from the stacks? Your personnel file, for example?" she asked.

"No. Irene said it was a prank, that Joey would be freaked out looking for that stuff, then get a laugh when he found it, that's all."

"Why did you run?" I asked.

"Because it was the car I'd broken into and you both looked pissed."

"And you're a thief," I pointed out.

"True. What happened to the key?" Sherlock asked.

"It's still in my pocket."

I fished it out. It was a key fob like Sherlock's, but without the Aston Martin branding. That the remote entry fob had been cloned seemed certain.

"When did you take what's in your backpack?" I asked.

"All that's from today. Why?"

I didn't say why out loud—Irene had asked Sherlock to find the jewelry before it had been stolen.

SHERLOCK HAD CALLED Straude, of course, and he and Saunders arrived to take Pfeiffer into custody. He was still protesting his innocence as Saunders took him to their sedan in police handcuffs.

"I think he may be telling the truth," Sherlock said to Straude as she put our handcuffs back into the duffel. "And while they're both clearly complicit, I'd like to keep Avery Parker and The Woman unaware of the fact that they're part of Pfeiffer's alibi, such as it is."

"Sherlock, if either one of them is the murderer I need to act quickly."

Sherlock shook her head. "I'm not sure what she's guilty of, Lee, just that it's something. And while Avery's guilty of stupidity in support of a friend and collusion to commit a felony, that doesn't mean he's a murderer. Keep tabs on them, but I'd prefer that they not know they're suspects. There are other avenues to be followed, first. Besides, if you arrest The Woman, she'll turn it into a circus immediately, and if we don't have ironclad evidence—and we don't—she'll find a way to embarrass the L.A.P.D."

Straude didn't like it, but he grudgingly agreed to hold off on arresting either Avery or my date for the evening.

Sherlock and I got into her car, but we didn't drive off. "Why aren't you ready to arrest Irene? Or Avery, for that matter?"

She drummed her thumbs on the steering wheel. "Because I feel, more and more, that the elusive 'better script' is truly at the center of all of this. Let's take what Pfeiffer says as true for the time being."

"If you insist."

"I do. That means that there was another writer Collin Toohey wanted to bring in. Perhaps Cliff was meeting with this person, which would be why he didn't want Dawn there. Jackson thought that Cliff had the new script with him when he disappeared, but Pfeiffer says he'd already lifted it. So what script *did* Cliff have, then? And what if the missing script was better? Maybe Cliff was planning to have this other writer take a look and see what he or she thought could be or should be improved."

"None of that sounds disappearance- or murder-worthy."

"No, it doesn't." Sherlock put the car in gear and headed off. "Which is why we're going to go visit the jumpy and antisocial Mister Toohey and see what he has to say."

Collin Toohey wasn't living the high life, but he was doing much better than Andy Pfeiffer. He lived in Westchester, near to LAX, in a larger apartment complex than Pfeiffer's. Sherlock found his parking place—his car was in it, and it wasn't one of the three we'd seen at the studio.

There was plenty of guest parking available, so that was a plus. We parked nearby, I grabbed the duffel as a matter of course for this day, and we went to Toohey's door. I knocked. There was no reply and no sound from inside. Sherlock rang the bell. Nothing.

We looked at each other. "What are the odds he's out taking a walk instead of trying to rewrite a script from memory?" she asked quietly.

"No bet, honestly."

"I'll stay here. You go around and see what you can from the other side."

I nodded and headed off. Toohey's apartment was on the ground floor, so I wouldn't have to climb up or over anything. There were small patios in the back of each apartment, however, and since the walls were six-footers, that was going to make seeing in a bit of a problem.

As I looked around for something to stand on, thinking that I should have stayed at the door and sent Sherlock to look over the wall, I felt rather than heard someone nearby.

I spun around to see a young teenaged girl looking at me over a nearby wall. "What are you doing here?" she asked suspiciously.

"Ah... my... friend isn't answering his door. I'm trying to see if he's at home."

"Some people use the phone."

"I have," I lied. "He hasn't picked up."

"I think I should report you as a creeper."

"You can. And, frankly, that would be wise since I'm a strange man sneaking around the place where you live."

She cocked her head at me. "You don't look like a creeper."

"I'm not, but I could be. So, you know, go with your instincts." If she called the police, Sherlock would fix it. Besides, a girl her age should be careful, not chatty, with strange men sneaking about.

"My instincts say you're not enough of a loser to be friends with Collin."

"You know him?"

She shrugged. "Yeah. My mom says that he's nice. I think he's weird."

"Weird how?"

"He never goes out."

"Wait, what? What do you mean? He goes to his job, surely?"

She shook her head. "He hasn't left the apartment for weeks. He used to, but then," she shrugged, "he got weird."

"How does he get food?"

"His friend brings it over. But Collin never leaves." She made a face. "And I don't think he ever cleans, either."

"How so?"

"My room's next to his. I can't be near the wall anymore—it stinks. My mom says it's just me being dramatic, but I have a very sensitive sense of smell and, *gag*, it's horrible."

I had a very bad feeling about this. "Could you go inside? I'm going to contact the police and I think we're going to need to chat with you more about Collin."

"I guess." She dropped behind the wall and I heard a sliding door open and close.

I hurried back to Sherlock and told her what the girl had said. We both pulled on gloves, then Sherlock tried the door. It was locked, so she picked it. Quickly. "Should we enter this way?" I whispered.

"Time is, as always, of the essence. We can always lock it up again if there's nothing sinister going on inside."

"And if there is?"

"Then we suspected foul play and shouted out before we entered." She opened the door slowly and sniffed. "The girl's right; there's something rotten in here."

"Could just be trash." Not that I thought it was.

We walked in. The place was spotless. It looked like a typical bachelor's apartment—heavy emphasis on audio-visual, some framed movie posters, a small bookcase, furniture built for wear and tear. Everything was arranged just so, as if this was a model apartment, not a place where someone lived.

Sherlock opened the fridge. "Fully stocked," she said softly. "Someone's living here."

It was a two-bedroom apartment; we could see the living room from the kitchen. Sherlock pulled the gun she wore at the small of her back and we moved to look in the hall closet. Filled with normal things and no person.

We checked the room and bathroom to the right. Nothing, though it was clear someone was sleeping here: the bed was hastily made and the toiletries in the bathroom had been recently used. No one in the closet, though there were some clothes and shoes.

Now we went to the bedroom on the left, first checking what looked like a closet but proved to house the small washer and dryer. There were some clothes with a big red "O" folded on top of the dryer. The smell was getting stronger.

"Brace yourself," Sherlock said softly. Then she opened the bedroom door.

THERE WAS A body on the bed.

I'd been prepared since I'd spoken to the young girl, but it was still a shock. The body was wrapped in heavy duty clear plastic wrap and, from the looks—and not least the smell—of things, had been decomposing for several days.

There was an inordinate amount of potpourri sprinkled all over the bed and parts of the room. There was also a partially used case of Febreeze near the door.

Sherlock checked the closet and bathroom, which were clear. Then she called Straude.

While we waited, Sherlock searched the apartment and sent me to prep our young witness.

I knocked and she opened the door, still looking at me suspiciously. "Yes?"

"You know, you thought I was a creeper. Should you really open the door the moment I knock on it?"

"You said you weren't a creeper."

"A creeper would lie about that."

"I guess. What's going on with Collin? Is he dead?"

"You're morbid. Accurate, but morbid. And why aren't you in school?"

She shrugged. "I'm home sick."

"You look fine to me, and I'm a doctor."

"Not that kind of sick. Girl stuff sick."

"Oh. Ah, you know, birth control pills can help with that."

"My mom says that's just an excuse girls use to get on the pill without their parents realizing they're doing the deed."

"Your mother sounds like a smart woman. Look, the police will be here soon. You're going to need to give them a statement. You might want to call your mother, too. I'm sure they'll want to ask her about Collin. And his friend."

"Can I see the body?"

"Not in your delicate condition."

She grimaced at me, then laughed. "You're fun. Okay, can I come over there and not see the body?"

I heaved a sigh. "Yes, because my partner wants to talk to you. Call your mother first, though, please. I'll wait."

She waved her cell phone at me as she walked out and closed the door. "These are really cool. You should get one. I've been texting with her the whole time. She's on her way home already."

We joined Sherlock in Toohey's apartment. She brought out a photograph she'd found on the bedroom dresser, showing an outdoor scene with a lot of people in the background and five men smiling and centered in the shot. "Is Collin one of these people?" she asked without preamble.

The girl nodded and pointed to the one on the end on the left. "That's him."

"That's very interesting," Sherlock said. "Watson, do you know why that's so interesting?"

A test, in front of my new friend in sarcasm. Meaning I didn't want to fail. So I studied the picture. The men were all white, very late teens or early twenties, some beefy, some slender. Four of them were quite tall and one was of average height, measuring them against the background, which was likely a fraternity house, going from the Greek letters Beta Theta Pi over their heads. All of them were wearing jackets with a big red 'O' on them.

There were some other people in the picture, hazy and out of focus, off to the sides and behind them. It appeared to be a barbeque or some other kind of party.

The man our witness had pointed out was one of the taller men. He had jet black hair, glasses, and a rather shy smile. The others looked like jocks, even the shorter man, but he looked more scholarly.

I took a closer look at the men in the picture. One was familiar. I'd met him earlier today. "That's George Benning." I pointed to the beefy man in the middle, who looked supremely pleased with himself.

"Our very own Campus King himself. Yes. What else?"

"He's one of Collin's friends," the girl said. "He comes over once in a while."

"What's your name?" Sherlock asked her.

"Amily. With an 'a,' not an 'e.' It's a southern thing, which we aren't but my dad was."

"My name is Sherlock, so, believe me, I'm not passing judgment."

Amily grinned at her. "I like you. And the creeper. Wish you were our neighbors."

"I'm flattered. Who else from this picture has visited?"

She pointed to the shorter man and another tall one on the other end of the picture. "Both of them. The short guy is the one who brings Collin his food and stuff."

What Sherlock wanted me to realize hit me. "That man, the shorter one; he's how everyone on the set described Collin Toohey. No one said tall with black hair."

"The man on the bed is tall, and his hair appears black. Whether he was murdered or died of natural causes is what needs to be determined, and as quickly as possible."

"Because the plot has thickened?" I asked.

"No. Because it's becoming clearer by the minute."

"Only to you, Sherlock."

She smiled, then went back into the bedroom and came back with another picture, this one of Toohey and a very pretty young woman with dark hair. They had their arms around each other and looked very happy. It was a more recent picture—he looked older than the other picture and they were standing on the Santa Monica pier. "Do you recognize her?"

Amily nodded. "She's his girlfriend. Well, she was." She paused dramatically. "She was murdered."

"Really?" Sherlock asked. "How?"

"I think it was like a rape at a bar kind of thing. Collin was hazy on it. But my mom probably knows all the details. Collin used to talk to her all the time before he got weird."

"Amily, I'd like to get a detailed statement from you, if that's okay."

"Totally. This is the most exciting thing that's happened since Christina came back to *The Voice*."

"I weep for the youth of America," I said quietly, as Sherlock's eyes lit up.

"A fellow enthusiast! Amily, this could be the start of a beautiful friendship."

STRAUDE AND SAUNDERS had joined us, along with a medical examiner and a host of crime scene officers. Amily's mother had also arrived, and between the two of them we were able to lock down a possible date of death: Collin Toohey had most likely died or been taken prisoner three weeks before he'd started work at the *Glitterazzi* set, but after he'd been hired. The ME felt that 'prisoner' was a good bet, based on a variety of factors that made sense to me, including the level of decomposition.

Calls to Jackson confirmed that Toohey had been hired via phone and email interviews and that no one had met him before he'd first come to the set. Apparently this was normal, since no one cared what the writer looked like, only that he or she could write well and fast. And Toohey had been finishing up another job, so his not wanting to take the time to meet in person, given the production company was known and established, wasn't seen as odd.

Amily's mother, Carol, said that Collin had suffered some tragedies in his life—an automobile accident that claimed a friend's life, the loss of his fiancée. She'd put his becoming a recluse down to depression and was horrified to realize he'd been held captive five feet away from her.

While Sherlock reassured Carol that there wasn't anything she could have done, she had Straude run the license plates of the cars parked in the Andenson spaces, but that was a dead end—the cars belonged to Antonelli, Jackson, and Irene. But Sherlock seemed pleased with the information.

The day had been a busy one and it was a shock to realize that we needed to get home so that I could get ready for my date.

"I'm not sure that I'll make it, even so," I fretted to Sherlock.

She cocked her head. "You know, Watson, you look fine. You could just go as is."

"I've climbed and almost fallen off a ladder, wrestled a man in an alleyway, and been around two dead bodies, Sherlock. That's not the look you should present on a first date."

"Except The Woman already knows what you've been doing all day. Besides, if you take my car, I'm sure she'll forgive you being a tiny bit rumpled."

"You just want me to see if I can get her to confess as to why and how she got a copy of your key fob."

"In part, yes. However, traffic is going to be terrible, and Lee can give me a ride home. Or," she shrugged, "you can be late for your first date. Up to you, really."

I knew when I was beaten. Besides, she was right: Irene lived in West Hollywood. Getting there from here during rush hour—which in Los Angeles was easily four hours long—wasn't for the faint-hearted.

Sherlock had me use the duplicate fob, but otherwise simply told me to have a good time and be careful about discussing the case. "What do I say when Irene asks me about *her* case?"

Sherlock's lips twitched. "If that happens, tell her that we've recovered the stolen property and see what she does."

I left Sherlock and Amily talking reality shows and headed for the car. I still had the duffel and put it back into the trunk. The stack of papers, which hadn't been tied or kept in a box, were now strewn all over Sherlock's trunk.

I plopped the duffel down on top of the mess, and noticed something bound, in amongst all the loose papers. I grabbed it as I did my phone rang. It was Irene.

I closed the trunk and went to the driver's door while I answered.

"John, I'm home now so I think we could still try for seven if you're willing."

"Willing and able as long as you don't mind that I can't get home to change first."

"Oh, you looked rakish and handsome today. No need to change."

Considering I was in jeans and a Henley, I hardly considered it a perfect look. But if Irene liked it, that was good enough for me. "Wonderful. Then I'll be to you as soon as traffic allows."

I dumped the bound pages onto the floor behind the driver's seat and put the light jacket I always kept in the car over it, so the wind wouldn't cause any issues with the paper. Then I headed off to the most terrifying thing I'd faced yet today—the 405 Freeway.

THERE WAS MUCH to be said for driving an Aston Martin, even in the worst traffic in the world. I felt far more attractive and successful when I was behind the wheel than I had a right to. The admiring and envious looks from other drivers didn't hurt, either.

I tried to focus on the case while driving, but had to give that up; I was getting nowhere and couldn't afford to get lost in thought. I turned on a classic rock station and just enjoyed being the coolest man on the road. By the time I reached Irene's apartment building, I felt like a million dollars.

She was dressed in another kimono-style dress, this one a pale yellow with black trim. Clearly they were her signature look, which I couldn't argue with. Same high heels, which I still approved of.

"What a lovely car," she cooed as I helped her in.

"Isn't it, though? I wish I could say it's mine, but it's Sherlock's."

"How thoughtful of her to let you borrow it."

"It was, wasn't it?"

Irene beamed at me. "I'd have been happy if you'd picked me up on a bicycle, John, but I'm flattered that you wanted to impress me."

I laughed. "Is it working?"

"Oh, definitely."

Sherlock had made reservations for us at Mr. Chow, which thrilled Irene. For all that she seemed to loathe her, Sherlock had gone out of her way to ensure that Irene and I had a wonderful evening. That was what friends were supposed to do for each other, of course, but I still found it touching.

We had to valet park, but if Irene noticed the key fob I handed to the valet, she didn't mention it. Instead, we continued the conversation we'd been having, which was what had brought us both to California.

"A degree in medicine from Oxford and here you are, working as a private investigator," she said as we waited for our table. "How amazing the world is."

"Private consulting detective. It's a little different. Not much different, but a little."

She laughed. "That's Sherlock's thinking, isn't it?"

"It is." I was about to ask her how she'd found Sherlock, since it was clear that she hadn't been referred by Andenson Productions, but we were taken to our table and the important business of choosing what to drink and eat claimed my attention.

I was careful to only have one alcoholic drink since I was driving, and Irene wasn't a big drinker, either. We decided on the Beijing Duck and weren't disappointed. By the time dessert arrived, I had to admit that this had been the best first date of my entire life.

"Penny for your thoughts," Irene said as she sipped her coffee.

"Sherlock's right."

"About what?"

"I'm smitten."

Irene smiled slowly, put her cup down, stood up slightly, leaned across, put her finger under my chin, drew me to her, and kissed me. A slow, lingering kiss that promised much more.

She sat back down and picked up her coffee. "I'm glad."

I knew I was blushing but I didn't care, though I took a good sip of coffee as well, to compose myself. "Where to after this?"

She shrugged. "My place? I wasn't joking earlier—I truly don't want to be alone tonight. Finding poor Dawn like that..." She shuddered.

I reached over and took her hand. "Don't worry. I'll take care of you."

She smiled. "I knew you were the man I needed the moment I laid eyes on you." She squeezed my hand, then stood up. "Powder room time. Miss me while I'm gone."

"Constantly." I watched her sashay off and considered that I might be the luckiest man in the world.

For lack of anything else to do while waiting, I pulled out my phone. One message, from Sherlock. *Whenever you see this, call me.*

Well, I'd seen it now, and Irene was in the restroom, so there was never going to be a better time. I called as requested.

"Watson, are you still with The Woman?"

"Yes, she's in the powder room. We've just finished dessert."

"Good. I'm glad you've eaten. And that she's not there with you at the moment. When she returns, just say that you don't want a subscription to the *Times* and hang up."

"Will do. What's going on?"

"The body of Frank Lawson was found about an hour ago on the Paramount lot. The uneven number of trash bins out there has been bothering me all day. Then I remembered that we'd seen that can off alone when we were tracking Pfeiffer, and had Lee's people investigate. The bin was originally near our soundstage and was moved."

"And no one noticed?"

"I presume it was moved at night, though Frank was killed during the daytime. Frank's estimated time of death is in the same general timeframe that Cliff disappeared."

"How was he killed?"

"Stabbed." She sounded slightly smug.

"You know where he was killed, don't you?"

"I do. In the writers' room."

"There was no evidence of foul play."

"There was if you consider that the only things in the room that could collect blood effectively were missing."

"They used the whiteboard erasers to remove the evidence?"

"Yes, they were found with his body. I had Lee's team go over the room. There's indication of blood cleanup in several places, including on the conference table near the stack of scripts that had been moved."

"So, they realized blood had gotten onto the pages and went back to get anything that was stained?"

"That's the prevailing theory. And the word 'they' is correct—there's more than one person involved in this."

"Involved in what, other than murder, is the question."

"I believe I have the answer. I just need one more piece of information."

Irene was returning. "Do you need me to come home tonight?"

"No. But I need you to get the information. You're the only one who can."

Irene was at the table. "I'm sorry, I don't want a subscription to the *Times*," I said in an annoyed tone. Then I hung up as instructed. "Sorry about that. Telemarketers call at the most ridiculous times."

She smiled. "They do. Shall we go?"

"The bill hasn't come yet. I'll hit the powder room and hopefully they'll bring it by the time I'm back."

So saying, I headed for the men's room. Once inside I went to a stall and sent Sherlock a text. But the phone looked fuzzy all of a sudden. And, as the phone dropped out of my hands and I fell to the floor, I realized exactly how Irene could have cloned Sherlock's key—the same way she'd drugged my coffee. Using distraction.

By kissing me.

I WOKE UP sitting up. In a car, as far as I could tell. My head felt fuzzy and my mouth was dry, but I was alive and that was something.

As my head cleared I was able to take in more of my surroundings. There were people talking, nearby but not right next to me. Men, and a woman.

Doing my best not to move in any noticeable way, I opened my eyes a crack. I was in the passenger's seat of Sherlock's car. Not a surprise, but I had a feeling that I'd be *dead* in Sherlock's car soon enough.

"It's not here," one of the men said.

"It should be," the woman replied. She sounded angry and a little afraid. She also sounded like Irene, not that this was a great surprise.

As the feeling returned to my body I forced my mind to work. They were searching for something they expected in the trunk. The only logical thought was that they expected to find whatever it was amongst the papers that Pfeiffer had put in there. I'd removed only one thing—the bound set of pages. Assuming that was what they were looking for, I wanted to keep them from searching the car's interior.

Of course, my hands were tied, in front of me, as were my feet. I wasn't going anywhere. Though I wasn't gagged, which was nice in a way and dangerous in another: if I could speak, I could learn, but I could also give things away.

I wondered where my phone was. At best, on the floor of the bathroom at Mr. Chow. More likely in Irene's possession.

It was dark, wherever we were, and I didn't hear the sound

of traffic. This didn't tell me much, other than that no one was going to chance upon us and rescue me.

"Look, it doesn't matter, does it?" This man's voice was familiar. I'd heard it before, I just wasn't sure where.

"I've done what you asked," Irene said. "Now tell me—is Cliff alive, and if so, where is he?"

"He's fine," the man said. "And you'll find out where he is once we get what we need."

"Avery and I got Andy to steal everything you asked us to and then some. We've done all you wanted."

"Let us go, give us Cliff, and we'll stay quiet," another man said. This voice I recognized as Avery's. He sounded frightened. I shared the sentiment.

"I told you I'd make you a star and you the head of a company," the first man said. "And it's happening right before your eyes, and all you two can do is complain."

"That remains to be seen," Irene said. "I'm complaining because you've left a swath of dead bodies across the southland. And how is it that you can run and skim a huge nonprofit for years, but none of you were ever smart enough to read the scripts, even when you were supposedly writing them? And I'm *really* complaining that you can't keep it in your pants, George. You've tried to have sex with every woman on the set, even the ones old enough to be your mother. It won't take long for someone to mention that you probably tried to do the same with Dawn and she refused. That's motive, and you don't actually have an alibi for her time of death."

"Neither do you," George said with a laugh. "Hey, Cliff was told what would happen. He didn't believe us. He does now. And again, it doesn't matter. They have Andy in custody. He'll take the fall—he has no alibi, he was there, sneaking on the set stealing shit. So he got caught and killed people to hide it. They want a killer, they have their best bet in their hands. He'll go down for it."

"How many 'its' do you think they can pin on him?" Irene asked. "By my count you've killed Dawn, Frank, and Collin, and I'm still not convinced that Cliff is alive, either."

"He is, but we *are* going to kill your new boyfriend," George said. "He's disposable."

"You can't," she said flatly. "If you kill him, then you make the police look at this in a whole different way. May I remind you that Andy is in police custody? He can't have killed someone who died after he was arrested."

There was a long silence, during which time I tested my bonds, which were solid, and considered how stupid George and whoever the other men with him were, which seemed to be quite a lot.

"You're not pinning it on me, either," Avery said. "Or on Irene."

"We could just kill them both," another man said.

"We have other problems," the first one countered. "You slipped up in front of the caterer, Freddy; who else realized you weren't the real Collin?"

"No one," Freddy replied. "I told you, Odie, it was the only time."

"Cliff was already suspicious," George said. "That's why we had to have Freddy suggest bringing on the 'outside expert.'"

"I know what to do, Avery," Odie said. He didn't sound southern, so I had a feeling this was a nickname. Based on Irene's nonprofit comments, I figured this was Oscar Odessa, the head of the Odessa Foundation. He was in the right age range and, if I squinted, could have been one of the taller men from Toohey's picture, aged a few years.

"That'll be a first," Avery snapped.

"Stop panicking. Bros before hos, man. And Irene, I have the fix. We'll just beat the shit out of him, turn his brain into mush. He was drunk when you left the restaurant, you were carjacked, he tried to stop them, they beat him up, you were able to run away to get help. I know you can sell that."

"I can." She didn't sound enthused, for which I was somewhat grateful. "But that still leaves us with the most incriminating script in the world floating around somewhere."

"You're not incriminated in it," a different man said. "So stop freaking out."

"I'm not freaking out, Lester," she snapped. "Or should I keep on calling you Mister Super Writer?"

"Jesus, Irene, calm down," Odie said, firmly. "I'll handle it. Like I always do."

"Bros before hos," George said.

"Yeah, tell that to Collin," Irene said.

"Hey, *she* came on to *me*," George said.

"If you call drinking a roofie you slipped her 'coming on,'" Freddy said with a snigger.

"And that's why all of you gang raped her and killed her? She was *asking* for it?" Irene sounded angry again.

"He deserved it," Odie said flatly. "It's his fault that Digger died."

"It was a car accident," Avery said quietly. "It wasn't done on purpose. And I had nothing to do with Talia's death, Irene, you have to believe me." I thought about the picture some more. The people at the edges, the ones who weren't framed by the camera—one of them was a shorter man. And Avery had been on campus at the same time George had. Meaning Avery was also a frat brother.

"Yeah? Then, after Digger's dead—what, three months— Collin and Digger's girl are an item?" Lester sounded angry. "He killed Digger to get her. He had to lose her in a way that hurt."

It was official—I wanted to kill every one of them. The positive of this is that I was making better headway with the ropes, and realized I'd gotten too angry to care that I was scraping my skin off. The negative was that whoever had tied these really knew what they were doing.

"'Gang raped by some gangbangers' flew for the police," Odie said. "They never dig too hard when it's not someone important." He laughed. "We'll do a charity event to support the families of those you've lost, Irene, don't worry. The Gala for Everything will come through for you."

"Besides," George said in a honeyed tone, "I heard they're rewriting the show. You're going to be the star now, Irene, just like you wanted. I'm getting a better role, too. It'll all work out."

Lights went on all around us. "Actually," Sherlock said, "it's only going to work out for the police."

I WAS UNTIED and out of the car, and, after tending to the slight wounds on my wrists, Sherlock was perusing the script I'd accidentally hidden. It was dawn, although light still blazed from police cars surrounding us.

We were at Forest Lawn cemetery, which explained why I hadn't heard anything. On the whole, it seemed an appropriate meeting spot to discuss murders. I had to give it to whoever was pulling all the strings—they had an interesting sense of humor.

"Well done, Watson," she said as Straude and Saunders read the prisoners their rights.

"I have no idea what I did, other than notice that, pull it out, and then promptly forget about it."

Irene came over to us. "I'm so sorry," she said to me. "I had to drug you, or else they'd have... hurt you."

"Excuse me, but why aren't you under arrest?"

Sherlock sighed. "Because she was helping us, Watson. The entire time."

"She was? And you knew that?"

"The moment I saw the jewelry she described in Andy Pfeiffer's backpack today, I knew she was trying to give us clues. So I looked at everything we knew from a different point of view."

"So you're a hero," I said to Irene.

Sherlock snorted softly. "Going to the police straight away would have saved at least two lives, possibly three."

"Collin was already dead before I found out," Irene said, without a lot of defensiveness in her tone. "I'd met him before, a few years ago. I knew the man pretending to be Collin was a phony."

"Collin wasn't killed until a few days ago. So, you *could* have saved him. If you'd bothered." Sherlock didn't sound as angry as I'd have expected. She also didn't sound surprised.

"Why didn't you tell anyone?" I asked.

Irene shrugged and didn't reply.

"Because blackmailing people is very effective," Sherlock answered. "Why do you think a star of her standing was invited to, let alone photographed at, the Gala for Everything? She used her knowledge to further herself within this group. She just didn't realize the lengths the 'bros' were willing to go to to protect themselves."

"Look, I wanted to move up, and getting the help of prominent people is the fastest way up. That's not a crime."

"Hiding the fact that you knew someone was being held against his will and impersonated is, however," Sherlock said. "As is collusion, though the case is very clear on you being under duress. It's foggier for Avery. Of course, you're not implicated in this script, and neither is he. So that's a good thing."

I took a good look around. Avery was in handcuffs, though he wasn't being put with the others. All the men were from Toohey's picture, though one of the tall ones was missing. Presumed this was the late and, in this circle, terribly lamented Digger.

"How did you find us?" I asked Sherlock now.

She snorted softly again. "You were never out of my sight, Watson. Not from the moment you left Toohey's apartment complex."

"You followed me?"

"In an unmarked police car, yes. Lee was kind enough to let me drive."

"I never saw you."

"You were far too busy being happy, Watson." She looked very sad for a moment, but in the next her expression went back to what I was used to—amused disdain tinged with compassion. "And I'd expected it. I barely had to try to hide us, you were having such a good time."

"Your car does bring that out." I chose not to mention that I'd been happy to be going out with Irene, and to both women's credit, neither one of them pointed it out, either.

"Yes, I suppose it does. I removed the script while you were dining, just in case. It was something for me and Lee to do while we waited for The Woman to drug you."

Straude came over. "Time for you to come with us, Miss Adler."

She nodded, then leaned over and kissed my cheek. "I'm sorry, John," she whispered. "I *do* like you. But I also have a standard of living I'm aspiring to reach."

As Straude led her away, she looked back over her shoulder and gave me her slow smile. Even after everything, it still got me.

Then she made eye contact with Sherlock. "By the way— James says hello, and that he knew you'd figure it out."

I felt Sherlock stiffen next to me, but she didn't react otherwise. I waited until Irene was in the car and being driven away before I asked. "Who is James?"

"Someone I'll tell you about another time, Watson. Though, apparently, sooner rather than later." She heaved a sigh. "In the meantime, do you have any other questions about this case?"

"So many I may forget them all. What do the scripts have to do with anything?"

"Collin had no idea that his friends had raped and murdered his girlfriend. While talking to George about the fact that they'd be working on the same show, George let something slip and Collin, being the smartest of this group, realized what was going on. There's no statute of limitations on murder, so he had to be shut up."

"Why the elaborate ruse, then?"

"Because George wanted to be sure *Glitterazzi* went on. He's tied quite tightly into Andenson—that unexpected cost, which left them floating all their employees, was due to them having to pay hush money to Amanda, Anna, *and* Julianna for George's unwanted advances. George needed to stick with the only place that would hire him, and protect him to boot; he needed this show to go on."

"Why didn't those women come forward?"

"They were paid off?" Sherlock shook her head at my glaring naiveté. "They, like George, needed *Glitterazzi*. And they were paid to be quiet."

"Why didn't he try it with Irene?"

Sherlock rolled her eyes. "Because The Woman was already blackmailing Oscar Odessa to do what she wanted. She was Oscar's girl, as it were, and off-limits to George. As hard as that is to believe."

"He's afraid of Oscar. I could tell. They all are, even Avery. Even Irene."

"Yes. There's more to Oscar Odessa than meets the eye."

"A connection to this 'James' that Irene mentioned?"

"And just when I think you've lost the ability to reason logically. Yes, that seems likely. He'll bear watching."

"He'll be going away for life."

"Sadly, probably not. He comes from money and he'll get the best lawyers. For himself, anyway. The others? I expect that whole 'bros before hos' nonsense to fade away under 'self-preservation before friendship.'"

"I still don't understand how you pieced it together," I said as Straude joined us. "I listened to them and I have no clear idea of why they killed who they did, let alone what the hell has happened to Cliff."

"Ah, well, Cliff Camden was found at Lester Tibble's house," Straude said. "Per Sherlock's information. Alive and reasonably well."

"Good, but...?"

Sherlock chuckled. "Follow me now. Collin was being held prisoner in his own home. However, none of these people could write a screenplay—it's not something you can learn overnight. So, they had to keep him actually alive and working. He, being smarter than all of them, was sending in terrible scripts. Remember that Andy Pfeiffer told us that the scripts were getting progressively worse, and that wasn't what anyone expected to happen."

"So, no one catches on, though, because they were all defensive, and Collin is trying harder and harder to get someone to pay attention."

"Yes, Watson. He finally realizes that the others are only skimming his scripts, and he also realizes that they're going to have to kill him. So he does a complete rewrite, where he tells the story of what's really going on—his story. Names changed ever so slightly. So the hero is in a car accident that kills his best friend, then hero and the ingénue fall in love due to shared grieving and such. The hero's so-called friends discover this, rape and kill the girl, and take the hero hostage."

Straude nodded. "It's very clear. The details of the young woman's murder match exactly with what we have on the cold case."

"So," Sherlock continued, "Cliff gets this new script and he finally realizes what's going on. But he needs to be sure before he starts making accusations. He's made an appointment to meet with another writer—one with a good reputation, who is also an expert on writing styles. Cliff wants to know if this is really Collin writing or not."

"Only, he never meets with that writer."

"Correct. He met with Lester, who kidnapped him. However, the script wasn't in Cliff's possession."

"Because Irene had told Andy Pfeiffer to steal it."

"In a way. She'd done a switch on the scripts and Cliff had an older version. She'd hidden the new script, then put it into the box of papers Joey was printing out for us. The rest you know."

"Not really. Who tossed Dawn's dressing room?"

"George, searching for the script, since The Woman had told him she'd hidden it there."

"Was there a real better writer?"

"There always is, but in this case, they were never in the loop. The rest of the gang handled the impersonation."

"Did they really think they could get away with it?"

Straude barked a short laugh. "They *were* getting away with it. Without Sherlock they *would* have gotten away with it. They were right—we have more than enough to convict Pfeiffer. But now, with what Miss Adler and Mister Parker will give us, we should have enough to prove conspiracy. Plus we have them on kidnapping Mister Camden."

"Some of them," Sherlock said. "I can guarantee that Odessa's going to worm out of that one for sure."

"Probably," Straude agreed with a sigh.

"Who killed Dawn?"

"None of them are copping to that," Straude said. "But it's a safe bet that it was Benning. Anything else, Sherlock?"

"No. You know where we are. I think it's time I got Watson home and into his own bed."

We got into the Aston Martin and Sherlock drove off slowly. The streets were fairly empty so we could have gone at a brisk clip. Only she didn't.

"What is it?" I asked her finally when we came to a stoplight.

She sighed. "The Woman's going to get off. She's quite bright, but then again, I already knew that."

"She was being coerced."

"It certainly looks that way." Sherlock wasn't looking at me.

"What am I missing? Besides everything? You saw Avery in Collin's photo, didn't you?"

"Yes, I did, even though he was hazy. I was prepared to find him, of course."

"Why so?"

"Him encouraging and assisting with Pfeiffer's theft was out of character. Meaning he had an ulterior motive. But Pfeiffer never said Andy was getting a cut. Plus he'd gone to Ohio State, and it was far too coincidental—in an industry as small as Pfeiffer rightly said this one is—that he didn't know Collin as well as George."

"George drove Irene's limo, didn't he?"

"Yes. And all of them are in photographs with her at the Gala for Everything. Establishing alibis for Collin's murder."

We started off again. She still hadn't looked over at me. "Seriously, Sherlock, what am I missing?"

"The scene they were supposed to be filming—the one that hadn't changed in any iteration—you remember that?"

"Yes. The one on the whiteboard, right?"

She nodded.

"What of it?"

"It didn't change in Collin's script, either. We were introduced to the heroine by a rival trying to hang her. A female rival."

"That's not enough to prove anything."

"No, it's probably not. And Cliff feels that Irene was trying to save him. Meaning she'll come out of this tied even more tightly to Andenson Productions. *Glitterazzi* was picked up for a full season, by the way."

"How? They haven't even filmed a useable minute."

"Notoriety is a strong motivator. Social media has been active since Dawn's murder, and with every new aspect of the case giving the show more coverage, they were snapped up by one of the major networks. Joey says that our fee will be doubled, and he's giving all the cast and crew who weren't trying to kill everyone a bonus for being good sports about being paid late."

"That seems awfully... fast... doesn't it?"

Now Sherlock looked at me. "Yes, it does."

"You think Andenson was in on it?"

"I never put anything past anyone. The Woman isn't the only one who wants to keep on moving up."

We were quiet again for a good few minutes. "It's because of that James, isn't it? That's why you're not satisfied with how this case has wrapped up. Your demeanor changed once she said that name."

"Yes. His involvement means things are far more complex than they appear." She sighed. "But, the case *is* solved; Cliff's kidnappers—and Collin and Frank's murderers—are going to be brought to at least some kind of justice."

"Why do you think it was Irene and not George?"

"Because we were told that Dawn wasn't allowing herself to be alone with him anymore. She was, in fact, getting one of the other women to be with her. And The Woman was not around where we could see her at Dawn's time of death. And she found the body. It all adds up. Circumstantially. There's no evidence it was her, of course."

"You could be wrong."

"When, Watson, am I ever really wrong?"

I didn't reply, because we both knew—never.

We drove the rest of the way in silence through the City of Liars with the top down and the wind in our hair.

half there/
all there

GLEN MEHN

THE WORLD KNOWS Sherlock Holmes through these pages as a calculating machine, seeking justice with cold logic, but I know another side of him. A soft side, a less serious side. Playful. Actually funny, even, if you can believe it, and one of the best friends a man could ever have, if you could get past his weirdness.

I first met Sherlock Holmes at the closing party of the first Factory, that silver box filled with pills and people, covered in tin foil, mylar, and plexiglass. He walked in, this tall, rail-thin man, white skin and black hair slicked back, cut short, like a banker or lawyer or something. Not my type, but I couldn't stop watching. He was the opposite of hip, but people noticed when he walked in and stood in the corner, smoking cigarette after cigarette, rolling each one himself. He watched everyone watching him, and, after an hour, came over to me, offering me a roll-up.

"It's only tobacco. That's all you smoke. You had enough of marihuana and opium In Country after you hurt your shoulder. You're more involved with things that are a bit more imaginative, something that might spur you to get up and do something, aren't you?"

His voice was low, with an accent that was hard to place, his flat vowels and clipped consonants emanating effortless cool.

A strange way of talking, too. Educated. Erudite, rejecting the language of the street, but also avoiding the affected language of the Factory pretenders, claiming European authenticity as a tiny bit of recognition. Style was the thing, convincing others that you were brilliant. Andy had a shotgun approach to catch whatever outstanding people happened to fall into the orbit of his ragtag collection of sexual deviants and junkies.

I didn't like him coming up and telling me things about myself.

"How'd you know I was In Country? And just what do you think I've got for you? I don't have anything to do with grass, or mushrooms, or any of that hippy shit."

I watched his thin face while he spoke, his jawbone etched out of granite there, though long and delicate, not like the ad men. I couldn't stop looking at him, listening to his talk. "You've got a shoulder wound, that's apparent from the hitch you had leaning against the wall, but you didn't grimace, so it's something you're used to. New Yorkers don't get much sun, but you're brown, with malaria scars. The way you move and stand shows a streetwise city upbringing. You watch other people around you, keeping an eye out for customers and the police, yet you've rolled your eyes at two deals, grass and heroin. So: you were in Vietnam, bored with common drugs. You're looking to sell something. I need something to occupy my mind and time. Something beyond even the delights manufactured in this Factory."

I didn't know what to say, so I took the cigarette he offered and lit it. It was a strong blend, thick, pungent smoke pouring out of the end, but nice. I looked up at him.

"It's called Drum. It comes to me from the Netherlands— from someone who owes me a favour."

He smiled at me, a crooked smile that turned my guts to water. I'd have a talk with him, and find out more about this observant, smoking man who'd just walked in to my life; for more than just a conversation, as it turned out.

We talked for a while, about what he liked. Up, but with a twist. Some psychedelic effect was useful, but nothing debilitating. I had just the thing, but back at the Chelsea Hotel. Blue beauties, I called them, stealing the name from the common black beauties, but they were as different as night and day. The chemical was amphedoxamine, but they wouldn't just take you up, they'd make you feel good, too. I made my rounds and sold a little to those I knew would be talking to me later, and came back to this Sherlock Holmes.

"I think I may have something right up your alley. It's in my more... private stash. There's just one thing, though. I need you to distract the landlady. We have a disagreement about the rent."

"You don't have it, yet she insists you pay it anyway?"

"Exactly."

"WHICH WAY DO you live, John?"

I don't know why I let him call me John. Everyone else calls me Doc, and I was qualified, though I hadn't lifted a scalpel, a stethoscope or so much as a band-aid since the year before, since I came home with shrapnel in my shoulder. My extensive experience in treating syphilis, jungle rot, and sucking chest wounds was of no use even at Bellevue. My hands weren't steady enough to practise any more. My licence and my knowledge of pharmacology kept me in high demand, however.

Grass was everywhere. Cannabis, mushrooms, and chemicals cooked up by burned out long hairs, as likely to contain strychnine as not.

The people who came to me weren't looking to turn on or tune in; they had more specialised tastes. They craved knowledge, the power to be creators, to be active participants in life, rejecting every custom, from money to their own sexuality and even gender. They who could only fit in here in New York.

I was a doctor, but it was good that the American Medical Society never saw my shaking hands, or the patients for whom I prescribed an increasingly esoteric variety of chemicals. Chemicals used for creativity, to give an edge, to support the frenzied, creative mind. Make something. Do something. Start something.

The news showed college kids burning their draft cards, dropping LSD, eating mushrooms, smoking marihuana, growing their hair long and burning bras on farms, trying to get away from everything, like that was going to change anything. Not so much in our little corner of New York. Downtown, making a living in empty warehouses. Staying up all night. Creating art out of anything, from cardboard to bodies, inventing superstars out of nothing. This was our buzz, our vibe. Sex. Drugs. Experiment and creation. Create something. Anything. Lots of things. Some of it would stick. We'd change the world, or at least our little corner of it.

"Which way, John?" Sherlock's voice shocked me out of my reverie.

"I live at the Chelsea, like everyone else," I sighed.

THE CHELSEA HOTEL. Heiresses desperately seeking disgrace with artistes. Writers and artists praying for a muse. Even in New York in 1968, you would be hard-pressed to find a more miserable hive of the desperate and demented.

The landlady was used to people making disturbances to get guests up to the rooms against the house rules. Someone would fake a fight, or try to sell drugs, or tip over an ashtray, and the rest of the people would run past the barricade. At two-fifty a night or fifteen dollars a week, the Chelsea was cheap, collecting youthful hope, grey enterprise, madness and decrepitude, along with any kind of bottom-feeding scamster. It also had an infamously liberal attitude towards rent, which meant that nearly every resident was constantly in arrears, and could be extorted for any money, valuables, or drugs they had while no complaints could be lodged against the owners about leaking roofs, flickering electricity, or the constantly failing boiler.

It was an arrangement that worked for most of us, particularly considering the heiresses and young men with rich fathers who came to spend time in this bohemian palace, tasting our lifestyle, but running back up to Park Avenue for Sunday brunch. They kept the place going, paying their rent for the few rooms in good shape on the second and third floors in the front. The only part of the hotel that ever saw the super's hands.

Sherlock walked into the Chelsea Hotel and demonstrated his useful observation trick. He walked straight up to the desk.

"I'd like to enquire about a room, please. I'd prefer monthly rates over weekly, if that's all right? I can pay in advance."

The hotel manager looked up through bleary eyes, and turned to get a resident's form, a cigarette dangling from his lip.

"Ah. I see that you only have rooms on the top floors available, and that it's been over a year since you've had your boiler inspected, and your exterminator certificate..."

I slipped past the doorway and up the stairs, listening to his sharp, deep voice tallying everything wrong with the building. It made me smile.

I checked the hair I pasted across the lock, and it was still in place. I opened the door and went straight to the loose floorboard under the mattress and pulled out my stash box, extracting a dozen of the blue tablets from the envelope. I didn't know how many he wanted, but ten, I thought, should do it. Plus a couple for myself, just in case. I didn't know what he was about, but the blues had helped my lonely existence for a night or two.

The room was dingy, the sheets dirty, my few belongings in the place making it look bigger than the closet it was.

* * *

SHERLOCK BROUGHT ME downtown from the Chelsea to Washington Square Park, a pale blue tablet dissolving in each of our stomachs after he interrogated me about its effects.

"Explain to me, John, what this is exactly, and why you think it's my sort of trip."

Even then, he called me *John*, and he was Sherlock to me, though Holmes, or even Mr. Holmes to everyone else.

"It's been around a while, tested by everyone. Big pharmaceutical houses. The Army. Someone died after an enormous dose, twenty times or more what we've just taken. It's been tested as a truth serum, a psychiatric aid, a cough suppressant, and a diet pill. It's mildly psychedelic, but more sensual and controlled than the tabs passing for LSD you can find cooked up all around the country."

"Groovy."

The word hung off the edge of his lip and I looked at him.

"What? I wanted to see what it felt like to say it."

"And?"

"It made me feel dirty. I suspect I may have lost some brain cells."

I stopped and stared at him, until he looked over at me, just with his eyes, a smirk breaking out on his face. We both dissolved into laughter there in the street.

Sherlock put his arm around my shoulders and breathed in. "This is good, John. Very good. Tell me something. The Chelsea. You like it there?"

"To be honest? Not really. It's not that cheap, but I can't afford better. It's good for me to be there for my clients. There are quite a few hangers-on with family money there, always interested in what I have. Prescriptions for amphetamines pay my way, and allow me to indulge in my experiments."

He put up a finger, asking me to pause, and walked past the chess players, observing their games.

"Would you bet on one of these, John?"

"I'm not a gambling man. I feel I've used up all my luck coming back from Charlie and malaria."

"It wouldn't be gambling, though. Some of the best chess players in the world are here, and it is a game of pure skill. I haven't the concentration for it, though I imagine I could do well if I put my mind to it. It's a fascinating blend of wit and strategy. The rules are simple, and it is good training for the structure of the mind. Look here. This man will lose, despite current appearances. He's playing well, but his opponent has the measure of him, playing a longer game with his lesser pieces. Ten moves, if I am correct, and I'm sure I am."

"You're a man of great power, aren't you, Mr. Holmes?"

"Not so much. I see what I see, and I am compelled by a sense of logic, a desire to unscramble puzzles. I need constant stimulation. Experiences."

"Hey. *S.C.U.M. Manifesto*? Only two dollars. Might change your life."

A short, dirty woman, obviously in and out of shelters, with short hair and a broken flat cap, but there was a sparkle of intelligence in her eyes.

Sherlock looked at her, with that look I would come to know so well. He was studying her, taking in details and making a judgement about whether or not to engage. Whether she was worth his breath, his attention.

"What about a proposition?"

"Oh, sure. I've had plenty of those. What do you want to do? Where? Under the pier? East or Hudson? Hudson's extra. It's dirtier, but if that's your thing..."

"Not that. Not at all. It's not your body I'm interested in, it's your mind."

"Conversation? Okay. Four bucks for thirty minutes, six bucks for an hour. We can talk about anything you want."

Sherlock glanced at me, a twinkle in his eye. "We're not what you think. Here's my proposition. Come have a coffee with us.

No strings. If we like what you have to say, we'll both buy your manifesto. If not, I'll pay for the coffee and give you a dollar for your time. Thirty minutes."

She looks at him, and at me. "Make it breakfast and it's a deal. You get as long as it takes for me to eat. Thirty minutes guaranteed."

"It's better and easier than getting a man to pay you for sex, is it?"

"Look, you want me to talk to you or not? Sure. I've turned tricks, gotten men to pay me to watch, to talk, whatever. It's no business of yours."

"Sorry, it's just that I don't want you to feel like you need to hide anything from me. I can see that you're occasionally homeless, but not always. That you're a lesbian, even though you seek the attention of men—that for money, you'll go with them, but that it's less attractive, miserable, middle-aged men that you end up spending time with. You've got moustache hairs and macassar on your fur-collared coat from at least seven different men, one black, three Italians—or Southern European descents, anyway—a blonde and two brown-haired professional men in polyester suits, and though I can see smudges of dirt from both the Hudson and East rivers, suggesting that you've slept under piers—though more often the Hudson—you're clean enough that you must shower regularly. At, if I'm not mistaken, the Chelsea Hotel, which is where my friend lodges. Shall we walk? There's an all-day breakfast place around the corner, Ms...?"

"Solanas. Valerie Solanas. Author of the *S.C.U.M. Manifesto*. I'm going to change the world."

"You don't say?"

"DON'T GET ME wrong. You guys seem all right. A girl's got to make a living, though. There's some real scumsters around."

Sherlock looked at me, an ice-blue sparkle in his eyes. He was feeling the blue beauty.

"Some real scumsters."

"Yeah. Like that guy, Andy, down at the Factory? My friend Irene brought me down there. She's this real Hot Girl. One of his so-called Superstars. She said that I 'just had to meet Andy.' When he met me, he asked me to do a screen test. Put me in one of his movies. Then I showed him a script I wrote. Brilliant play. *Up Your Ass*. He read it, said it was well-typed. Well fucking typed. Can you imagine that? Then he asked me if I was working with the vice squad to entrap him, it was so dirty. I told him, 'Andy, Irene told me you liked it dirty. I told you it was called *Up Your Ass*, didn't I?' He didn't have much to say to that, but told me that he couldn't produce it because the cops would be all over him. They were just looking for a reason to come in and shut him down. He's really paranoid.

"Then this guy Maurice had me out for dinner the next day. French guy, he says, talks with an English accent, though. Says he's published Anaïs Nin and Henry Miller. I was explaining the *S.C.U.M. Manifesto* to him and he said he wanted to publish it. Bought the rights. Wrote me a cheque right there and then for five hundred dollars and put it there with a contract. Said he could sell it and sell some more of my work, too. I could write some adult books, maybe. So I signed. Paid my bill at the Chelsea. Paid back some friends. Made some more copies of *S.C.U.M.* to sell. Got my typewriter out of the pawn shop. I had to get up onto the roof and get typing. Maurice wanted an expanded version of the *S.C.U.M. Manifesto*, a novel based on it, so I got typing. Working on it. Trying to make it into a novel. I made characters who got screwed over for each fucked-up thing that men did to women. Each grievance a character, like Greek Furies.

"I was all wound up, telling this Maurice Girodias about Andy and how he was stealing my script. He said to me 'That's your next novel, after *S.C.U.M. Up Your Ass*. Just what you need to get into the big time.' Maybe I should publish *S.C.U.M.* as it is. He wanted me to call it *The Manifesto for the Society* for *Cutting Up Men*. Said to get ready with *Up Your Ass* right after. But I don't have the script anymore. I was worried. I wanted another five hundred bucks. Maybe more. You should get paid more for a second script, right? But he disappeared. Later on I look at the contract, and it says it's not just for the two books, but for future writings, too. I think it must be all my future writings. Now he's split, back off to France or L.A. or somewhere. I don't know. I can't get any answers."

"Have you got a copy of the contract? I could look at it if you like. I know a thing or two about the law. About a few things."

"Yeah. Hey. That'd be good. I just... I get all excited when people are nice to me. Hey. You two. What are you after?"

"Us? We've just had a... what was it, John? A blue funk? It's anything but. A blue buzz, maybe."

I found myself grinning like an idiot, pushing my hash browns around on my plate, watching pale yellow egg yolk run over them in the harsh fluorescent light. "We've just... had a couple of pills. They're a bit..." I pointed to my plate. "Strong."

Sherlock looked at me and grinned. "Have you met John, Valerie? Call him Doc. That's what everyone else does. I think he could be a candidate for the S.C.U.M. Male Auxiliary. He is a very, very good friend to have."

I smiled at Solanas. My feet were itching, tapping the floor in a syncopated rhythm that only Sherlock could understand. "I would really like to walk."

"EAST, TOWARDS THE Alphabet! Beyond the Village, there's a city, a city of the Alphabet, Avenues of letters!" I said, exiting the greasy spoon six dollars lighter but carrying two copies of Valerie Solanas' self-mimeographed *S.C.U.M. Manifesto*, inscribed '*Too bad you're men. You'd make O.K. broads— Valerie.*'

The grey New York light was coming up, and you could see

dark shapes shuffling, junkies twitching in failed sleep in East Village Park, behind iron railings. A shaft of light pierced the gloom and murk.

I looked for the street sign. "Avenue A. Direct sun, at dawn, every now and then. I thought I had enough of sunlight In Country, but I like it over here, in this quiet corner."

"It's not so quiet, John. There are plenty of dark things prowling these streets, and I don't mean rodents. People, John. The worst kind that skulk in shadows and desire harm to their fellow man. I've been considering this area."

He looked at me, up and down, appraising.

"John, what would you think about leaving the Chelsea Hotel? Moving somewhere a bit more permanent? Shall we turn here, on Avenue B? There's something I'd like you to see."

We walked along another two blocks, shapeless husks huddling in doorways, nestling with the bags of garbage on the street, shopkeepers opening their doors to conduct business through bars. Downtown New York.

Sherlock stopped in front of number 221 Avenue B. A bakery, the bars on its front window painted white, a bright sign over the door. There was a bell over the door that rang as we walk in.

"Mrs. Hendrix. How are you this fine morning?" He grinned at her, his teeth glowing almost blue in the light of the fluorescent tubes overhead.

Mrs. Hendrix was a well-kept black woman dressed in a navy blue chef's uniform, with a white starched apron and a few stray smudges of flour dusting her arms. "Mr. Holmes. You're here mighty early, aren't you?"

"My colleague and I have just had our breakfast over near Washington Square Park, and I thought I might show him the rooms for rent. Alone, I might be a little worried about making the rent, but with a second person... well, if he's willing to come in with me, then we'd never have a thing to worry about."

She looked at us, with her big smile on her face, and as it

dropped off, the temperature dropped by several degrees. "My husband and I like you, Mr. Holmes, and we're not worried about what you do in your rooms, but the rent. You have to make the rent. Every single month, due on the twenty-fifth, late on the first, understand? Or you're out on the first, that day."

"Mrs. Hendrix, I wouldn't dream of being late. You and I are going to be the best of friends. Frustrating, I'm sure, at times, but I think we understand each other, and you'll have nothing to fear from me, as long as you don't bother about what we do. I will do experiments, sometimes, and Doctor Watson here will assist me with his medical and chemical knowledge."

Her smile reasserted itself, erasing any hint of malice and covering the world-weariness she felt. "Okay, then, want to have a look?"

THE SECOND FLOOR was filled with ovens, sacks of flour, paper bags, the leftover junk of running the bakery. "You have to pass through here, but just stay on this side of the tape, and try not to track any mud through or anything. Health department rules. Not that they inspect much, but you never know. Not with a 'spade' business."

She pointed to the ovens, with the pipes running from them. "My husband worked on ships in the war. We heat the water from the bakery ovens so there's plenty of hot water until around midnight. Building heat, too."

We went up to the third floor. It was a massive, open space, swept clean but could use a good scrub. "Used to be storage for a magazine company during the war. They had some clerks up here before that. Hot in the summer, cold in the winter, but the heating's covered and the windows open, top and bottom. You get a good airflow in summertime, here and on the fourth floor. I've done enough stairs, though, so you can go up to the fourth yourself."

"There's another floor?" My entire room in the Chelsea wasn't a tenth of this space. Fourteen-, maybe sixteen-foot-high ceilings of bare wood. You could dance in here. There was nothing but a couple of hard chairs and a simple table.

"Yep. There's an old bed up there, too. Just the one. My husband and I lived up here while we were fighting with Stuy Town, before that Mr. Lorch let us move in to his place."

I remembered them. The *Post* had written a scathing editorial about letting 'that spade family' move in and 'corrupt' the all-white enclave.

Sherlock looked at me, rubbing his fingers against his thumb. I reached into my pocket and gave him the ten-dollar bill he had given me a few hours before outside the Chelsea. I was overdue there, and I wasn't going to pay them another dime. I was going to live here.

"Mrs. Hendrix, we're happy to take the floors, effective today. Right now, if that's all right?"

She turned from the top of the stairs. "That's no problem. Y'all do what you need to do. I've gotta get keys cut, but y'all stay here if you need and they'll be ready as soon as we can get them out. Breakfast rush about to start. First of June, now. See you on the first of July, if not before." The bills disappeared underneath her apron.

Sherlock looked at me. "This floor alone is worth it, isn't it? Shall we look upstairs?"

The next floor was the same, if a little cleaner. There was a bed, made up, with a dust cover on it, and a small rough wooden dresser.

"We're allowed to do what we like. Put up walls if we want, or not. And Mrs. Hendrix wanted to keep the furniture up here, said that it was too much trouble to bring it down. And free breakfast. Anything left over from the day before. I think your trim waistline may expand, if you're fed enough."

I yawned.

"Poor John Watson. I've tired you out with my manic walk the length of Manhattan Island. We should lie down." He pulled back the dust sheet.

"This is the one thing. The blue beauties will make you yawn, tired and exhausted, but you'll have trouble sleeping."

"I'm sure we'll find something to do." He pulled me to him, to those lips and that lovely long face I'd been dreaming of all night.

A SINGLE RAY of actual sunshine wandered across the floor, motes of dust sprung up from our bodies twinkling in their slow journey to the floor. "Look at the dust, Sherlock. Floating there, swirling. Lighter than air. It's like magic."

"Not at all. They're very light, but not lighter than air, or they'd float up and we'd have far less sweeping. They're just light enough that the lift from swirling air molecules, from tiny temperature changes can slow their descent. The sunlight is heating the air as it streams through the window. That's your magic, John. Motes of dust are simply pawns in the sun's game."

"Take the joy out of everything, don't you?"

"Not everything, John." He smiled at me, then, the first time I saw his secret smile; the one he only shared with me, and only when we were alone. That smile told me that this, that we, were special, but that it wasn't to leave the confines of the private lair we would build for ourselves, there above Alphabet City.

"Pawns." He sat up, moving faster than I could even think of moving. "Tell me something, John. Do you remember Valerie Solanas? Did she strike you as a pawn? Someone who would do something, unasked, for someone else?"

I thought about her. "Not really. She seemed more... more like someone who was used to playing her own game, changing the rules of the game she found herself in."

"Exactly, John. She's a queen, able to make any moves,

playing her own game, but she is without the luxury of her own board. Acting as a pawn. Driving towards the opponent's back row, to regain her crown."

He got up and walked to the window.

"But she's not in control, is she?"

"That's exactly it, John. She's not in control of her life, and she's trying to work out who the king is."

"Or the player of the game."

"Or the player of the game. She's the most resentful pawn ever committed to the game, and that makes her dangerous. She's a puzzle, isn't she? Where's that manifesto of hers? I'm of a mind to read it. Ms. Solanas, you are a bit of a puzzle, aren't you?"

He padded back from the window, casting a long, lean shadow across the floor, rifling through the pockets of my pants looking for those ragged sheets with purple writing on them.

OVER THE NEXT two days, I'd packed my few belongings for my new home at Avenue B, and Sherlock had turned up the next night with an array of tough youths carrying boxes and crates of notebooks and chemical apparatus, a coffee table made from a cable spool, and a few chairs that looked like they'd spent some time on the street.

It was starting to look more like a home than anywhere I'd been since before the War.

Sherlock was still talking about Valerie. We'd run into her once more on the street, and talked to her about her *Manifesto*. Sherlock wanted to know more.

"Go on, John. Find out what you can about Valerie from your contacts at the Factory. Keep an eye out for her, and talk to her if you have to, but if you can follow her without her noticing, that would be helpful."

I didn't know why we were so interested—why *he* was so

interested, that is. I would have been happy to have whiled the weekend away with day-old cakes and bread. I had some deliveries that could be made to the Factory, though, so I went ahead, not knowing what to expect. Everyone had the same reaction. Nothing outstanding, for the Factory. Billy and Paul were there, ready to get their prescriptions, only too happy to share catty gossip.

"Valerie? Who?"

"You know. The street dyke. Twitchy."

"Oh, yeah. Creepy. Did you see her screen test?"

"Eyes like dark holes, staring into your soul."

"Not attractive, really. Could be, if she put on makeup or something. Could be better, anyway. Better than street chic. Eau de Hudson, like she usually wears."

"There was something about her, though. Something interesting. She was clever, when she wasn't too twitchy. Maybe if she'd been fed."

"Some days she'd be so angry, railing about men and scum. Other days, she'd be real personable. Friendly. She used to come in with Irene, sometimes, but we haven't seen them together in months. She just keeps coming in shouting at Andy about her script. He gets so many scripts from people. What's he supposed to do?"

"And money. She's always asking everyone for money."

"Speaking of, Doc. What have you got for us? We loved those black beauties last time. Got us right through the move. What do you think of the new digs? Union Square? Next big thing?"

"Orange OPs. Phew. Those things'll keep you going, all day, and all night long"

I finished my business and walked back to the Chelsea to see a few patients for some business there.

It was strange, heading up there. I had a pocket full of money, and another full of tablets, and I was ready to see the back of that place. Sure, lots of people had written loads of stuff there, and it was a collection of plenty of interesting people, but did it matter anymore?

Sherlock was in the coffee shop next door, sitting with a greasy-looking man in a brown suit with heavily macassar'd hair. Pencil-thin moustache, impeccably dressed, like he was just catching up with the Beats. They were out, man, didn't he know? Sherlock saw me and took his lovely long hands and knocked on the window. I went and ordered a coffee.

"John! How are you? Can I introduce you to Maurice Girodias, of the Olympia Press? Mr. Girodias is a fascinating individual, having published some of the more influential works over the last twenty years. Arthur Miller, Nabokov and others. Mr. Girodias, this is Doctor Watson. He's called Doc by his friends. Don't call him John. He hates it. Just indulges me."

"Pleased to meet you?" He half-stood and gave me a limp handshake. My impression was cheap macassar and a cheaper suit, though he had quite the breakfast in front of him: eggs benedict, fresh-squeezed orange juice, and coffee with the sugar jar next to him.

Sherlock went on. "We appear to have a mutual friend. Ms. Valerie Solanas. You remember her, John?"

He was up to something, but I had no idea what. I made a show of screwing up my face for a moment. "Short woman, flat cap, sheepskin coat?"

"That's her. Mr. Girodias is her publisher. Or will be, when he can find her, of course. He's got a manuscript, and is hoping to get a second, maybe even a third, isn't that right, Mr. Girodias?"

"It is, actually. We call them the Travellers Companion books. Great literature that offers a... a traveller, one on his own, a break from the day-to-day grind. That traveller might need some stimulation. That's what we provide. Dirty books, sure, but dirty books for the discriminating reader."

There was something about this Girodias. His accent was English overlaid with French, but a coarse English and the

287

French sounded more like it was from the movies than from growing up in Paris, but what did I know? Just that I didn't like him. I spent a lot of time with unsavoury characters, freaks, and cast-outs of prestigious families. I didn't mind *strange*, but desperation rolled off of him, despite his rolls of money and the way he encouraged us to order whatever we wanted on his cheque.

"How did you and Valerie come to meet?"

He looked at both of us as though we were part of the vice squad. To be fair, Sherlock's clean-cut face and short hair would make him look like a bad rookie who has put on civvies and been thrown out into the wilds of Southern Manhattan to catch gamblers, pimps, and johns. "Nothing like that, I assure you. No, no, no under the bridge and down the alley liaison for me." He strained so hard to pronounce "liaison" in a French fashion that I was afraid he was going to pull his larynx.

"No, we were introduced by the daughter of one of my *financiers*." (That strain again.) "Adler. Irene, I think? Lovely family. Lovely woman, actually. Intelligent. Spent quite a lot of time at the Factory. The only one of the Superstars that was a real Superstar, if you know what I mean. Knew of my taste for *la controverse*. Good for *le commerce*. You know. She told me of the *manifesto* of *Valérie* and I knew I should meet her. With such an endorsement, I knew I should meet her and get her on my author list. So I did."

Sherlock looked at me, his expression unreadable, a look I would come to puzzle over many times in our life together. "Valerie has asked me to look over this contract you've sent her—it's so vague as to be legally questionable, you see. She'd like to, hm, clarify her position."

"Ah. Well. Tell her... tell her to talk to me, not to send some agent out. I'm a reasonable man, but I am a man of business. She needn't be concerned. We can... we can discuss the terms. Of course. She is an artist, and I want to make her some money, and myself some. She doesn't need to send someone to speak for her."

"Oh, no. She didn't send me, she only mentioned it, and since I ran into you, I thought I would ask."

"Fine. Well. I must be going. I have a printer to meet. You'll get that? Very kind, thanks."

Girodias left the impression he was running, leaving us with the bill for his breakfast.

"John, John! What have you found?" Sherlock was looking at me with a sparkle in his eyes.

"You didn't think I'd want to share with you?"

"What? What are you saying, John?"

"You've found some pills, someone's shared something with you. We're barely down from the blues and now you're up again. I thought... Nevermind."

"John. John. Look at me." We were sitting on the same side of the table, across from where Girodias had been. He put his hand under my chin and turned it to face him and his eyes softened. "I haven't had any pills. I just get excited when I'm stimulated. I just take pills to keep myself going in times when I can't find something to keep my interest. Please. What did you find out at the Factory about Valerie?"

I could have kissed him, deep, his stubble raking against mine, there in the coffee shop. I wanted to, but I held myself back. I waded through the pile of information that the hangers-on and buyers had given me. "Not much more than we knew. You have to filter it out of the language they speak over there. They mostly made fun of her, like she was part of the scene but not any longer. Irene Adler did bring her in, and used to be friendly towards her, but no one seems to have seen them together for months."

"Hmmm. Interesting. There's something there. This Adler. What do we know about her?"

"If we weren't in America, she'd be royalty. Rich. Very rich.

Glamourous. Gorgeous, too, even if she's not your sort of thing. Her family made money in ice in the early 1800s, and then diversified. Lumber. Newspapers. Radio. The Midas touch. Always on to the next big thing.

"The open secret is that much of Andy's generosity comes from her. Most of the big expensive dinners out she pays for, but he gets all the credit. She bought a few paintings, has been in a bunch of his films. Lives at the Chelsea. She's the original Superstar."

"Ms. Adler. How did you come to be friends with Ms. Solanas? And why these introductions? What is it you want Valerie to do for you?"

"Sherlock, really? What could she possibly want? Maybe she was... moved by her writing, or something?"

"A woman like that? No, John. It can't be. Come on. Let's go to the Chelsea Hotel."

Just like that we were out of there, five dollars left on the table: more than double the bill, but it was enough for him. Not for the last time would I follow on the heels of Sherlock Holmes with only the tiniest idea of what was going on.

The Chelsea Hotel was buzzing with hushed excitement. Billy, Candy, a couple of other transvestites were lying on the sofas, arms artfully arranged in a pose of fainting, affecting stricken. One of the writers—Paul, I think—was standing in the corner, smoking cigarettes; a line of butts on the ground showed where he had been pacing.

"He's been walking there for at least an hour and a half. Twelve butts on the ground, seven minutes a cigarette, one in his hand. Something's happened. I don't like this, John."

I went over to Candy. She was normally a rock. As dramatic as she could be, she was someone to trust in a crisis. "What's going on? What's happened?"

She looked up at me.

"Oh, god, It's Andy. He... Andy's been shot. Valerie shot him. She slept in my room last night, went out for coffee, and came back crazy. She was running around, looking for Maurice, angry. Pacing back and forth. Got all dressed up. Make-up, can you believe? Said she was going to go talk to Andy. I thought maybe... but I don't know. I helped her with her makeup. She looked nice."

Sherlock had his concentrating face on. "This can't be right. This can't be it." He looked at me. "Do you know Irene Adler? What she looks like? Her room number?"

I didn't know what to say. I could hardly believe the strange, gregarious woman we'd met, so canny in teasing money out of us, had just shot Andy Warhol. "I know her from sight. We've met a time or two, when I was accidentally invited along to dinners, but I don't really know her. She wouldn't know me. I assume she'd be in the front on the second or third floor, where the nice rooms are."

He turned on his heel and strode to the counter. "Excuse me. I need to speak to Ms. Irene Adler. It's a matter of some urgency. Could you ring her room, please, or let me up?"

The desk clerk looked up, his ever-present cigarette dangling and burning. He muttered "Adler. Adler. Hm. What was your name, sir?" as he pulled out a slip of paper.

"Holmes. Sherlock Holmes. She may be in danger."

The clerk turned and looked at the keys on the wall behind him "Red tag. She's gone away for a while.

Sherlock stared at him. "Danger. She may be in serious danger. Can you tell me where she is, or anything useful?"

The clerk sighed and lit another cigarette, taking in Sherlock's lean frame and rumpled, but well-cut clothes. "Let me just have a look..." He thumbed through the guest ledger. "Says here she booked a taxi to LaGuardia. Gone at least a week, maybe longer. There's the forwarding address... now why would you go to Los Angeles in June? Surely you'd go in the winter?"

He closed the book with a thump and looked up at us, but Sherlock was already pulling at my arm.

"John. She's off to Los Angeles. What's happening there? We

need newspapers, and time, and perhaps a little something to focus the mind..."

He led me away towards Union Square, muttering to himself. I listened, but could not make out very much. "Los Angeles... Irene Alder... Andy Warhol... The Factory... John!"

I was startled out of my reverie, walking along past Sherlock. "What is it?"

"You're around the Factory a lot. Has anything happened in the last few months? Anything peculiar?"

"Not that I can think of. People are always coming and going, at least a little. They fall in and out of favour according to Andy's whims."

"Would you know who was in and out?"

"I don't know. I don't particularly pay attention. I notice when people are gone for a while."

"What about Adler? She's the common thread."

"She was definitely in. Belle of the ball. She was in quite a few of Andy's films, Billy's films, too, two or three years back. Paul just loved her. She was starring in them. Andy even conceived of a series of films just about her. A series of series. She was the centre of the Factory's fleeting attention. She would take them all out; fifteen, twenty people. More, sometimes. They'd have champagne and oysters. Steak. And pills, Plenty of pills. She left, though, a while back. Peak of her stardom. People started talking about her afterwards. She'd been involved with a musician. She'd gotten pregnant. Couldn't handle the drugs. Bored. Lots of things."

"She's the key, John. She knows something. She was there. Somewhere. Important."

"I think she may be as crazy as Valerie."

"Right, John. The thing for this is to sharpen the senses. I want to know what's going on. Anything in those pockets to aid in focus? An upper?"

"I have some of the black beauties—cut with methaqulaone,

though—Quaaludes, so maybe not so good for concentration, and some Obetrol—Andy Candy."

Sherlock took one of each and upped his pace, to get the blood flowing. I wasn't sure about the combination. Doubling up on the amphetamines, but, then, I was still a bit edgy from the blues, so I figured it couldn't hurt.

We headed to Midtown, East 47th Street, to the site of the original Factory, walking fast to get the pills into our bodies.

He stood in front of the scaffolding surrounding the pile of bricks, facing away, looking up and down the street.

"Sunlight. Grand Central. There's a YMCA nearby. Hmmm..."

He turned left and stalked away towards 3rd Avenue. I had trouble keeping up with his long, muscular legs, despite my own enhancement.

I was getting jittery, and the methaqualone was sending shivers down my spine as we strode down past Grand Central and towards the Chelsea.

Sherlock stopped in front of a newspaper stand and looked at the papers.

"Gum, please. Spearmint." He handed over his fifteen cents, scanning the headlines. "California Democratic primary. California. Los Angeles." He picked up a copy of the *New York Times*, and the *Los Angeles Times* for good measure. He handed me the *New York Times*. "Here, John. Back to Avenue B. We've got to get through these newspapers."

I was worried about him, but I thought that, back at Avenue B, we would have water and blankets and the comforts of home. I wasn't sure that we hadn't overdone it for a Monday evening, and I didn't expect we'd get any sleep tonight.

It was good that it was evening, because we were a giggling mess when we got back. We have had—still do, I suppose—our share of late-night or very early morning entries through the bakery, Mrs. Hendrix constantly reminding us that what we do is not her business, as long as the rent comes in on time.

"I'll take L.A., John, and you take New York. Systematic. Let's first spread the paper out in even numbers across the floor. We're looking for *patterns*. Something to do with the Presidential primary. Set aside advertising circulars and sports sections for now. Keep Arts and Culture."

I looked at him, peeling apart the newspaper, page by page, setting it down. "Sherlock, surely we'd be better off leafing through normally?"

"Nonsense, John. Trust me. Unless we can see the whole of it together, we can't see the patterns. Lay them out. Even pages up. Facing inwards so we can scan across the whole paper. Don't overlap the pages at all."

I laid them out, end to end, looking back at Sherlock crouched there, muttering at the pages as he read them. "We should have bought two copies of the papers, John. We could have them spread to see the entire pattern."

At last it was set out, and he walked back and forth in the centre of the room, looking at the newspapers spread there on the ground.

"Turn them, John. We need the odds, quickly."

We went through the laborious process of turning the papers over, one by one. Sherlock's fingers were crumpling the edges, twitching with overstimulation and speed. "Fuck it, John. I'm in a hurry. Just national and local news." He was stalking back and forth, wild-eyed, his own movements stirring the air to make the papers move around underneath his feet.

"Stop, Sherlock. Slow down. Listen to the sounds outside. New York at night, even on a Monday." Sirens whirred in the distance. Shouts came up, from the street and from the light-wells out back, one more scream. Laughter, and the tinkle of broken glass. "Take a breath. Let's have a glass of water. Maybe some wine."

He looked at me. "You're right, John, thanks. Get that."

I went upstairs to the third floor and our kitchenette. There was a jug of dry red wine that I poured into a couple of jelly jars and filled a coffee can with water from the tap, recoiling at the chlorine smell. I ran a handful of it over my hair, feeling the tingle of the water drops roll down my scalp and neck.

Another breath.

"I've got it, John!" Sherlock was shouting from downstairs. "We need the telephone. Long distance, direct to California."

I staggered down the staircase in a succession of freeze frames, like Duchamp's nude, glasses clattering in my hands, feet skittering over the steps one by one in a controlled fall, my heart bursting with fear and pride at the bottom. I hadn't fallen.

Sherlock was there, holding a piece of the *L.A. Times* in his hand, his pupils the size of quarters. "This is it, John. She's after Bobby Kennedy. We've got to tell someone."

"Sherlock, what the hell are you talking about? Valerie Solanas is after Bobby Kennedy? She's the subject of a citywide manhunt. She can't fly. That doesn't make sense. Here, let's sit down and have some wine. Settle, remember?"

"No, John. Don't mistake the pawn for the queen. Irene Adler, if that's even her name. She's played everyone. Had her revenge on Warhol for spurning her. Solanas is just an unpredictable bomb, tossed into the Factory. She'd hurt Andy somehow, but it's only chance that she's actually shot him."

He stops and thinks, looking at the ceiling.

"I can't figure it out. It would make sense, though, that she would focus her rage on Warhol himself, not just the hangers-on. That's who I'd go after. The leeches. The grovelling assholes who build egos out of propaganda and then think they're important. I understand Warhol and what he's built, but there are all these people around him, inserting themselves into his orbit. They don't have an original thought of their own, but they take delight in playing political games, talking down to people. Making fragile people like Valerie Solanas feel more isolated and alone."

He was spitting with anger, staring out the window, the sheets of newspaper crumpled in his hand, his forearms rippling with muscle. I stood behind him and put my arms around him, kissing him lightly behind the ear, rubbing his stomach through his shirt.

"It's okay, Sherlock. Really okay. They are shitheads. Everything they hate. I know. Andy, I think, knows."

He turned in my arms. "Maybe some of that wine?"

I handed him the wine. "I don't know if it's any good. It's just what was upstairs."

"I imagine our taste buds aren't working anyway. Just so long as it's not sweet. I can't stand sweet wine. Hippies and grassheads and those with no imagination. They should just drink Coke."

He put the papers down and took up the wine and toasted me, slipping his arm through mine for the sip. "You're good to me, John. Good *for* me."

I blushed and picked up the papers he'd put down.

"There's something there. I can see the whole thing, but I can't explain it all. My head is buzzing too much.

"Listen: Adler was been pushed out of the Factory six months or a year ago. Must have met Valerie at the same time. It doesn't make *sense* that she's a real socialite. She might have taken Warhol out in that case, but not all those people. The rich hang on to their money exactly by not giving it away. No. She wanted them to believe that she was wealthy. Buying her way into stardom? She had money, clearly, but the class? Breeding? I find it hard to believe.

"She met Solanas, and Solanas would have been the perfect bomb. Chaos incarnate. Delicate. Wounded. Fractured in places. If she could get Valerie angry enough, and directed, she'd go off in some unpredictable way. Hurt Warhol? Damage his reputation? Scare him? Could be anything.

"Why would she run, though? She didn't do anything.

Introduced Valerie to Girodias and Warhol. Possibly stoked the coals of resentment, a bit, but nothing that would be out of the ordinary in the circles she ran in.

"But here's the thing: Valerie suddenly got set off. She turned from building up a head of steam to murderous in a few days. She was fine when we met her, just a couple of days ago. Solanas was a practice run, I'm sure of it. I don't have enough data, but she must have been grooming someone else, someone fragile and vulnerable. Someone poor. Getting her ready. Why would she go off now? Solanas has claimed friendship with Warhol on the most tenuous of links. There's no way the pigs would go after a rich socialite. Warhol is a distraction. Important, but something to get people to look at New York.

"The polls are opening any time in California for the Democratic Primary. Bobby Kennedy is the only candidate campaigning in Southern California. It's all there, John."

"I know, Sherlock. Just relax. It makes sense. It's plausible, but there's no way we can let anyone know now. I could possibly get one of Andy's groupies to trust me, but who would we call? The FBI? The LAPD? The NYPD? They're all pigs. One of the newspapers? They'd have us out as crank callers in a second. We can barely string sentences together."

He put his head in my lap. "I know. I know. I just... I'm sure of it."

"Could be the amphetamines or the 'ludes. We've had quite a lot."

We sat there for a few minutes, the morning sun bouncing off the windows of the building opposite, the smells from the bakery coming up and turning our stomachs. We drank the water, and the wine, and then Sherlock turned to me and kissed me again, and in his kiss was hunger and desperation. We made love on and on and it was like nothing I've experienced before or since. It—he—was filled with an intensity and urgency that was simply indescribable.

He was right, of course. Probably, anyway. Bobby Kennedy was shot just after midnight as the polls closed, and Nixon went on to win the election. It was the beginning of the end as well. The Factory stopped being so open. The hippies grew up. Irene Adler disappeared, and was forgotten by pretty much everyone. She would become a footnote in the Factory, a face flashing by in some of Warhol's films.

Sherlock was devastated.

He spent three days and the six blues that he had left wandering around the apartment, listless. He smoked cigarette after cigarette, shouting out the window into the night at the girls downstairs. He went down onto the street and bought bags of grass, then bags of brown powder later, cooking them up and, for want of a syringe, snorting the brown liquid.

I went out and bought a deadbolt and locked him into the bedroom on the top floor to let him dry out, leaving him newspapers, a carton of orange juice, some bananas, and water. After twenty-four hours, I went in to him, and he was sitting on the floor in the beam of the setting sun, holding his knees and rocking, my newspapers strewn all around him in a disordered mess, all the articles on the Kennedy and Warhol shootings arrayed around him, and a book open in his lap—Voltaire's writings after the revolution.

"It's my fault, John. I did it. I had it all figured out. I could have saved him, if I was able to speak. Knew who to speak to. Solanas was the practice run. Revenge on Warhol. She wasn't even really an heiress. She came in, flashing around money, acting the type, wanting something from Warhol, but her star fell too fast. Solanas was an opportunity, but Sirhan Sirhan was the long game. Irene Adler probably wasn't even her name.

He held up the Voltaire. "With power comes responsibility, John. I've got to make my work mean something. Save lives. Stop the corrupt.

"And for my diversions, and distractions, you and your

magical tablets, those are for afterwards. When the lives are saved and the city is safe. To keep us from being bored."

Soon enough, we had a string of people coming in to 221 Avenue B, eating one of Mrs. Hendrix's cakes or bean pies, explaining to Sherlock and me their unsolvable riddles, which he'd go and unwind, rooting out evil and corruption across America.

Bored? We were never bored.

Sherlock got harder, colder. I think I was the only one who ever saw his sense of humour, and hardly ever again. He never spoke about our lovemaking, not after that one time. We were friends and associates. People suspected, sure, but they never found anything concrete. The times changed, the world got darker.

He never forgot Adler, though. She was always The Woman. I think he was a little in love with her. The only one to ever outsmart him, and to get away. He'd only find shreds, suggestions of her existence. A few lines in the Solanas transcripts. Scenes in Warhol's unwatchable films. Occasional cuttings from the newspaper.

She created him, in her own way. Would 221 Avenue B have given such hope to the hopeless? Would those we've caught have killed and stolen more? Would we have been something more than friends? Happier? Would New York be as safe, or any more—or less—interesting? Where would we have been without her?

the power of media

GLEN MEHN

one
PIECE IT TOGETHER

WE USED TO believe in the future. Not just Sherlock and me, but everybody. Andy and his hangers-on were changing the means and process of production. Women were going to be equal; Blacks, Irish, whatever. Wars were going to end.

Until it all wasn't.

Sherlock was just getting started and was right in the middle of it, of course. It was the littlest things that indicated a bigger story; maybe the biggest story ever. I'll never really understand how it wasn't, except... well, you'll see. The people involved are good at making things go away.

I'm writing out how it really happened. I'll take out the choice parts before anyone sees it. Most of the drugs and the sex, and some identifying information. People need to be protected, probably even their children. I have to write it all down, though, even if it never sees the light of day.

It's hard to know where to begin. The stuff Sherlock would want me to write—how he'd built a case up on top of a tiny scrap of hair or a smudge of grease. He'd want me only to write a dozen pages on grease viscosity or paper stock and leave all the interesting parts out, the parts about people and how they work.

*　*　*

IT REALLY STARTED right after the Adler thing, when Andy Warhol and Bobby Kennedy got shot in the same week and Valerie went to jail when Andy was stuck in the hospital, for weeks on end. He died, you know, for a few minutes there on the table, but he came back, bigger than ever before. I still had my business—using the doctor's license that the Army had left me, along with the shrapnel in my shoulder—to procure and provide mental, physical, and chemical support to those bright young things inside and out of the Factory. It's not as bad as it sounds, now—no one thought of me as a drug dealer. There was no war on drugs, not yet, and a lot of people, respectable, everyday people, then and now, thought that a little chemical help was just what they needed to get through their day. I just served societal outcasts instead of well-to-do housewives. As a doctor, I could prescribe what people needed and it was better than buying things on the street. Sure, some things were off-label, but my feelings on the Hippocratic Oath have always suggested that you should do what works.

It was a different time. We still thought we had a future, something to look forward to. We actually believed that if we could just fix the rules, then the country would change, and our problems around race and class, war and peace, they'd just... evaporate, I guess. Fat lot of good that did. People wanted to turn me and Sherlock into gay icons, but in that time and place, we didn't really consider ourselves gay or bisexual or anything. Little Joe used to joke that we were all trisexual: we'd try anything sexual. If you gave yourself a chance, you might find you liked something different. For me, it was more about who people were. I didn't like people very much, but Sherlock was different. For others, for Joe, or Irene, or some of the other Factory hangers-on, it was more about who they could introduce you to, what you could get out of it. People were honest about that, too. Who or what you could get out of a good screw.

two

AN INTRODUCTION

ANDY FINALLY CAME home, weeks later, after the New York summer was in full swing, dripping air conditioners everywhere, the heat beating up through the soles of your shoes, the concrete soaking up the energy of the sun all day and throbbing with heat after the sun went down. Everything made it hotter—the subway poured steam out of the sidewalk grates and pumped flat, dry air past commuters. That time of year, it seemed like everything was hot, even the ice in your Coke would melt in seconds. If you weren't lucky enough to have air conditioning, you could only sleep with all the windows open, spread eagled and not touching. No sheets, needless to say.

My wallet was thin since I'd just spent the better part of two weeks nursing Sherlock back to health and what I thought was a fragile sanity. He hadn't left the house in all that time. Hadn't left the room, after I installed the deadbolt. I had to be doctor and nurse and swap out buckets for a toilet while he was sleeping. Mrs. Hendrix kept what would become her legendary calm, but her eyebrows would go up all the time, waiting for the police to come in and arrest her for whatever we were doing.

"It's time, Sherlock. Time to face the world."

"I know, John." He looked up at the bedroom door with its shiny new deadbolt over the old knob. With a sharp intake of breath he stood and looked down to touch my face. "You're right."

"Andy's home. We could go and see him, see if we can be of any kind of help. Be nice to see everyone, if you're up for it?"

Sherlock looked at the floor. It was Adler's manipulation of Solanas that had led to his week-long binge of amphetamine and Amphedoxamine. He closed his eyes and shook his head. "Yes. We absolutely should. Maybe there's something out there for me."

I didn't know what he meant, but I went to the floor and tossed our clothes onto the bed and started picking mine out, dressing myself and watching him armor himself against the outside world.

On our way out we were stopped by Mrs. Hendrix. "Dr. Watson, Mr. Holmes? I want you to meet my nephew Joseph. He'll be working for us from time to time. He'll be up on the second floor, moving stuff around sometimes, but he'll stay out of your floors, though, won't you Joseph?"

"Yes ma'am."

Joseph was young and wiry, his hair cut short and dressed, just like Mrs. Hendrix, in clean clothes despite working around loose flour all day. He looked down at his hands, which were fidgeting with each other.

"Mrs. Hendrix, we're not worried about that at all. Joseph, it's very nice to meet you." Sherlock stepped forward and stuck his hand out to shake. Joseph looked at it, then shook it. "If you're around sometimes and not too busy, would you be averse to running errands or messages? Nothing dangerous, and we'd pay you, of course."

Joseph risked a glance up. "As long as my auntie says it's okay, sir."

"Great. We've got to go. Thanks, Mrs. Hendrix. Great to meet you, Joseph."

* * *

"WHAT WAS THAT about, Sherlock?"

"What do you mean, dear John?"

"About running errands and all that? Do we suddenly have errands to run we can't do ourselves? We're not exactly flush with cash."

"Oh, I don't know, John, but I think there are places where a young man like that could go that he would be less visible than you or me, so I just thought having the option couldn't hurt. He seemed really uncomfortable, didn't he?"

"He did. Colored people often are. They have the Civil Rights Act now but it'll take time, a couple of generations, before they work their way up and are completely equal. They've got to get doctors and lawyers and, you know, artists and everything. But we've crossed the main bridge now, right?"

"You think so, John? Really?"

"Well, no, but getting the laws in place is the most important thing, isn't it? Society can and will change, but it takes time. Look at women's rights. They got the vote in 1920, and now they've got woman's lib. You can't expect people to change overnight."

Sherlock stopped talking and looked forward, walking in silence for a couple of blocks. "That young man was so nervous he wouldn't even meet my eye. He's a good-looking, strong-backed young man of, what, sixteen? Eighteen? Standing there in his trousers that had been hemmed short and then let out three times as he grew. Mrs. Hendrix is intelligent and works hard. It would be reasonable to believe that he would be the same, but can't he look at his aunt's lodgers in the face? He did risk a glance, though, when I shook his hand. He looked at me, up and down, glancing ever so briefly at my face. You don't look at someone like that unless you're trying to figure them out. He's intelligent and observant, but he's short of opportunity."

* * *

"THIS IS THE elevator that she ran up and down that day. She rode it up and down for a couple of hours before she went in."

Sherlock stood in the corner, where Solanas had stood, looking around, riding up to the floor below the Factory and then back down, then back up again.

"What do you think had been going through her mind as it cracked, John? Girodias had disappeared, and maybe something about Adler's conditioning redirected her anger on Andy?"

"I can't even imagine. She was on the news the other day, shouting about scum. It's awful, but it sounds worse on television, like there's no filter to it, no context.

"I still don't completely understand it, Holmes. I can believe that it's possible, maybe, if a little crazy, but how can you be certain about such an off-the-wall idea? Some master criminal somewhere that can find unstable people, groom them, and point them at their intended victim like a gun? It would make a good movie, maybe, if you could get all the twists and turns right."

"Look at the evidence, John. Why did Adler disappear? She hadn't been cut out of the inner circle at the Factory. Nothing was wrong. She went to Los Angeles on the same day. Two unhinged murders in the same week, unexplained, with the same person in place at both of them? Conspiracy theories are already boiling up around the Kennedy shooting, but they're missing the insight that we had over here. If you examine the facts, and you eliminate the impossible, then what remains, however crazy it sounds, has to be true."

The elevator door opened on Billy Name and Ondine in the reception, studiously not looking at each other. Billy's face lit up with a smile when he saw us.

"Oh, hello there, Doc. You got something for us?"

"As always. Something to help Andy feel better, if he's up to it? How's he doing?"

"He's all right. Quiet. More quiet than usual. Working on the edit of a movie for Madame Ondine there."

"New movie, Ondine? What's it about?"

"Wrestling. Women. College."

"Oh, really? You're the star?

"Of course. It's all about me, honey." He lit a cigarette and looked out the window, blowing smoke out of the side of his mouth.

Billy looked at Ondine and decided to change the subject. "Did you hear that that Maurice-fucking-Girodias is publishing that bitch's book? *SCUM Manifesto*. She writes about scum because she is scum, and he's nothing but scum. He's the worst."

"Yeah, I met him. He was horrible. When he spoke, it was like macassar dripping into my ears. Awful."

Ondine didn't respond, just stared out the window flicking his cigarette. Odd. He never missed the opportunity to be catty about someone, especially an enemy.

"Where's Little Joe? I heard he was looking."

"Oh, Doc, you know Joe. He's not actually going to pay you. Maybe a little hustle if you want it. You're better off finding somebody who wants to sleep with him if you need cash. Plenty of those down at the Chelsea. Speaking of—how's the Alphabet, huh? They miss you back there. Especially the landlady. She keeps asking us where her forty-two dollars' back rent is."

"She can hold her breath, the way she treated me when I was there. Okay if we head in and pay our respects to Andy?"

Ondine perked up. "Pay your respects? He's not dead. He's just in there moping, last I saw of him. Not doing anything. Unnerving everyone, like when I first met him. Went to a big old orgy and sat there chain smoking and just watching with that annoying smile on his face. 'Throw that thing out of here, would you?' I said. I wish I could throw him out of here, but he'd probably bleed everywhere."

I was surprised—Ondine wasn't the nicest of the Factory hangers-on, but the tone in his voice could strip rust off of a bumper faster than Coke. I nodded at Sherlock and went around the corner towards the door.

"What are you doing? I just told you to leave him alone. Not now. He's got to finish my movie. Besides, he's a bummer. Away with you. Get out!" Ondine flipped his hand—he thought he was the Queen of England—and shooed us out. "Go find Silver George. He's looking for you." He stood there and watched the elevator doors close behind us.

"Goodness," Sherlock said after we started back down.

I had to laugh. "You're funny, you know that?"

"I wonder what's the matter with her?"

"Got up on the wrong side of the bed this morning? Got dumped? Bad comedown? Hasn't slept for a few days? Ran out of pills before I came back?"

"He's preoccupied in the worst way. It's uncharacteristic. This was... actually mean."

Sherlock—

Congratulations on the living arrangements. Alphabet City. You always did like your letters. And a Doctor. Mother would be proud. Well, on the surface anyway.

If you're looking for a vacation this year, I'd skip Chicago. The heat is worse than the cold.

—Mycroft

BY THE END of August the eyes of the nation were on Chicago. No one had any idea who the Democratic party was going to nominate, with Bobby Kennedy dead and buried and his votes up for grabs, and there were the Yippies threatening to put LSD in the water supply and riots breaking out in the Windy City. The FBI had put out a warning about Black Panthers threatening violent uprising, and no one knew if the war or peace movements were going to prevail.

"What do you think about all this Chicago business, Sherlock?"

"I don't. Who's going to be President won't make even a bit of difference. Politics doesn't have to do with society, or anything that really matters. Johnson hasn't done anything different since Kennedy was shot. You think McCarthy or Humphrey or whoever comes out of Chicago will? Those aren't the real men in power, John. You should know that by now, with the shrapnel in your shoulder and your medical practice focused on servicing the Factory's eclectic needs."

"I saw Andy yesterday. I asked him what he thought about those Yippies and their pranks. They're nominating a pig for President, and they tried to levitate the Pentagon with their minds, but it didn't work. 'Something should have happened.' he said. 'Snowflakes or flashing lights or something. It was unsatisfying, like a story without an ending.' Then he got sidetracked as to how Abbie Hoffman compared him to Castro, like they were the different types of medicine the world might need. 'I never felt so manly.'"

"So what, John? Does any of this matter to the people out on Avenue B, or to Mrs. Hendrix? We're just shuffling the faces of government, the ones who face the music and pay for the sins of those with real power, the faceless, enduring people you don't hear of. You think the elected control things? You don't believe in the creation myth of this country, do you?"

"My god, Sherlock. What's gotten into you?"

He looked at me, then, his eyes flashing with indecision. "I've had a message from my brother Mycroft. Any understanding I have of how power works is because of him. He works for the government. The real one. The one that actually runs thing. He sent me a note congratulating us on our new housing situation. Reminding me that, despite the fact that I never talk to him, he knows where I am, what I'm doing. He supposedly serves law and order, but who watches over him, Watson? No one. It's people like my brother who decides what laws are made and what they mean. He is—he might be—more intelligent than I am. He's certainly more in tune with American values, from his too-big house with its white picket fence in Virginia, but his American values are the only ones that really count."

"You didn't tell him about moving in here? How did he know?"

"I don't talk to him if I can help it. I don't even go home for Christmas. It's meaningless. I'm not a Christian, so why would I celebrate the birth of their god, any more than I would celebrate Hercules Day or the passing of Zeus down from Olympus? No. No, I didn't tell him anything, but he knows anyway. He knows about you."

"What does he know?"

"Doctor, Army captain, that you've been 'treating' a lot of the satellites of Warhol's world. Doesn't seem to mind, at the moment, but that's probably so that he can have something to use to get me to do a 'favor' for him later, or maybe you. That's how they work—they get information on you and then use that to make you do things for them. Mycroft is particularly good at it."

"What kind of things?"

"Well, right now he wants to make sure that we stay away from Chicago and all the people there. He doesn't have the faintest actual understanding about me, really. I have no interest in going to Chicago. That's the kind of thing he cares about. Public relations and perception. Manufacturing complacency and a docile public. I know that something as inconsequential as a Presidential election can't cause them any real problems. I don't know what would, to be honest. Anyway, we're not going to Chicago."

I changed the subject, trying to find a happier mood. "There's a party at the Factory next month. Andy's decided to come out into society again, like a debutante, presented back to his adoring public, or at least the two hundred or so closest of them. He's decided to stop moping."

Sherlock looked up. "I suppose. I'm not sure that the Factory is living up to its reputation. There isn't much in the way of work coming out of it, nor much of interest—ideas and so forth. I get bored, John. So bored. It was all very fun for a while, seeing how that world worked, but now I'm getting tired of navigating all the petty personal politics. It's exhausting, not really challenging. Honestly, if Andy hadn't been shot, we would have drifted away from them when they moved to Union Square."

I didn't know what to say. He was right—it had gotten tiring, having to keep up with all the different factions and Andy's whims—but that's where Sherlock and I had met, and I wondered if *I* hadn't become boring. The target of Sherlock's acidic sense of humor. Boring was the worst thing you could be.

"Oh, for God's sake, I don't mean you, John. You're the best thing that came out of that place. I just mean... it's an interesting idea, a factory where you can manufacture culture out of drugs and the lives of broken people, but there's the persistent influence of money creeping in to it, isn't there? Ever since Adler and the society types came in. The profit motive, maybe. It's always been a little bit about what who could do for you, but now... I think our days there are numbered. We should find something interesting to occupy our time."

three

TURNED AWAY

THE STICKY EDGE came off the heat of summer as August grew into September. The nights cooled off just like the mood of the country once the news stopped showing young people being beaten up. There wasn't any LSD running out of the taps, and Sherlock was right—nothing more lasting than broken bones came out of all that protest in Chicago, even though the politicians on both sides tried to use it to their advantage. Nixon talked about bringing law and order back. Humphrey's victory showed that the Democrats still didn't care about the war, or anything but being elected.

Andy's coming out party rolled around and I brought over a nearly full prescription pad the day before, and left with it nearly empty, Edie's money bulging in my wallet.

When we showed up for the party, Paul was out front. He made a show of shuffling through the paper on his clipboard twice.

"Sorry, Doc, but you're not on the list. It's intimate tonight. I think if we had a few more you'd be fine, but Andy said he didn't want anyone coming in."

"Really, Paul?" I was at a loss for words. "I saw Andy yesterday, remember? He said he'd see me tonight."

Paul pointed at the list and shrugged.

"Come on, Doc, let's go to that party in Hell's Kitchen."

Sherlock to the rescue. I was stunned. I'd been to all the Warhol parties, even the most exclusive ones. I had a standing invite to dinners at Max's, and usually didn't pay, even though we drank more than we ate. I knew I wasn't 'cast out,' because Andy had actually been friendly with me the day before. He was getting more and more reclusive. I guess he was a target now that he was so famous, so recognizable. They were talking about him everywhere, and you couldn't blame him for being afraid after being shot.

We stood outside in the cooling evening air, wondering where we should go.

"Don't look now, John, but we're being watched." Sherlock took out his tobacco and papers and rolled cigarettes for both of us, leaning over to light mine with his match. "It's hard to see, but I think it's Ondine over in the square, see there on the bench next to the subway entrance? Just the perfect spot to see who comes and goes into the Factory. I think he was writing in a notebook."

"It is him. He's staring at us like a dog looking at an open can of dog food. Like he's panting. What the hell is he doing over there?"

Sherlock smoked for a moment, looking at me. "Let's actually go to Hell's Kitchen. I have a little game I'd like to play: you point out people to me and I'll tell you what their story is. I want to stretch my brain out a little. You know, when you have a problem turning around in your head and you gnaw on it, worry at it, and then when you *stop* thinking about it, the solution comes to you? I need distraction. Come along. Let's go and see what we can shake out from the hidden corners of my mind."

I didn't know what to say to that. I was partly devastated. I felt lost and adrift, cut off from anything, except Sherlock, and he was... not what I wanted right then. "No, Holmes, I'm... I'm going to go home, I think. I'm suddenly very tired."

He looked at me for a full minute, then nodded, and turned and walked away.

*   *   *

I watched Sherlock walk across the street and over to the subway station, wondering if I'd done the right thing. Should I have gone with him? I could just about catch him, probably, if I ran now.

"Excuse me, Dr. Watson. Forgive the intrusion."

A tall man, taller than Sherlock even, with a loud rumpled yellow plaid jacket under a London Fog overcoat. He reeked of cigarettes and yellow nicotine stains vied with the blotches of ink on his hands.

"Call me Doc, please. What can I help you with?"

"My name is Richard Wellsley. I'm with *Collins* magazine. You're familiar with it? Good. I was down here, trying to get in to see Andy or someone from the Factory at Max's, hoping to do an interview with someone about Valerie Solanas, and the Factory and Warhol, and all of that, but no one would talk to me. They said Andy wanted to put all that behind him. I was sitting there wondering who I could talk to, and then I looked up and recognized you. You spoke at Solanas's arraignment, didn't you?"

I laughed. "I did. She said she wanted me as her doctor, if you can believe it. She told me that Holmes and I were just about the only men she almost trusted."

"Could we set up some time for an interview?"

I didn't know what to think. *Collins* wasn't your regular magazine. It was widely read, but also insightful. Not quite the *New Yorker*, but deep, thoughtful, and well-regarded. Still, I was wary. I didn't really want to spend my time talking to someone who would go on and twist my words. Sometimes people didn't get what I had to say—I had to explain it in a different way for them—and no matter how good a magazine, the writers were after a story; and maybe not the story I had to tell. This is also how I got started, being more famous as a writer than a doctor.

I had notes, where I wrote down most of what happened around the time of the shooting. Sherlock was raving, locked away in our bedroom, and between caring for him I had a lot of downtime. I'd tried to get all of what he talked about straight in my head, piecing together what I could from the nights around the Blue-induced haze and the shock of Andy's shooting. The story was convoluted and I wanted it straight, laid out on paper. I'd almost got it straight, I thought. I wouldn't really know if it sounded crazy unless I wrote it out.

"There is a story in it. It sounds crazy, though. I don't really want to do an interview. It's complicated. Convoluted. I'm not sure I could explain it, but I could write it for you, maybe? My friend Holmes and I knew Solanas, talked to her a lot right before she got the gun. I've been writing it down, trying to make sense of it. What if I finish it and then you could polish it up if it's not fit to print?"

He looked right through my flimsy excuses with his unlit cigarette hanging out of the corner of his mouth. "So you wanna be a writer, eh? All right. Writing's tougher than you'd think, you know, but we can start with that. We'll have to share the byline, but I haven't got any other leads and this story's going to go cold. Think you could get me something by next Thursday?"

I thought about my journal and the unlikely hero that shared my bed, just waiting to be typed up, with a few excisions.

"Sure, I can do that."

"It's just that, see, if I can get it by Thursday I'll have time to read it, see if I need to work on it on the weekend. If you can't do it by then, I can still get that interview, right? I know there's a story. I'm happy to share the byline with you, but I want the inside scoop."

"No problem."

four

A FAVOR, AND A CASE

Oh Sherlock—
Nice article. Sounds like you're having an
exciting life up there with Dr. Watson.
—Mycroft

THE LESS SAID about that winter the better. It was cold, and long. It took me a few weeks to write up the story, and then it went back and forth with Richard and the editors. Richard had liked it well enough, said it just needed a polish, but they were waiting for the trial to go to print. Or, as it turned out, a slow news week.

"Good morning, John. Or should I say good afternoon?"

I woke up, bleary-eyed in the cold March light, to Sherlock standing over me with a smile on his face; a smile that had less warmth in it than the wintry sun outside. It was practically cruel.

"What's this here? I wasn't aware that you'd gotten a job at one of the nation's more prestigious journals. Congratulations."

When he was angry he got excited. This was something else. Something that made me feel small, like a child who'd walked in on his parents making it. He was waving a folded-up copy of *Collins* with Valerie's picture on the front. I'd almost forgotten about the article. The trial wasn't for months, but for some reason they'd decided to run the feature. At least I'd get paid now.

"I don't have a job, Sherlock. I just wrote up what happened with Solanas. I thought it was an interesting story, and one that nobody else would tell. Or *could* tell. What's wrong? I didn't put in any of the stuff about the Blue Beauties or you and me. Just enough to suggest that there was more to the murder than Sirhan Sirhan, that you were trying to figure out who would believe you if you called the FBI or the LAPD, or someone who might believe you. I was there. It happened. Just because we were high doesn't mean that everyone shouldn't know how brilliant you are." I laughed, it was so preposterous. "You figured out something even the FBI doesn't know, and you were high. That's the story that should be told."

"No, John, I'm not talking about that. I don't care about fame, real or imagined. That's not the problem. You just made it all sound glamorous, like I'm some kind of magician. You didn't talk about how simple it was. It was fascinating, but you didn't simply write about the patterns that are all right there in front of our eyes. The mud on Valerie's clothes. The clear and obvious signs of coercion. The easy availability of guns. Adler's inexplicable movements. Anyone could have figured it out; they just didn't pay attention. But you make it sound like... a novel or something. I look like an idiot."

"You don't, Sherlock. Really. But it's cool, what you do, man."

"Then why can't you just focus on the facts? I heard Girodias was a problem, so I went and talked to him. I was able to see that he was a power-hungry, money-grubbing bastard. I could see what Solanas was, how she was selling herself and devoting energy to running scams for money. Her life was just affected by a specific range of problems: cash, money, talent, and abuse. If you can put those things together, you can easily triangulate where the stresses were coming from and find out who was trying to use her as a puppet. It was really straightforward. She wasn't anything like what you've written. Focus on what matters, John, not the... speculation about emotions. Or leave me out of your new writing career."

I snatched the magazine. "You can be a real bastard sometimes, you know that? I was just trying to be nice, and I think you come off really well in the piece. I worked on that, even when the editor wanted to cut some of it out. It was important to me."

"Well, maybe you should have some other priority."

He turned to the window and picked up his brown, smoky tobacco, rolling a cigarette without looking at it and staring out the window.

"Fine. I've got to be at Max's at eight if you want to come."

I went downstairs for a glass of water, and sat, looking out of the kitchen window. I hated it when he got like this. We smoked cigarette after cigarette like that, one atop the other, until around 7, when we silently got ready to go.

"EXCUSE ME, MR. Holmes, Dr. Watson? Have you got a few minutes?"

Sherlock looked at me and glanced at the door. "Of course, Mrs. Hendrix. How can we help?"

"Well, you remember when you stomped through with muddy shoes the other day, and made such a mess and a racket during the morning rush, and said you owed us a favor?"

I don't know if Sherlock remembered any of this, but I certainly did. I thought she was going to throw us out, and I'd had to take hold of my high and force myself straight. "We did. I'm really sorry. It was... Holmes here was sick. Really sick.

Mrs. Hendrix fidgeted for a few minutes. "Look, this is a little strange, but have you heard about those Black Panthers up in Harlem?"

"Sure, I've heard about them," I said. "They're in the papers all the time. They've been having shoot-outs with police in Oakland and Chicago and they're loud and they shout about killing the white man and overthrow the government and everything. They say they're activists, but it seems to me that they're just thugs with guns, ruining the civil rights struggle for reasonable people."

Mrs. Hendrix looked at me, then at Sherlock. A look passed between them that left me completely out of the loop. Not for the first time.

"John, please, don't. Mrs. Hendrix. What can we do for you?"

Mrs. Hendrix looked at me and I missed the warmth in her gaze. "It's my nephew. You know Joseph—works down here sometimes."

"I do. He's a good boy. He went out and got pizza slices for us the other day, and wouldn't take any money. I had to force him to let us pay for his."

"That's Joseph. Always has time to help people out. He can be a little hot-headed, but my sister and me, we kept him away from gangs and all that. He's bright. Very bright. Too bright for school and everything. Can't stay focused, always looking out the window, wanting to read his own books. Not inspired by school, you know."

"I do know. I don't think that either Dr. Watson or I had good experiences with traditional schooling."

"Joseph's supposed to be learning a trade. My sister asked me if I could take him on, teach him a few things, but he was always more interested in other stuff. Typical young man. Girls. Music. Lord knows. Plus, he's all the way up in Harlem. He's so far uptown he's past uptown. Don't want to spend an hour getting all the way down here all the time. No jobs up there, though.

"Anyway, now she says she found one of them Panther newspapers in his room. Out of her mind with worry. All you hear on the news is like Dr. Watson says. Gunfights with the police. California, Chicago, probably here in New York next.

Seems like anywhere black folks try to organize themselves, there ends up some kinds of trouble. He been coming home late, leaving real early. Was supposed to come in and work today, but he never showed up. Do you think you could go up there, have a look around, see if he's getting in any kind of trouble with those Panthers? Find out what's going on?"

Sherlock looked at her, at the pleading in her eyes. "Why would you want us to do that? Isn't there someone else you could talk to? We don't exactly fit in in Harlem, Mrs. Hendrix."

"I know. My sister and I can't go up there. Mothers and aunties chasing after their boys. Wouldn't be right. We'd be taking away his manhood. I read this thing Doc wrote about you in *Collins*. Thought you might notice something if you talked to the Panthers. See if they look like the type to be fighting. If you do talk to Joseph, he might listen to you. Hasn't got a man around the house since the police knocked his daddy round his head for being in the wrong place at the wrong time, then arrested him. Here, let me give you my sister's address. I'll let her know to expect you."

Sherlock looked at me. I shrugged, trying to tell him no. No, please, no.

"I'm not sure when we'll make it up there—sometime in the next few days, I guess. I'll see how long our errands take today but we'll see what we can see. I can't make any promises."

"Even if you just go have a look it'll be a big relief to me."

I WAS BOILING over with anger that Sherlock had agreed to go to Harlem. First, he shouted at me about telling the world about his genius, and now he was dragging us uptown on a fool's errand likely to get us robbed, shot, or worse. I had to get into the right kind of light-hearted mood for spending time with the Factory hangers-on.

We walked in silence over to Max's. Andy waved us over

and then we were forgotten as soon as people shuffled to make space for us. We were at the end by Ingrid, who harangued us with her stories of her epic poetry reading a few nights before.

I watched Andy suck down a white cross with his coffee. He didn't even nod back at me. I knew he'd been in hospital again for some follow-up surgery, but he wasn't going to talk to me about it.

Ingrid's voice was grating. "Oh, and did you hear, Viva's writing a book? It's supposed to be a surprise tell-all, but she keeps calling everyone to get their secrets, but she got all wired and told Andy she was recording her calls. Says she's publishing as fiction so we can't sue her. I told her it could be an art project, a comment on the falling value of conversations, making a book factory out of her phone calls, the rest of the book is essentially manufactured but she can't see how that would work. She's lost it since she went to Paris. Trying to scam some money out of us. Oh, and did you hear about poor Candy Darling? Beaten out by Raquel Welch, of all people, for this movie, and you want to know why? They said Raquel-goddamn-Welch would make a better transvestite than our very own Candy Darling. Isn't it just not right? Hey, Doc, you haven't got a pick-me-up, do you?"

I looked at Sherlock and he flicked his eyes at Andy, and then at Ingrid. I had never realized I could be so stupid. "Sure thing, darling. Here you go." I palmed her a white cross and stood up. "We have to go, um, to another meeting. Sherlock's..."

"I'm giving someone a hand. An investigation."

"Like Perry Mason? I used to love watching that as a kid, when my dad wasn't home. 'I don't like people who prey on other people's weaknesses.'"

"Not... quite... Oh, God, John, look at the time. Will you excuse us?"

I had to hold my face straight, half from anger at both the Factory two-faces and Sherlock, half trying to keep from laughing at Ingrid. People who don't know their place in the world. Ingrid and us, being flung out of the orbit of the sun like a dirty rock in space.

"WHAT DID I tell you? Nothing but petty politics and recycling the same old camp stories." Sherlock walked over to a phone booth and pulled up the yellow pages. "We could go up to Harlem, get our favor to Mrs. Hendrix out of the way? I'm sure there are baked goods in it for us."

"What the hell, Sherlock? Couple of white boys in Harlem? We can't go up there. Not on our own. We'll be arrested by the cops for looking for cocaine or horse. That's if we're lucky. Most likely we'll be beaten up or stabbed. Why would you agree to that, at least without asking me?"

"You're clean now, aren't you, John? Dropped everything off with the boring artsy elite? Come on. It's daytime. We'll be fine."

I didn't want to go to Harlem. I mean, sure, I was glad the blacks had made strides, with Martin Luther King and all that stuff. I didn't want to see any more riots and beatings on the television. It was just terrible what had gone on down south, in Alabama and Arkansas. Those peaceful marchers and the little girls. Those people were a thousand miles away from Harlem, though. Harlem had its own problems. Knives. Guns. Gangs. I knew. I'd seen it with my own two eyes.

WHEN MY PAPERS came through and my tour finally finished and I came home from the war, I didn't have any place to go, really. My parents died before I finished college and joined the Army to pay for medical school. The ETS interview officer asked if New York was still my home of record, so I said, "Sure, sure it is."

I had just finished at CUNY back in 1962 when my number came up. I had good enough grades and an acceptance to med school. Turned out my parents were just about broke once the funeral home and the lawyers all had their cut. Dying is surprisingly expensive. I had just enough left over to pay for my undergrad degree fees. That's when the letter came. I could defer if I was studying, but I couldn't afford even a single day.

I had two dollars in my pocket and I put them down on a pint of whiskey and a pack of smokes and sat up, drinking coffee with whiskey in it and smoking cigarettes, trying to think of what I could do.

I scrubbed up the next morning, put on a white shirt and a tie and took my jittery, half drunk self on down to Whitehall Street, a month before the date on the letter in my back pocket. I had my degree and my transcripts in my hand. I asked the sergeant if the Army would put me through medical school in exchange for service putting together the kids blown up over in Vietnam.

He said he sure thought they might be interested in that. Brought me upstairs and sat me on a bench.

I SPENT THE next eight weeks crawling through mud and being shouted at by men who had to call me 'sir' and who didn't really care how many push-ups I could do, and then I was in Bethesda for my accelerated battlefield surgery training.

I don't know what most doctors go through—all the time I've spent with doctors has been up to my elbows inside of bodies that have been blown up, shot, or burned—but my residency was spent in blistering, steaming heat looking at men who had been burnt to a crisp by white phosphorous and napalm. Weapons that Charlie didn't have.

I got my full medical license in a Quonset hut handed over by the CO. The incoming alert went off before he could even pour me a drink, and I shoved the certificate in my pocket as I went off to get scrubbed up. Two years of blood-spatter later and I got off the bus at the Port Authority with twenty-five dollars and that crumpled-up medical license in my pocket.

I didn't have anywhere to go and I didn't care about anywhere except that it be not Vietnam. I wanted a slice of pizza, an icy grey cold winter and a bottomless cup of real coffee and that was it. I didn't have any change for the subway and I was tired of being cooped up after the bus, so I turned my feet south and walked down the long blocks of Seventh Avenue towards the YMCA.

"I'm sorry, sir, but we're all full up. Hold on, let me call around and see if there's a bed at another Y."

New York looked pretty much the same in May of 1967 as it did in 1962. Dirty, like the leachate dripping from the bottom of a dumpster. Flashing lights. Longer hair on the men. Brighter colors. Mostly, though, just the same yellow cabs and bright lights and people walking fast, more important than you were, to get where they were going.

"Okay, here we go. I called around and the only place there's a bed tonight is at the Y in Harlem. You can take the A-C-E train or the 2-3 up to 135th Street and it's between the two stops, right on 135th Street."

"Harlem? I can't go to Harlem."

"Oh, honey, we integrated all the YMCAs this year. It's all right. If you want a bed at a Y that's your best bet. Plenty of hotels around if you want to spend your money on that."

She turned back to her crossword and I didn't have much choice but to put my bag on my shoulder and go find a hot breakfast that would leave me with two dimes for the subway and 135th Street.

"Reds, whites, horse, whatever you need, young man, I got."

I knew negroes in Vietnam, but this was a different kind of

jungle. It was dark and terrifying. Garbage was spilling out of the cans on the street. People were out and walking all around but aimlessly, like they didn't have anywhere to go. It was late, and I was the only white person in sight. A lifetime lived in New York—I wasn't counting my time in country—and I'd never, ever set foot in Harlem.

I knew colored people, sure. We had negro porters at school and a couple of nurses in Vietnam, and I'd heard of a good surgeon from another unit. I was friendly with the people that worked the dining halls at CUNY. But Harlem was something I hadn't ever experienced. Everything was loud. There were men sitting on stoops and women walking around and everyone was talking as though they all knew each other, like the street was their living room. They shouted across the street at each other and said all kinds of incomprehensible things.

I wasn't a racist—I signed a petition supporting the Civil Rights Act in Vietnam, and I thought that Martin Luther King was right about just about everything. It wasn't fair that blacks and whites had separate schools, not to mention all the lunch counters and all that. Still, I wasn't exactly comfortable in this situation.

I'd walked forward like I knew where I was and where I was going, heading for the corner to turn on to... what street was that, 133rd? I couldn't see the sign in the dark. I couldn't tell any of the men on the street's faces apart without more light. Were the streets darker here? A man in a red sweatshirt, too warm for the April night, walked up to me, and started talking.

"Hey, man, I'm talking to you. I know you're only up here for one of two things. You either want brown sugar or some color, brown, white, or red, so tell me what you need."

"I'm fine, thanks. Just fine."

"Man, look, don't get me wrong. I don't mean nothing, but you got a look about you. You looking for some good soul food, maybe? Come on, man, I'm just trying to help you out."

I turned onto the street, trying to get a glance from the corner of my eye. Damn, I thought, that's 134th Street. I've got to go up another street with this guy following me.

"I don't need anything, thanks. I'm just going up here."

"Up where, man? I can show you. I know where you should walk, and where you shouldn't, know what I mean? It ain't safe up here for honkeys. Not safe at all. Might need some protection, know what I mean?"

"I made it through Vietnam. I think I'll survive walking a few blocks in New York City, buddy." I know I should have just ignored him, but his chattering just got to me. It just made it worse. Now he knew that he'd got me talking.

"Think so, huh? Different kind of jungle up here. You been killing the yellow man, maybe the black man don't appreciate that, you know what I'm saying? Maybe the yellow man, the red man, the black and the brown man, maybe we all got to stand together, huh?"

People were watching, now. I knew I'd draw stares, my white face standing out, but his constant shouting made me the center of attention, and I was bone weary and just wanted to get some sleep. "What do you *want*?" I asked him. "I just want to walk down the street without being harassed."

"Brother, I'm just trying to keep you safe. You want to walk down that street you best turn around and go down them subway steps, take the train downtown or out to Queens. Only one reason for you to be up here, and that's to participate in the local economy. Contribute to our economic activity. See? I ain't stupid, just because I be using words like 'ain't.' Now, you looking for something I can help you find it, otherwise, you might become a less willing participant in the economy, you know what I'm saying?"

I didn't like the way he was talking. Worse was the attention I was getting. It wasn't just stares, but I could swear that at least one person was following us as we walked down the street. I couldn't turn and look, though, because I didn't want to look like some racist honky. I wasn't. I mostly didn't want to get shot.

I picked up my pace, slinging my duffel bag full of stuff I didn't want over my shoulder. Uniforms. Ribbons, Paperwork. My medical degree. Everything I owned, and most of it was from the damn Army.

"Oh, you got some step in you, ain't you? Maybe you got some good fighting moves, too. That's what's going to protect you, huh?"

I saw two beat cops ahead of me. I've never been a friend to the police, but I'd never seen a sight that made me so relieved. It was like the weight of the street was off of me, except this guy who would not shut up.

"Hey there, something bothering you, friend?" The dulcet tones of Brooklyn were never more welcoming to me than now.

"No, I'm okay, officer, but..."

Before I could even answer the man had his arm behind his back and his face against the brownstone on my right. One of the cops was patting him down while the other one was holding him in a way that, I knew from basic anatomy, could dislocate his shoulder in a second.

"Can't leave well enough alone, can you, boy? You gotta get up in everyone's face. Shooting your mouth off. Well, you listen to me, son. You got no reason to be chasing people up the street."

I'd never seen someone roughed up like that by the police, but I figured they were the beat cops up here, they must know the neighborhood. It must've been a pretty bad character that was following me. I nodded to the officers and turned to go.

"Now just wait a minute there, you. Stick around. Don't go anywhere."

I stopped and turned around—yes, he was talking to me. I stopped and waited, the habit of taking orders from people in uniform, while he shouted at and berated the man. It was awful—he kept calling him all kinds of mean things—but I was torn between thankfulness that I didn't have to put up with him any longer and discomfort at how the guy was being treated.

"Now you run along, boy. Get out of here and stay out of other people's business. Now you—what on earth would have you up here anyway? Boy there says you're looking to buy drugs. That what you doing? You don't want to be doing that. Look at this place. Trash everywhere. They won't even respect themselves, so why you expect them to respect you? Well? What are you doing up here?"

"Why is it any business of yours? I'm not suspected of a crime, am I? Has one been committed?"

"Don't you get fresh with us. There ain't no reason for you to be up here. We just stopped this guy from jumping you."

"Really? On a crowded street? Come on."

"You'd better get a civil tongue in your mouth before we—"

His partner put a hand on his shoulder. "Look, buddy, we're just trying to watch out for you. Just tell us where you're going, huh?"

I was tired and I just wanted to get some food and some sleep and make some kind of life tomorrow.

"I'm headed to the Y. I got off a bus at the Port Authority a couple of hours ago and this is the only place I can get a cheap bed for the night. That okay with you, officers?"

It wasn't good luck in the end that the two pigs had turned up. When I woke up the next morning my bags had been gone through and I was missing my captain's bars and twenty dollars. I was down to a buck fifty seven and I didn't have a job or even an actual address to get a job on.

"Here's the address. Should be up by 135th Street."

I sighed. I made it out of Harlem that time, and I was still here. "All right, but let's take the 2-3."

"The A-C-E would be faster."

"Yeah, but I don't want to go up that way. I don't want to come out by the park."

five
RACE WAR

THERE WAS A sheet of black-painted plywood over one of the windows at the Black Panther office. Sherlock pointed out broken glass glinting in the corner. "That window's been broken, but someone's swept up the street outside. Just a few pieces of broken glass there."

The bustling office fell into a dead silence when we walked in the door. Two dozen black faces stopped dead and looked up at us as one. Staring. It was terrifying. It was like a needle had been ripped off a record just as we walked in, and their attention was focused directly on us.

No one said a thing. They just stared. People had watched us since we got off the subway, but it wasn't as obvious as this. We could feel every eye on the back of our necks. These stares were direct and shameless, demanding to know what we were doing there without saying a word.

"Hi," I tried, trying to sound casual. My voice may have squeaked a bit, under those stares.

"We, um, that is, we're looking for Joseph Hendrix. For a friend. His aunt. Down in Alphabet City. Is he here? Can we talk to him?"

The group exchanged looks, and then a man with a voice like gravel spoke up. "Can't help you with that."

Sherlock stepped in and tried to get us into trouble.

"Do you want to start a race war?"

I had to stop myself from running out the door. I stared, mouth agape.

"Man, are you for real? What are you talking about?"

"That's what they say in the papers. You're trying to start a race war. You've armed yourselves, your groups are getting into shootouts with the police in Oakland and ending up with burnt-out offices everywhere. We thought we'd come uptown and see what the truth was. So tell us: do you want a race war?"

The self-appointed spokesman's face fell. "Man, we want the same thing every black man wants. Yellow, white, red man and brown man, too. We want equality. A decent place to live. Decent food to eat. Jobs. An end to the random oppression of our people. We want to protect our children from the police, who are supposed to protect them but manage to be their biggest threat. We respect Dr. King, may he rest in peace, but we also take on the teachings of Brother Malcolm X, that we must defend ourselves and our rights by any means necessary. We don't need any more brothers blown up or shot, and we're tired of waiting on jobs and education, and getting stopped and beat up for no reason at all."

"Why the guns, then? Why not a policy of nonviolence, like Martin Luther King or Gandhi?"

"Man, they been trying that since the end of the war. Know what we got? Plessy v. Ferguson. Separate but equal. Jim Crow laws. Little girls blown up going to church. Southern eyes looking at strange fruit. We got the Civil Rights act now; Dr. King paid for it with his blood, for all the good that it does. We respect nonviolence, but we prepare for violence. Violence that we did not start, and that our bodies have borne for centuries. We will have our rights by any means necessary. We sharpen the mind as well as the sword. We know our rights, every woman and man here studies the law. We're studying and educating ourselves, because we have been denied these things in the past. Law. History. We frighten you because we have guns, books, and the mind to use each of them."

It went on like this for a while—Sherlock arguing, digging into the practicality of what they were doing, what they wanted to do. I had to admit that it actually sounded much more reasonable than I expected, even if I was still frightened, all these men in their makeshift uniforms with guns right there on the wall. Their stone cold faces were dark and betrayed no emotion. They were talking about providing free breakfast and health clinics, social services for the most needy that the City wouldn't provide. I didn't see a junkie in sight. Guns a-plenty, but no dope. Something was different.

Sherlock enjoyed himself, as he bantered with the Black Panthers. I was scared the whole time that one of the men would pick up his guns and fill us full of holes. I lost track of time until Sherlock was satisfied with his queries. We left, eventually, with flyers about the Ten Point Program and a self-printed *Black Panther* newspaper.

WE WALKED BACK in silence, Sherlock smiling with a bemused look on his face, the *Panther* newspaper folded under his arm. I was still angry but banked my fire—I didn't want to call any more attention to ourselves than we already had, just by the color of our faces. I couldn't believe that he'd just go up and have an argument with a bunch of men with guns, who insisted they'd go after their rights by violence if necessary. One of their leaders had been shot in a gun battle with the police just days after King was killed.

I couldn't hold it in any longer. I kept my voice low.

"What on Earth were you doing, Sherlock?"

"What do you mean, John?"

"We went up there to talk about Mrs. Hendrix's nephew. You wanted to debate morality and politics."

"No, John, I went up there to see what I could about these Black Panthers, and partly as a favor to Mrs. Hendrix to see if I could find out anything about her nephew. I didn't think that I would be of much use getting information out of that group, so I thought that I would have a discussion with them, which should tell us—or Mrs. Hendrix—if she should be worried.

"Here's what I observed, John. I observed some type of sergeant-at-arms keeping watch over the guns that were so prominently displayed on the walls, even when every other person crowded around the honkeys in the front who came to argue with them. I could see that those guns gleamed. They were cleaned, oiled, and polished. Well taken care of. None of the serial numbers were filed off, as you'd expect if they were being used in crimes. We didn't get very close, but although the weapons weren't all the same—it's obvious that they bought what they could rather than equipping an army with matching weapons—the barrels hadn't been swapped to confuse rifling or anything. Military bearing on the leadership, John. I'd have expected you to notice that.

"Remember when we walked in the door? There were teams of people who knew how to work together, all focused on their tasks. Compare it with the Factory. This was a disciplined enterprise. An actual factory. Not a gang flophouse. I don't understand this, John. It isn't like you. This outburst is strange. You're normally very open-minded."

"I'm not a racist, Sherlock. Of course I want equal rights for everyone. I stitched up black, white, and yellow men in country. Not because I thought yellow men were evil, like they told me in training."

I stomped along for a few minutes while Sherlock walked in silence. "I got robbed in Harlem the night I came back from Vietnam."

"Not by these people, John. You have got to separate the individual from the class. They are no more responsible for

334

your misfortune than you or I are responsible for blowing up that church and killing those four girls in Alabama. Possibly less so, come to think of it. Hmm."

Sherlock pulled out his notebook and scribbled a few notes. It was maddening, but he had a point, I supposed. I just didn't see why they had to have all those guns.

"DID YOU SEE Joseph?" Mrs. Hendrix looked worried, still.

I looked at her and she saw the answer in my face. "You haven't heard from him either, ma'am?"

She shook her head, looking down at her spotless apron and muttering to herself.

"Sorry, Mrs. Hendrix. He wasn't there. We talked to them at length about their programs." I looked at Sherlock. "And their guns."

"The way they talk on the television. So angry! I don't know why they have to be like that. Militant."

Sherlock didn't agree. "They are their own army, Mrs. Hendrix. In their eyes, they have to be the army, the police, the hospitals and schools for the community, because the world they were born into has completely failed them."

Sherlock held out the papers they'd given us. A newspaper and some handbills, one of which listed the ten-point program that the Black Panther Party for Self Defense put as their demands.

Mrs. Hendrix sighed. "You know how it is. We colored people have to fit in somehow. You don't never know what's going to happen. You don't know what it's like. People look at you, know they're better than you, even if they're not. Invisible when you want to be seen, and standing out when someone's looking for whoever done something wrong." She shifted through the papers, at a loss for words. Sherlock pointed to the newspaper.

"Here's what we did see, Mrs. Hendrix. The news shows us the Black Panthers using their guns and rioting in the streets;

or, as I've noticed, more often give the police an interview in front of the shot-up, burnt-out shop fronts. What we saw was organization. Stacks of literature. Writers writing. A very civil argument about the place of women in the Party—many of the women weren't satisfied making coffee, but wanted to be on the front lines.

"Guns, yes. All in a rack, with one person standing guard. I asked about the guns and was informed that they were there for their own self-defense. That the police had come after them and that they were issued arms as part of a regulated militia—all in keeping with the aims of the Second Amendment. I don't think the pigs—sorry, the police—see it that way, of course.

"They claim a few things: that they have a zero tolerance policy for drugs; that the guns are only issued as needed, for official business; that everyone is given comprehensive weapons training; that their guns only ever go out fully loaded. I don't know about any of that, but they certainly had clear rules on how and where weapons could be carried openly, specifically visible at all times, without a round in the chamber, and not pointed at anyone. They even quoted the section number and actual text of each law. It was impressive."

"So what about Joseph?"

Sherlock turned to go, and stopped at the door. "I don't know what to tell you, Mrs. Hendrix. The people I saw don't match what J. Edgar Hoover or the *New York Times* headlines say about the Black Panthers. I don't think that your nephew is safe, exactly, but I wouldn't say that it's the Black Panthers that are a threat to him. He only suffers from the circumstances of his birth." His face looked troubled, like he wasn't sure what to say next. "There was something about one of them..." He shook his head. "Something just wasn't quite right, but I can't put my finger on it.

"We'll keep looking. I'm interested in these Black Panthers."

six

THE FIRST REAL CASE

MRS. HENDRIX KNOCKED on the door the next morning, late, and Sherlock answered it, disgustingly alert for the hour. "Excuse me, Mr. Holmes? I thought you might want some coffee and these leftover rolls from yesterday. There's a bean pie in there, too, if you're interested. Someone came in asking for you. I didn't know what to do, so I took his name and number. I hope that's all right."

"Did he say what it was about?"

"Didn't say. Just seemed... upset about something."

"Tell me everything you can recall about him."

"White fella. Not too many white folks come in to the bakery, you know. They like to buy from whites. He looked around for a while, looked at the pies and the rolls, and then he asked if this was the bakery that Sherlock Holmes worked out of. I was so surprised, you know, at him pulling your name out of the hat. I thought at first he might be the Health Department or something. Dressed normal. Not too pressed. I don't think he was rich. Tweed jacket. Bow tie. Not poor, but not rich or stuffy."

"John! Do you hear our Mrs. Hendrix here? She's a marvel. You, Mrs. Hendrix, might be the most observant person I've ever met except myself. Please, come in and sit down."

"No, no, I don't have time. There's a pile of dough proofing and I've got to make three birthday cakes and a whole mess of cupcakes. He was—oh, I don't know—middle height, brown hair, a little greasy. Needed a cut. Seemed nice enough. Didn't sound like a New Yorker."

"Sorry. I know you need to go. Why did you say he seemed like he was upset about something? What did he do, exactly?"

"Well, he was nervous, like he felt like he didn't belong. That was normal. Then when he was talking it was like he didn't want to talk to me. Like he'd made up his mind he could talk to you but didn't want to bring anyone else into it."

Sherlock raised his voice slightly, irritated. "But what did he *do*, Mrs. Hendrix? What was it he did that made you think those things? Please."

"Oh, okay. Well, he was wringing his hands, kept putting them together then apart. Tapping on the glass, and talking to himself when he was looking at the other stuff in there. That's why I thought he might be from the Health Department. Like he was quoting regulations or something, trying to find some reason to fine me or shut me down. He kept stopping, then starting to say something else, once he started to ask for you. I can't remember all what, now. There's the number. You give him a call, now, and let me go make some bread."

Sherlock looked at the note, scrawled on one of the white bags used in the bakery. He took it over to the window, turning it this way and that in the light. "Damn, I wish he'd just left it on the counter. I can't tell which of these creases are hers and which are his. Well, he's obviously left-handed, and in a rush. See where the ink is smudged there? Even with a ball-point pen it takes a bit of time to dry. Lefties have to curl their hands around but if they're in a hurry they'll smudge the ink. He's nervous—his writing is inconsistent."

I was awake, but in my skivvies, so I'd just listened behind the door to Mrs. Hendrix's description. I couldn't make heads or tails of what Sherlock was doing. "What's going on, darling?"

He looked at me, annoyance flashing across his face just for a moment. He was excited. As excited as I'd seen him, since we'd met Valerie.

"It's something interesting, John. A puzzle. Something to distract us now that the Factory people have turned boring and I'm limiting my intake of your delightful tablets, as you recall. So. Want to find out what this is about? It's most probably some simple, ridiculous story, but maybe it'll keep us occupied for a few hours. Let's find out, see what we can see."

Sherlock—
   Harlem! My, my! Best to keep a clear picture of who your friends are. You never know who you can trust.

—Mycroft

SHERLOCK PRACTICALLY BUZZED with excitement as we went down to the phone on the corner to make the call. He was wired. The phone booth was missing several of its Plexiglass panes, and the ones that remained were gouged with unreadable graffiti.

"What do you think, John? Should we get our own telephone? Mrs. Hendrix needs hers and we can't keep coming down to the corner. First of all, I only have so many dimes, and second, some of the youngsters in the neighborhood seem to have nothing better to do than to smash the booth up and tear the receiver from its mooring." He picked up the receiver and dialed.

"Oh, hello there, is that 'Bill'? This is Sherlock Holmes calling. You left a message for us at the bakery on Avenue B? Yes. Yes, I understand. All right. Sure. In an hour? Not a problem. There's an all-day breakfast place just down the street from the Chelsea. Oh, you know it? Great. In an hour or so, then? All right. See you there."

The remnants of the aluminum door shrieked as Sherlock pulled it open. "He wants to meet."

"Near the Chelsea. I heard. We'll have to hurry if you want to get there in time."

BILL WAS MEDIUM height, thin, with wavy brown hair and sallow skin. About as nondescript as they come, but that didn't stop Sherlock.

"Bill? Hello. Sherlock. Is it mathematics or physics? I can't quite tell, but I'm sure it's one. This is my friend and... colleague, Dr. Watson. I presume it's Dr. Bill, but you're not bothered by titles. What seems to be the problem? Anti-war activities spilling over into your personal life? You may have some reminiscing to do with my friend Dr. Watson here, about Vietnam. Lost your notebook? I suppose your friend in the bathroom hasn't taken it?"

'Bill' looked up at Sherlock with his mouth open for a full five seconds.

"Mind if we sit?" I asked. "I could really go for a cup of coffee. Don't bother about him. That's what he does. He'll explain it all away in a minute."

Sherlock's eyes flashed and his brow wrinkled as he looked at me. If I didn't know him I would swear that he was angry, but the storm disappeared from his face almost as quickly as it had brewed.

"It's pretty straightforward, really. You're a professor—I could hear your voice hitch when you said 'Bill' to me when I called. You'd started to say 'Doctor' but caught yourself. The silence was a little embarrassing to you as you moved on to Bill. You weren't hiding your identity, though, just trying to avoid casual familiarity. Your hands and jacket sleeves are smudged, but with graphite, not with ink. Pencils, of course, are the tools of the academic, physics and mathematics specifically, assuming you aren't using your doctorate to teach elementary school. So much writing and rewriting; only, eventually, going over the work in ink when it's finalized. You've got a peace pin on, so I suspect that you're involved in the anti-war initiative, and you have a pencil out that you've been fidgeting with, and you keep reaching to your breast pocket, like you're going to write something down, but no notebook, which is why I ask why you're nervous, whether or not it has to do with your anti-war activities, and if you've lost your notebook. A second place is set, and here's the waitress with the coffee for the mysterious other person who seems to have disappeared. We'll have the same, thanks. Black. Oh, and the sweetened condensed milk in your coffee is, if I'm not mistaken, a distinctly Vietnamese way of drinking coffee."

Bill blinked at Sherlock's revelations. "I did a Fulbright a couple of years back, went to Vietnam, where I picked up the habit. Vietnamese coffee never tastes right here."

"You need a really dark roast, and it's not a bad idea to add some chicory, to get a little bit of a burnt flavor, like you were roasting coffee over a fire by yourself. Sorry. I thought it would be useful to know about a country we were at war with. Even if it's a fake war. It's real enough to those with the bullets. You were saying."

Bill stared at Sherlock with the look I'd come to see all too often. "Yes, I've lost my notebook, and you're right. Physics is what I studied, actually, but it involves a lot of math and I've been doing more and more math so, yeah, lots of pencils. I was going to go to the five-and-dime after this meeting and get another notebook, but I ran out of time. So, okay, you've impressed me. Figured some things out right away. That's good. I wonder if you could help me now, though, with something a little bit odd?"

Sherlock smiled, and it was like he was settling into a chair that he'd had for many years. This is what he does, I realized. This is who he is.

"Tell us everything. All the details... Oh, Joseph! Fancy meeting you here."

Mrs. Hendrix's nephew sat next to Bill and took a sip of his coffee. He was a Black Panther, sure enough, in full uniform: turtleneck, black leather jacket, only missing the beret. "Mr. Holmes. Dr. Watson."

"I like your new style. Don't worry about us. We like the Black Panthers, don't we, Watson?"

Joseph cracked a smile. "They told me about you stopping by. I wished I'd been there to see it."

"Your aunt is worried about you. Your mother, too."

Joseph looked down at the table, then back up at us. "I know. They shouldn't worry. Can't you tell them not to? I know they're trying to get by. We are, too. Why can't they be proud of me, of us? Things are starting to change. We have to show that we can't be stopped by the pigs. They bash in our window, we gotta fix it. They smash in our faces, what should we do? Doctor won't see us. Nobody listens. They tell you and my mom and my auntie that we're thugs with guns, that's what you all believe."

I had had just about enough of this. "Now listen here, Joseph. You want to run around with guns, blowing stuff up, go ahead. But don't get mad when people are scared of you and call you thugs. Every change that's come has come about from peaceful protest. Violence never solved anything."

"Violence never solved anything except creating slavery while stopping it. You really don't see it, do you? You don't see the black brothers and sisters being put down on the street, stopped, searched, groped, and beaten for no reason at all? Those people you see on your televisions being hit is news to you, but it has never been news to the black man, the red man, the brown man, or the yellow man. The world you operate in is a different world than we live in. We do not advocate violence, but we will not have violence done to us, do you understand?

We will demand our rights and maintain our dignity ourselves. We will create change, and if it must come from the barrel of a gun, then so be it."

"Well said, Joseph. Well said." Bill was smiling at me. "All this military industrial complex is tied up together, doctor. The war isn't the problem. It's a symptom. Like if you have a patient with a cancer who's vomiting. You don't give him Alka-Seltzer. You don't treat the nausea. You find the root cause and work on that. Cancer. What causes the cancer? Stop them smoking. Mr. Holmes is right. I'm an anti-war activist, but I also work for civil rights. Women's lib. I do the dishes as does my wife. The Panthers are an enviable organization. You should go up there and see for yourself. The women work just as hard as the men. They train with guns. They do the front line work."

Joseph spoke back up. "That's not how it used to be last year, they say, but the sisters started explaining a few months ago how they were being treated like second class citizens. They could shoot a gun just like we could cook the children's breakfast. They were right. Like Mao says in the little red book: 'We're all resources for the revolution.' Every one of us receives the blows of oppression on our backs, so every one of us can live and die for the revolution. We lost a few people, but after it all shook out, it seemed like it was the right ones who remained. The only ones we lost were people not committed to the struggle." Joseph looked at his watch. "Anyway. I got to go. Bill, I'll let you know when Chairman Fred's coming into town. Might not be till springtime, maybe even the summer."

"Okay, Joseph. Please pass on my regards. I look forward to meeting him."

Joseph stood up and shook Bill's hands, then Sherlock's, and finally mine. He stared me in the eye like he was daring me to look away, and I could see the controlled rage burning in him.

* * *

"WELL, THAT YOUNG man has changed in the past six months, hasn't he, Watson?"

"He sure has. He's gotten all angry and strident; sounds like a young Malcolm X in training."

Sherlock looked at Bill. "The last time we spoke he was so timid he barely shook my hand, and wouldn't meet my eye at all."

"I don't know which is worse, to be honest," I said. "I'm glad he's got some self-confidence, but he's so angry about everything. Racial relations've made great strides in the past ten years. Hell, just in the three years I was away stitching people up in Vietnam things changed so much I almost didn't recognize America. He would have had trouble coming *in* here, in '62, '63, but today he hardy drew a glance. All that... I don't think they really appreciate all the strides, how far things have come."

Bill was watching me with a look of horror on his face. "Now hang on there just a minute, sir. Just try, just imagine, for a few minutes, that everything he says is right. That the police go after him, stop him on the street for no reason. If you spat on the sidewalk, you might a dirty look, but if you were black, you might get brought downtown. Stopped for no reason, imprisoned on trumped up charges. That you couldn't get a mortgage in a good neighborhood, weren't allowed to buy property, that if you lost your job, someone just said, 'Oh, it's the troublesome whitey again. We shouldn't hire them no more.' What would that be like, do you think? What if you had all that, plus a history of slavery and Jim Crow and all that to boot?"

"Well, that... that would be terrible. I couldn't believe it's that bad."

"Maybe that's why you don't have any sympathy for him. Try an exercise, just for a little while. Try believing what he says, see where it gets you."

"Do you know Joseph well, Bill?"

"First time I've met him, actually. We're trying to build alliances off the back of the disruption in Chicago. We need more than laws. We need social change. Black people need to come over for dinner, and we need to go to their churches, and find out what each other's like. It's not as easy as you might think. You have to work at it. I called and asked if I could meet with a representative of the New York Black Panthers, and Joseph is the one that showed up. That's about all I know. How do you know him?"

"Believe it or not, he's related to our landlady. A formidable woman. I think you may have met her, in the bakery where you left your message? Speaking of, what seems to be your problem, that you would seek out the services of myself and Dr. Watson? I must warn you, I did not approve of the story which Watson typed up for *Collins*, and I imagine that nothing we do will prove to be very exciting." This he said looking at me. "Tell us about your trouble, and please, don't leave out any details, no matter how unimportant."

"You're going to think it's crazy."

"I promise you, Bill, I take great care to not prejudice my opinions on anything but bare facts. Ask Doc there if you want, but I have no reason whatsoever to judge you for your problems."

"Okay. Well. I'm an academic. Maths and physics, as you say. It seems like someone's stealing my research. I published a paper last year, and then within six months the formulae became obsolete. I've always been better at doing research and coming up with formulae and proofs than I have been at writing up, but in the past two years I've submitted half a dozen papers only to be told that there was similar work already under consideration, that I'd been beaten to the punch. I'm afraid that people are starting to think that I'm spying on my colleagues, but I haven't even met any of the people who appear to be publishing my work."

Sherlock put his hand up. "So this is... six papers in the past year? That's fast work."

"It's a new area, reasonably wide open. And, like I say, I'm slow at writing up, but my head of department suggested that I might get sidelined for funding if I didn't publish soon, so I've been trying to focus, get some work out, but it's almost like people have access to my notes."

"Surely this isn't so surprising? That people would be working in a new field, and that others might have come up with some of the same ideas or the same proofs that you have? There's a long history of people coming up with the same ideas in science over the years. Fermat and Descartes; Darwin's discoveries in the Galápagos and Wallace's voyages near Indonesia."

"It could be, but it seems really unlikely. It doesn't seem to be happening to anyone else. I got asked to peer review one of the articles, and it repeated a mistake in my first pass."

"Who are these other researchers? Do they know each other? Are they at the same university, or conference, or members of the same academic society?"

"They're spread out: at Cal Berkeley, Purdue, Case Western, MIT. Some of them work in different areas. None of it's impossible, but it seems incredibly unlikely: I've been essentially unable to publish for over a year. Maybe it's just bad luck.

"The weird thing is that my notebook keeps disappearing. I did lose it today. And the last time I came to New York. I carry it with me everywhere. My research and work has gone beyond physics into more pure math—set theory and mathematical logic. Inspiration might strike anywhere, and you need paper and pen to write it down. Thoughts. Theories. All that. Pretty boring stuff, unless you're a mathematician. It's always here, in my breast pocket." He patted the pocket of his tweed jacket, flashing his suede elbow patches.

Sherlock perked up. "Oh, really? That *is* interesting. Tell me everything about these notebook disappearances. Anything you can remember."

"I came down yesterday. I had my notebook on the train; I was trying to work out some puzzles about bounded sets of infinity, and how they would work using different laws of physics. Doodling, mostly. Then I put it in my pocket. I got to NYU and the boilers must have been on overdrive because I had to open my window a crack just to breathe. They'd put me up in a dorm room this time. I put my notebook down on the desk and went down the hall to the toilet and had a quick wash and a shave, then came back to get ready to have dinner with my colleague. My notebook wasn't there, and I looked through all the drawers. I didn't think much of it, but there it was in the top drawer the next morning before I went out. I might've put it in there—I remembered the drawer being opened before I came in, like the student who'd stayed there before had forgotten to shut it when he unpacked, but I could swear I looked through the drawers when I came home.

"I know how this sounds... crazy, right? I thought so, too, the first time it happened; I didn't give it a second thought. But then I was thinking about it on the train going back the last time, and I could swear—I know, the mind plays tricks on you about this kind of stuff—that it's happened every time I've come to New York for meetings.

"I was telling my wife about it, how crazy it was, and she said, 'Wait a minute, Bill, I have just the person you should talk to about it,' and she pulled out her copy of *Collins* and there it was. New York, and the way you'd pulled all those threads together— well, that sure was something. I'd basically dismissed the whole idea, but then my notebook went missing again this morning, and I thought that maybe you'd have some ideas. You sure impressed me with that thing you did, knowing all that stuff about me when you came in. Maybe you could tell me if there's anything to worry about, or if someone's stealing my ideas or... or whatever. Or maybe that I'm just actually turning into an absentminded professor, and I'm actually not good enough."

"I didn't *do* anything coming in here, Bill. I just observed and paid attention to what I saw, which is what most people don't. Tell me, what's in these notebooks of yours?"

"Just mathematical formulae, scribblings, charts, sets. Doodles, sometimes, but I pretty much always use them when I'm working on some math problem. I don't use it for anything else—look, I do grocery lists and things like that on deposit slips from my check book. Drives my wife crazy, because she's always afraid I'm going to run out. There might be a doodle but it's just that I can look at a doodle and it'll jog me back to what I was thinking."

"And these formulae and data sets. Who could understand them? What are you working on, and with whom?"

"It's pretty abstract stuff. You'd have to have a PhD in mathematics. Most of the last six months we've been looking at ways of finding the roots of derivatives of multidimensional problems."

"So. Useful, but not an applied science; not likely to be corporate espionage, say."

"Not really. Some of it could be exciting to other people in bow ties and tweed jackets, but there aren't so many like that out there. Certainly not cat burglars."

"And who have you been working with this on?"

"A couple of guys from England. They come over a couple of times a year. There's someone at NYU as well, though we're mostly using him for his stock of Master's students that we can get to think without paying them. We had a breakthrough a few years back, but I think we might be getting somewhere else, soon."

"Could the notebook disappearing be a prank?"

"Maybe. I don't stay in the same place, though. I get put up in student housing, and I stay with friends sometimes. Mathematicians and people I met on the Fulbright. There's some anti-war activists as well. I've... I've been known to demonstrate against the war. It's no secret. I've even printed up cards for people to carry in their wallets if they get arrested. Sometimes I stay with friends, most of whom are anti-war activists. They're all over Brooklyn, in the upper east side, Spanish Harlem. Everywhere."

"Do you lose the notebook at the start of the trip, the end? Any pattern?"

"Nope. I always find it again within a day, and it's always when I come to New York, but never quite where I've left it. It's maddening. Almost like..."

"Like someone's out to get you, undermine your confidence in yourself? Ruin your reputation?"

"Something like that."

"Is there anyone you've made angry? Not necessarily someone in academia, now. And, this is important, it could be anyone at all. An ex-lover, friend, rival mathematician. Even, especially, if it's someone for whom being kept out of the spotlight would be advantageous."

"I'm... I'm pretty boring in terms of enemies, as far as I know, Mr. Holmes. I've never cheated on my wife or anything like that, and I'm pretty sure she hasn't either. I win research grants, but I'm not especially good at it, and it isn't so hard, really. There's always use for math and physics spilling out of the government, NASA and the Army and all that. Maybe I beat someone for a grant or a Fulbright and they're jealous? But I don't think so. I've been arrested and done sit-ins and all that." He leans over and lowers his voice. "I'm, uh, very sympathetic with civil disobedience. I refused to pay income tax in 1966, and went public about that. I've also helped people plan break-ins to burn draft cards. There are a lot of Catholic priests and nuns who do the same kind of thing. Bishops, too, sometimes. They think that, despite what the government is saying, there are greater issues at stake. I can get behind that, you know?"

Sherlock stared into an area about ten inches off of the top of the table, his chin on his fist. "Can I have a look at your notebook?"

"But it's lost, I've just told you. I could call you when it shows up again, if you want."

"Have you looked in your overcoat pocket?"

Bill looked at Sherlock, his pupils dilating and his cheekbones flushing. He reached over to his London Fog overcoat folded on the chair next to him, and pulled it up, feeling in the pockets. He looked up at Sherlock with widening eyes. "How on Earth did you?"

"I noticed it as soon as we walked in. I *observed*. I was beginning to wonder if you were testing me, but I wanted to hear you talk. Let's assume that this is as you say, however. May I?" Sherlock pulled the notebook out with two fingers, holding it up to the light, and turning it this way and that, looking at the edges, and carefully at the spine and cover, before laying it on the table. "Can you see anything that looks different? Anything at all—a smudge, a crease, anything? I can see that you're left-handed, see, there, where you open the pages. That's your thumbprint. Let me see your hands." Sherlock grabbed Bill's hand and held it up, stretched the finger and thumb out, and then put the notebook in it. "Go on, open it up. Let me watch you. Yes, that's what I thought." And then he took it right back out of Bill's hand, holding it up to look at the edge, and then spreading it open and looking in at the stitching. "Write in it. A formula. The quadratic equation. Anything will do."

Bill took it and laid it on the table, holding it open with his hands and bent over to write in it, and had barely drawn a sigma when Holmes snatched it away again, laying it on the table. "Why do you hold it open, hmm? Look. It lies perfectly flat."

"I don't, not usually. My father was fanatical about books. He knew too many people who'd lost books to Hitler. We were brought up to be careful. In our house, you didn't break the spine."

"But this... this is completely broken, and I think someone else has been flipping through it. Look: that's where your thumb goes, but see how it's wider there? That's another person thumbing through your notebook. Doctor Bill, you have yourself a fan, or someone interested enough in your work that they're liberating your notebook from its resting place when they think you're not looking. Okay. Here's what we need to do. You send me a list of all the articles that have been published with your work. Professors involved, their journals, universities, all that kind of thing. If you can, include photocopies of the relevant pages of your notebooks. Think you can do that? Don't send it to the bakery. Send it to this address." He handed Bill a preprinted card that I had never seen before. "Don't put my name on the envelope, just 'Baker Street Ltd.' We'll do some research and plan our next steps. When are you next in New York?"

Bill looked at Holmes, then at me, then back to Holmes. "What... what do you mean?"

"When are you next in New York? I think, yes, I'm pretty sure that we can come up with a way to uncover the plot against you, but there's no way to do it unless you're in New York, so when will you be back?"

"Well, this time of year it's pretty busy. Exams coming up. Probably not till after we mark them and get the grades recorded. June, probably, but maybe July, I guess."

"Where will you stay?"

"Good question. It usually depends."

Sherlock sighed and put his head in his hands. "Bill, listen. I'm interested, and happy to help you, but you've got to be straight with me, you understand? You've got to tell me what you're really doing in New York, not lie to me. I can't answer your questions without facts to build a chain of logic around."

Bill looked down, sighed, and then reached over and took his notebook back from Sherlock and shut it. He stood up from the table and took a deep breath, looking at the table, and then breathed out again.

"You know I'm an anti-war activist. I'm against all types of oppression. I'm working with some other movements, and I can't tell you about them, not without their consent. It's delicate, not to mention that I actually, at this point, do not know where I'm going to be or when. We're trying to create something, but it's about more than just me, here. All you have to do is listen to people like Joseph, what happens to them. Black people. Hispanics. It's reasonable that I'd be nervous."

Sherlock looked at me, then back. "It is. That's why I'm still here waiting to see if you're going to trust us or not."

"I'll most likely be staying up in Spanish Harlem. I don't know when, exactly, and I don't have the address on me. Can I let you know?"

"See, John? We're going to have to get a telephone. Tell you what, I'll give you the number of the payphone near us. I'll get someone to watch it. Call, say, between seven and seven-thirty on Tuesday evening. Any Tuesday. Leave a message with whoever answers—just say 'this is Doctor Bill,' and then give the details, the date and the address, and we'll come and meet you."

Bill looked at the number he was writing on a scrap of paper. "You act like you know more than you let on, Mr. Holmes."

"You can't be too careful, Doctor Bill. No, no, don't tell me your full name, not yet. I don't want to know. Could be paranoia, but I really think it's best, don't you? Sorry, I'm a little bit hungry. I'll get your coffee, and Joseph's. Watson, do you mind waiting with me while I eat? Doctor Bill, thank you and goodbye."

Bill stood up, looking a bit flustered at his dismissal. He stood there for a moment, as Sherlock turned his attention away.

"Excuse me, miss? Could we get a plate of French fries over here, and some more coffee? Do you want anything, Watson?"

"Sure, make it two orders of fries." Hell, I was hungry, why not. Bill was wandering away from us, looking a bit like a lost puppy. I'm sure he was wondering if he'd made a mistake, talking to Sherlock. I sure was.

Sherlock's voice dropped. "Don't be too obvious, but look for someone really square. Short hair, probably blue eyes, chiseled jaw. You know. All-American. Elliot Ness. Anyone who gets up to leave and follow Bill there."

I turned to look at Holmes after scanning the room around me. "I don't see any cop-types. You think that's his real name?"

"Yes, actually. Despite my own precautions I think Dr. Bill is telling the truth. Did you notice his pupils when I pointed out his notebook? He wasn't lying, so unless he really is completely absentminded and left it in his pocket, he's as surprised as you were when we got blanked by Andy. I do think Bill is his real name, and I think he's in quite a lot of danger. The question is, of course, is it because of something he's done, something he's going to do or something someone thinks he might do?"

I woke up to Sherlock's absence all day on Sunday; he came to find me Monday afternoon. The day's light was fading and Sherlock brought us outside to stand shivering next to the payphone on the street corner. I was uncommonly tired, and almost ready to sit on the two-foot-high pile of the compacted grey snow that lined the New York streets in the winter. A tall black man walked up, at least six-foot-six, and beautiful. Half black, short hair, black leather jacket, thin and lean. He moved with power, and he was intimidating. I might have been a little in love, and it was confusing to me. Black, in this case, certainly was beautiful.

"Dr. Watson, this is Tyrone. Tyrone has agreed to be our answering service. Tyrone, this is Watson, or you can call him Doc. He's as good to receive messages as I am."

"Tuesdays, right? Between seven and seven-thirty?"

"That's right. Remember an extra five when he calls. Somebody's got to wait for it, every week. And to watch out if you see any funny characters hanging out, okay?"

"Me and my boys'll be on it, don't you worry, Mr. Holmes." He and Sherlock shook hands, and it was like an earthquake went off in my head, right there in Manhattan. It was the same handshake that I'd seen negroes in Vietnam using when they were handing off heroin. Sherlock wasn't interested in street drugs, though, and all he had to do was talk to me. I had a clean, guaranteed supply of whatever he wanted.

Tyrone walked away, smiling to himself.

"This is our new answering service, Sherlock?"

"It's helpful to have someone invisible, John. Tyrone and his 'boys' are always out on the street, and they're just the type to be ignored by... anyone who might be watching for us. It's good for us to have eyes and ears everywhere."

"How did you get him to agree?"

"He had a little problem. I helped him out with it. It was interesting, in a way. His mother was getting consistently underpaid for her work at the two hotels she cleans at. It was pretty simple for me to put on a tweed jacket and red bow tie and make up a card identifying myself as a city auditor. I've been reading this book, *An Actor Prepares*, by Konstantin Stanislavsky. It's important to the Soviets, but it isn't widely available in translation, and I thought I could try out some of his methods. A quick audit and the discovery that the owner was... well, pocketing the worker's wages isn't exactly right. Accidentally underpaid, I think is what he said. He paid the arrears and I've promised to re-audit in a few months, and I handed the number around to all the workers to call for a re-audit just in case, and the city—well, I suppose, myself as an undesignated representative of the city—graciously decided not to fine the hotels. Tyrone offered to pay me, but I asked him if he was interested in doing some odd jobs for us from time to time. He's going to get us some work, too, John. Send people over to us who have problems that a little bit of knowledge and a modicum of brain power could solve. The thousand mysteries of the daily lives of the proletariat. He liked the idea, and so here we are."

* * *

Sherlock—

You've always been such a Nice Young Man. Keep helping people out like that. It's a good outlet for your creative energies.

—Mycroft

SHERLOCK CAME IN with a thick envelope from Bill a week later. It was full of photocopies and a typewritten list of journal articles, names, and addresses—but we didn't know that, not yet. Sherlock had the envelope in a bag, and he had a pair of gloves with him, thin cotton ones like a Disney character. He drew on the gloves, pulled the envelope out, and examined it, turning it over.

"Check it out, John. The postmark is from Haverford, Pennsylvania. Hmmm. Look here, see the smudges on the flap? I don't think they quite match up." He turned on all the lamps and held the envelope up to look at it from the edges. "This has been examined. I'm not sure, but I think it's been opened. Let's see what it contains."

He got a letter opener and slit the envelope open, but he didn't pull the contents out right away. He pulled back the cut edge of the flap, gently, looking at the glue where it was sealed. "Oh, hello there. You *have* been opened." He looked at the edge of the stack of papers in the envelope, holding them up to the light, then motioned for me to clear a space on his workbench. He poured out the papers without touching them, setting the envelope aside. He examined the stack of papers, their edges and all over the top, then went through them, one by one, looking at each one in turn.

"This is getting boring, Sherlock. I might go for a walk."

He ignored me and kept paging through the pile of papers, looking at the corners and the edges of each one. I watched him for a while, completely captivated in the moment, and then turned to go. I was at the door when he finally answered.

"How can you go, John? This is so captivating. Have you seen anything like this? The variety of the areas is... This is surely bigger than any... I need some quiet, please, John."

I hadn't spoken in at least five minutes, standing there like an idiot, waiting for a response. Sherlock returned to his examination. I didn't know what to make of it. It was idiosyncratic, like he was so often. The things he did that made me want to be his friend were exactly the things that he did that drove me away. I left the apartment in a brown study.

seven

THE WAITING, THE GARBAGE

BILL'S CALL DIDN'T come for months, but we didn't spend all that time waiting. Tyrone made good on his promise: he brought in people who had problems, and we—well, Sherlock, actually—untangled them. I have to say that I was wrong most of the time, but it made Sherlock look good. Once or twice my medical knowledge helped out. It was during that time, April or May of 1969, that Sherlock found and identified the Wandering It Girl, which got him more press and another article in *Collins*. They didn't want me to write it, this time, but Sherlock told them he wouldn't be interviewed by anyone else. We had another fight about the content, but I made sure to put in some of his careful explanations of bloodstains and footprints. He thought the article was too focused on him rather than how he solved it. Soon after, we had a line of people coming to the bakery most days. At first he would take ten, twenty, fifty dollars off people, depending what they could afford, listen to what they had to say, and then, usually without even bothering to leave the bakery, tell people where to go or who was in the wrong, and give them an idea how to fix it.

Richard Wellsley from *Collins* came to me and asked if I would write a regular feature. Sherlock's two exploits made for fascinating reading, and bumped up sales quite a bit, and the advertisers loved it, too. This was the time Sherlock started to get famous, at least partly due to the articles. The Wandering Heiress confirmed that people wanted to read about Sherlock, and cases like the Park Avenue Bachelor and the Secret of the East Village Tunnels really got people hooked.

The problem was, Sherlock started to get bored. He wanted more interesting work. The first time he rejected a case was when a lady walked in in a short raincoat with a tied up belt. Fashionable. Makeup done just so. He just looked her up and down as she walked in the door and sighed, loudly. "No, thank you. He's not going to be found. He's gone. He knows you cheated on him. Knows, not suspects. And you haven't even stopped. I can see by the way you're walking. You've been *in flagrante* with your other man—the one whose picture is in your purse—on your way here? Your hair is still a mess. Shameless. No, I don't want your money. Just please leave and don't come back. Watson, can you tell them all, no more lonely hearts, break-ups, cheating husbands? No matter how much they're paying. I'm just not interested."

And that was the end of the profitable few. We did fine, though. He loved the attention, but he had to take fewer cases. He'd do half of them free; he'd charge those he thought could afford our fees. He liked being a show-off, too. I liked being around someone so smart. I was no dummy, but I felt like one next to Sherlock Holmes. All of his explanations seemed so goddamn obvious once they were out there. Sure, sometimes you might not know the difference between East River and Hudson mud, but if you could see two different colors of dried mud, it must mean something.

The springtime grew hot, and Sherlock's patience started to fray. We had the windows open, but the ovens from the Bakery just didn't quit; no matter how much we opened the windows, we felt like we just couldn't breathe. Summer was coming, and it was already brutal in June.

"I feel like an accountant doing multiplication tables all day long." Sherlock sat and drummed his fingers. "No word from Tyrone. All I can think about is Bill and his notebook, even when I'm solving these little problems."

Sherlock looked around at the stuff we'd accumulated. It was nearly a year since we'd moved in together, and I had a strongbox full of interesting chemicals upstairs. Sherlock had his own clutter: he'd got a chemistry set that he'd fiddle with, and an Erector Set that he was definitely using to test out some kind of theory. He had a drafting table and books on engineering, economics, politics, criminology, and current events as well as incomplete sets of different encyclopedias. He was making himself a lock picking set and he had a door with six slots for locks in it, and a tool bench a mechanic gave him for showing him how his tire guys were skimming off of him, littered with cloth and sewing supplies, different kinds of cigarettes, and boxes of bugs. We talked about putting up a curtain or a wall up, but I think Sherlock liked the effect it had on people, his mad scientist's lair.

"We've got three days, John, before Tuesday. I've told Mrs. Hendrix to turn away anyone else this weekend. Let's go on a private vacation. What exactly are these? And these?"

Sherlock had clearly got further in his lock picking than I'd given him credit for. He'd been through the strongbox and had enough pills in his hands to keep us occupied all weekend.

I WON'T GO into details about that weekend. We survived, and the New York Police Department ended up standing around and scratching their heads at the sudden appearance of correct solutions to dozens of unsolved cases under the windshield wipers of unmarked detective cars across the city. Six officers were reported in the *Times* for stellar casework. Sherlock took note of who they were. The rest apparently showed the notes to their superiors, so we were in the news again, but unnamed. Sherlock and I laughed and laughed, imagining what kind of idiot would let a case go based on mistrust of an anonymous tip.

We crawled through Monday with the aid of a half-dozen pecan pies, two dozen doughnuts, and all the coffee south of 14th Street, but Sherlock thought we shouldn't take the edge off with anything stronger than coffee—it "might dull the mind."

"Tomorrow is Tuesday, John. Every Tuesday for the past month I've been afraid of being at anything but my peak performance. I want to hear Tyrone's voice, and get the information from Bill. We should make sure to get some rest, to be at our best for tonight. We might have to go. Who knows when we'll next sleep?"

We didn't sleep, couldn't really, but we found ways to relax ourselves.

The shadows of the evening were drawing in by the time we went out to find Tyrone. The summers weren't going to get much longer, and you could still see blue up above, but the buildings blocked everything out, kept us in a fake twilight, from four o'clock until dusk. He was there, on the corner, in a tank top and an afro with the comb sticking up. He was lean and muscular, his triceps flexing as he played with the toothpick he was chewing on. A mint toothpick, I bet. I knew that trick. Try to trick your body into thinking part of it was cool and that would get you to pretend the rest of you was, too.

"Hey there, Mr. Holmes, Doc. How you doing tonight? I got something for you. That phone rang and it was some man named Bill. Gave me his number and everything. Been watching for one of them cars, too. Plymouth Fury was right over there, a while ago, man sitting in it. Blonde, blue-eyed, square jaw. Looked like he should be a football player from, I don't know, Iowa or Kansas or something. Like the pictures on recruitment posters. Sitting there looking at Hendrix Bakery like something was going to happen. Plymouth Fury. Six cylinder, three hundred and thirty horsepower. Man, I'd love to get behind the wheel of one of them, yeah. Drive around fast, late at night. Maybe I should go be a pig, huh? He's gone, now, anyway, about twenty minutes ago. Back to his little piggy family."

"Thank you, Tyrone. Just in case, though, I'm going to need you to visibly 'sell' me something, which obviously won't be drugs, but just the address." Sherlock took out a twenty dollar bill folded it in quarters and walked over and shook Tyrone's hand in the passing maneuver known to everyone from chief of police down to the lowest street dealer, and then spoke, loudly. "No thank you, but, young man, you should get over to the soup kitchen on Fourth. They'll give you a hot meal any night from seven o'clock."

Sherlock walked away and around the corner, heading for the subway, and I followed him.

"Holmes, you didn't think that was going to fool anyone, did you? Everyone on the planet who's ever seen a drug knows that handshake."

"That's what I'm counting on, John. Tyrone doesn't have anything on him and neither do I, but I am hoping to flush out anyone who might be watching. He knows the risk that he's going to be stopped and searched."

Sherlock paused there, around the corner, out of sight of anyone who might be listening. "Wait for it, John. Ah, yes. There it is."

I heard Tyrone's protest from around the corner, a voice that managed to be outraged while at the same time sounding bored, repeating a litany of arguments it had used a hundred thousand times. "What? What have I done? What's the probable cause for this stop? Or the one last week, or the two the week before that? This is an outrage. I want my lawyer. I demand my rights." On and on it went, while the voices spoke in their clipped New York accents, voices that had grown up idolizing Sam Spade and Eliot Ness. They'd imagined they would grow up and get their man, until they were faced with the tedious reality of everyday policing in New York. Polyester uniforms in cold winters and hot summers, and nothing they did made a damned bit of difference. No wonder they hid behind their badges.

"Damn. Now they're on to me. We're going to have to find a new way of communicating, Watson."

"Jesus, Holmes. Haven't you got a scrap of heart for Tyrone there?"

"I do, John, but he'll be fine. We've discussed it. They'll have nothing to hold him on. He'll be freed in a few minutes, or a couple of hours at most. Our casework has given us the financial freedom to pay lawyers if we have to. We're going to have to set up a network of people who can help out. The invisible to society. Weirdos and irregular people that can travel anywhere to get and pass information."

He had a spark in his eyes, the one that meant that things were looking up, that we were on to something, and that ideas were bursting outside of the three seams of his skull. I wished I'd had a better night's sleep, but the effects of the weekend were still resonating.

"Uptown, John. In Spanish Harlem, on Thursday. Let's get some newspapers and refresh our knowledge of what we missed over this weekend. I think it might prove useful."

He paused, and looked at me, thinking.

That look of his was annoying. "Go on. You want to say something to me. Spit it out. Don't soften it up or dance around it. I'm a big boy."

He narrowed his eyes. "You remember when we talked to Joseph in the diner in midtown? When we go uptown, just... keep your opinions to yourself. Listen for a while. I don't have any idea who's going to be up there, and neither do you. Observe. Reserve judgment. See what you can see, and draw conclusions unsullied by your personal prejudices."

I didn't know what to say—I didn't actually have anything to say—so I just nodded.

*   *   *

THURSDAY AFTERNOON, WE braved the heat of the subway all the way uptown, exiting into the east side of South Harlem at 125th Street. The subway blew a blast of hot air as we came through the turnstiles and up the stairs, and it was like we'd entered a war zone.

"Jesus, Holmes. I don't think I can breathe here for long."

The stink was overpowering. The smell of unwashed people in the summer, excrement, and the crud from the bottom of a thousand dumpsters. The overwhelming sweet smell of rot that could make a thousand people sick in an instant. I could see the cause. Stacked by every vacant lot, burned-out shop, and apparently bombed-out building was a pile of black plastic bags boiling in the heat, oozing black sludge into the gutters.

"That's gotta be a public health hazard, Holmes. Why doesn't the city get on to these people to clean up this garbage? That's just... the bacteria alone, much less the rats..."

And that's when I saw them: the rats, swarming over the piles of garbage, almost obscured by flies, visible only by their shocking pink tails. It was an echo of a nightmare I once had in country, and I turned around and grabbed the rail of the subway exit, leaning over it to breathe in the hot air exiting from the incoming train. I never thought I would be refreshed by the smell of burning grease and ozone, but it worked, kind of.

Sherlock put his hand on my shoulder and gave me his handkerchief to put over my mouth. His voice was calm, the voice he used with me in private. "Come on, John. Let's get moving. Let's hope that Bill's friend lives up some stairs where there's a breath of fresh air."

We walked two blocks uptown and one block east until we got to a six-story walk-up. There were garbage cans and piles of black plastic bags outside of every building. "Five-twelve. Fifth floor. I don't think there's going to be an elevator, do you?" The security door was shut, but opened when we tried the handle. "Kicked in."

It wasn't any cooler inside, and the air was stifling, though there was a tiny bit of breeze. Somebody must have left the door to the roof or some windows open. The smell was stronger. It was dark inside: the only light was a few floors up. We trudged up the stairs to five, Sherlock stopping to look out the window at each floor. He stopped at the landing, holding his hand up for me to stay still, and crouched down, looking along the floor. Satisfied, he stood up and walked down the hallway, knocking on the door to 512.

A tall light-skinned black woman with an afro that was a yard wide if it was a foot answered the door. "You Bill's people? I'm Juanita. Come on in." She had a Spanish accent. Puerto Rican, maybe. There were seven people around the room: Juanita, Bill, Joseph and two other Black Panthers, one with a chinstrap beard that neither of us recognized from the last trip to Harlem, and another one, taller and thinner, standing back watching us. Two Hispanic men were sitting, holding purple berets and listening to the Black Panther with the chinstrap beard, captivated by the urgency in his voice. Joseph was watching him with frank admiration on his face.

"Look, I don't want to get into your own internal conflicts. This is up to you, not us. We've had good work building the Rainbow Coalition in Chicago, the people building on their shared experience of poverty and having been kept down by the Man, but in my experience, you gotta stop waiting for the Man to come up here. All that garbage down there? Look at what our Black Panther brothers and sisters are doing a few blocks over. The people and the city can't feed their children? We'll feed the children, like we're doing in Chicago and Oakland with the free breakfast program. Nobody can afford a doctor? Get together and run a free clinic. Children can't get to school because of an unsafe road? Turn up in uniform with your guns and escort the children across that road. Find some people who want to help bring power to the people. Help the people stand up and demand respect."

The people were nodding, talking amongst each other. The woman who let us in looked around. Chinstrap beard said, "Speak up, sister. The voices of the women should be just as outspoken as the men. And you all, don't you interrupt her, neither."

Juanita spoke up. "Why can't we get our brooms and everything together and sweep all that stuff up? I bet the churches would help us out."

One of the two men waved his purple beret. "No, now, that's their job. We pay our taxes. How can we make them do their damn job and come get the trash we been putting out for months?"

Chinstrap spoke back up. "Now hang on, brother. First, of all, let the sister speak, and second of all, the whole Black Panther party got started because Huey Newton and Bobby Seale got tired of seeing kids in their neighborhood get run over trying to get to school. They wouldn't put in a stop light, so Huey and Bobby got some other black people to escort those children. Power from the people, to the people, for the people. Getting the people together to take care of their community. You want to see power to the people? Get the people working on something they can believe in. Look, now, I gotta go, but you can swing by the Panther office tomorrow before I get on the train back to Chicago."

He stood up and left, nodding at us on the way out. The taller, thinner man followed him out.

"Hello, Bill. Who was the inspiring gentlemen who just left?"

"Mr. Holmes, Dr. Watson. You've met Juanita. The gentlemen are Paco, Ricardo, and George, and you know Joseph. That was Fred Hampton, chairman of the Illinois chapter of the Black Panther party, and his bodyguard, William."

We all nodded to each other.

"Fred left us with these newspapers. Look here, they've announced their Rainbow Coalition in Chicago. All the political movements of poor people are getting together, sharing knowledge and resources. Publishing together, too. The Young Lords: supposedly used to be a gang over in Chicago, but now very similar to the Panthers. They're the Puerto Rican community. They're doing free breakfast and all kinds of things. And they've got these Young Patriots." Bill looked up at us. "They're basically rednecks from West Virginia. There's the Brown Berets, the Hispanic—"

"Chicano."

"Right, right, sorry. The Brown Berets are a *Chicano* organization also in Chicago. They've announced that, and Fred came out because he heard about the garbage situation going on here in El Barrio. How long's it been since the city picked up the trash?"

Paco looked up. "Seven weeks now. They got plenty of trucks. They drive right past it all on Third Avenue every day going downtown. They keep saying they don't have the hours to do it, with all the strikes and everything."

Juanita said, "Now look, what we need to do is make up a list of important things. Windows not working. The garbage in the streets. Food for the children in the community. What else?"

George stood up. "Lead paint all over these houses. Nobody knows what's what, and our kids be getting lead poisoning."

"Yeah. Health in general. Maybe we should make up a program for health." Juanita seemed very organized.

Sherlock and I sat down in the corner, and he rolled up cigarettes for both of us, and then, at a nod, one for George. Joseph came over and sat next to us. "You see what I'm talking about, gentlemen? This is the power of the people coming together, here. These ideas are like a seed, made by the people, watered with their tears. That seed can grow and create fruit for the people. You met a good man tonight. Fred Hampton, he knows about the people. You get the chance, you should talk to him. You saw the Panther office here? You should see the one in Chicago. Dozens, hundreds of people. They been fighting the pigs for years. Fred's Rainbow Coalition? He's bringing all the gangs in Chicago together. Thousands of soldiers to get educated and fight the Man for the people, you know what I'm saying?"

We sat and smoked and watched Bill and the Puerto Ricans discuss what needed to be done. Bill had a slight smile on his face, and he occasionally looked out the window.

WE SAT THROUGH hours of ideas and planning based on hope. I kept my mouth shut, like Sherlock asked. We smoked and filled ashtrays, and when Juanita went to clear them, I jumped up and found the garbage cans in the corners. I emptied the ashtrays twice, before the Young Lords left. Juanita came back from letting the men out.

"You guys need anything? Water? Coffee? I've got to get to bed, I think." Juanita stretched with a yawn.

Bill smiled at her. "It was good work here, I think. This is the kind of stuff that changes things, you know? We're okay. We'll take a pitcher of water but we're just going to talk about some stuff."

"You do what you want," Juanita said. "You know where everything is. I'll see you in the morning. Your sheets are there behind the sofa. At least all this smoke will keep away the smell from the street."

We bid Juanita good night and went to sit down.

"Well, Mr. Holmes? What have you discovered?"

"At the least, Bill, someone's opening your mail. At least some of it. You're being watched, by persons unknown, and you should be very, very careful with what you do and say."

"What? Why? Who?" Bill seemed calm, calmer than I would be. It was almost like it was an intellectual exercise, to understand the forces at work around him. Like it was just confirming that the world that he knew was actually just as awful as he'd thought it was. "How do you know?"

Sherlock opened his bag and pulled out the thick envelope that Bill sent us, the one that, months before, he'd dissected with such attention.

"I didn't just tear open this envelope when I got it. I examined it. Look, here, where the flap was glued down. See that? That's been steamed open and re-glued, but you can tell it's a different glue from the original, if you look on the inside. I suspected as much, so I slit it open with a knife rather than tear it. Whoever did it was careful enough to line up the glue on the outside. It's careful enough to pass an average examination, but when you peel it away from the inside, you can see it right away. See where it peels, then sticks again? That's the re-gluing line.

"Then, when you get to the contents, look here, at the corners of each of your photocopies. See that faint crease? That's where someone picked them up one by one. They've been put on a copier glass, photocopied, and picked back up. Someone's hands pinched the same corner of each paper. I assume you didn't copy your copies? No. I didn't think so. You can see two sets of thumb smudges on your notebooks—yours, and someone with larger hands. Remember how I showed you on your other notebook? We haven't even got into the actual contents, but we have evidence, Bill. Someone's reading your mail, and I can only hope that they haven't figured out who we are. I rented the PO box under a pseudonym but if they were watching it... well, we can't stop that.

"I reviewed the papers that were published out from under your nose. You'd appear to be right. None of the people who published your research seemed to be a particular expert in number theory or set theory, but they did groundbreaking work, seemingly out of nowhere. They're from all over the country, some top-tier institutions and some second-tier. I can't find any pattern as to why these academics would take your work, or why someone would send it to them. There are a couple of interesting points, though. First, I can't find out who's funded the research in any of these cases. That may not be unusual for a single paper—sometimes people forget, or it isn't significant enough to mention—but in six papers, it suggests a pattern. Second, I've read the papers and gone over your notes and in two of the six cases you have notes on additional pages that go beyond what's been published. They've published papers based on flawed reasoning, reasoning which you've already solved in your notes. There may be more, but I didn't have the entire contents of your notebooks. I would hazard a guess that you could publish responses, cleaning up the others' work; show your work as evidence and get the credit for yourself. But I'd ask you to wait. There are a number of possibilities as to who's watching you, most of which are unpleasant, if not downright dangerous. I've got an idea, though, how to flush them out, if you were willing to work with us?"

"If you've figured out all these things, Mr. Holmes, then you'll know that I'm not one to resist tweaking the nose of those in power. I'm a fan. As long as it gets results."

"Excellent. Did you bring your notebooks? I have some suspicions and I'd like to spend some time with them."

Sherlock and Bill shook his hands, and we spoke late into the night. I had known that he was brilliant, but now I realized I should never, ever get on his bad side.

eight

GARLANDS ON A STONE WALL

JUDY GARLAND DIED that Sunday, and the world went into mourning. A least, that's what you would have thought if you put on the television or picked up a newspaper. We got a message, via Tyróne: we were summoned to the presence of Andy for the funeral. Andy was going to tape record everyone's reaction as they passed by the casket, and we were an essential part of his vision. It would be some sort of happening, or something. Bring Obetrol.

"Why don't we blow it off, Sherlock?"

"No, John, I think there's something in it. We should go. Believe it or not, there might be the thinnest of threads between Bill and his young people and Andy's world downtown. It's definitely worth a little time to have a look."

We took the subway uptown and went to the funeral home on 81st Street until we realized just how long the line was going to be. It went out and snaked down to 80th at least.

We wandered down the line until we saw Andy and Candy Darling. Candy had her hair curled in finger waves and Andy was, despite the heat, in a white turtleneck with a tape recorder over his shoulder, pointing his microphone at people and fiddling with the buttons.

"Mind if we join you?"

"Oh, hello, Doc. Yes, I've been saving a space for you. We hardly see you around anymore, do we, Candy? Why is that, Doc?"

"What do you mean? I come around, but no one lets me past the desk out front. It's all turned into business." I had an idea for a joke. It was stupid, but I liked the idea of stupid at this moment. "Speaking of, Andy, look: Andy. Candy." I pointed at each of them, and then opened my hands. "Andy Candy."

Andy smiled daggers at me, but he helped himself to what was in my hands. Candy wasn't shy either. They both looked like they could use a cup of coffee, or something stronger. I didn't have any coffee, just something stronger.

"Oh, look, there's Ondine. Hello, darling. You haven't been around much at all. Where have you been keeping yourself? Got yourself lost in a big old orgy? You know you should let me watch."

Ondine looked tired. Not in a strung-out Factory sort of way, he looked like a normal person who was just tired after a long day. It was odd. He'd put on weight: the hollows in his cheeks were gone, and he had the color of someone who saw the sun, and not just after a long night out.

"Hey, Andy, Doc, Candy Darling." Ondine performed a perfect cheek kiss with Andy and Candy, raising and lilting his hands. He stood there smiling. "How are you, Holmes?"

Sherlock nodded and looked him up and down. "How's life over in Brooklyn, Ondine? Working for the postal service, are you?"

"I just can't see how he does that. Do you know, Doc? Andy?"

Andy actually looked surprised, for a second, before settling back to his typical sneer.

"Uniform pants, and the shoes. I'm sure you wouldn't be caught dead in polyester otherwise. You're spending time outside and it hasn't killed you. That smudge of mud on your feet has the characteristic multi-colored hues of Gowanus mud. Letter carriers start off in the worst routes of New York, figuring that if you can't handle the canals and back streets you wouldn't be of any use. Rites of passage, hazing, whatever you want to call it. How am I doing?"

Ondine smiled the stupidest grin I'd ever seen. It reminded me of Ward Cleaver. This was a different person from those who had tossed us out of the Factory back in October. This was someone I didn't even know.

"It's amazing, Holmes. You know just what to tell a girl."

"I never thought you'd be the monogamy type, though, Ondine. You were so free-spirited. I assume you've stopped taking speed completely, or just for a bit?"

"See? Right again. Can you imagine that? Me, off speed and with just one steady lover. Freddy. We started off less exclusive, but he was the first person that wasn't interested in getting into the Factory scene, you know. It's nice, though. Yeah, Andy, I'm working as a mailman, can you believe it? I'm in Brooklyn with Freddy, and we've got this place, just a little place, half-basement of a brownstone, really, but it's ours. Steady job, hot in the summer, cold in the winter, but neither drugs nor orgies nor crazy art will stop this courier from his appointed rounds. Something like that, anyway."

Andy shuffled forward, the microphone hanging limp in his hand. He was looking around like he didn't know where he wanted to point it, like there was nothing of interest to tape in the entire world. It was a look I knew well enough. This was Bored Andy coming on with Andy Candy, and I wondered what was going to happen.

We fell into an uneasy silence. Ondine shifting from foot to foot, trying to keep his relentless sober enthusiasm from pouring out. Candy didn't say a word, just smoked one cigarette after another, looking over the top of Andy's head and anywhere but Ondine.

Candy Darling spoke up. "I was thinking about changing my name."

Andy didn't even look.

"What do you think about Candy Warhol?"

Ondine looked up. That go this attention.

"Well, I think that would be wonderful. Interesting, anyway." Andy's gaze passed out over the people arriving at the line, their faces filling with shock and then resignation as they either marched to the back of the line or turned around and walked away. "See those two there? I can't bear to imagine them and their lives. Look at them. They just can't decide. I can't imagine having friends like that, friends that don't think the same way as you. It would be like a little betrayal. It would be so boring. Just stand in the goddamned line or go get a cup of coffee. Standing there arguing in the street is just so boring, wouldn't you think? How would you do it? Would there be a wedding? You're not trying to legitimize me, are you?"

"Me, Andy? You know better; I'm good for nothing but scandal. What would you want? St. Patrick's Cathedral and carriages through Central Park, or should we go to city hall and invite everyone along? We could make this entire line sign our papers."

"See that? That's exactly what I'm talking about. Friends that think like you do."

Andy started pointing his microphone at the people around us. We could see the funeral home now. Our arguing and shuffling had gotten us that far.

"Don't you have headphones?"

"No. I don't want to know what I'm listening to. That's sort of the point. Chance. Ondine's so goddamn boring I need to do something."

"You should try life clean, Doc. A little clean, maybe. It's nice. Earning an honest living. Coming home to your lover. Making it in the summer heat. A cold beer and a cigarette afterwards." Ondine looked up and down the block, like he was waiting on someone else.

"See what I mean?" Andy wasn't impressed by Ondine's anything, and kept talking to me in his almost whispery voice.

In the studio, everyone would shut up and listen and laugh, even though what he said usually wasn't funny. Out here on the street, you had to be a foot away from him to hear a word. "I just can't tell what it is that I'm listening to. Or who. It could be your Aunt Tilly. I suppose I'm glad he's off drugs. I suppose I'm glad he's clean and happy with his little suburban life, but he hasn't got any sparkle. He's like the Silver Factory. Gone with the wind. He's a goddamn non-personality now." Andy paused and looked up at the length of the line. "Ah, now we approach greatness."

We were nearly under the red 'Frank E. Campbell' awning when a halt was called. We were almost the next people in the door, standing there for almost ten minutes on our own, until a man walked out of the funeral home door. He should have been good-looking, but the weight of the world had settled on his shoulders and let all the air out of his tires.

Candy knew the score. "That's her husband, Mickey Deans. He doesn't look anything like he did in their wedding pictures. Not glamorous at all in those wrinkled clothes. He looks devastated."

Deans looked at the assembled crowd like it was completely overwhelming. He started to say something and then turned, sober as a judge, and got into his waiting limousine, holding back a shudder. People were filing out with their handkerchiefs up against their noses and clutching anything: old movie posters, LPs, pictures. It was like they wanted to just have her records in the room with her body. Andy was riveted, in his disinterested way. I turned to Sherlock.

"What are we doing here, Holmes? This is... voyeuristic, at best."

"I know, but I think we should stick it out. Trust me."

"Jesus. They were only married for a few months," I heard from someone just behind us in line, while we waited. Deans had had enough time alone with his bride after about fifteen minutes. Andy smirked, holding his microphone out. He gave me a look that I didn't understand as he pushed the leather case of the tape recorder behind his back.

The security guards in their pale grey suits pulled aside the velvet rope and let us go on in. Candy Darling strode forward with purpose, drawing us along in her wake. The place was drowning in flowers. There were displays from everybody, from Fred Astaire to Irving Berlin.

There was an actual rainbow made of flowers in front of a glossy white and gold coffin. Glossy. Classy, I supposed. It was sad, sure, just like the death of anyone is sad; but I thought this whole setup was really weird. Thousands of people lining up to pay their respects to a person that they'd only known from the movies and their record players, maybe the stage if they were lucky enough to get tickets.

"She's really gone away over that rainbow now, hasn't she?" Candy was conferring with a woman whose mascara had run down the side of her face. She'd buried her face on Candy's dress, probably smearing her makeup all over. I looked at Sherlock, wanting to grab him and get out of this festival of chintz and manufactured feelings, but he was standing back, head down, watching Ondine, his eyes flicking to the entrance and away.

There were piles of roses, records, playbills, and stuffed Toto dogs. You name it, it was piled against that coffin. One of the ubiquitous security men in his pale grey suit came up to Candy and held out a box of Kleenex. He put his hand on her shoulder and whispered to her. She took the strange woman by the arm, patting her, and began to pull away. Andy hovered, glancing into the coffin but standing back, catching the people as they passed. I turned and walked out, trying to pull Sherlock with me, but he shrugged off my hand and ambled in behind Candy, Andy, and Ondine.

"What do you see outside, John? Anyone watching? I think someone should be."

"Have you dipped into the Obetrol? You're on edge and I don't know what you're talking about."

"Just wait, John. Just you wait." He looked up, "Ondine—why don't we go for a drink and catch up? A night like this"—Sherlock nodded at the line of thousands still standing ten abreast on the sidewalk—"would be a good night to go down the Village and dance with some short-haired women and long-haired men, don't you think?"

Ondine looked around, at the cars up and down the street. "Oh, I don't know. I've got to get home, Freddy'll be expecting me."

"Oh, come on. We've got to celebrate the night of righteousness and send off Mrs. Garland in style, don't we? Look, there's a pay phone. Here's a dime. Why don't you give Freddy a call? I'd love to meet up with him. See this person that's got you going down the straight and narrow. Well, clean, anyway. What do you think, Andy?"

Andy looked off to the side, almost rolling his eyes. "Sorry, I've got to get home and dissect my tapes."

"Come on, Ondine, Doc. Let's go dance downtown."

THE STREETS WERE steaming as we exited the subway at Christopher Street. A curl of vapor was rising out of the grate on the right and we crossed 7th Street to walk past the little park on the right and cross the street.

"This is a little place I've heard about. Ondine, you should be able to get us in."

It was a nondescript brick building with blacked-out windows. There was a neon sign above, but it wasn't lit up. You could hear some kind of music coming from somewhere. It sounded like black music, but I couldn't be sure.

"Oh, hang on." Sherlock knocked a pattern—three short, two long. "You have to know a few little secrets. Go on, Ondine. They only let you in if you look a certain way."

We all heard the hatch slide back from over the keyhole. "Yeah?"

Sherlock prodded Ondine.

"Oh, um, can we come in?"

"What for?" The voice was gruff, very old New York, like a truck driver or a fireman.

Ondine looked at me, then Sherlock. Sherlock gave him a nod. "A drink?" Sherlock raised his eyebrows. "We're here to dance away our sorrows at the ending of a legend." Ondine cocked his head and put his hands on his hips.

The bolt slid back and the door opened. The music was coming from inside the bar, of course, and it was black music, with its incessant beat. A massive Italian stood there in black work pants and a black jacket. We filed in, and Sherlock came last, entering backwards. He turned around and gave me a smile.

"We've been followed. I'm certain of it. It's good to know I'm not paranoid. Let's let the evening play out into night and see who turns up following darling Ondine."

We paid our three dollars and signed the register with false names. There were more John Smiths at this nightclub than lived in the five boroughs. Sherlock signed himself Inspector Clouseau. I signed as Doc Holiday. The bouncer gave us each two drink tickets. Ondine smiled at the beat and looked at me and nodded. Clearly his cleaning up his act didn't extend to booze or dancing in underground Village gay bars. Sherlock walked me through the smoke-filled bar, looking around.

"Let's go to the bar. Look at that—retail duty stamps. Naughty naughty. Illegal booze sales. Probably no liquor license. Hiding behind the pretense of being a private club." He got us both gin and seltzer—no lime, unfortunately, not in this hole, and barely any ice. It looked all melted, and there were fingerprints all over our glasses. Not the strictest hygiene standards.

The dance floor was a riot of color: shirtless men, drag, butch girls with short hair, and anything in between. There were at least four people dressed up as Dorothy. Whether these were regular transvestites or just there to honor Her Imperial Majesty I didn't know. Blacks and Hispanics and whites dancing like the world outside didn't matter. It seemed lighter in here, somehow. I pushed my way across the floor searching for the bathroom, which required not a little bit of dancing, and between the flashing and the blacklight it was enough to bring on the tiniest hint of a flashback. The toilets were foul, with a chiseled farm boy wearing overalls and cowboy boots kissing a skinny little thing in a tight pink shirt. It must've been the only space they could get enough room for their roaming hands.

When I pushed my way back across the dance floor I saw Sherlock standing there, looking amazing. Almost exactly like he looked the first time I saw him, leaning against the wall and scanning everybody, but I understood now what it was he was doing. I could see that he was where he could watch the front door and where he could see Ondine dancing. He had one foot up and was rolling a cigarette of his strong brown tobacco.

It seemed like Sherlock had turned favors into a type of currency. Everyone owed him something, and while he used money from time to time, favors were a better currency. They got him things that money couldn't. Loyalty, information, attention—or the lack of it.

I went and stood next to Sherlock and he handed me the extra cigarette he'd rolled. "I saw you watching me there. What time is it?"

"Jesus Christ, it's almost one o'clock. What happens to time in these places? It's like it loses its shape. Another drink?"

He looked troubled. "Perceptions change. You're enjoying a collective unconscious experience, getting a little bit high off the people here. Time is elastic, according to our experiences. You needed to blow off some steam anyway, John. Ondine seems to be getting along all right. Is one of those his Freddy, do you suppose?"

I looked around, and spotted Ondine wrapped in the arms of one man, with another writhing away behind him. "I don't know, but something tells me not."

"Do you think I could have been wrong, John?"

"About what?"

"About being followed. I would have expected the raid to come before this."

"What are you talking about?"

"Come on. Let's go outside."

We moved to the door. The bouncer looked us up and down. "No ins and outs. You go, you're gone, fairies."

We shrugged at him and went outside. It was like hitting air conditioning, even that evening in New York, after the sweat and smoky haze of the club. Sherlock nodded across the street at the tiny park with the knee-high fence. We stepped over the fence and sat on a bench facing the Stonewall Inn, and Sherlock rolled us both a cigarette.

"Damn Ondine. There was something about him the last time, when we saw him outside the Factory, remember? He was watching. He kept acting oddly, asking strange questions, probing for information, and then he suddenly goes clean. Can you imagine? Ondine? Clean and straight? The only reason he'd do that is if it could get the heat off him somehow. He's been using going straight as an excuse to stop spying on Andy and the Factory. I laid the trap today, and he came, and I'm pretty sure I saw his handler."

"What are you talking about?"

"He's been a spy. For the police, or somebody. Someone's been using him. They've probably got something on him, some charge they're holding over his head to make him deliver more information. I've been thinking we've all been watched, but they should have come by now. The NYPD can get a few dozen officers together pretty quickly, if they want to bust some gays. I can't see why they wouldn't... Wait. Sssh." He held up one hand and took both of our cigarettes with the other and silently crushed them under his foot.

Two cars had blocked off both ends of the block, and around twenty of New York's Finest walked up to the Stonewall Inn and pounded on the door.

"Police! We're taking the place!"

They hammered on the door until it opened, and they held up their badges and billy clubs and marched in. I was glad we'd left.

"Look, John. The suits. Those two are NYPD, but that other one, in the navy suit? That's no police officer. He's a Fed."

"What? How do you know?"

"The suit, for one. Charcoal or navy blue. Classic Fed. You can see that he knows he's in charge. See the other ones? They're deferring to him. Look, see there? The first ones coming out in handcuffs? They've just looked at him to see. He's watching, but for us, or for Ondine? Let's stay here."

More people came out of the nightclub, one by one, all of them looking down. They were the most normal, no one dressed up, no one in drag, no one too effete. The good homos. Some of them stood around, waiting, and that was the pigs' mistake. They let them wait for their friends or neighbors or whatever. There was silence for a while. The pigs in suits conferred with one another; there was some sort of disagreement. The Stonewall's managers were brought out in handcuffs, and the staff from the bar. A few ragged cheers came out from the assembled homos. "Good going! Make them pay for their shitty drinks! Get us some running water in there, why don't you!" There were five uniforms standing around ten handcuffed Mafioso types. They looked around, and when they brought a couple of drag queens out in handcuffs to a murmur of protest from the crowd, shouted into the bar to, "Hold on till the paddy wagon arrives."

The cops standing around guarding the prisoners started to look nervous. There must've been forty people standing around; way more than they could shoot or club. A murmur went across the crowd, punctuated by shouts. "Why the hell you guys gotta bust our balls? We ain't doing nothing." "Gay Power!" "Who complained?" "Oh, no. Harass the homo!"

The cops looked nervous. Some of them drew their billy clubs and some of them put their hands on their guns, and the crowd quieted down, a little bit, but murmurs went across it. A police wagon came up, driving over the edge of the sidewalk at the end of the street. Sherlock put one finger up, urging me to stay still here in the shadows where we could watch unobserved.

Two cops got out of the wagon and went around and opened the doors. They looked over at their pig brothers, and laughed. "What are you, scared of a bunch of pansies? Come on. Let's get 'em in here." He called through the door. "Okay, bring 'em out. The cavalry's here."

Four cops exited the door with three drag queens and a short-haired, short, muscular woman in a tank top, her hands cuffed in front of her. She was fighting, and she pulled away from the cops and ran a few steps. Two cops broke off from guarding the door to help out the pigs chasing the woman. She stopped, smiled, and made as though to allow herself to be arrested again, and then when the pigs were close she smashed one of them in the nose with her forehead and kicked the second one in the shin, missing a strike at his testicles.

The murmurs from the crowd changed in tone. They sounded bolder, more sure of themselves. The woman backed away from the four pigs now approaching her and looked around at the good homos and shouted, "What the hell are you guys just standing around for? *Do* something already!"

Memory is fleeting, and changes all the time. Ask two witnesses to an event what happened and you'll get two conflicting statements. Even what they agree on might be demonstrably wrong. Camera evidence, for instance. My mental image of this moment fills me with shivers each time I recall it. It probably didn't really happen quite like this, but here's what I remember.

"Do something!" shouted the woman, and the cop stepping towards her came face-to-face against the perfect, silent parabola of a brick spinning in from the hand of a tall black transvestite in an outrageous hat made of pineapples. I don't think it hurt him, not really, but it shocked him. It's lucky for homos everywhere that those four cops reached for their billy clubs and not their guns, that they backed up as the crowd found the power in their own limbs. A bottle flew, along with the shouted words "It's the revolution!" and more bricks. Another drag queen stomped a cop with her heel, and a big beefcake slammed his forehead into a pig who was looking like he was ready for the woman. After that, it was like a flood. Shouting and hooting rose, the drag queen in the Carmen Sandiego hat was there in the middle of it, kicking and punching. The pure force of numbers had the pigs in complete disarray. I wasn't really a military man; I was really only in country to patch up boys so they wouldn't die too quickly. I could recognize a rout, though. The pigs had no discipline, no coordination, and they fell back more like a mob than a retreat into the bar, one of them bleeding from his nose.

"Hey, there, darlings in your bracelets. Come on over here, they don't suit!" A tall, thin man in a rainbow tank top and a big afro near the front had a big smile on his face: he was holding up some keys he'd snatched from one of the cops.

Sherlock tapped me on the shoulder and pointed down the street. The three suits were getting into one of the cars at the end of the block, their movements interrupted by wild gesticulations. It was an odd scene, like watching the television with the sound turned off. You'd expect to hear shouting, but they were controlling their voices, avoiding attention as they got in the car and drove away.

"Well, this isn't going how they expected tonight would go. The homos have some courage after all."

Ondine was nowhere to be seen. He must have been inside the

bar, still, unless he got out without Sherlock seeing him, which wasn't likely.

We watched in amazed fascination as the homos took up arms together, a tangle of colored limbs, breaking windows and hurling abuse at the police barricaded in the Stonewall Inn, along with more bricks and bottles. Someone somehow ripped a parking meter up and two street queens started using it as a battering ram, trying to break the door down. People pulled trashcans from somewhere and lit them on fire and dumped their contents in through the windows, trying to smoke out the pigs.

We stuck around for a while, watching the chaos, until the tactical pigs showed up with their body armor and riot shields. It was excellent at first. The homos didn't disperse, and when they were talking tactics, a bunch of the girls started a chorus line, jeering at the cops. They started to form up into ranks, which I recognized all too well. I tapped Sherlock on the shoulder, and pointed at them, mouthing *Time to go*, and we slipped out the back of the park and walked east, with the splendor of the day and the night gleaming in our minds.

> *Mycroft—*
> *I found your friend in the Factory. It would appear that he's managed to get himself away from you and yours. You may have accidentally stirred up some trouble trying to get him back. Your misguided policies are going to bear this fruit. I hope you enjoy the harvest.*
>
> *—Sherlock*

"Look at that, Sherlock. Another riot in Christopher Park last night. Imagine in ten, twenty, fifty years, looking back and thinking we were there. It'll be like the moon landing, but for homophiles."

"Someone was directing that, John, and it didn't play into their plans to have a bunch of queers rebel. If anything actually comes from it, it'll be because they've got more important fish to fry."

"Look here, they think that the Black Panthers might be involved, and the Students for a Democratic Society. 'Conspiring to organize the homos.'"

"That's exactly what I'm saying, John. The media have the link already. 'Gays are getting together with both the scary black men with guns and the evil people who started the riots in Chicago, disrupting the Democratic convention.' Message received."

"What's wrong with you, Holmes? This is a big deal for people like you and me."

"Are you a gay, John? A homo? Do you identify with that place we've been, dancing late at night? Sure, it's a fun group of people, but those people aren't us, and we aren't them. I've never seen you put on a dress or affect an accent or be particularly attracted to men. We spend time together, like each other, get naked together and, yeah, we sleep together. It's not anybody's business who we make it with. That's only between me and those people I choose to have in my bed. It doesn't have to have a deeper meaning. It doesn't mean we have to be part of a movement. The important thing that I learned last night? Ondine's definitely mixed up with something. Something federal. There's no other reason for a Fed to be there directing the raid of a tiny gay club in New York City."

"What are you talking about, Holmes? What's Ondine mixed up with?"

"I've been pretty sure he's been some kind of informant for the pigs of some stripe. He's been on edge for ages. Remember when we saw him outside the party? Writing down who was coming and going? Why did he go clean so suddenly? Maybe as a reward for something. More likely he's been taking the edge off his usefulness, and the Factory's not stirring up trouble. That's why we went, John. I brought him down there because

I knew someone would come after him. I expected someone to grab him and drag him into a car. I didn't expect a full-blown raid. Ondine's the informant, but we've managed to use him to get information. It's too bad he's probably compromised. We could have passed him false information, followed the trail." Sherlock paced for a minute, and then looked at the wall above his cluttered tool bench.

"Come on, help me clear off this wall. I've got too much of Bill's problem in my head. Time to get it out of the attic of my brain, store it on the wall, and reserve the analytic abilities of my mind for understanding the connections between these disconnected facts."

nine
JUST BECAUSE YOU'RE PARANOID

A MONTH WENT by and it seemed like the gays were winning. I didn't know what to think. Sherlock was right, but I was still excited. Maybe I was partly gay, like Kinsey said.

Sherlock came in the door in a huff. "Libraries, John. You can get me into the CUNY library, right? Come along and read some academic journals?"

"What?"

"I think I can convince NYU to give me an alumni card as well, even though I'm not technically an alumnus. Come on. We need to read up and find out what we can."

So we started to spend time in libraries. It was tedious work, weeks and weeks of cross-referencing and pulling down information. I didn't know what he wanted, but I followed his lead, until it turned out that I was too slow for him, most of the time, and I just stood around. I started reading journals that Sherlock was done with, and then started ordering my own. There was tremendous work being done on the brain and neurochemistry. I thought I owed it to my patients to explore the edges of research in the areas of the brain. I wanted to explore the possibilities of actually using chemistry to expand the mind, increase intelligence, creativity. Writers were infamous drunks, but also terrible depressives. There were promising chemicals that seemed to be stimulating empathy as well as reducing appetite. What if we could isolate the euphoric effects and remove the adverse effects? What if you could remove the hangover, but keep the fun? Boost intelligence? Creativity?

I read, and I experimented, while Sherlock read, building a constellation on the wall of photocopied notes, pictures, all linked to a map with colored pins all over it.

Tensions started boiling all over New York that summer. The gay rights movement started, and the Young Lords organized themselves and their neighborhoods in their purple berets. They somehow got all that trash in the middle of Third Avenue, blocking the streets in the early mornings when the garbage trucks were supposed to head down to the Upper East side. When the cops came out, they burned the garbage and threw bottles and stones and trash at them. Then the Young Lords took over a church, saying that it was the property of the people. They set up a clinic in it, nurses and doctors volunteering their time. I don't know where they got their equipment, but there was an x-ray machine when we went to go have a look. We were told it had been requisitioned for the struggle.

"DID YOU KNOW that there's been a significant increase in university funding over the last ten years, John? There's the spillover from the Space Program, but this seems even bigger than that."

"Hmmm?" I was reading in our growing collection of academic journals about the active component of grass being identified, and being posited as an analogue to a neurotransmitter. There was also a modification to Amphedoxamine: a very old chemical reaction, but it seemed promising and I thought it was worth an attempt at trying myself. I'm no chemist, but this seemed fairly straightforward. I was used to being interrupted by Sherlock, but it wasn't usually anything important.

"Patterns, John. That's what this research is all about. Finding them. Where are the patterns, where is the power, and why would someone want to discredit Bill? The Ford Foundation has been spending tens if not hundreds of millions growing universities over the past four or five years. More buildings. More research grants. More growth. They've been getting government matches or other foundation matches for a lot of it as well. Some universities have doubled in faculty size, and gotten new buildings and libraries and laboratories and everything. Did you know that? When in doubt, John, look for the money. Who benefits? In America, that's money. Look at this list of universities that have been funded by Ford and received matching grants from the US government."

"Yeah? So? There's two or three dozen schools there."

"What about the ones who have good math departments? That cuts it down to sixteen. If you look only at universities publishing number theory, there are seven."

"But Bill's only got beaten to the punch on six papers."

"Exactly, John. And after talking to him I've identified at least two other potential papers in Bill's notebooks. Two different theories that he'd worked out but not yet written up or submitted for publication. One of them is in a notebook that was 'lost' and found again over a year ago. Why don't we go talk to some mathematics professors at the University of Chicago?"

ten

WHY CHICAGO

THAT'S HOW NOON a few days later found us at Grand Central finding the platform for the B&O Capitol railroad. It had fallen off from its heyday, and it was nice, even though we didn't get first class tickets. I couldn't remember the last time I'd left New York. The air in August was stifling, and the town was quiet with all the power brokers away in the Hamptons. Andy hadn't been in touch since the whole Garland thing. I guessed we were on the outs, or he'd found another supply. I was happy with the air conditioning on the train. We didn't splash out on sleeper tickets, but we had plenty of space to ourselves.

There was something pleasant and relaxing about beating the heat while watching the miles roll past, out first through all those commuter towns that people moved to: Jersey City and Wilmington, passing the water on the left and going through Baltimore and DC. I should have probably read a book or something, but I just wanted to stare out the window and watch the miles get eaten up.

Sherlock stared out as well, appearing lost in the countryside, but I knew he was thinking, pondering, planning his move. He turned to me and spoke up.

"We'll get in in the afternoon, John. I want to do two things while we're here. I've got a list of math professors that I want

389

to chase up. Could take a few days, maybe a week. We're in too early to go straight to the University, but I thought we could go to see about these Black Panthers in Chicago. I like the idea of seeing if the praise that Joseph has heaped on them is true, and I suspect... something involving them. It may or may not be relevant to Bill's situation."

I nodded to him, then sat back in contemplation, watching a world slide by. The railroad was the dividing line of cities. The neighborhoods framing the tracks in the outskirts of Baltimore and Pittsburgh; little nondescript towns with good and bad sides of the tracks, but I couldn't ever tell which was which.

It was still early morning when we pulled into Chicago's Grand Central station. We'd had fitful sleep in our seats.

"They're talking about knocking down this station. Not enough traffic, it seems."

I looked around at the Art Deco splendor of the building. "It would be a shame. An awful shame. But maybe Chicago has more important things to preserve or fix now than an empty station. Now, it's the El and a walk."

WE COULD HEAR the crowd from a couple of blocks away on Western Avenue. It was dirty, this part of the city. Not as dirty as Spanish Harlem had been, but older, with more burned-out shopfronts and tumbledown buildings. You could see why the Black Panthers, or anyone who brought stability, would do well here. Schoolchildren walked past derelict and collapsed tenements. Men in stained tank tops stood around all over the street, sweating in the August heat.

We heard the cadences of political rhetoric, the call and response of the leader working his crowd from around the corner. Madison Street. Fred Hampton was there in front of what looked like a bombed-out office with the same scraggly chinstrap beard. There was a crowd, probably a hundred people, maybe more. It was a motley crowd, mostly black, but some Hispanics, and quite a few whites as well.

"Is that Dr. Spock, Sherlock?"

It was, indeed, the famous author and doctor. We listened to Hampton.

"So that's how I got convicted, and out on this appeal bond. The people got together and collected the money to get me out, and for that I am humbled and honored. Every one of you knows that I've given my life and my body over to the people, and I'll fight and die for the people, whether those I'm working for agree with me or not. I was not born to die in a car wreck. I was not born to die slipping on a piece of ice, or of a bad heart, or of lung cancer. I'm going to die doing the things I was born for. High off the people. I'm going to die in the international proletariat revolutionary struggle, and you should come along.

"Now, you want to know what the funniest thing is about this so-called trial? They talked about me stealing all those Good Humor bars after beating up the driver. Seventy-one dollars' worth. Seven hundred and ten bars. Me, I know I'm big, so I asked what I was supposed to be doing, eating all them bars. The prosecutor said I did it to give those ice cream bars out to children. They lie about me, just like they lie about you, but the only thing they're going to try to convict me for is some kind of Robin Hood thing."

A murmur of laughter pealed across the crowd.

"Now, this here, the office getting raided and shot up. You know and I know how our training works in the Black Panther Party. They're going to be saying the Black Panther Party shot at them, but we're just exercising our rights. Second Amendment says the people have a right to their weapons. Our training, everyone will tell you, is shoot second. We have the right to defend ourselves from a tyrannical government who has visited upon us a long train of abuses and usurpation. We shoot if we're shot at, whether it's a murderer, a robber, a rapist trying to come up in our homes and offices, or the government's pigs, being all three of those.

"Now, two weeks ago when I was locked up and waiting for my trial, the Chicago pigs came in shooting up the offices, illegally. They put it in the papers that we were arming ourselves, that we're devils coming out to shoot cops down in the streets, but you can see we're just defending ourselves. You count these bullet holes, you know they shot us out, ran us out. We got those motherfuckers, though. Only one Black Panther died and one wounded, but we wounded six of those pigs and killed two of them. I don't celebrate the deaths of people, but these were soldiers, agents of a tyrannical system that was trying to murder us in our beds.

"After they ran us out of there, you know what they did? Went upstairs and burned up all our records, burned up boxes of cornflakes and oatmeal we had for the free breakfast program. Taking food out the mouths of children in this neighborhood. They had no reason to do that. They want to shut us down. They don't like that we've been doing their jobs for them. They don't like the idea that black, brown, and yellow children get an education and some breakfast. They don't like the idea that we can turn gangs into revolutionaries. They want us to keep being angry with the Young Patriots there, with the Young Lords. They know that if we keep fighting each other, none of us will notice that they're the ones keeping us down.

"Well, I'm here to tell you, each and every one of you: I—am—a revolutionary. Now, you could say it too. Repeat after me: I—am—a revolutionary. Power to the people."

The crowd had been chiming in with nods, and "umm-humms" and "uh-uh" here and there, but they all chimed in together, a hundred voices there in the street. "I—am—a revolutionary!"

Fred spoke back up. "If you say, 'I don't want to make a commitment, cause I'm not ready to die,' what you did, you're dead already. You have to understand that the people have to pay the price for peace. If you dare to struggle, you dare to win. If you dare not to struggle, then goddamnit you don't deserve to win. Now listen here what we're going to do. The man, what he wants is for us to shut up our shop and leave our storefront. Do you think that's what we're going to do?"

"Oh, no!" said the crowd.

"No, no, we're going to go right back in and fix up our offices. Get new glass in the windows, but put some plywood up there if there isn't any. We going to sweep out the upstairs and get this office back open. Fortified again, better this time. If the pig wants to come, he can come. We got a lease on this place, so we going to open it right back up, starting right now. Power to the people!"

The people responded, right back, "Power to the people!" and Fred Hampton and his bodyguard William and Dr. Spock and all of these people, filed inside and just got to work. I turned to Sherlock, and he was gone. I looked for him—with his height he should be immediately visible—but I couldn't find him anywhere. I was alone, and I was in a strange city, standing outside of a Black Panther office that had recently been the scene of a gun battle. I put my hands in my pockets as I turned to stroll, and there was a note from Sherlock. Odd. He must have slipped it in while Hampton was talking.

> *John—*
> *I'm going to go to the University. Stay here and see what you can see. Keep an eye on the Panthers. I think one of them may be some kind of informant. Keep your eyes and ears open.*

I WENT INTO the room and found Fred, asked him if he remembered me from Spanish Harlem. He said he did, but he looked completely worn out. "Look, I'm a qualified medic. I'd be happy to lend a hand in your free clinic if you'd like."

"Sure thing, man. It's down the street a couple of blocks. Talk to that sister over there. She'll take you over. She's a nurse."

"Maybe you should come, too. You look like you're about to faint."

"No, man, I'm okay. I just got a lot on my mind, you know. Got this appeal thing to worry about, got a baby coming in three months. Then there's the whole overthrowing the capitalist system and fomenting a revolution, redistributing all the power and the wealth to the people. You know." Fred's smile erased the pain from his face for half a second, and I realized I quite liked him.

"You've been eating prison food, right? Why don't you come down to the clinic, I can look at your bloods. You might just need a supplement, or maybe a couple of day's rest. Here, hold on, step over here, those guys are trying to get through with a ladder."

A white guy with a brown shirt and a Confederate flag patch on it passed through, working with a man in Black Panther uniform. He looked me up and down, and spoke to me in a thick Southern accent, skipping over his consonants and extending his vowels.

"What's the matter, son? You never seen no white boy working hand-in-hand with a negro before? These are some honorable blacks, here. Good people. Chairman Fred, there, he showed us how we were all pissed off at the nig—er, blacks and browns and whatever, we should've been fighting with the men in their suits downtown. Fight the power, power to the people."

Fred smiled and shook his head. "Maybe I should come with you. Seems like I'm just in the way of the people here. William! Over here. We're gonna go on down to the clinic... What's your name?"

"John Watson. They call me Doc, mostly."

"Doc, this is William. He's in charge of security. He'll keep an eye on me, make sure I ain't going to go get killed or nothing."

I remembered William. The tall, skinny black man who had stood in the corner on that hot June night and watched everything. He made me uneasy then, and he didn't make me feel any better now. I couldn't put my finger on it.

We'd got to the clinic. "This here is Janelle. She's a powerful sister with a needle and thread. If she was a white man, she'd be a surgeon."

"Hello, Doc. Pleased to meet you. Can I get your blood type and are you allergic to anything, please?"

I hadn't been asked for my blood since I had been in country. "What for?"

Fred spoke up. "Anyone working here, we keep records on everyone, just in case anything happens to them. Better forearmed in case we don't get forewarned, know what I mean?"

I looked over the holes in the walls of the Panther offices and the spent shell casings in the street as we left. I did know what he meant. "A-negative. NKDA."

THE CLINIC WAS small, but well laid out. There were a few people there, waiting to be seen. And Fred wouldn't let me examine him until we'd looked over the 'people,' particularly the children.

There wasn't anything especially wrong. The first patient was a kid, maybe twelve, with lacerations on his hands from a rusty fence. We didn't have records of his vaccinations or anything, so we gave him a tetanus booster and cleaned it up well.

Janelle was, as Fred said, excellent. If I'd had her in Vietnam, I'd have put her in charge of the nurses, if not recommended her to be sent for medical training, although of course the Army doesn't work that way. I couldn't imagine a 'negro officer' in command anywhere except in the front lines. She was more than up to the task of running anything that came through the door that day, and I told Fred.

"I know. She should be a doctor herself, maybe a famous

surgeon. We told her we'd send her to medical school, but she said no way. 'Five years away from the people wouldn't do nobody no good, now would it?' is what she said. Made me proud, man, of what we're building down here. Still, it's short-term. I start to worry about the bigger movement. What we're gonna do when the revolution comes, you know? We're gonna need revolutionary surgeons and engineers just as much as pipe-fitters and academics. Hard to think that far ahead when we got the pigs coming by and shooting at us every couple of weeks."

There was something infectious about Fred Hampton. I had trouble explaining it, but I found myself imagining the future right along with him. "The Declaration of Independence was 1776. The constitution wasn't ratified till 1789. Thirteen years. Some of that was wartime, but it took a while. You've got time."

"We're not no American Revolution, though. Rich white men landowners fighting to create their own country where they could go on being white landowners. A system built on slavery and oppression. A capitalist, oppressive system built on the backs of the people. No, Doc, the revolution has to be built up carefully, it has to be a *people*'s revolution, shifting power to the people where it belongs."

"I never thought about it that way, you know. I should be ashamed."

"No, man. No reason why you should be ashamed. The people have been made to feel ashamed for being ignorant for centuries. Ignorance just means you ain't found something out yet. Einstein was ignorant before he developed that bomb. Little children are ignorant before we teach them to read. You never had a reason to think about the revolution like that. Better to think about the coming revolution than glorifying the ones in the past, though."

"Hold on there, Fred. Your eyes are drooping. Nurse Janelle, could I have that flashlight please? Here, follow the light." I started to examine him. "Dehydrated. You need to drink more water and less coffee. Look at your nails, here. See how they're all grooved and brittle? More iron in your diet. Nurse Janelle?"

"Sister Janelle, or just Janelle, please."

"You earned that title, I'm going to give it to you. Sorry to make you run around like this. Have you got any IV iron supplement?"

"We had some. May have used it all on some pregnant sisters. I'll check."

"Fred, you need to get more iron in your diet. That'll probably do it. Get a bit of rest for a couple of days. Eat stuff like liver, beef, oysters. Beans and greens are good, too. How much do you sleep at night?"

"Man, I don't even know. You're not going to get me to sleep much more, though, Doc. I'll try to get some better food. Drink more water and stuff. The revolution ain't gonna come if we sleep in every day."

"Okay, Fred. You eat better, and try to get a little more sleep. It's not just about you: an army can't march if they're sleeping or tired. I saw enough young men ruined from lack of sleep in country. You're a leader. You can die serving the people, but if you fall asleep before you make it to the battlefield, it won't be of any use to anyone. Now, where's your blood fridge? A-negative is pretty useful. I could give you a unit if you like. I gave enough blood in the Army to bleed myself dry a few times. I suppose a pint here couldn't hurt. What do you think, William? You up for a donation?"

William looks at me from his chair next to the door. "I ain't so big on needles, Doc, but you go ahead on and bleed yourself out for the people."

eleven

A WEEK

I SPENT A week in that clinic, patching up burnt hands and treating dehydration and malnutrition. Kids told me how much they liked their free breakfast, which was back the next Monday. A group of people went out and came back with huge boxes of cereal and oatmeal, and then a whole shopping cart filled with bottles of milk. The upstairs was barely swept out and it was already being filled up with food.

I think some of Sherlock's lessons may have been making an impression. I wasn't just seeing people come through, I was noticing the money changing hands. People were leaving coins and notes for the Black Panthers, which must have been what was paying for the medicines and gauze I was using, and the food disappearing into the children's bellies. People were bringing sheets of wood and cans of paint, too.

Sherlock would disappear every morning, leaving like a man on his way to work, and coming home in the evening. He didn't talk about what he did during the day.

"You remember Solon, John? 'Count no man happy till the end is known'? It's the same with investigation. We mustn't draw conclusions with partial information. A few more days. We'll talk through what we've found out on the train back to New York."

That was it, for a week. We were staying in a cramped apartment that was part ammo dump, part meeting hall, and part sleeping den. They gave us a room, and Fred shushed several people who started to ask about the sleeping arrangements. "Ain't no business of yours, now is it? Besides, it ain't like there's a whole lot of spare rooms going. Two men big enough to share a bed. Ain't like none of us wouldn't, neither."

It was nice, doing something with my medical education. I'd spent half a year just trying to make ends meet in New York, before I lucked into the gig with the Factory. We didn't really know about PTSD then, and if anyone brought up the war, we got to hear about how much worse it had been for our fathers and grandfathers, in Korea and the Pacific and the trenches. I didn't know what those guys that I sewed back together were going through, but most of what I remembered was malaria, mosquitoes, and blood. All for what, for the pride of something or other? Dominoes. I was starting to see the Black Panthers' point. Using my hands, doing something, day after day, was a good thing. I could wash up in the morning, and at night, and go to sleep and sleep the sleep of the just, for the first time in a long time.

"YOU KNOW WHAT I'm going to miss, Sherlock? The sky. Did you notice? The buildings are all lower, and you're not in perpetual shadow like you are in New York."

"It's too slow, John. I'm not sure we could survive outside of New York."

"No, I don't know what I'd do without the incessant buzz, but it is nice to see the sky, one without helicopters riddled with bullet holes buzzing around it and so much goddamn blood."

Sherlock looked at me, and I could see his mind searching for the right thing to say. "Looking at the sky is a distraction, John. You miss what's right there on the ground in front of you."

The train rocked back and forth, crawling its way along

the rails north of Washington DC. We'd spent another night onboard, resting and waiting for the other to speak first.

"Okay, John. What did you find out?".

"I spent a week taking care of people, Sherlock. It was good. I felt useful, and useful to something that mattered. My hands didn't shake. I'm not sure I'd want to do surgery again, but wrapping up burn victims, stitching cuts, giving tetanus injections to children? That was good."

"I don't mean about your feelings, John. What did you see? I hoped you noticed something, some important detail. For instance I noticed that the guns in the apartment we stayed in were kept unloaded, except for the guard who sat up at the front. That the back door led to a blind alley, so it would be easy to trap people in the apartment. That despite the Panthers having plenty of pistols, no one, not even William, the head of security, carried one as a matter of course. That's the arms discipline. What did you see? And more importantly, what did you *observe?*"

I watched a small town pass by. A boy in a striped vest, waving out of the back of his house. I wondered if he had floorboards, or a floor open to the dirt below. "Malnutrition. The free breakfast is a genius idea. Children going to school need glucose in their brains. It's not enough, though. There's iron deficiency everywhere. The people there are eating the cheapest food they can get. Oatmeal's actually pretty healthy, but the children are mostly very thin. Not enough protein. Sugar's a cheaper calorie than beef or vegetables."

"Good. What else? What about the people, the people in the office and the people running the clinic?"

"The nurse they have, Sister Janelle. She's amazing. She's got more raw talent than some of the white doctors I've worked with. Ones that went to good medical schools. Fred Hampton is going to work himself into a coma, but he seems like he's convinced he's going to die fighting. He said something, I can't remember exactly what, but it was to the effect that he might have died anyway, in a gang or something, so he didn't mind if his life got used up for the people. Something like that. William is an odd choice for security. He doesn't seem like he really knows what he's doing."

"What do you mean, John?"

That's when it hit me, that he was doing his job wrong, and it wasn't just at the clinic, either.

"Wait a minute, Sherlock. Let me think. He sat in the clinic when I was watching Fred, and he watched us. But he sat next to the door, with his back to it. Not on the side where he'd be behind the door if it opened. If someone came in he'd be the first thing they saw, and presumably shot. He was observant—he was watching—but he was watching us. Fred and me. Not the door. He wasn't paying attention like someone in charge of security who was being attacked with some regularity. It was the same in East Harlem, remember? He stood up there, and he watched us, listening to us, but he hardly paid any attention to the door."

Sherlock nodded, drinking up my words, the mask falling from his face. He was visibly excited, thrilled.

"What about you? What did you find out? What new information have you got? You have to share, too, you know."

"It's big, John. Very big. It might be the biggest. One of the math professors—someone who's on a course for tenure, but hasn't quite got there—received a letter, a thick packet of photocopied notebook pages, about a year ago. He had no idea what they were, at first. Were they meant for him? Were they the work of a student? If so, it seemed that it was an exceptionally brilliant student. He teaches mostly the big survey courses and some advanced classes, but strictly undergraduate level. He realized it was someone else's work, unlike six of his colleagues at other universities that Bill, you, and I could name, but he set the papers aside, not sure what to do with them. Said he'd come across them from time to time, and pick them up. There was part of him that was interested in the work. Some of it was just doodles, but most of it was what looked like number theory. Not his area of expertise, but interesting to look at. You could see his morality playing out with his curiosity across his face. He just wasn't sure what to do, or even who to tell. He thought there were people in the department that would work on it for the intellectual challenge alone, and then maybe publish, either forgetting where it came from or assuming that their work was the greater part of the discovery. He went back and forth on it for 'a month or two,' he said.

"That's when he had a visitor. A clean-cut, all-American type. 'Ice-blue eyes, blond crew cut and with his jaw practically shaved off' is how he described him. Asked him if he received his package. Said that 'the government did research' sometimes, and that they couldn't really publish it themselves, for one reason or another. 'Think about the Bomb. Think about the Russians, now. It's good for us if we're publishing plenty of research, but we don't want the Russkies to look too closely at government priorities. So we pass on some stuff like this to people we like. A helping hand, you know. Makes America look more innovative, better at science and engineering.' He then went on to suggest that it would unlock further funding down the road. This is lifeblood for an academic. More funding equals more publishing equals more prestige equals more research grants."

"Well, Sherlock? What did he do?"

"He put him off. Told him it was fiendishly complex, and that it would take some time to understand it all and then finish it. A month later, he got two more sheets in the mail. And three after another month. He gets calls at random, usually when it's inconvenient, like right when he's walking out of a class, or a few minutes at the end of his office hours. He was fifteen minutes early for a date once and the visitor sat down, bought him a drink, and gave him the sales pitch all over. I looked over the photocopies. They're extra pages from Bill's notebooks. The thing is that some of the pages don't seem to be exactly relevant to the core work. There were several pages of doodles. The only thing connecting them is that they're all from the same notebook."

"But what does it mean, Sherlock? Who on earth would want to steal Bill's research? And what does it have to do with William?"

"All will be revealed in time. We'll need to either get Bill to New York from Philly, or else get ourselves there. Not just yet, though. A week, I think."

twelve

WHAT WOULD YOU THINK...

"WHAT WOULD YOU think about breaking into an FBI office?"

Bill went pale, and his eyes got wide over the dark ever-present dark circles surrounding them. "What?"

"It's a shock, isn't it? I think it's the only way to find out the rest of the truth. Sorry, hang on, let me back up. Here's what we've found. Someone's taking your notebooks, but only when you're in New York. Ergo they have access in New York. It's someone who's good at thievery. They've got both resources and political leverage. We've uncovered informants inside the Factory. They've got resources inside several universities.

"They're trying to discredit you, personally. I'm sure there are others. Someone's been following you, someone with access. Reading the mail you send. Copying your notebooks, and sending snippets out to other academics, so they can publish and you'll languish. They can both promise and deliver academic funding from the government and at least one major research funding body. I identified seven likely candidates for your notes. Six of them had already published your work as their own. The last one had received photocopies of your notes but put them aside, intriguing though it was, and he was stopped by a Fed, again and again. 'This is how things work,' they told him, and gave a cover story that it was work done in a government lab.

He was offered funding and tenure just for publishing your work.

"I'm pretty sure that one of the Black Panthers in Chicago is an informant, and it's not for the Chicago police department. I saw the sergeant-at-arms in the Harlem Black Panther office, he was watching us carefully—too carefully—when we went in there. Dr. Watson, there, he noticed something similar in Chicago. He was Hampton's bodyguard when he was in New York. There was something odd about him, and I couldn't put my finger on it, but Watson *observed*. He sits in exactly the wrong place to be a bodyguard. He watches Hampton, not the people Hampton's with. He's keeping tabs.

"Now, we have informants across state lines. Infiltrating and observing anti-war protesters and civil rights activists. Mail being opened. Professors being bribed. If you know anything about blackmail, this is how it starts. Once you accept the easy paper, the extra research, then the briber has something over you, and if the carrot doesn't work, the stick will do. Who does this sound like, with all this power? It could be the President, I suppose. It's someone at that level. Who's been in power for over forty years, enough to build a power base? J. Edgar Hoover, that's who. He not only survived the failure of McCarthyism, but he and his FBI have thrived. What threat is there, really, to the FBI's power? What do they do? How many agents do they have? When was the last time you heard about them breaking a big case? Why have they been ready with 'credible sources' after the Stonewall uprising, after the Spanish Harlem garbage offensive, and the Warhol and Kennedy shootings? They've got one villain, and that is subversive groups. I know for a fact that they were wrong about the last one.

"If you eliminate the impossible, whatever is left, no matter how ridiculous, has to be true.

"If nothing else, the FBI is a bureaucracy. And bureaucrats love paperwork filed in triplicate above all else. That's their weakness.

We've seen their footprints across our daily lives, but we need to find out what those footprints mean. Why you, why Hampton? What's the connection? I've spent the last month since we came back from Chicago in the public library, where there's so much information flowing around it should be impossible to keep track of one person's research. There are some small, satellite offices—little more than regular business offices. Many of them don't have alarm systems or even real safes, just locking filing cabinets. It would be very instructive to see a selection of FBI documents. Some of their general orders. Find out what kinds of people they're watching. I've identified four of these satellite offices within two hours of New York that should be easy to break in to. One of them isn't so far from you, Bill. Look, there, just another suburb of Philadelphia. Media, it's called."

"Wouldn't that be treason?"

"Isn't burning draft cards treason? What about breaking into Army recruitment offices? I'd call it civil disobedience. Our own tea party. Citizen's oversight over the FBI. Who are they accountable to? We'd look over everything we found, and anything that could damage an investigation or put an agent in danger we could redact, or just burn the records. We're only looking for stuff that suggests that people are being followed without probable cause. *Quis custodiet ipsos custodes*? The traitor is the one breaking the constitution he's sworn to uphold."

Bill looked at us, and then looked back down. "This is crazy talk. Thanks for the investigation, but I think you're loony. There's no secret conspiracy, not beyond global capitalism and a military industrial complex. It's not... it's not possible. They couldn't have followed me, done all that stuff. I'm sorry, Mr. Holmes, Dr. Watson. I'm afraid I've wasted your time. Thank you and good day."

Bill stood up and walked out, looking around him like a paranoid.

Sherlock shook his head. "I rushed him. He believes me, but he doesn't want to. I hope that nothing happens to him. They're surely after bigger fish than one mad professor who's burned a few draft cards. I really would like to know, though."

thirteen

THE FOURTH OF DECEMBER

CHICAGO IN DECEMBER is dark. The wind coming off Lake Michigan is crippling, cutting through whatever clothes you wear. I'd thought summer in Chicago was brutal, but the winter was worse. There was snow and sleet everywhere, and they said the winter was just starting.

Fred Hampton was dead. Killed overnight in a raid by the police. There were stories about a gun battle, how he and his compatriots shot at the police when they went to serve a warrant on him. Sherlock got us on the first train out.

He was fidgety, didn't sleep the whole eighteen hours of the journey. I was worried. It was the kind of manic behavior that he'd displayed when he'd found out he was too late to save Bobby Kennedy. That time, it had led to a two-week fit of drugs and depression. There was a cold edge to him now. He was usually aloof, fascinated by mysteries, but not emotionally invested. This was like Solanas. Like when he felt it was his fault.

When we got to the apartment—the same one we'd stayed in—it was locked up, but there were signs of a struggle everywhere. We went to the Black Panther offices and everyone stood around with a vacant look. I saw Janelle, the nurse, and went to speak to her, but Sherlock interrupted.

"Does anyone here have the key to that apartment?"

Janelle looked at him. "Why? What do you want to do?"

"They've told a story and I want to see for myself."

"I don't think they want us in there."

"That's what they told you with their guns, once again. Let me go in, Janelle, before anyone else does. I want to see for myself what happened there. If it was a sealed crime scene, they would have put a guard on it."

I spoke up. "He's good at this kind of thing. He might be able to make sense of it. Trust me, Janelle."

She went to the desk and pulled out a ring of keys. "Let me get my coat."

SHERLOCK ASKED US to wait outside when the door opened, and he stepped in, looking around, carefully, bending and squatting to look at different things, being careful not to step on anything. I watched him in this dance that I would see again and again; gathering evidence, sifting and sorting. He was beautiful. He swung a door back and forth and looked at it.

"I can tell you one thing. There has been no gun battle here. Every shot was done by the people entering. Except that, there. There are shotgun pellets buried in the wall. This is where the guard would have sat, wasn't it?"

"Mark Clark was there. He got killed, too. He was on the roster to stay up at night."

"He died right in that chair. This shot, it doesn't make sense. If he was going to shoot at someone attacking, the pellets would be near the entrance, but they're all over the wall and the floor. I'd wager that the gun went off when he got shot. That's it. Everything else is incoming, from the front or the back. Look at that. A trail of bullets across the wall right at bed height. This is where he died, right? Look at this trail of blood. He was dragged off of the bed and left here in the doorway. Here are two bullets in the floor. They shot him on the floor, just to be sure. This wasn't a gunfight or a raid, this was an assassination."

Sherlock was the first one to name Hampton's death an assassination. He spent an hour there that morning, talking Janelle through the evidence, and that's what gave the people the idea that they could refute the story that came out from the pigs. The investigation into Hampton's murder kept coming out, and the Chicago pigs got deeper and deeper into shit. They stonewalled, but the court of public opinion swayed against them. The *Chicago Tribune* ran a big story, swallowing the police story hook, line, and sinker, and somebody leaked information to the media that the FBI thought the Panthers were planning a big shoot-out.

The problem with their narrative was the evidence. The Chicago Panthers, the lawyers, and even members of the public took Sherlock's evidence and added their own, unpicking and disproving every one of the FBI's assertions. The Chicago pigs showed pictures of what they called bullet holes that turned out to be nail holes. They tried to say that the defense attorneys went to a lumberyard and got a fresh door and painted it to confuse the evidence. It was desperate. Eventually, it even came to a grand jury, and the pigs stuck to their story. Point by point, they were refuted. The grand jury agreed with the people and Sherlock in the end. Ninety-nine shots fired by the pigs, including the two that killed Hampton in the end. The pigs were in the wrong, the grand jury found—eventually—but not one of them served a day in jail. They didn't even get charged.

But I'm getting ahead of myself. It took years for the grinding wheels of justice to exonerate the Chicago Panthers, by which time they'd disbanded and the Chicago PD had consolidated their power.

Sherlock watched this unfold from New York, thinking we'd never know the reasons behind the shooting, who was pulling the strings of the FBI and why. It was a depressing thought.

fourteen

EPILOGUE

SHERLOCK WOKE ME on a cold March morning, over a year after Hampton's death. Spring hadn't quite broken through, but the grey snow had started to melt. I was hiding in bed with the blankets over my head when Sherlock poked a copy of the *Philadelphia Inquirer* under the covers, open to page 12 of the local section.

"He's done it, John." He gestured to the small article, just a few inches: *BREAK-IN AT FBI OFFICE.* The article went on to mention how no guns—the presumed target—were stolen, as they were locked in a safe. There weren't any details as to what *was* taken. I was groggy.

"Sherlock, it's too early and too cold for you to be pulling me awake. What's this about?"

Sherlock slowed down, the urgent edge still raising his voice. "It's Bill, it has to be. Remember the small FBI offices I tried to get Bill to burgle? Well, he's done it. Someone has. The Media office just a couple of suburbs over from Haverford. Broken into overnight, during the Fraser-Ali fight, when the whole world was watching men hit each other.

I thought about this for a minute. What information they could have gotten away with. The risks they took. "My god, Sherlock. This is amazing. We should go see him. Find out what they know."

"No, John. That's exactly what we shouldn't do. We need to give them time to uncover whatever they've stolen. My curiosity is beyond piqued. I'm hungry for the knowledge of what they've found out. We have to wait, though. I'm sure that if it *is* the FBI following us, they'll go on high alert. We've been watched, and associated with Bill. Any contact now, anything abnormal, could tip their hand. We can only hope that he contacts us once the heat dies down."

THE *WASHINGTON POST* published the first of the stolen papers two weeks after the burglary. They came in the mail, anonymously, quoted as the 'Citizen's Commission to Investigate the FBI.' A lot of people in the nation went into an uproar, both for and against the publication. The FBI documents talked about 'enhancing paranoia' in political groups and black activist groups, from the violent Black Panthers right down to peaceful movements. One document said the FBI should be giving the impression to political movements 'that there was an FBI agent behind every mailbox.'

The public didn't like that, not one bit. It was clear that the FBI was at the very least exceeding its authority, if not downright breaking the law.

WE NEVER KNEW for sure, but I always assumed that the Hampton murder was what set Bill off—assuming it was Bill. He wouldn't return our calls or answer letters after that. We tried to go meet him in Philadelphia. It must've been spring of 1970, but he refused to meet us. He called Campus Security on us when we went to his office in Haverford. Sherlock and I went and passed by that FBI office in Media. The papers said it was perfect—no alarm, and just a normal deadbolt that had been picked by a professional. Every document in the office had been taken.

*   *   *

HOOVER'S REACTION WAS predictable: close ranks and rally his troops, both agents and the public. Every week there was a new Public Enemy Number One. There was a woman who'd visited the FBI office—long brown hair and glasses, like pretty much every third woman in Philadelphia at that time. He talked about how disclosure of these documents 'endangered lives' and 'encouraged criminality.' They tried to get a court order to stop the publication of the documents, but the *Post* kept publishing, and the rest of the papers soon followed.

What the FBI was apparently doing was beyond the most out-there conspiracy theories. They spied on everyone, from presidents to Black Panthers. They'd spied on Martin Luther King, and other clergy members. The vast majority of the spying was on left-leaning groups. The only right-wing groups were real reactionaries like the KKK. In some places, it seemed like FBI agents were spying on *everyone*. After a while, someone went through the papers and found that in one all-black college, every single student and staff member was either an FBI informant or under surveillance; sometimes both. Postal workers. University professors. Activists, and regular students, too.

Eventually, the term COINTELPRO turned up, and any chance the FBI had of holding the moral high ground started to fall apart. Hoover lost his ability to act with impunity. Then Watergate came out and no one trusted anyone in government for a while, elected or not. This might have been the biggest story of the twentieth century—the illegal and incompetent mass surveillance of Americans for no reason other than their birth or beliefs. There was a Senate investigation, and it seemed like it could almost have brought down the government.

No one served a day, though. Hoover's name was dragged through the mud, and he died with a cloud over his head, if not behind bars. Watergate and the Church Committee restricted the powers of the FBI until we all forgot about it, with the oil crisis and the economy and inflation. By the time Reagan came along, everyone'd pretty much moved on.

That's the thing that really gets to me. If you ask the man in the street today about COINTELPRO, people don't remember. From that time they remember these things: the Summer of Love was amazing, the Black Panthers were bad, Martin Luther King was good, and Kent State a tragedy. No one remembers that this was the time when the government engaged in the illegal mass surveillance of anyone it didn't like. I think it only fell apart because they were limited to paper and carbon copies, and the amount someone could hold in their heads. The FBI thought they had an army of Sherlocks, but they didn't. They really didn't.

But we ignored their treason in the end.

I did find a note from Sherlock's brother Mycroft, though, in a book on a shelf years later. It was yellowed with age and clipped to that first article from the *Post*.

> *Sherlock—*
> *I actually don't know how you did it, but this has to have been you. Good job avoiding getting caught yourself. You know nothing can touch me.*
> *—Mycroft*

about the authors

Although she's best known for science fiction, paranormal, horror, and fantasy, **Gini Koch's** (ginikoch.com) first literary love is mystery and suspense, and her first literary crush, at the tender age of 7, was on Sherlock Holmes. Gini writes the fast, fresh and funny *Alien*/Katherine "Kitty" Katt series for DAW Books, the *Necropolis Enforcement Files* series, and the *Martian Alliance Chronicles* series for Musa Publishing, and as G. J. Koch she writes the Alexander Outland series. Gini's made the most of multiple personality disorder by writing under a variety of other pen names as well, including Anita Ensal, Jemma Chase, A. E. Stanton, and J. C. Koch. Her dark secret is that pretty much everything she writes has a mystery in it—because mysteries are the spice of literary life.

Glen Mehn (glen.mehn.net) was born and raised in New Orleans, and has since lived in San Francisco, North Carolina, Oxford, Uganda, Zambia, and now lives in London. He's previously been published by Random House Struik and Jurassic London, and is currently working on his first hopefully publishable novel. When not writing, Glen designs innovation programmes that use technology for social good for the Social Innovation Camp and is head of programme at Bethnal Green Ventures. Glen holds a BA in English Literature and Sociology from the University of New Orleans and an MBA from the University of Oxford.

Glen has been a bookseller, line cook, lighting and set designer, house painter, IT director, carbon finance consultant, soldier, dishwasher, and innovation programme designer. One day, he might be a writer. He lives in Brixton, which is where you live if you move from New Orleans to London. He moved country five times in two years once, and happy to stick around for a while.

After a misspent adulthood pursuing a Music Education degree, **Jamie Wyman** (www.jamiewyman.com) fostered several interests before discovering that being an author means never having to get out of pajamas. She has an unhealthy addiction to chai, a passion for circus history, and a questionable hobby that involves putting a flaming torch into her mouth. When she's not traipsing about with her imaginary friends, she lives in Phoenix with two hobbits and two cats. Jamie is proud to say she has a deeply disturbed following at her blog.

Jamie's debut novel *Wild Card* (Entangled Edge, 2013), and the follow-up, *Unveiled* (2014), are available wherever ebooks are sold. You can also find her short story 'The Clever One' in the anthology *When The Hero Comes Home 2* (Dragon Moon Press, August 2013).